Penguin

THE WADDI TREE

Kerry McGinnis was born in Adelaide and at the age of twelve took up a life of droving with her father and four siblings. The family travelled extensively across the Northern Territory and Queensland before settling on a station in the Gulf Country. Kerry has worked as a shepherd, droving hand, gardener, stock-camp and station cook, eventually running a property at Bowthorn, near Mt Isa. She is the author of two volumes of memoir and now lives in Bundaberg.

Also by Kerry McGinnis

Pieces of Blue
Heart Country

THE
WADDI
TREE

KERRY
McGINNIS

Penguin Books

PENGUIN BOOKS

Published by the Penguin Group
Penguin Group (Australia)
250 Camberwell Road, Camberwell, Victoria 3124, Australia
(a division of Pearson Australia Group Pty Ltd)
Penguin Group (USA) Inc.
375 Hudson Street, New York, New York 10014, USA
Penguin Group (Canada)
90 Eglinton Avenue East, Suite 700, Toronto ON M4P 2Y3, Canada
(a division of Pearson Penguin Canada Inc.)
Penguin Books Ltd
80 Strand, London WC2R 0RL, England
Penguin Ireland
25 St Stephen's Green, Dublin 2, Ireland
(a division of Penguin Books Ltd)
Penguin Books India Pvt Ltd
11 Community Centre, Panchsheel Park, New Delhi – 110 017, India
Penguin Group (NZ)
Cnr Airborne and Rosedale Roads, Albany, Auckland, New Zealand
(a division of Pearson New Zealand Ltd)
Penguin Books (South Africa) (Pty) Ltd
24 Sturdee Avenue, Rosebank, Johannesburg 2196, South Africa

Penguin Books Ltd, Registered Offices: 80 Strand, London WC2R 0RL, England

First published by Penguin Group (Australia), 2006. This edition published 2007

1 3 5 7 9 10 8 6 4 2

Text copyright © Kerry McGinnis 2006

The moral right of the author has been asserted

Design by Adam Lasczcuk © Penguin Group (Australia)
Cover photographs by AAP Image/Richard Durham, Australian Scenics, Getty Images
Typeset in 11/18pt Fairfield by Post Pre-press Group, Brisbane, Queensland
Printed and bound in Australia by McPherson's Printing Group, Maryborough, Victoria

National Library of Australia
Cataloguing-in-Publication data:

McGinnis, Kerry, 1945– .
The waddi tree.
ISBN-13: 978 0 14 300604 6.
ISBN-10: 0 14 300604 5.
I. Title.

A823.4

www.penguin.com.au

For Judith, for the summer of 2002.
And for Norma, for autumn, winter and spring

ONE

The bay pony came thundering down the track from the horse paddock, stubby ears pricked, red dust clouding behind his feet. On his back a boy gripped the hide with bare legs, his eyes sparkling as he urged his mount on. The house was within Jim's peripheral vision now and he saw his mother step out onto the verandah, drawn by the noise. Satisfaction buoyed him – his father, standing by the bore, was already looking, so they would both see.

'Watch me!' he yelled. The trough was six feet away. He clenched Jake's barrel tighter in readiness, but the pony swerved violently and stiffened his legs, front hooves sliding in the sand as he stopped dead. Without time even to yelp his surprise, his rider shot up his neck and over his head to land with a rib-shaking thump in the sand.

Mortified, Jim lay for a second collecting his wits while the pony shook himself until the bridle rattled, and blinked big eyes at his fallen rider. 'Toad!' he spat.

He could see his mother running towards him, her dark hair flying, and he scrambled up.

'Are you all right, Jimmy? What in the world did you think you were doing?' Jenny McAllister was out of breath, flushed from heat and effort.

'Course I am. I meant to do that.' He saw the laugh forming on her face then, and grudgingly backtracked. 'Well, Jake was supposed to jump the trough.'

'Then it's a good thing he's got more sense than you have,' his father said. He had arrived with grease on his hands, the spanner he used on the pump-jack in one of them. He scratched the side of his nose, leaving a black smear across reddened skin. 'You can think up more ways of getting yourself into strife . . . ! You could have broken Jake's neck. Where were you off to?'

'Just up the paddock. I came back for Nipper – there he is.' Jim clambered onto the pony as a skinny black boy of the same age with a shock of wild hair came running up and jumped lithely on behind him.

'I seen you,' he cried delightedly. 'You fell off.'

'Did not.' Jim kicked Jake, who ambled placidly away. Nipper grabbed Jim's middle, his slightly longer legs hanging below the white boy's, the woolly width of his hair masking Jim's red mop.

The sight of it jogged Jenny's memory. 'Not so fast, you two. Where's your hat, Jimmy?'

'We're gunna find it, Mum.' Jim was too wise to stop. The pony, picking up a sense of urgency, swished his tail once in protest then lengthened his stride, carrying the boys rapidly beyond recall.

Jenny rolled her eyes and felt for the pins in her escaping hair. 'Dear God, that boy will kill himself yet. Why didn't we have a daughter?'

'Ah, come on love,' Sandy said, 'a few tumbles won't hurt him. I had my share. Though I must say,' he broke off to chuckle, 'I never thought of claiming any of 'em were intentional.'

'No, that's a new one.' She reached her thumb to the grease smear by his nose. 'Come home, I'll make us a cuppa and you can tell me again how Daring Danny is going to make it through childhood in one piece.'

Sandy's pale eyes crinkled into a smile. He was a short stocky man with a round face and sandy-coloured hair and brows. His face and arms were reddened from sun and wind, the skin about his eyes puckered into tiny creases. Nearly fifty, he seemed younger – a tolerant, easygoing man with an unshakeable faith in his ability to snatch a living for himself and his family from the harsh country that was their home. He adored his wife, whom he had married six months to the day after his discharge from the army. Jenny, a former nurse, was farm-bred and settled easily into life at Arcadia Station. They had taken up the unimproved property in 1947, the year their son was born.

Despite the changes brought by ten years of unremitting labour, Arcadia remained a lonely and isolated spot on the edge of the Simpson Desert, midway between the Queensland border and Alice Springs. There were cattle on the property now, and tanks and mills for the three bores, even a couple of paddocks, but none of this had altered the distance separating them from their far-flung neighbours, or brought the conveniences of town any closer. Kharko Station, forty miles to the west, was their closest contact, but forty miles was a long way on two-wheeled tracks and their visits there were infrequent.

Kharko was a big property, even by desert standards. It was company owned, and managed by Sandy's brother Rob, who was as different from his elder sibling as it was possible to be.

'He's a buttoned-up sort of bloke,' Sandy said one day when they were driving home after a visit, and Jim, looking at the rolled sleeves and open throat of his father's shirt, had silently agreed. Uncle Rob wore his pressed khakis buttoned to the wrist, and his shirts always seemed to be spotless. He spoke slowly and deliberately and never tossed his hat about or hugged Aunt Mary when he came home, the way Sandy did with Jenny. He was very strict too – far too strict for Jim's liking. Even his nine-year-old cousin Rosemary agreed with him on that, calling her father Old Grumpy behind his back. Her brother Oliver, who at fourteen was four years older than Jim, chipped her for it but Rosemary paid no attention. Rosemary never did. She was the most aggravating person Jim had ever met.

'How come,' he demanded of Sandy, 'Uncle Rob doesn't look like you?'

'That's because Rob takes after your grandfather. Just like you do. Brothers don't have to look the same, any more than they have to think the same.'

Jim, who was a literal-minded boy, pondered this. The closest thing he had to a brother was Nipper, from the Aboriginal camp down on the creek bank, and if all proper brothers were anything like Uncle Rob then he was better off without one. Nipper was clever; he could throw straighter and track faster than Jim and was an eager participant in all his friend's undertakings, even those that sometimes led them into trouble.

There had been a time back when Jim was six when he desperately wanted a brother. But his mother – who as a nurse was an expert in such matters, and was occasionally called upon to help the Aboriginal women in their birthing – had told him there was no guarantee he wouldn't get a sister instead. Jim, properly horrified, settled for Nipper and had never raised the subject since. If he thought about it, his life was perfect anyway. He had everything he wanted – the freedom of Arcadia, friends to share it with, the best father in the world, and a loving mother to return to each night with the tales and foragings of his day.

These last often found a place on the shelf beside the kitchen sink, where special treasures were displayed. The good teapot lived there, and a narrow-necked, gold-lipped jug Sandy had once brought home from the Alice. Jim's drawing of Jake was there too, along with a bangle he had plaited for his mother out of the pony's tail hair, and a posy, now dried and pale, he'd made for her with the everlasting daisies that spread like a vivid carpet across the land after rain.

The shelf was homemade, as indeed was the entire house. Sandy had built it himself from bush timber, concrete and iron, squaring the roof rails with an adze, which he'd also used to shape the coolabah doorframes. There were three rooms: two bedrooms with hinged shutters that could be closed over the bare window spaces, and the kitchen, which also served as their store and living room. Jim did his schoolwork at one end of the table, where he would lift his head from the problems of long division, or the spelling of difficult words, and marvel at the way things fitted in. For besides the kerosene fridge and sink, and the stove that added unbearably to the heat of the room in summer, there were shelves of tucker – flour and sugar, tea, rice, oatmeal, jam, and all the rest. His mother grew vegetables in winter; they kept goats for milk and meat, and, thanks to the camp dogs, an ever decreasing number of hens. But everything else had to be stored on the shelf in the crammed little kitchen.

There were other things in the room as well – his mother's sewing machine, his father's accordion, and the tea chest in which his school papers were kept. A large box containing the best cups and plates, which they never used, was stored under the sink, together with his mother's crystal dressing-table set. They would all come out of their wrappings, Jenny told him, when they built the new house.

'When's that gunna be?' Jim asked. He saw no need for another house.

'When our ship comes in,' Sandy would say, which made no sense at all to the boy.

In summer they lived mostly on the verandah, a square of shade in front of the kitchen roofed over with a spinifex thatch and shaded on the eastern side by a desert acacia, which Sandy maintained must never be cut.

'That's a waddi tree, son.' He slapped the dark trunk. 'They're real desert battlers. Like us. The first night we spent on Arcadia was under this tree – and all the rest till the house was built. It's practically a family member. And it'll be here long after I'm gone, I shouldn't wonder.'

Sandy had carted gravel in for the floor of the verandah and Jenny hung creepers and ferns from the rafters, planted in cut-down oil drums. On the hottest days they soaked the gravel with the garden hose and ate and worked out there, drinking from the big canvas waterbag while the breeze, channelled through the leaves of the waddi tree and over the damp ground, cooled the air. In the hurtful light beyond the shade, the horizon shimmered and swam as the thermometer touched a hundred and thirty. The blacks, straggling slowly up from their camp for water, looked like trees walking.

Winter nights were just as extreme. The temperature plunged until frost crisped the ground and the stars snapped white and sharp in the midnight sky. Even the call of the curlews sounded cold, and on full-mooned nights the tiny bats that lived in tree hollows squeaked shiveringly across its yellow face, as if with their darting movements they could outrun the chilled air.

'This country'd fair give you the fan-tods,' Sandy grumbled one cold morning, rubbing swollen, chilblained fingers. 'Jesus, even the Eskimos have it better. At least they miss out on the heat.'

Jenny, her black curls spread about the shoulders of a red rollneck sweater, took his hands in hers to rub them warm. 'Only they miss out on the figs too, and the lemons and tomatoes. Jim, stop dawdling there. Teeth cleaned, please, and your books out.'

Every day he had a half-hour lesson on air with an unseen teacher in Alice Springs, but his real teacher was his mother. It was she who marked his work and helped him make sense of unfamiliar sums and guided him through the School of the Air program.

Now, to gain time, he asked, 'Don't Eskimos have gardens?'

'No.' Unconsciously Jenny looked out at hers – the cauliflower like great white blossoms, the tomato plants swaddled against the frost. There was a lemon, a mandarin and a fig tree, and in a tub by the gate her precious rose bush that produced wonderful yellow blooms. Jim, who had heard the story many times, knew that it had come all the way from Victoria with the sheets and saucepans and other household goods. It spent its summers on the verandah, sheltered from the hot desert winds, and Jenny picked the short-lived buds for the kitchen shelf.

Later, struggling with his sums, Jim laid down his well-chewed pen and looked at his mother kneading bread at the other end of the table. Through the door behind her the sky was a clear pale blue, and if he rose just a little in his seat he could see the ochre face of the distant range, its gullies slashes of purple that cried out to be explored. He and Nipper would go there one day – perhaps next year when he was eleven.

'Mum?'

'Something you can't do?'

'No, I just wondered – I mean, if you hadn't met Dad I wouldn't be here, would I?'

'That's true. Maybe another boy would, or even a girl, but not you.'

'So how did you meet him?' Jim's brows contracted in puzzlement. 'Where do you find ladies to marry?'

Jenny smiled at her son. 'Oh, there're plenty around. Your dad, for instance, found me in a pea patch.'

'Like a garden? Did you grow them?'

'No, they were Grandfather Grantly's peas. You wouldn't remember him. He grew for the markets. Acres of peas and carrots, and other things too. Your father came as a picker. I used to take smoko out for the picking gang and I met him there. We fell in love and got married. Not straight away, of course – we waited until the carrots were finished.'

'And then you came here?'

'That's right. It took a while, eighteen months in fact. We came by train and horse and cart, and then in an old bomb of a ute your father bought. It was always breaking down. I remember we spent four days on the side of the road once until someone came along. But we finally got here.'

Jim sighed with a mixture of satisfaction and envy. 'I wish I'd been with you.'

'You were. You were born very soon after. Now then, what about those sums?'

'In a minute. Tell me about Uncle Rob. Where did he meet Aunt Mary?'

Jenny pushed a strand of hair from her face and flipped the dough over. 'At her father's stables. You know how keen your uncle is on racing? Well, Rosemary's grandfather had quite a famous training stable and your aunt worked there as a strapper – that's someone who looks after the horses. She used to ride track work too, even though she wasn't a jockey, and that's how they met.'

Jim's mouth fell open. 'Aunt *Mary*? She rode horses?'

'Certainly did. Your aunt . . .' Jenny hesitated. 'She was different back then, full of fun and high spirits. And a good rider, I believe.'

The boy tried to reconcile this information with the colourless woman he knew. 'So what happened?'

'Well, nobody talks about it because it's sad, but she had a little boy – not Oliver, another little boy called Todd. He was born before Rosemary, and the year we were married he drowned in the Goola soak. That's why she didn't come to our wedding. She changed after that. Of course I hadn't known her before, but everyone says she did, and she no longer takes any interest in the horses, though I'm sure she knows quite as much as your uncle about them.'

'Poor Aunt Mary.' Jim thought about the little boy dying and was sorry for his aunt. He didn't know her very well but she was kind to him. She had always been quiet, unlike his mother who laughed a lot, and sang, and played boisterous games with him when he was little. He could still remember those days when he was too young to leave the garden. Of course Jenny shouted at him too, sometimes, whereas he'd never heard his aunt raise her voice in anger, or seen her more than politely pleased about anything, even a win at the races. She made nice cakes, he supposed, and always asked him how his schoolwork was going, but he didn't have much more to do with her than that.

'Come along.' Jenny was brisk again and he knew there would be no more talk until the lesson was done. He looked longingly out the window to where Nipper and the other camp kids were sailing stick boats in the trough, then sighed and drew the sheet of sums towards him.

TWO

But even school ends, and one hot December day on the verandah Jenny, marking a page and shuffling it with other papers into an envelope to be returned to school, smiled at her son.

'Okay, Tiger, that's it. You're finished for the year. Off you go.'

'Whacko!' Jim shot out of his chair. 'No more sums for six weeks. How long till Christmas, Mum?'

She sighed. 'One day less than when you asked yesterday. Forget Christmas. Just concentrate on the party – that comes first.' She flapped the skirts of her pinny to create a breeze, then used it to wipe her face and neck. 'And maybe a bit of rain before that, if we're lucky.'

'Not too much.' Horror visited the boy's features. 'What if the road was cut and we couldn't get into Goola?'

'Of course we'll get there. When have we ever missed a Christmas party? Now, run along – and don't forget the goats.'

'Righto.' Jim, scooting out the door, was impatient with the reminder. The prospect of missing the best outing of the year through an untimely fall of rain was of greater concern than his evening chore of penning the goats. What if, he thought, it was to rain enough to make the Tallee River run, or even Condamine Creek? Nobody would get there then. The Maddisons certainly wouldn't make it, and without Bill Maddison's fiddle the evening wouldn't be the same. Even though it was desert country, vehicles still got bogged.

He scanned the sky. The closest clouds lay above the range, too small and far off to worry about. As quickly as they had fallen, his spirits rose – it would be all right. And school was over at last. Holidays were magic times, all those days and weeks stretching ahead with nothing to do but please himself. He could spend them riding Jake, or playing with Nipper and the others, or driving about the run with his father. Sometimes his mother accompanied them and they'd picnic at Marvell Creek, boiling the billy on a fire of gum sticks gathered along the bank, getting back home with just enough daylight left to pen the goats. Then it would be a cold supper on the verandah and maybe later Sandy would unhook his accordion from its peg on the kitchen wall and play for them. Jim loved the way the music sounded in the night, wrapping around and rippling over things, the way the wind did.

Another highlight of the summer holidays was sleeping outside. Sandy would bring the camp stretchers out of the shed and set them up under the soft white stars, with the curlews calling in the dark and the swish of owls' wings overhead, and perhaps the distant bawl of a beast or the sough of the wind through the waddi tree. It meant getting up if it showered and dragging the bedding inside but nobody minded that. On such nights he fought sleep until his eyes closed of their own accord, then woke in grey light to the chatter of birds and the sight of Sandy pulling on his boots.

'You can stay there, son,' he invariably said. 'It's early yet.' But Jim never did. Summer days were far too precious to waste in bed.

This afternoon he was going riding – if he could catch Jake. The bay pony was dozing in the shade near the trough with half a dozen other horses that stood with lowered heads and shadow-dappled hides, flicking their tails at the flies. The boy studied them from the corner of his eye, pretending not to. He idled closer, moving quietly but humming a little too, in case one of them should startle at his sudden appearance and send them all bolting down the paddock.

The tails swished on undisturbed as he paused by the trough, then the brown packhorse, Peddler, shifted his feet and lopped an ear, making Jake lift his head. He stared suspiciously, but the sight of Jim's empty hands reassured him and he settled again, ears splayed and his bottom lip hanging open to disclose yellow teeth. Jim breathed slowly out and reached to pat Dolphin's chestnut rump. A step up to her ribs, another to her shoulder, then he ducked under her neck and as Jake snorted and began to wheel aside, he hooked his fingers into the pony's mane.

'Gotcha!' From his pocket he pulled a length of twine, already knotted into a flimsy halter, and slipped it over the pony's ears. Jake snorted again, as if in reproach at the trick played on him, but allowed himself to be towed across to the corner of the shed where the saddlery was kept.

Five minutes later, Jim, bare feet firm in the stirrups, was riding out. Somewhere in the paddock, in a tree hollow, was a sugarbag, the hive of the stingless native bees. Their honey was dark and delicious, and from the moment he first spotted them crawling with laden pollen bags from a wild convolvulus on the tank pipe he had determined to find their nest. It would be a treat for them all, a change from the endless golden syrup.

Heat and daylight were draining from the afternoon. Long shadows lay across the red sand of the paddock where whitewoods massed and the tougher supplejack and bloodwoods grew. There was spinifex on the ridge, scattered clumps of conkaberry bushes between the white-woods, and where an elbow of the creek intruded into the paddock, the pale trunks and silver glinting leaves of gums. They were the most likely hosts of the hive and Jim rode blindly, gaze high, eyes screwed against the light, his bare heels drumming an impatient tattoo against Jake's ribs whenever the pony lowered his head to snatch at grass. Eventually, with the sun westering beyond the creek timber, he found what he sought: a steady stream of bees flying in and out of the high crotch of a gum where a hump of scaly brown growth marked the hollow.

Finding it was one thing, reaching it quite another. Jim measured the distance with his eye. It was a tall tree, thick through the base but tapering as it rose, and with a slight bend in the trunk. Easy enough to climb if he cut footholds with the tommyhawk. He'd bring a bucket and get Nipper to help, but it was too late today – he could already hear the clang of the goats' bells as they headed home. Still, it wouldn't hurt to look.

He nudged and pulled Jake into position beside the tree and spoke sternly to him. 'I'm gunna stand on the saddle and jump, see? So don't you move. Forget about your belly and stay where you are – understand?'

Jake's snort sounded resigned. He was a biddable pony, used to being crawled over and under, and Jim was confident of his ability to understand human instructions, though less certain of his willingness to obey them. Jim pulled his feet up onto the saddle and straightened his knees, but just as he launched himself Jake, with impeccable timing, stepped neatly away beneath him. He grabbed as much tree as he could but he had counted on a narrower trunk at a greater height and gripped in vain at the smooth bark. The ground accelerated towards him and he landed with an agonising thump on his tailbone, and found himself staring through smarting eyes into Jake's quivering nostrils, which flared in surprise above a mouthful of half-chewed grass.

'Guts-ache,' Jim said bitterly. He picked himself up and rubbed the painful spot. 'If I was a dog I wouldn't eat yer.'

The goat bells dinned again; the animals were almost at the trough and if he didn't catch them before they drank they'd clear out to avoid being yarded. Muttering his disgust, he climbed back onto the pony and set off at a canter, the brittle summer grasses crunching under Jake's hooves.

He caught the flock in time and drove them to their post-and-netting yard. By the time he'd penned the kids daylight was bleeding away beyond the range and shadow filled the paddock. Back at the shed, Jake rubbed his head against the boy's shoulder to scratch an itchy spot, then swished his tail and trotted off, his whinny riding back on the dust behind him.

Jim hung his bridle up and stood sniffing the air, filled with a vast contentment. Lamplight spilled from the kitchen doorway, along with the smell of roasting meat, and behind that was the indefinable scent of the land – of dust and spinifex resin and smoke, and faint olfactory echoes of baking stone. Headlights flashed along the track from Two

Bob bore, accompanied by a distant pulse of noise – his father was coming home. Tomorrow Jim and Nipper would chop out the hive and there'd be honey for tea. He shoved his hands into the pockets of his faded pants and headed, whistling, for the house.

Next morning his plans received a check. Jenny, learning about the hive, shook her head.

'Maybe tomorrow, Jimmy. You're going to Kharko with Dad to spend the day with your cousins. Your hair wants a bit of a trim first, and you'll need shoes and a better shirt than that one. I want you to keep your shoes *on* too – and for goodness' sake remember your manners at lunchtime. I won't have your uncle thinking we're raising a savage.'

'Mum!' Jim stared in dismay. 'Can't I stop home? There's nothing to do at Kharko. Dad'll get talking and I'll have to hang around for hours and hours. I don't want to go.'

'But you are,' Jenny said firmly. 'I wish I could too but I'm baking bread today. As for having nothing to do, Oliver will be there and you can play with Rosemary. She'll be glad of your company, and Aunt Mary would like to see you too.'

'I don't want to play with girls!' Jim's eyes flashed indignantly. 'They can't *do* anything. Aw, Mum, do I have to? Nipper and me —'

'Nipper and I.' The correction came automatically and he breathed out a martyred sigh.

'All right, Nipper and I then, we're gunna climb that honey tree and —'

'Tomorrow. Right now you're getting a haircut.'

There was nothing for it but to hope they would be home early enough to salvage something from the day, but even this seemed unlikely for the land rover spluttered into grudging life only to die again, then would not start at all. Jim waited until the third attempt had failed, then jumped eagerly from his seat.

'Does this mean we can't go, Dad?'

'Nope.' Sandy lifted the bonnet and stuck his head under it, his words coming muffled. 'It'll just take a bit longer, thassall. Slide across behind the wheel and try the starter now.'

The sun was higher than the mill head when the engine finally caught. Jim kicked disconsolately at a front tyre, expecting his father to stop for a drink of tea before they left. Not that it made any difference, he told himself, the day was already ruined. But Sandy simply scrubbed the grime from his hands and climbed behind the wheel, checking automatically as he did so that the water drum was full. Sweat stained his now rumpled shirt and put a shine on his red face as he backed the vehicle out of the shed.

'We won't get back till midnight,' Jim grumbled. 'Dad, do I *have* to wear shoes all day? Can't I take them off till we get there?'

'Well . . .' Sandy waved to Jenny standing in the doorway, then turned to his son. 'Just between the two of us, why not? But mind you keep them on while we're there. Your mother doesn't want you looking like a poor relation when we're visiting your uncle.'

'I don't want to visit him,' Jim muttered rebelliously. 'I don't like Uncle Rob.'

'He's a good enough bloke, son – and the only uncle you've got. Remember that.'

'Why? I mean, how come Grandma McAllister didn't have more kids? And Mum's an only child too, and then she just had me. Look at Mrs Maddison – she's got five.'

'That's the way it goes.' Sandy swung the wheel as the station track merged into the slightly wider one that was the main road, then he coasted to a halt beside the mailbox. 'Nip out and stick the bag in it. And be quick, we'll be running it fine to get there in time for lunch.'

The mailbox was a concrete pipe of enormous dimensions left over from a Main Roads job on the bitumen between Alice Springs and Darwin. Sandy had carted it home and set it up on a stand, fixing a hinged lid to one end and stopping up the other. It was, he liked to say, roomy, unbreakable, and not a bad signpost either. Jim, dropping the lid shut behind the canvas bag, noticed as he always did the trickles of paint that had dribbled down from the 'r' and 'i' in 'Arcadia'. A sturdy wattle overhung the box itself, and plainly visible in the red sand before it was the tyre track of last week's mail run. Nobody else had driven the road since. Jim squidged his bare toes luxuriously through the fine sand and climbed back in beside his father.

It was a long, dusty, bumpy drive to Kharko as the morning heated towards noon. They saw nothing for long stretches, just the endless red track with scrub or spinifex off to the side, and the purple range, cleft with folds and shadows, creeping ever closer. Further on, cattle pads looped like thin snakes across the track and euros lifted their heads from mulga shade. Sunlight glinted on distant millwheels and the way ahead danced and shifted, smoothing itself into phantom blue lakes where emus wavered some ten feet high between trunkless trees. The wind, coming through the quarter windows, blew furnace-hot on Jim's skin. 'Perishing weather,' he announced, as he'd heard his father say.

'Not far off it,' Sandy agreed. 'Hello, what's wrong with Chummy?'

Chummy bore stood within a few hundred yards of the track. At this time of day there should have been no more than one or two head on the trough, while the rest chewed their cuds in the shade. Instead there were hundreds of cattle milling about, bawling at the brazen sky.

'They're outa water,' Jim said knowledgeably.

'We'll check.' Sandy swung the wheel and they bounced along a cattle pad to pull up in the shade of the tank. The stock scattered at their approach but continued to jostle and bawl, and Jim, who had shinned up the tank for a look, dropped down again dusting his hands.

'It's empty, Dad, and hey,' he lowered his voice, 'there's somebody camped there, the other side of the tank. It's funny, though, the mill's still pumping – why's the tank empty?'

Sandy stood, hands on hips, looking at the trough. 'There's a beast in the trough. Looks like he's kicked the end out and the water's running straight through. Get the cable, son. I'll tow him out, then we'll see what we can do about blocking the end till Rob can get someone out here.'

Jim jerked his head at the tank and sank his voice to a whisper, as if the stranger behind it might hear him. 'But who could that be? There's an old blue truck there.'

'Dunno. But if he's done nothing about it yet he's not likely to. So I reckon it's up to us. You can't leave stock to perish.'

The beast, a red bullock, was dead. He lay with his legs in the air, the bulk of his swollen body filling the upper half of the trough but leaving a channel for the water to escape below him. It had soaked the red sand for yards around without pooling and was wonderfully cool to Jim's feet.

'How long you reckon he's been there, Dad?'

'A long time, judging by the size of him. Righto, hook that cable up to the tow bar, then get well back in case something gives. He's stuck so damn tight I might pull the whole shooting match outa the ground before I shift him.'

Fortunately this was not the case. It took longer to belt and hammer the end of the trough back into position and it was the racket of accomplishing this that finally brought the stranger from his camp behind the tank, two wide-eyed black kids hovering behind him. Jim saw them first. The kids ducked back out of sight while a shuffling white man with unkempt stringy hair and greasy clothes approached. His bare feet, and as much as the boy could see of the rest of his body, were filthy; his pants were held up by a piece of rope and his hat was a shapeless mess. He had a queer, sidling way of moving and avoided direct eye contact, looking down and shooting quick, sly glances up at them both. His blue eyes were veined and pouched in a face of broken capillaries, and he stank worse than a wet dog.

'G'day.' He addressed Sandy in an ingratiating whine. 'Know yer, don't I? McAllister, is it, from up the track a bit?' He snapped his fingers. 'Yeah, Arcadia. You couldn't spare a man a bit of baccy? I'm fresh out.'

Sandy fished wordlessly in his shirt pocket for his Log Cabin. He opened it, saw it was less than quarter full, and tossed it to the man before him.

'Keep it. You can find your own matches.' He stood up and toed the finished job with his boot. 'It never occurred to you to do something about the trough? Or at least shut off the valve before the tank emptied?'

'Why should I?' The man's hands were shaking as he fumbled a cigarette together, but the acquisition of the tobacco had made him bolder. 'Station's done nothing for me. 'Sides, that bastard of a manager warned me off the place. Let 'im see to his own stock. I'm a sick man.'

'Yeah, well, if you're travelling east you can keep off mine as well.' Sandy gathered up his tools. 'I don't want you there and neither do the blacks.' He jerked his head at the wide-eyed boy. 'C'mon, son.'

'Who was that?' Climbing into the land rover, Jim looked back over his shoulder at the man now shambling out of sight behind the tank. 'Boy, he was dirty! And how come he smelled so bad?'

'He's what most people would call a white blackfella,' Sandy said. 'There's nothing wrong with being a blackfella, but a white blackfella's one that's given up on his responsibilities. He's usually a drunk and he takes up with a black woman and breeds half-caste kids that don't belong in the tribe or anywhere else. And worse than that he corrupts the blacks with grog. Blokes like Diamond or old Nimrod'd rather see their young women dead than living with trash like him.'

'Oh.' Jim blinked, readjusting his ideas. Nimrod, who was too old to work, was Nipper's grandfather, and the father of Diamond. Black men and white worked together, Jim knew, but they never lived together. His father always ate apart from the blacks when they were mustering and they never shared a camp at night. And at Kharko the white men had huts but the blacks lived down in their own place where no white man was allowed to go, though nobody had said why this was so.

'But,' he pondered aloud, 'I bet you couldn't smell so bad even if you didn't wash for a whole year.'

'Probably not,' Sandy agreed. 'That's the metho. He lives on the stuff.'

'Are you gunna tell Uncle Rob he's there?'

'No need. He'll find out soon as his bore man gets out to see to that trough.' He changed down a gear for a gutter. 'The horse-paddock gate's coming up. You'd better get those shoes back on.'

Sighing, Jim fished under the dashboard and, knee to chin, began struggling into the hated footwear.

Every time he visited Kharko, Jim suffered an initial shyness brought about by the sheer scale of the place. At Arcadia there was the house and the shed. At Kharko the big house, as the homestead was called, was larger than both, and double-storeyed as well. It was set in a shady garden and surrounded by a complex of sheds and outbuildings, so that approaching it as they did from the horse-paddock gate was, to Jim's eyes, like driving into a town.

There was a separate kitchen for the men, a store that held everything from rations to new truck tyres and which had a loading-dock round two sides of it, and a bookkeeper's office tucked just inside. There was a meat house where the beef they killed was salted and kept, the men's quarters, the head stockman's cottage, four or five sheds, the stables, a blacksmith's shop – and that was without the fowl house, the stockyards, the tanks and bore, and the tennis court at the rear of the garden.

Jim alighted reluctantly at the front gate and walked beside his father up the gravelled path to the screen door at the side entrance.

'Anyone home?' Sandy bellowed cheerfully, and Mary McAllister, quiet and plump and the same height as her brother-in-law, came to meet them, a look of relief on her face.

'Sandy, there you are. We were starting to think . . . And Jim, dear me! How tall you've grown. Well, go on, go through, the rest of them are at the table. Did you have trouble, Sandy? Jenny said you left hours ago. I radioed when you didn't turn up.'

'We stopped at Chummy. The tank was empty and there was a beast in the trough.' Sandy hung his hat and nudged Jim to do the same. 'Hope we haven't put you out, Mary?'

'Of course you haven't. How's Jenny?' Their voices faded as Jim stared about, conscious as he always was at Kharko of the space and colour of the place. There were rooms for everything, for cooking, for eating – and even one in which his cousins did their schoolwork. It seemed strange to have so much space in a house when at home the kitchen served all their needs.

His uncle and cousins were seated about the long table in the dining room, with Mr Baker the bookkeeper occupying the chair to Rob McAllister's right. Mary indicated a seat between his two cousins and Jim slid into it, muttering a hello to Oliver. Rosemary he ignored, but at sight of his father she jumped up, crying, 'I want to sit next to Uncle Sandy.'

'Stay where you are, Rosemary,' Rob said, and she subsided again, looking mutinous. 'Trouble along the way, Sandy?' he asked.

'Bit of a hold-up at Chummy bore, that's all.'

Listening to his father's light, easy voice, Jim thought how different to his uncle's it was. Rob's words were round and hard, unfriendly-sounding, and he never swore or dropped his 'g's the way Sandy did. He didn't tell yarns either, or laugh until he choked over the funny ones. In fact, the boy decided, glowering down the table at his host, he was not so much buttoned up as sewn into his clothes.

Jim remained quite unaware of his own strong physical resemblance to Rob. Oliver, a gangly, freckle-faced teenager with ginger hair and glasses, could more readily have passed for Sandy's son. Rosemary was different again; she had her mother's broad cheekbones but was small and slender, with flaming curls and hazel eyes. She was poking at her plate now, wrinkling her nose at the slice of tongue that lay beside the vegetables.

'We've finished our schoolwork,' she told Jim smugly. 'Have you?'

'Course I have – yesterday.' He turned to Oliver. 'I found a sugarbag in the horse paddock. Me and Nipper are gunna chop her out when I get back.' He remembered something else. 'There was a bloke camped at Chummy this morning with some blackfellas. He had a blue truck. Dad said he was a metho drinker.'

'That'd be Sammy Deane. He was here cadging off the blacks a couple of days ago and Dad hunted him.' Oliver's pale eyes were solemn behind his spectacles. Then abruptly he changed the subject. 'Hey, did you know we've got a new horse? From Adelaide. He came up on the train and Barney brought him out Friday. You oughta see him, he's a real beauty. Got the legs of everything on the place, Barney says.'

'Yes, and his name's Castlelee,' Rosemary put in. 'But Barney calls him the Rook.'

'Why?'

'Because his sire was Chess-something, and Barney said —'

'That's wrong, Ro.' Oliver buttered his bread with calm superiority. 'His registered name is Castling and *that's* why Barney calls him the Rook. His sire's name was Chessman.' He took a lusty bite of bread and spoke through a full mouth. 'It's in the form books. He's an entire, Jim. A big, raking brown – and you ought to see his shoulders. Barney says it's the shoulders that make a racer. He reckons we'll clean up at the next meeting – the Rook'll win everything. Well,' he qualified in his pedantic way, 'not the Maiden, obviously. But he'll take the Cup and all the distance races.'

Jim's mind was stuck further back in the conversation. 'If his name's something else why's he called Rook?'

'It's *the* Rook. That's a game piece in chess,' his cousin explained. 'It – oh, never mind. It's just a name. Barney thinks horses oughtn't to have silly names. Except it can't be helped with registered horses sometimes if you want to link their breeding in. Old Chessman sired heaps of colts – there's Chessboard and Chessgame and Chessmove. I suppose they just ran out of names beginning with Chess. You would, after a while.'

'Who cares about racing, anyway?' Jim blurted. 'I'd sooner have a stockhorse – at least you can do something with them and they're fast enough.'

'Only because company places like Kharko buy good stallions to breed from,' Oliver argued. 'Otherwise they'd all be runty little nags like the brumbies. Anyway, racing's fun. Barney's teaching me to ride on the track, and next year, soon as I'm fifteen, Dad says I can start jockeying.'

Jim, impressed but determined not to show it, shrugged. 'I'd sooner go mustering.'

'Vegetables, Jim?' his uncle asked. Then he added in a pleasant voice, 'No boomerang today? So the windows are safe, eh?'

Jim scowled. Any reminder of his last visit, and the thrashing his uncle had promised him in the heat of the moment, was unwelcome. Rob, unaware of offending, went on, 'Get Oliver to take you down to see the new horse.'

'Yes. Thank you, Uncle.' Jim looked at the plate his aunt had set before him and with a sinking heart saw that he too had tongue. His mother would expect him to eat it, he knew, and there was no help to be had from his father, who was deep in conversation with the adults across the table. Reaching reluctantly for his knife and fork, deaf to Rosemary's incessant chatter, he began gloomily quartering the meat. If he cut it small enough, perhaps it wouldn't taste so bad.

The meal over, Jim followed his cousins down to the stables, where the new horse was in feed. Barney O'Dowd, a youngish-looking man with a wiry frame and bright blue eyes, was there before them, smoking a cigarette as he leaned on the rails and watched the stallion. Every now and then the horse lifted his nose towards him, taking his scent.

'How's that for a horse, eh?' he said as they lined up beside him. 'You could write pomes about them legs.' Barney had a pleasant face – lean-jawed, and creased about the eyes. His rumpled hair fell to his collar, curling there as he turned to glance at Jim. 'Where you from then, mate?'

'He's our cousin —' Rosemary began, but Jim cut her off. He could speak for himself.

'Arcadia.'

'Ah. Seen your mum and dad at the races. Your dad plays at the dances, don't he?'

'Yes.' Jim was pleased at the recognition. 'And my mum's always the prettiest lady there. That's what Dad says, anyway.'

'Does he? Well, what you reckon of Kharko's new racer, eh?'

'He's all right,' Jim conceded, adding defiantly, 'I like stockhorses best.'

Barney shook his head sorrowfully. 'And you a McAllister . . .' He reached through the rails to rub the Rook's face. 'I gotta go, big fella.'

'Where?' Rosemary demanded. 'Can we come too?'

'Nope.' He winked and wagged his head. 'See you round, kids.'

They watched him stride away. Jim saw that his legs were bowed and he wore his spurs turned round on his instep so the rowels wouldn't catch as he walked.

'He's our best friend,' Rosemary said importantly. 'He lets us help bring the killers up, and he showed us all the fancy ways to plait. He can make a man's head knot –'

'Don't be daft, Ro!' Oliver scoffed. 'It's a *Turk's* head. Turks wear turbans and the knot looks like one.'

'So what? Man or Turk, it's still a plait, isn't it?'

Mooching along behind them on a tour of the sheds, Jim listened to the quarrel. Rosemary was as irritating as a fly buzzing about your ears. He was suddenly glad he didn't have a sister to contradict everything he said. Oliver bore it patiently, even when she called him by the hated nickname of Specs. Jim didn't know how he put up with it, but he and Nipper would never let any of the skinny little camp girls get away with half of what Rosemary did. Still, when it came to leapfrogging the feedbags in the feed shed, she surprised him by flying over them more easily than her brother, whose gangly legs got in the way and sent him sprawling face first into the baled hay.

Afterwards they had cake with raspberry vinegar in the kitchen, courtesy of the cook. He was a big man in both girth and height, and as hairy as a gorilla save for his head, which gleamed in naked splendour. Bushy eyebrows and a huge black moustache hedged his face, as if all the hair from his pate had come to rest there instead. Tight curls of body hair spilled from the neck of his navy singlet, and south from where his shorts ended. He wore sandshoes, their uppers slit to accommodate his bunions, and had a tea towel tucked into the waist of his shorts. Everyone on the station knew him as Pommy John.

'Been out here thirty years,' he said, 'and I'm still Pommy. S'pose it's better than being a bloody wog.'

Back at the house, Aunt Mary had packed a cardboard box for Jenny – tomatoes from the garden, plants wrapped in newspaper, and a pile of old *Women's Weekly* magazines. Sandy folded the top of the carton shut and secured it in the back of the land rover. Rosemary suddenly broke away from her mother's side and ran to hug him round the waist.

'Goodbye, Uncle Sandy.'

'Bye, sweetheart.' He caught her up to kiss her cheek. 'Thanks for the lunch, Mary.' He looked at Jim, who added his own thanks, then waved to Oliver in the background.

'See you at the Christmas party,' Rosemary yelled as they moved off. Jim raised a perfunctory hand and the little group waving at the gate fell away behind them.

The afternoon heat was waning, the sun sitting low above the western range, veined now with deep purple shadows. They would be late home, Jim thought, but his mother would expect that. He hoped she'd remember to yard the goats. The dingoes had killed two kids last time the flock went unpenned. And he hoped she'd made rice pudding for tea – he was starting to feel hungry again. They rejoined the main road and the land rover's shadow ran east before them, the wheels never quite catching the dark, fleeing shape.

Sandy stretched his neck, holding the wheel firmly in his big, sun-reddened hands. 'Well, did you enjoy yourself, son?'

'It was all right, I suppose. Oliver showed me Uncle Rob's new horse. How can a horse have blue blood, Dad? What makes it blue?'

'It isn't. That's just a way of saying he's got a fancy pedigree. And he belongs to the station, you know, not to your uncle.' Sandy's eyes crinkled into a smile. 'He told me he was gunna win the Cup with him next year. Wouldn't be the first time Rob's reckoned that.'

'Barney said he would too – and Oliver. Even Ro,' Jim remembered. 'D'you think he will, Dad?'

Sandy shrugged. 'D'you think it'll rain Wednesday? It's probably easier to forecast that than tell what'll happen with racing.' He fished in the glove box for a new pack of tobacco, then nodded at the wheel. 'You can steer for a bit while I roll a smoke.'

Jim, concentrating on keeping the rover in the wheel ruts, let the conversation lapse.

The moon was up when they rattled down the last stretch of track and stopped for the horse-paddock gate. It was not quite full but shed enough light to sail alone in its patch of sky, the nearest stars dimmed by its brilliance. Jim, who had slept through the last twenty miles, yawned as he pulled the gate back. He could smell chimney smoke and see the yellow wash of lamplight in the kitchen window, the night held like a cupped hand behind it. His stomach rumbled as he pulled the gate shut and climbed back into the rover.

'I'm starving.'

'What's new?' Sandy slowed again and stopped by the garden gate. He cut the engine, stretched, grunted in his seat, then swung the door open. Jim yawned mightily. He could hear an owl calling, and the tic of cooling metal was sharp in the silence. They had no generating plant at Arcadia and the night sounds came uninterrupted. Now it was the whiffle and snort of brumbies along the paddock fence.

'There's horses, Dad!'

'I hear 'em.' Sandy cocked his head. 'Not to worry, the fence is sound. I thought you were starving.' He scooped Mary's carton up under his arm and they walked together through the warm darkness towards the lighted house.

THREE

They chopped the hive out next day, climbing up cuts they made in the trunk of the tree. Nipper was a human lizard. Jim watched enviously as he swung himself into the fork, locking his skinny legs about a branch. Jim had to stick to the footholds, chipping away with the tommyhawk until he had a place to stand.

He had brought a cut-down kerosene tin with him and they took turns to reach into the hollow, break out the chunks of honeycomb and transfer them to the tin. Their fingers sank into the wax; honey oozed stickily over their palms and thumbs. These they licked, transferring honey to their faces. Bees crawled and buzzed through their hair, straying into their ears and up their noses. Brushing at them only spread the honey further over their bodies.

When Jim, puffing repeatedly at the bees crawling into his eyes, could stand it no more he called a halt. 'I reckon we've got plenty. Anyway, they're all gunna drown in the stuff unless we get outa here pretty quick.' He lowered the tin to the ground by a rope tied to the handle and looked across at Nipper, who was foraging another piece of comb for himself. 'C'mon, we gotta leave 'em something.' Then his sticky hands lost their grip on the bark and with a startled yell he shot down the trunk to land beside the honey tin, his left ankle twisting beneath him.

'Aauugh!' He rolled, clutching his foot, red spikes of pain behind his squeezed eyelids.

Nipper shinned down from his perch and looked helplessly at him. 'Hey, what happen?'

'It's broke, you idiot,' Jim roared. 'My ankle's broke – and the party's on Saturday.'

'More better we tell the missus,' Nipper said practically, and set off at a run.

But the ankle wasn't broken, not even very badly strained, Jenny declared when she had her patient ensconced in one of the greenhide chairs on the verandah. 'You'll just need to rest it for a couple of days,' she said, snipping through the bandage and pinning the end. 'And I mean rest. Every time you get tired of sitting around, remember the party. You don't want to miss out on the cricket, do you?'

Jim sighed and leaned palely back, his injured foot propped up on a second chair. His toes looked very dark against the bandage and he could not believe the bad luck that had overtaken him. 'It hurts, Mum.'

'Well, it will for a bit.' Passing behind him with the basin, Jenny stooped to kiss his forehead. 'I'll bring you some aspirin to make it better. Just be glad it wasn't a broken leg.'

'We got the honey, though.'

'You did.' Her grey eyes twinkled at him as she pushed at the mass of hair on her neck. 'And what if you'd landed *in* it, dirty feet and all?'

'Well, I didn't.' Wanting to keep her there beside him, he said, 'Why don't you cut your hair off, like Aunt Mary? I'm glad you don't, cos it's pretty how it is, but it'd be cooler if you did.'

'I suppose. But I've always worn it long, even in New Guinea, and that's hotter than here.' She smoothed his own hair back from his sweaty face. 'Poor old Jimmy. Such a boy for being in the wars. If it's not squashed fingers or gravel rashes, it's split heads and sprains. Lucky for you I'm a nurse.'

'Mum, if you're going away can you get me a book?'

'I'll do that when I bring the aspirin. And mind, foot up and still.'

She brought him *Treasure Island* but he laid it aside after the first chapter, fired with a sudden ambition to have his own boat. He and Nipper could chop a canoe out of one of the gum trees if his father would let him borrow his tools to hollow it. Then when the rain came they could launch it into the creek and paddle for miles. He wished Arcadia had a dam like Kharko's so they wouldn't have to wait for storms to use it. They'd start looking for the right tree as soon as his ankle was better, Jim decided, and with luck they'd have a boat by Christmas. He wiped his face and flapped his shirt to create a breeze. It was so hot that rain would surely have come by then.

Jenny was right about his injury. The swelling soon subsided, and by the following evening he could hobble about with the aid of a crutch Sandy had cut for him from the fork of a mulga. By Friday the idea of a canoe had palled and he had become a pirate instead, clinging to the now unnecessary crutch, which he considered added to his role as Long John Silver, whose adventures he was still reading. He was thoroughly bored by his confinement to the house, but his mother insisted he give his ankle another twenty-four hours before his next attempt at destroying himself.

'Oh, Mum,' he said crossly.

'Nevertheless.' She had a way of saying that word that put a full stop to objections. Sighing, Jim crutched himself out to the waddi tree and leaned there, looking over his island, seeking a glimpse of sea between the headland of the tank and the jungle that was the yards.

Nights of distant thunder followed, when lightning played for hours across the eastern horizon. On the eve of the party, Sandy returned from a day spent pumping at Two Bob bore carrying an emu egg he'd found. This Jim knew to be a good sign – emus bred only when seasonal weather prospects were good, but as far as the Christmas party went it couldn't have been worse. Rain from the isolated storm had followed the course of Marvell Creek, whose upper reaches crossed the main road. Sandy was happy. It had been a good fall, he said, enough to lay water on the claypans and fill the gutters with boggy clay.

'It's coming, love,' he said to his wife. Mud streaked his trouser legs and was splashed across the rover doors. 'A fall like that at Two Bob and I could quit pumping.'

'That would be wonderful.' Jenny poured tea from the chipped enamel pot, adding matter-of-factly, 'It's certainly hot enough. You could've cooked an egg in the kitchen today without using the stove. Was there an inch in it, do you think?'

'Thereabouts. Slippery as buggery too. And while I was waiting for the ground to get a bit of a crust on it I found this.' He lifted the large, densely green egg and Jim, forgetting his crutch, crowded his mother to see.

'An emu egg.' Jenny weighed it in her hands. 'It's heavy. What'll you do with it?'

'Drill the ends and blow the yolk out. It's easy enough when they're fresh.'

'Have a cuppa first,' she urged, and he kicked the chair round and sat, casting his hat onto the gravel.

'Take a team of draughthorses to stop me. You walking again, Jim? Well, nip down to the shed and bring back the drill. And the box of bits. May as well do the thing scientifically.'

When Jim had left, Sandy stretched in his chair and took a swallow of tea. 'Ah, that's better. You know, there were ducks there already, on the claypans. I stood and watched them and I swear I could smell the grass coming. How's the boy's foot?'

'It's fine. But I think we'll have to live with the crutch until Long John Silver wears off. I give it till tomorrow. Paper pirates can't compete with other kids.'

Sandy reached across the table and put his roughened palm over his wife's hand. 'Ah, Jenny. We're lucky, aren't we?'

'Yes, we are,' she said simply, and turned her palm up under his, dimpling a smile. 'Considering I could have had Pete Miller.'

Sandy frowned. 'You've never mentioned him before.'

'You don't know about Pete?' Jenny raised her brows. 'He was the pig man on the farm next door. About sixty, lame, and he smelled a lot like his pigs. I could have had him like that.' She snapped her fingers. 'Only I took you instead.'

'It was my money! Knew it'd come in handy sometime.'

Then Jim was back, staring disapprovingly at them. 'Here's the drill, Dad. Wotcher holding hands for?'

'Arm-wrestling.' Sandy got up. 'Right, stand aside and let me at it. This sort of stuff takes brains.'

The eggshell proved tough. When the drill finally penetrated, Sandy drove it right into the egg. 'That should have broken it up a bit. Now comes the hard part.' He closed his mouth over the top hole and blew until his face was crimson with effort and his eyes were about to bug from their sockets, but nothing happened.

Jim hadn't been so entertained in months. He stamped his feet gleefully, crowing encouragement. 'Do it again, Dad. You look like a turkey.'

'I'll do you in a minute,' Sandy promised without heat. He drew breath like a diver going under for a week, jammed the egg to his mouth and blew hard, with no result save the breaking of a tremendous fart. Sandy lifted an astonished face to see his wife and son convulsed with laughter. Jenny's mouth would prim, then break again, while Jim shrieked with mirth beside her.

'That'll do, the pair of you.' Sandy took control of his embarrassment. 'I beg your pardon, my dear,' he said quaintly to Jenny, who was still trying to stifle her laughter.

'All right, Jim.' She mopped her eyes on her pinny. 'It's not polite to laugh at . . . I mean, you should just pretend you didn't notice. Anyway,' she peeped at her husband over the cloth, 'I think you'd better stop while you're ahead, don't you?'

Jim, who thought only boys and horses farted, let his laughter leak away and was struck by a sudden thought. 'Why don't you just leave the egg for the ants, Dad? They'd clean it out in no time.'

'Well, bugger me.' Sandy stared at his son. 'Good thinking, cobber. There's a big meat-ants nest down behind the yard, just near —'

'I know it.' Jim was already halfway to the door. 'I betcha they'll have emptied it before we get back from the party.'

It was growing late. The cattle were gone from the bore and cockies now lined the trough, heads dipping to their last drink of the day. Hopping on his bare feet to avoid being bitten by the ants, Jim deposited the egg beside the nest and went to pen the goats. The air felt still and thundery and a bank of clouds had crept up in the east to lie like a twisted blanket along the horizon. He watched them uneasily as he headed off to the hens. There were only three eggs today. He shut the door of the chookhouse and abruptly reached a decision.

Hiding the third egg where the crows wouldn't find it, he ran down the well-worn pad past the yards to the humpies on the creek bank, and threaded his way through the smoky evening fires to Nimrod's gunyah. He made a rapid deal with the skinny old man: two eggs for him not to sing for rain tonight. The blackfellas had sung every evening for the past fortnight, and Jim was guiltily aware that his father had given the old man a plug of tobacco to do so. But waiting an extra day for rain wouldn't hurt the country or the cattle, he reasoned, not when something as important as the Christmas party was at stake.

Jim wrestled with his conscience all evening and went to bed torn between triumph and guilt, half expecting to wake to a flood. It would serve him right. But the part of him that craved the fun and excitement of the day ahead applauded the precaution he'd taken.

Next morning he was astir at first light, helping Sandy in the goat yard. When they returned to the house the table was spread with food – chops and gravy for immediate consumption, and a cold leg of mutton, potatoes boiled in their jackets, jam tarts and a sponge cake, which Jenny was packing into a box.

'There's a melon in the garden, Jim,' she said. 'You can bring it in as soon as you've eaten. And no running, mind! It won't be worth taking if you drop it.' To Sandy she said, 'It's going to be stinking hot. We need a couple of wet corn bags to wrap it in. And I can't find the billies.'

'They're already packed, along with the water and the chairs. Stop fussing and have your breakfast. There's plenty of time.'

To Jim, hovering about in a fever to get going, there seemed both too much and not enough time. It took for ever to get the food loaded to his mother's satisfaction, and even longer to collect the cutlery and plates and tin pannikins. The party would be half over before they even started, he thought.

They were finally getting into the land rover when Sandy, patting his pockets, said, 'Where's my pipe?'

It took fifteen agonising minutes to search the kitchen, then backtrack over all the places he'd been, without result.

'I'll check the truck,' Jim said, and ran to the shed, casting a cursory glance into the cab of the old Ford. 'Not there, Dad,' he panted when he was back.

'I had the damn thing in my hand twenty minutes ago,' Sandy protested. 'Nip down to the bore, son. See if I left it on the fuel drum, or maybe the ledge of the tank.'

Jim took off again, but was soon back empty-handed. 'Can't you take the other one, Dad?' he begged, desperate to be gone. The sun was unthinkably high. Suppose the road was sticky from rain, or they had a flat tyre? If they didn't start soon they might as well not go.

His mother gave voice to his thoughts. 'Yes, leave it, Sandy. We really haven't time.' And to his infinite relief his father gave up the search and got into the rover.

'Right,' he said and they were off, Jim on the outside where he could wave at Nipper running beside them for a dozen paces, and to several women standing with empty water buckets at the bore. He bestowed a passing glance on Dolphin and Peddler, who in response to the vehicle rushing past put their tails over their backs and took off, heads high, up the paddock. He hopped out for the gate, closed it smartly and ran back, slamming the door. As he settled in, his mother nudged him. 'Happy now?'

'Yes. But why are grown-ups always so *slow*?'

'We're not, you know.' Jenny smiled, touched by her son's excitement. It had been a long time since her last day out and the chance to see her neighbours. 'We're just thorough. You wouldn't want the cakes left behind, for instance.'

'No fear!' There would be a packet of sweets too, he knew. His mother would have bought them some time back and kept them especially for the occasion, although he wondered how she could bear to have them in the cupboard so long without trying one. He hugged her arm in sudden gratitude. Most of their treats appeared on his birthday or at Christmas; the rest of the year was what Sandy called bread-and-scrape, which made a day like today doubly exciting.

It was too noisy to talk. The engine roared as the land rover tackled the straight lengths of sand; it growled around the turnings and shook bone-jarringly across the corrugations. Jim whistled to himself, then realised he was echoing his mother. Jenny could whistle like a bird and the sound carried better than words in the noisy cab. They ran through 'Old Man River', with Sandy joining in for the chorus, and after that 'Ten Green Bottles', but then a dingo ran across the road, causing Jim to yell and point, the whistling forgotten.

Slowly the miles fell behind them. They passed the bend where Sandy had once bogged the rover so badly it took him three days to pull it out, then the turn-off to Chummy bore, and then the sign for Kharko Station. The next landmark was the wide, shallow-bedded Tallee River, and finally, a little short of noon, the tiny township of Goola, with a population and travelling public too small even to support a pub. There was a store, a one-cell police station, a couple of houses, and, set back behind them, a racetrack and the local hall.

Sandy drove past the buildings, heading for the mill head poking above the giant river gums along the banks of the Tallee River. The mill was built above Goola Well and was connected to two tarred stock tanks and a long steel trough under the trees. There was no grass, but the litter of fallen bark crunched satisfyingly underfoot, and the spaces between the trees were filled with vehicles. To Jim's eyes there seemed to be dozens of them, but his attention was immediately diverted by the sight of the Maddison boys and he was out of the rover almost before it stopped and off to join them.

For Jim the day passed in a whirl of activity, with a cricket game during which Roy Maddison was hit in the eye with the ball, a tug-of-war with all the women and kids pulling against the men, followed by a noisy barbecue lunch. Afterwards Sandy, who had disappeared behind the stock tanks during the cake-and-watermelon stage of the meal, came striding back in a moth-eaten Santa suit, carrying a chaff bag of presents. Besides Jim himself, only two older boys, Wally Maddison and Oliver McAllister, knew the identity of the sweating, red-faced man who roared out the names of the expectant children. One by one they came shyly forward to receive their gifts. Jim's was a clockwork train and a dozen lengths of track that fitted together to form a loop. 'Keep it out of the sand, son,' Santa told him in a whisper. 'You having a good time?'

'It's great, Dad.' He wrestled the tin loco out of its box and ran to show his mother. She turned the key and examined the tracks quite as if she'd never seen it before.

'Aren't you the lucky one? Don't play in the sand with it, Tiger, it'll wreck the clockworks.'

Jim left it in her keeping. He couldn't spare the time to try it out while there were other boys to run and wrestle with and trees to climb. When he fell out of one and winded himself Jenny came from her place in the circle of chairs under the gums to minister to him.

'Settle down, for goodness' sake. You're as red as a beet already. Just play quietly for a while.'

'Yes, Mum.' But a moment later he was running again, tagging Rosemary then somersaulting in the sand. The rest of the children scattered laughing before his scarlet-faced approach.

Jenny shook her head and returned to the shade, where of the older children only timid little Gina Colson remained, sleeping on a towel at her mother's feet. In the chair beside Kathy Colson, Brenda Tillet nursed her fretful six-month-old, patting him over her nappy-draped shoulder. She looked pale and tired, and the strands of hair that had escaped from the knot at her nape were stuck to her sweaty forehead. The policeman's wife, she was new to the district. Her twin daughters were down amid the flurry of shrieking children in the riverbed.

Jenny held out her arms. 'You look worn out. Would you like me to take him for a while?'

'Thank you.' Brenda smiled weakly. 'It's just the heat. I don't think I'll ever get used to it. It doesn't seem to bother the girls, though.'

'Oh, nothing will bother them today, except the prospect of it ending.' Jenny rocked the grizzly baby. 'Luckily they'll be too tired for tears when it does. It's understandable, though – how often do they see each other? And my boy's luckier than most because his cousins live at Kharko. Not,' she admitted, 'that we get there often.'

'It was him that fell out of the tree, was it?'

'That's Jim. Blue shirt and red hair. Not so red as his cousins', though. They're Mary's children.' She nodded across the circle at her sister-in-law. 'Have you been to Kharko yet?'

'No.' Brenda sighed and knuckled trickling sweat from her chin. 'But I hope – I mean, it's so close to Goola and I'd like to have a woman friend I could visit without bothering Jeff to take me. It would mean a lot.'

'I'm sure it would.' Jenny looked down at the now sleeping child, wishing her words unsaid. She had been thoughtless to implant the idea. She'd never seen her sister-in-law nurse or lift or even touch someone else's baby since the death of little Todd. Older children presented no problem, but it was as if she could not bear to be reminded of the infant she'd lost. Jenny bit her lip. Perhaps Brenda would forget, or Mary would find some way to discourage intimacy between them.

That shouldn't be hard. Her sister-in-law was kind to a fault but she presented a calm, standoffish manner to the world that had the effect of holding people at arm's length.

Suddenly, like a flock of raucous parrots, the children were back wanting cake and the warm, flat lemonade left over from lunch. Rob raked the fire, dropping an armload of sticks onto the embers, while Sandy, dressed once more as himself, filled the billies for tea. Big fluffy clouds shone white against a vivid blue but it was pleasantly cool under the trees.

Jim, wiping jam from his fingers onto the hem of his shorts, thought the day was like an illustrated page in a book, a series of bright little paintings all crammed together into a larger one. Only better because you could taste and smell and feel and hear it all: the sweetness of jam, the wonderful tang of burning gum, the sun and the shade, and the sound of the cicadas pulsing in the heat – throbbing with life like the day itself. And as far as he was concerned, the best was yet to come.

This happened after tea, a meal of leftovers mixed with cold chicken brought by Kathy Colson and two enormous meat pies that his Aunt Mary fished from the bottom of the Kharko tuckerbox. He wondered if she'd made them herself, or Pommy John had. He cooked for the big house as well as the kitchen, Jim knew. The men built up the fire to make light to eat by, and afterwards, when the plates and table had been packed and everything but the chairs put away, Sandy brought out his accordion and Bill Maddison his fiddle and the music began.

Jenny, to Jim's disgust, sent him off to wash his hands in the cattle trough just as Bill began to tune his instrument. 'You too, Ro.'

'I already did, Aunt Jenny.' Smugly she showed her palms, which the boy was prepared to swear had not seen water all day, and was rewarded with a smile.

'Good girl. Off you go, Jim.'

When he returned he scowled to see that his young cousin had appropriated his mother's lap. Not that he would have sat on it here – even though he still did sometimes at home – but she was *his* mother, not Rosemary's. Jealous, he contrived to kick her leg as he sat down beside their chair, but Ro ignored his spite and simply tucked herself more firmly into his mother's arms.

Then Bill Maddison, a tense, thin-looking man with a pinched mouth and worried eyes, nodded across at Sandy. 'It's the time and the place. Let's warm 'em up with "Jingle Bells".'

They played through all the carols with everyone joining in, Jenny's rich contralto soaring over Rosemary's shriller piping and Jim's own voice. Rob wasn't singing, or Wally Maddison, although his uncle, Jim saw, was patting time with his foot. Wally's voice, like Oliver's, had been going squeaky and deep by turns all day, so that probably accounted for his not joining in, but there was no excuse for his uncle. Something his father had once said floated into his mind. 'Rob's a regular kill-joy, takes after the old man.' Jim had never known his paternal grandfather, and observing his uncle's dour look, he was glad of it.

Watching his neighbours in the fireshine was like standing outside a house and looking in at a lighted room. Aunt Mary looked sad, Sandy beamed happily as his thick fingers danced over the buttons, Bill Maddison had a dreamy look and his body seemed to have spread as the tautness went from it. They all liked the music, Jim thought, but none as much as he. Wally Maddison was picking at a pimple on his

44

chin, the identical brown eyes of the little twins from Goola were wide and bright as stars, and their parents were leaning forward, faces rosy in the firewash, singing together.

They finished all the carols everyone could remember. Sandy dragged his accordion open and said into the expectant hush, 'This one is for my wife.' The first strains of 'I Dream of Jeanie With the Light Brown Hair' bounced into the silence under the gums, then the fiddle caught it up in a silvery shower of notes. It was as if a door had suddenly opened for Jim. It wasn't Jeanie, he realised, but Jenny his father was singing about, with a smile that was making his mother blush. Jim glimpsed the fire-enhanced pink of her face, and little actions he had witnessed between them unaccountably returned, fitting into place like pieces of the puzzle that made up the adult world. Things like them holding hands yesterday, or the way his father would wrap his arms around her from behind and hug her tight when he came home of an evening. Looking at the other fathers – Rob, Bill Maddison, big Sam Colson with a voice to match his size – he wondered if any of them did the same.

The song ended and was followed by 'Molly Malone', 'The Yellow Rose of Texas', 'When Irish Eyes Are Smiling', the music spilling out into the warm dark like rings in a dam, Jim thought, only they were brown and muddy-looking while the music was silver. It went further too, beyond the fire and the trees, spreading upwards as well as out until it joined the stars shining soft and lustrous overhead. They danced with the silver notes, twinkling for joy, and Jim fell asleep with his head drooped against his mother's leg and the memory of her hand holding it in his dreams.

FOUR

'C'mon, son.' Sandy's hand was shaking his shoulder.

Jim stared blearily up at him, then around at the empty spaces to either side. Most people had left. Tail-lights winked like crimson eyes as another vehicle – the Maddisons', he thought – pulled out. The policeman and his family were leaving now, and he could hear Sam Colson's big voice loading up his wife and sleeping daughter. Beside him his mother was folding a canvas chair, shaking out a towel, and gathering other oddments into her capacious straw bag. The night smelt late and the Southern Cross had moved while he slept.

The flames had died to embers. His father kicked the burnt ends with the toe of his boot and Jenny tugged at his arm. 'Up you get – that's right. The rover's over here.' He stumbled beside her through the dark, disappointed beyond measure that he had slept and missed the rest of the music. His lids felt heavy and grainy with sleep; he wished they could camp here and go home in the morning. He yawned, eyes closing again. 'Tired.'

'I know you are, Tiger.' Jenny pulled the door open and steered

46

him in. 'You can sleep in a minute. Just slide across – that's it. Leg over the gearstick.'

He felt her presence beside him, the scent of her powder, the touch of her hair on his cheek. Light cut across his eyelids, then the thump of Sandy's body hitting the seat and the slamming door rocked him against Jenny's shoulder. He heard his father's voice.

'Rob's gunna follow us.' The engine ground into life. 'The rest of 'em are gone. Good day, eh love? The young fella asleep?'

'Just about.'

'Am not.' Jim spoke thickly without opening his eyes as they crawled towards the road. A horn tooted goodbye. 'Mum, where's my train?'

'It's safe.' Jenny put her arm around him. 'Go to sleep.'

The night reached out and took him, carrying him deep down into its billowy folds where no stars shone and his father's whistling did not sound. It rained in his dream, and Nipper ran through puddles, splashing and laughing, dark skin gleaming and his wild hair plastered like wet cat's fur to his skull. The rain splashed on Jim's head too, but he screwed his eyes shut, remembering the eggs he had given to Nimrod to prevent this happening. The old man had cheated him and now they would never get to the party. Jim moved his head to make the rain stop and that was when he heard the sound – a *shush, shush*, like a big snake slithering through sand.

Desert snakes were deadly. He froze and gave a little whimper of terror, ears straining as the scaly hide rippled towards him; he imagined its cold touch and the sharp pain of its bite. It was too close, he would never get away in time. He tensed himself to roll, then his hands clutched sand and he tore his eyes open into a painful beam of light.

Somebody had lit the lamp in his room. He went to push himself up from the bed only to fall back in bewilderment because he wasn't in bed. He wasn't even at home, but lying on fresh tyre tracks on the ground – he could see them in the headlights – with tree branches spread above him. The rain had wet his face and hair but the rest of him, along with the sand he lay on, was quite dry – as his hands informed him.

Then the boots that had roused him ran past, scrunching the grainy sand, and a man's voice cried, 'Sweet Jesus! Sandy – Jenny!' But it sounded more like praying than swearing.

Other feet were coming. A woman's voice yelled, high and funny, '*Stay in the car!*' and then she was on her knees beside him, her hands light on his face.

'Mum,' he said gratefully, and fell back into darkness.

When he woke again he was lying on the horsehair sofa in the lounge at Kharko, a blanket over him and water running into his eyes. Everything looked muzzy, and for a moment he mistook the shadow above him for his aunt. She had been washing his face and was now pressing hard against his brow, which stung fiercely. He moaned and rolled his head sideways. 'Don't – hurts.'

'There, dear, nearly finished.' Her face, like her voice, swelled and receded. He watched the light shrink and grow and felt the sofa spin a little. His right hand found the studs at the edge and gripped hard, which stopped the movement but left him feeling scared.

'Mum? What happened?'

'It's all right, dear. There's been an accident but you're all right.

Just lie still now, there's a good boy.'

His sight was clearing and he saw it *was* Aunt Mary. Aunt Mary with bloodstains on her dress, carrying a bowl of bloody water out of the room. Jim felt his head and encountered a thick pad over the place that hurt worst. Now that he was awake enough to notice, most of him hurt.

For what seemed a long time he lay there not thinking at all, except about the fierce ache in his head, and how it must still be night because the lights were on, and that his mother would be mad as fire about the rip in his good shirt, not to mention the dried bloodstains down the front. He could hear the hissing crackle of the transceiver from another room, and voices that talked and stopped and talked again, and something in the quality of the silence between woke a vague alarm in him. Why did nobody come? Why was his mother not here, bandaging his head and looking after him, instead of Aunt Mary? His mother was a nurse – she looked after everybody, and always had.

He threw the blanket off and was pushing himself up when the door opened on his aunt, carrying a glass of water.

'No.' She hurried towards him. 'You musn't get up yet, dear. The doctor wants you to lie quietly till morning. I've brought you a tablet to make your head feel better.'

'I want Mum.' The room was rocking and the sofa seemed to be moving again. 'Where's Dad? I want them both.' He could feel he was going to cry.

'Yes, dear. Your dad will come presently. He's just a bit . . . well, you know, shocked. From the crash. Here.' She scooped his head up and presented the tablet, following it with the glass, its smooth edges cold against his lips. He swallowed obediently but pushed at her arm, feeling the water spill over his chin as he struggled to rise.

'I want Mum. Tell her my head hurts. I want her *now*!' There was a treacherous wobble in the demand.

'You must wait a little, dear. Please. Come on now, there's a good boy. Lie down again and I'll turn the light off and wait with you, and we'll talk about it in the morning. Nothing seems as bad in the morning. Your head will feel better and your dad will be here with you . . .'

His eyes seemed to be closing of their own volition and his body felt woolly and light, as if it might float away somewhere by itself. Aunt Mary's voice faded, dwindling with the yellow glow from the open door, and the strange panic he had felt drained from him. It would be all right. Whatever had happened, it would be all right in the morning.

But it wasn't. In the morning Aunt Mary, sitting closely beside him on the sofa and speaking as if he could remember nothing of the previous night, told him about the accident.

It was much later than he usually woke. There was a patch of sunlight on the floor and the day was no longer fresh, as it was in the early morning. The air hung stuffily in the room, so that when the grandfather clock chimed nine it sounded muffled – as if it had a blanket wrapped around it. Aunt Mary was different too. She held both Jim's hands tight in hers and her face looked strained and pale, as though she had not slept. Beyond the tick of the clock he heard a crow cawing, and the far-off thunder of an engine, but for the rest the house was quiet – so quiet that panic began building in him as his aunt's voice went on and on. He wanted her to stop because a part of him already knew, had guessed last night, but his ears would not close and once the words were spoken his world would change for ever.

'It's not true!' he shouted. 'Where's Dad? He knows, he'll tell you. Because she isn't. She isn't! It's a lie!' He was struggling with her, yelling into her face until he saw the anguish there, and then it was as if the whole of his insides fell away, leaving ice in their place.

'I'm sorry, dear. Your mother loved you very much, and she'll love you still from heaven.' She let go of his hands and whisked a hanky to her eyes 'It's . . . I shall miss her too, you know. But though we're all sad now, by and by we shall be able to remember her without pain. You must be brave, Jim, and help your dad all you can.'

Jim's green eyes burnt like lamps in his pale face. 'Is he . . . ?' He started to his feet. 'Is that why he hasn't come?'

'No, no, he's not hurt. Well, a cut on his arm, but he's all right. Only very, very upset. Your uncle's with him now. Shall I get him?'

'No. I'll go.' Then his composure broke and he ran to the door, feeling the sob building in his chest. 'Dad!' he cried. 'Where are you, Dad?' Skidding down the hall, plunging through the dining room. '*Where are you?*'

Mary's face twisted. She hoped he would find the father he sought, although it didn't seem likely at present. Sighing heavily, she wiped her eyes again and rose to fold away the bedding.

Sandy and Rob were in the office, a ground-floor room in one corner of the house. Jim had a general impression of yellow curtains at the window, a large desk, a filing cabinet, charts and pictures on the wall, and the quick lift of his uncle's head as he burst into the room. The air in it felt empty, as if neither man had moved or spoken for hours. The bandage on Sandy's forearm was shockingly white. He sat with his head in his hands until his son reached him, and when he looked up his appearance stopped Jim in his tracks. This was not his father, this shrunken man with pouched eyes and tear tracks down his cheeks.

'Dad.' Jim's voice came high, sharpened by the agony of his loss, but Sandy seemed unable to reach beyond his own pain.

'She's dead, son. Your mother's dead.'

The boy whitened. It was true then. He stepped hesitantly closer, begging for reassurance. 'What will we do, Dad?' But the huddled figure beside him spoke as if Jim weren't there.

'Jenny,' Sandy murmured. 'Oh, Christ! Jenny.'

He was going to cry, Jim thought in paralysed horror. His mother was dead, his world destroyed, and his father was going to sit and cry. He whirled for the door and felt his uncle's hand close on his shoulder.

'It will be all right, lad. And your dad will be too – in a little while.'

Rage blossomed in Jim like fire in spinifex. It was easy for Uncle Rob to say. She was his *mother*. How could anything ever be right again? Eyes blazing, he wrenched himself free and fled the room.

Jenny McAllister was buried in Alice Springs. Although most of the district made the long journey in to her funeral, of her family only Sandy, Rob and Oliver attended. Mary kept Rosemary and Jim home. A funeral was no occasion for children, she claimed.

Sandy still walked like a dead man and it broke Mary's heart to see Jim hovering about his father, waiting for a spark of recognition in eyes that no longer seemed to see what they looked at. Jim avoided the awed and awkward company of his cousins in favour of the stables, where he had gone that first morning to huddle in the stallion's stall with his choking grief.

The Rook had been out in the yard, pacing the rails and occasionally coming to a prick-eared stand, head lifted at the distant horse shapes in the paddock. It was cool and dim in the stall, and comforting, with the familiar ammoniac reek of dung and horseflesh mixed with the green tang of lucerne hay. Barney, when he slid through the rails with a head-stall over his arm, was casually unsurprised to see him there. 'G'day,' he said.

For a moment Jim wasn't sure whether he was talking to him or the Rook. He wiped hastily at his cheeks and stayed where he was while Barney caught the horse.

'There's me fine beauty.' Barney slapped the stallion's neck and ran a hand over him, teasing his forelock straight and rubbing his ears. Then he led the horse to the water trough in the next yard and stood beside him, rolling a cigarette while the Rook drank. His cigarette lit, he looked across at Jim.

'Doing anything, mate? Want to bring his oats from the feed shed? There's a measuring tin in the drum – half a tin'll do.'

It was the first time anyone had spoken normally to Jim since the accident.

'Yeah. Sure.' He jumped up and fetched the grain, tipping it into the feed bucket and watching as the horse thrust his nose after it, mobile top lip gathering the kernels into his mouth.

'You don't give him much.'

'Well, he's going out to the mares soon, see,' Barney said. 'He's been on hard feed for months, so you gotta wean him off gradually. Can't just cut his rations and shove him out on dry grass. He does all right, don't you big fella?'

The Rook lopped an ear at the familiar voice and one bold dark eye watched them both as he ate. 'Tell you what,' Barney said, 'there's a coupla brushes on the shelf in there.' He nodded at the shed. 'You can give us a hand currying up his coat. The boss likes him smart.'

For an indeterminate time then, Jim lost himself in the soothing rhythm of the work, polishing the satiny skin until the Rook's coat shone. Barney spoke only to direct his strokes and his silence was companionable and undemanding. He hissed as he brushed and made no effort to tell Jim that everything would be all right.

'Looks a picture, don't 'e? he said at length, standing back to admire their work. 'Know what? I reckon he likes yer – hey, old man?' He drew his hand down the horse's nose and the Rook snorted and pushed up against it. 'You can help out again anytime.'

Jim took him at his word, and most days found him down at the stables. Rosemary occasionally spoiled things by accompanying him, but mainly he went alone. It was some years before he realised that his aunt must have deliberately kept his young cousin away, to give him that time alone with his new friend.

It was strange, but all the things he couldn't talk about to Oliver or Rosemary or his aunt were easy to tell Barney. Sitting on the top rail with him, watching the Rook eat, or helping to shovel manure from the stall, he told him all about life at Arcadia. About his pony, about the blacks' camp on the creek, about old Nimrod and Nipper, and the big goanna he and Nipper once killed. In turn Barney told him about the racehorses he'd trained and ridden.

'Are you a jockey then?' Jim asked. Looking at Barney's light, wiry frame, he could see how he might be.

'Yeah. Started me apprenticeship when I was fifteen. Rode in the city for a year or two before I come bush to be a ringer. Now I do the breaking for the station as well, and the boss gimme the stable to look after. We've had some good bloodlines here. The company ain't afraid to spend on bloodstock, I'll give 'em that.'

'Why did you stop? Being a jockey, I mean.'

'Ah.' Barney rubbed a thumb reflectively over the lump on his cheekbone, a mannerism Jim had noticed before. 'Wanted to get away, I s'pose. City wasn't really my style and there was nothin' to stay for.'

'What about your family?'

Barney shrugged. 'Never had one. Orphan child, that's me. They hung me old man when I was six, so the Sisters of Charity brung me up.'

'*Hung* him?' Jim's eyes bugged as he stared at Barney's unconcerned face. 'Cripes, why?'

'Murder.' Barney spoke as if he were talking about somebody else's father. 'He come home drunk one night and beat me old lady to death. Found a bit of pipe, see? Most times he just used his fists, but he found the pipe, so they hung him.'

Jim was speechless. Barney slanted a look at him. 'Sounds tough but it was a long time ago now. I guess I prob'ly loved me mum.' He drew thoughtfully on his cigarette and blew twin streams of smoke out through his nostrils. 'But I got over missing her. You do, you know. And they coulda took me old man away the day after I was born and it wouldn't have bothered me none. Proper bastard he was.'

'What did he do?'

'For a living? Nothing. For a pastime, knocked me and me mum around. But that's history now. They're dead and I'm here and life goes on.' He flicked his cigarette to the ground. 'I was gunna take a run out and find the mares this arvo and start them into the yard. You want to come?'

'You bet.' Then his face fell. 'I suppose I'll have to ask Aunt Mary.'

'Oh, don't worry 'bout the missus, she'll be jakes,' Barney said comfortably. And so it proved. Being with Barney made things feel almost normal again.

Two weeks after the tragedy, with Sandy's land rover still at the crash site awaiting salvage, Rob drove Jim and his father back to Arcadia. Jim, who had initially longed to return home, found himself dreading the prospect. He'd barely seen Sandy at Kharko. His father's room had often stood empty even at daybreak, although on some days the door stayed forbiddingly shut well into the forenoon. Jim could sense his father's presence behind it, but a new timidity prevented him from bursting in on him as he would once have done. His anxious queries had been brushed aside too often. 'Not now, son' and 'Later' had become Sandy's most frequent utterances. Sometimes, while Jim was in the middle of talking to him, he simply got up and walked away, as if unaware his son was there. At the meal table he stared at his plate, eating little and answering vaguely when anyone spoke to him.

Now, climbing hesitantly into the cab of Kharko's land rover, Jim thought of their lonely house filled with his mother's emptiness and his father's silent grieving and wished he could run away. There would be Nipper and Nimrod, and Jake of course, and plenty to do – caring for the stock, checking the bores, keeping the firewood up, looking after the goats. But how would they manage all the things his mother had done? Making out the store orders, mending clothes, knowing what to cook for dinner? If his father would only come back it would be different, but Sandy had gone away inside himself. Jim, remembering his mother's laugh and the way her undisciplined curls sprang about her head, was suddenly swamped with such pain that he knew he must cry. He turned his face to the window to hide his tears.

The trip was largely silent, broken only by Rob's comments on the country and his reminders that help, if needed, was available. Charlie Attwood, a Kharko boundary rider, had been camped at Arcadia pumping and taking care of things since the day after the accident, so the fridge would still be working and the goats looked after. Mary had packed enough cooked food to see them through the first week, and if anything came up Sandy could always give them a call on the radio.

The older brother roused himself. 'I know. Thanks. It's good of you, Rob.'

'For God's sake, man!' Rob sounded irritable. 'We're family, aren't we?'

'Yes, of course. It's just . . .' Sandy left the sentence unfinished but Jim knew what he meant. His father would help anyone who needed it, but accepting help was a different matter.

Now they were charging up the rise through the wattle, to the bend where the house was visible. Jim shut his eyes, opening them only as they coasted to a stop at the gate. He stared about him, shocked, for the scene, though essentially the same, was subtly altered. The house looked small and drab; its chimney was blown crooked, probably by the same willy-wind that had lifted part of the roof from the shed and tumbled the chairs across the verandah. Small signs of neglect became apparent as they pulled up. Jenny's oil-drum plants hung dead in the shade, along with her precious rose; the waterbag swung empty on its hook. And spread against the netting of the garden fence was a table-cloth that had been left to dry on the line on the morning of the party.

Old Charlie had made his camp down by the stockyards. 'Didn't want to interfere with your stuff,' he said gruffly as he poured tea for them from his blackened billy. 'I checked the bores yesterdee. Started the diesel on the one south of the creek – there's a good three hundred head running there and she was down a coupla sheets. Goats is fine. My dog's been gutsing himself on the milk.'

Jim, glancing sideways, saw the heeler panting gently in the shade. 'Woulda got the blacks up to do the milking,' Charlie continued, 'only they cleared out the second day. Nary a sight of 'em since.'

They had heard, Jim thought. In that mysterious way the black-fellas had of knowing things. And Nimrod had moved them away. They feared to encounter the spirits of the dead. Jim had already seen the blown ash of cold fires and the abandoned humpies along the creek. It was something he hadn't counted on, and that night, when they were alone with the lamp between them, eating one of Aunt Mary's meals, he asked his father about it.

'Will they come back?'

Sandy pushed his plate away and reached for his tobacco. 'Next season, after the rain, maybe. The old blackfella's got a lot of taboos, especially about death.' He rubbed a hand over his face. 'Jim, how would you feel about stopping with your uncle for a bit?'

'No!' Panic fluttered within him, and his voice reflected it. Only that morning he had dreaded returning to Arcadia, to his mother's absence, but already the familiarity of home had settled about him. 'I want to stay with you. I can help – there's lots of things I can do. Don't make me go away, Dad, please. I don't want to live at Kharko.'

'Sometimes,' Sandy said, 'you can't do what you want. But we won't decide anything now. Only I have to work, and when the holidays finish there's school, and I don't see how we'll manage that.'

Outside in the moonlight a curlew wailed. 'We'll talk about it later,' Sandy told him. 'Finish your tea.'

'I don't want it.' Jim pushed the food away. His face had whitened and his stomach churned rebelliously.

Sandy's shadow moved on the wall as he stood up and swept his plate and cup together. 'Well, clean your teeth then and off to bed.'

Jim watched his father pick up his swag. 'Where are you going?'

'Outside. I'll sleep on the verandah tonight.'

But if he did it was only briefly, for when Jim got up hours later for the toilet, he found him smoking in one of the chairs, his swag still rolled at his feet, and the empty waterbag creaking in the wind.

FIVE

Christmas, so long awaited, was the failure it was bound to be. They had tinned plum pudding and lumpy custard because Sandy, who could cook a respectable feed of curry or corned meat, wasn't much of a hand at dessert. There had been pressing invitations from Kharko to spend the day there but Sandy turned them down.

In previous years there had always been a tree – usually a gum sucker that Sandy cut on Christmas morning – decorated with gingerbread biscuits shaped like bells and stars and Santas. Jenny piped icing for eyes and buttons onto the Santas, which were Jim's favourite. Christmas smokos, they called the dark, chewy biscuits, and ate them straight off the tree. This year, Jim waited to see if his father would go out with the axe before breakfast, and when he didn't said nothing about it. Who would make the gingerbread biscuits, or tie the bunches of ribbons on the branches?

But beneath Jim's silent exterior a hot rebelliousness seethed. One part of him felt that he and his father should not give up – it was Christmas, and even without his mother they should do as they had always done. Not the biscuits, perhaps, but they could still cut the tree; his father could still go out as in past years and shoot a bush turkey for their dinner. It wouldn't help the pain but it might make the day seem a little more normal. Then his lip trembled and the stock tank grew swimmy in his gaze, for the rest of him knew that life could never be anything like normal again. The emptiness inside him was a worse pain than toothache. The times he'd suffered from that, his mother had twisted cottonwool onto a matchstick, dipped it in oil of cloves, then pressed it into his aching tooth – and the pain had vanished, like magic. He remembered the relief of that moment, and the touch of her gentle hands on his throbbing jaw. But there was no Jenny now to heal the pain, in himself or his father.

Jim's Christmas present was a large parcel of string and balsawood struts that assembled into a box kite with a red fabric cover. Sandy helped him put it together after breakfast, but there was no wind and no one to fly it with. His father claimed he was too old for kites. He sat on the verandah reading a month-old paper while Jim waited disconsolately for a breeze that never came.

In the afternoon they went for a drive around the bores to check the water, coming back at dusk when the black cockies flew crying to roost. Jim stared through smarting eyes at the unlighted house with its hot little kitchen, and in that moment he hated his cousins, and little Gina Colson, and the policeman's twins, and even Nipper – they all had a mother and he didn't. But most of all, in a sad, desperate way that made him want to weep, he hated his father for not helping him, for not even trying to pretend that his son still mattered. Dispiritedly he went to feed the chooks and pen the goats for the night.

In the kitchen the unlit stove was overflowing with ash because Jim had forgotten to rake it out over the past few days. Now the fire would not draw. Sandy swore and stamped outside to light one beside the woodheap. The bakelite handle on the kettle melted in the flames, and they ate Aunt Mary's leftovers in a silence broken only by the pinging of insects hitting the lamp. When Jim went drearily to bed, he cast his unflown kite out the bedroom window. It hit the ground heavily and he hoped vengefully that the fall would wreck it.

Later that night he heard his father raging in the kitchen, and then the smash of breaking things. He pulled the sheet over his head, holding himself small and tight under it, too miserable even for tears. It was so unfair. His mother was dead but his father still had him: that was what he wanted to shout, if he could only have got the words past the hurt in his chest. *You've still got me!* He was trying to adjust to life with just his father – why couldn't Sandy do the same?

In the morning, the good teapot and Jenny's little gold-lipped jug were both gone from the shelf. When Jim carried the ash can out to the rubbish bin he found them there in pieces, amid the Christmas wrapping and empty tins. The teapot had shattered to bits but the jug had broken more moderately, into two fragments. He remembered the day Sandy had given it to his mother, and the way her hair had tumbled down as he swung her in his embrace. Jim's throat ached with longing as he carried the jug to his room. Later, while Sandy brooded over his pipe at the kitchen table, he took the shovel down to the stock tank and dug a hole under the gate valve and buried the pieces there.

There was rain at New Year, enough to lay water and bring nine-day grass springing through the red earth. The sky, rinsed a darker blue, arched over clear distances where the new grass was so green it glittered in the sun. Ducks came planing in to the watery claypans and the cattle deserted the bore. Pumping was unnecessary now. Sandy turned all the mills off and he and Jim drove home through the mud, leaving deep tyre tracks behind them.

More showers followed, the grass thickened and seeded with the rapidity only desert vegetation knows, and Jim waited impatiently through the lonely days, hoping that Nimrod's mob would return. Each morning, he woke with the glad certainty that today he would look up and spy the string of dark figures, hung about with toddlers, coolamons and dillybags, drifting across the landscape to their old camp by the creek. Grass now grew where their fires had been, and the weather had taken their gunyahs, but sometimes, wandering at a loss under the gums, Jim caught their laughter in the cry of birds, or the whisper of their voices in the rustling leaves.

And then, at breakfast one morning towards the end of January, the final blow fell. Aunt Mary, Sandy told him, was coming over to pack up the house. The wireless was on, the rattle of static and voices drowning his father's words, and Jim gaped uncomprehendingly, having caught only half the message. His aunt had been an infrequent visitor to Arcadia; mostly it was they who had made the visits, not the other way about.

'Why is she coming here?' he asked, thinking hopefully that she might bring some cake with her. They had had no cake since the Christmas goods had finished.

'I just said. We're leaving, Jim. She'll pack up your mother's things. I'm moving on. We can't stay here, I couldn't stand it. An agent's coming out from the Alice to look at the stock, and if he ever finds someone willing to take over the lease the land can go too.'

'Sell Arcadia? But . . .' Jim's face whitened. 'It's home, Dad. You can't! What about Nipper and Nimrod and everybody? What if they come back, or the bore breaks down when there's nobody here?' He leapt to his feet. 'You can't sell Jake, or Dolphin – I won't let you.'

'Listen, son.' For the first time in weeks Jim had his father's undivided attention. Sandy's pale blue eyes were really seeing him as he reached across to grip Jim's clenched fist where it rested on the table. 'We have to go, for your sake as much as mine. Just look at you. How long since you combed your hair or scrubbed your nails? And you could grow spuds in your ears. It's my fault for not . . .' His voice cracked momentarily. 'What would your mother say, eh, if she saw you like this? And there's your schooling as well. It's just no good. I have to get away, and you need more looking after than I'm giving you.'

'Well, aren't I coming too?' Jim said anxiously, but Sandy was already shaking his head.

'No, you'll go to Kharko. Aunt Mary will take you back with her. You'll soon settle down there with your cousins. Probably get to like it better than being here with only the black kids to play with,' he added with a horrible heartiness that rang false to them both.

Jim shook his head, lips pressed together to hold in the tears, but Sandy hurried on. 'I'll get things sorted out, find someone to muster the stock, then come by Kharko to drop old Jake off for you. We won't sell him. Or Dolphin. Or any of the rest. And we'll make arrangements for the goats too, so don't worry about them.' It was the most he had said in any one stretch since the accident and every word cut like a knife at his son's heart.

'But . . .' Panic turned Jim weak and he felt the blood drain from his head. 'What do you mean you'll drop Jake off? Why? Where are you going?'

'I don't know yet. Away, that's all. Just for a little while, Jim. I'll be back soon, and you know Mary and Rob will look after you better than I can right now.'

'How long is soon?'

Sandy rubbed his brow with his stubby fingers. 'I told you, I don't know. I don't know anything, except that I can't stay here. I'll go mad if I do.'

'No!' Jim's voice was shrill. 'I want to stay, and if I can't then I'm going with you. I won't go to Kharko. I won't!'

'You have to, son.'

There was such finality in his father's tone that, hearing it, Jim hit the table with the palms of both hands, blood flooding into his face. 'I do not! I hate Kharko and I hate Uncle Rob! You can go and leave me if you want, but I'll stay in the camp with Nipper. Mum wouldn't have left me behind, ever. She —'

'That's enough!' Sandy's voice was hard as a whip.

Jim fell silent and a sick hopelessness filled him. It was going to happen. His father would leave him too. He wished he were dead, or that his uncle and aunt were. Vindictively he pictured the homestead on fire, the family unable to get out, but it was no good. Death only came for the innocent, for people like his mother, and baby Todd.

Sandy sighed and his voice softened. 'You'll understand when you're older, son.'

Jim had heard that one before. And it had proved no more satisfactory then than now. Rage and desolation smarting within him, he whirled and ran from the house.

Aunt Mary arrived mid-morning in a truck driven by Kharko's mechanic, Dino, whose black curly hair reinforced his Italian ancestry. By late afternoon everything had been packed up – pots, pillows, the sewing machine, his mother's best china, his father's tools, even Jim's saddle and bridle. It went into tea chests and was loaded onto the back of the white Dodge. Dino, whose nose was so crooked Jim thought it must have been broken at some time, thrust the last screeching rooster into the netted crate and dusted stray feathers off his shorts. A hen had clawed his arm and another had knocked his hat into the water dish so that the brim now hung soggily over one ear.

'Thank Christ we're not taking the goats as well,' he muttered, then he flushed and looked at Mary. 'Sorry, Missus. You ready, young fella?'

Jim ignored him. His whole life was parcelled up into tea chests. The house had been gutted of everything but furniture, a few cooking pots and Sandy's swag. The kettle with the ruined handle still sat on the hob, and the fridge hummed against the wall, but the rooms echoed as if they were empty. As empty as the blacks' camp, for they had still not returned. He wouldn't even be able to say goodbye to his friends.

Standing at the door of the truck, Jim looked searchingly across the horizon, ducking his head to see under the thick new growth on the gums, but nothing moved except a pair of emus, stalking with bobbing heads through the scrub. Sandy came to rumple his hair and pull him roughly against him. Jim's heart swelled painfully and he shut his eyes, smelling sweat and tobacco and a whiff of diesel.

'I'll be along in a week or two, son. And I'll have old Jake, don't you worry.'

Jim nodded mutely, wondering how a horse, even one as dear as Jake, could make up for his father's absence. He climbed into the truck and Aunt Mary reached across him to shut the door, as if he couldn't do it for himself, and then they were moving. Leaning out of the window, he watched his father dwindle in size until the bend of the road took him from sight and there was only the mill tower and the crooked chimney of the house.

It was closer to three weeks before Sandy turned up at Kharko, and by then Jim was back in school. He had a room at the top of the stairs, next to Rosemary's, and a place for his saddle and bridle in the shed beside the stable. Aunt Mary had cut his hair and thrown out the shirt he'd been wearing on arrival. Uncle Rob greeted him with, 'Glad to have you, Jim,' then laid down the rules. He must inform somebody every time he rode out. He must keep away from the blacks' camp, the old mine shafts and the machinery shed, and he must try hard at school.

'Yes, Uncle.' Jim eyed the tall, unsmiling man with dislike.

'It's a bit different to what you're used to but you'll soon settle in. Just give it a try. We all want you to be happy.'

This was so insultingly absurd Jim would not dignify it with an answer.

Later he had gone to his cousins. 'Where're these mine shafts supposed to be?'

'In Crimea.' Oliver was practising his shuffling technique, the cards making little kissing sounds as they slid between his bony fingers. He was a bony sort of boy, Jim thought critically, all angles and elbows, continually catching his feet on things. Before he could ask more, Rosemary spoke up.

'You go out past the yards, miles and miles away, where the hills curve round. There's heaps of tunnels and shafts. A cow fell down one once and died.'

'It did not, Ro.' Oliver pulled the cards out in a long string, then clapped them shut again before they spilled. 'Dad just said it ought to be fenced off because cattle *could* fall down the shafts. And it's not that far away, only about a mile. It's the old Kharko copper mine,' he explained to Jim. 'It was here first and they named the station after it. Some of the shafts are supposed to be eighty feet deep.'

'Who says? I'll bet you've never been to look.'

Oliver hesitated but his sister was less reticent. 'Course we have. We don't tell Dad cos he'd go mad. We aren't supposed to go there at all, but it's fun. There's sheds and engines and a big old slippery dip you get onto from a ladder.'

'It's a conveyor belt,' Oliver said shortly. 'And Dad'd have our hides if he knew. But we just stay round the sheds and they're nowhere near the shafts, so it's quite safe, really. We'll take you there if you promise not to tell.'

'Me? I wouldn't tell him . . . tell him . . .' Jim couldn't think of anything trifling enough to complete the sentence with, and the anxious look faded from his cousin's freckled face.

'That's all right then. We'll take you as soon as your horse comes.'

The range was purpling at the end of a hot day when this happened.

Rosemary and Jim had climbed the mill tower and were sitting swinging their legs on the platform, enjoying the breeze gained from that elevation, when a travelling dust cloud hove into sight. It was moving too slowly for a vehicle and Jim, narrowing his eyes to discover the reason for it, felt his heart leap with sudden foreknowledge.

'It's Dad!'

'How do you know?' Rosemary screwed her eyes up and squinted ferociously into the light. ''Tisn't. It's just wind.'

But he was already on his way down. It was indeed Sandy, although it took half an hour for the horses to reach the yard. By that time Jim and Rosemary were waiting for him there, and presently Barney and Dino drifted down on foot, then Rob, driving the land rover.

'Dad!' Jim flung himself on the dusty, unshaven figure, careless of Dolphin's snort and upthrown head. 'How far did you come today? Where's the truck? Are you going to stay here now?'

'One thing at a time, son,' Sandy said, and squeezed him with his spare arm. 'How you doing? Let's get the packs off first, eh? They've come a good thirty miles today – that's a big up for fresh horses. I camped at Cobbler's bore last night and come across bush to the main road. How're you getting on with your uncle and aunt?'

'All right,' Jim said impatiently. Sandy had forty-odd horses with him, five of which carried pack bags and camping equipment. The bags were plumped out by their contents; one had a folded tarp over the top and his father's swag was on another. A shovel handle poked out from flaps below it, along with an axe and a canvas rifle case. There were buckets, billies, a camp-oven. Hobbles swung from each horse's neck strap; some carried bells and the packhorses wore headstalls.

'What happened to the truck?' Jim asked as he held Billy, the old brown gelding, while Sandy unpacked him. Barney had caught and tied the other packhorses and was busy pulling the gear off them. After weeks of waiting, everything was suddenly moving too fast. Jim had known his father would come, but not like this, poised on the edge of departure.

'It went with the stock. The herd's gone already.'

Jim steeled himself. 'How long are you staying here?'

Sandy pulled Billy's headstall off and met his son's gaze. 'Just tonight. I'll be away at daylight, but I'll write you from further up the track.'

Jim swallowed hard, conscious that Barney and Dino could hear every word. 'How long till you come back?'

'I don't know exactly, son. You want to unsaddle Dolphin for me? Let's say next Christmas, shall we? Now, mind her girth – it's a bit galled and she might have a poke at you with her hind leg.'

He turned away to shake hands with Rob, leaving Jim standing numb with shock beside the mare. Next Christmas! That was nearly a whole year away. He was distantly aware of Barney's cheerful tones and the horses moving about him but all he could think of was the desert of time stretching before him. He had hoped it would be only weeks, had suspected it might be several months, but had never dreamt it could be a year. Sick with despair, he fumbled the flaps up and tugged at the chestnut's girth.

Sandy left at sun-up next morning. He had gone out in the pre-dawn darkness to bring the horses up, and Jim, who woke to the sound of booted feet descending the stairs, was waiting on the yard rails when he returned astride Peddler. The light was on in the kitchen by then and they ate breakfast there, Jim nibbling silently on toast while Pommy John, brown eyes curious above his huge moustache, talked to Sandy and tended the big wood stove. The rest of the men came in as they were finishing, jostling each other at the pans of steak and gravy, screeching the backless benches across the floor as they sat.

Pommy John stuck his head through a hatch in the outside wall and slammed down plates of steak, with bread and treacle on the side, for the blackfellas waiting there. Everyone was happy, Jim thought, it didn't matter to them that his father was going away for ever, or as good as. He could hear the blackfellas laughing out on the woodheap where they ate, and Dino cheeking old Charlie – who was a regular misery-guts, according to Pommy – just as if it were an ordinary day. He supposed it was, for them.

After breakfast, Sandy thanked the cook, stuffed the first of the morning's ready-rubbed into his pipe, and went back to the house to finish packing. Barney walked across to the yard with Jim. Jake was standing in a corner with Dolphin, nipping her flank whenever her tail stopped moving, for the flies had come with the daylight. Jim bridled him with cold hands, adjusting the fly veil on the brow band and mechanically rubbing Jake's ears for the sake of something warm to hold. It was all he could do not to cry when his father returned and put his arms round him.

'I'll be back, son,' Sandy said gruffly, and rumpled Jim's hair. 'Behave yourself. I'll see you round Christmas time.'

'Okay.' He could trust himself no further than a single word.

Yellow light was breaking over the range as the plant trotted from the yard, pack loads creaking in its midst. Jake, aware of his mates' departure, paced at the end of his reins, whinnying after them. Jim watched the square of his father's blue cotton back going steadily away from him. He would always remember the way the dust hung, and the sun glinting on one of the packhorses' whiskery jaw, and that fading blue back.

Jake whinnied again, reefing at his reins and pawing the ground, and Barney clicked his tongue.

'What say we put him in the stable yard for an hour or two? You don't want him over the paddock fence. What do you call him?'

'Jake.'

'Good-looking pony.' He reached to pat him and Jake, as he always did with strangers, snapped at his fingers. Barney gave an admonitory tap to his muzzle. 'Got a bit of devil in him, eh?'

'A bit.' Jim was hardly listening. Then abruptly he said, 'Where's Mara—, Maratanka?'

Barney rubbed his cheekbone. 'You wouldn't mean Mataranka? It's up north in buffalo country. Wild place that – they've got crocs and snakes. The little ones grow to about nine feet, I heard.'

'That's where Dad's headed. How far is it?'

Barney shrugged. 'Dunno. A good distance, I'd reckon.'

'It'll take months just to get there.' Jim spoke despairingly. 'Then he's not coming back till Christmas.'

'That's no time, really,' Barney encouraged. 'The other side of winter. He'll be back before you know it.' He clapped Jake on the neck. 'C'mon, fetch the pony along. Is he any good with stock?'

Jim answered crisply, begrudging the words. 'Handy but slow. That's what Dad says.'

'Well, tell you what, next time I bring the killers up you can give us a hand and we'll see what he can do. Oliver usually helps. It's a bit of a job yarding up by yourself.'

'Righto.' Jim would have given the same answer to an invitation to dance. What did it matter? His father was gone.

SIX

Jim had never known a year could be so long. Gradually, as the weeks passed, he settled into life at Kharko. There was always something going on, and visitors were far more frequent than they had been at Arcadia. All manner of people came for all manner of reasons: the Inland Mission padre and his wife, to hold a service in the garden; the carrier, when the rain had finished, to unload a ton of fresh stores onto the loading dock; and the Flying Doctor and his nurse, who came each month and took over one end of the verandah, where they ran a clinic for anyone who turned up. There were fourteen extra people for lunch during the March clinic, and two less to go home afterwards, because Gina Colson fell off the loading dock and broke her arm. She and her mother went into Alice Springs with the doctor, bringing Sam Colson roaring across to Kharko to glean details of the accident first-hand.

'He's besotted with that girl,' Mary said to Rob as they stood at the gate watching their visitor charge off again. She shook her head. Mary had dealt with the usual run of childhood scrapes, fractures and sprains, and was almost as handy with a bandage as Jenny had been.

To see the big, tough cattleman begging for reassurance over a simple greenstick fracture amazed her. 'Still, I suppose she's their only child.'

Apart from these regular visitors, there were other, more interesting ones. Some, like the contractors and men looking for work, he met in the kitchen; others, such as the company's managing director, cattle buyers and travelling clergymen, dined in the big house. One day, an artist turned up. He was a funny, bearded little man with a thick accent who wore a cloth hat and long shorts with baggy, button-down pockets. He drove in to the station in a battered van and stayed for a week, camping in the quarters at night and spending his days wandering about the sheds and yards, all the while drawing.

'Bastard's mad,' declared Pommy John. 'He ain't a proper artist at all. Take a look at this.'

He held up a charcoal sketch of himself drawn in bold, sweeping strokes. It was more like a cartoon than a proper picture, Jim thought. Only half of Pommy's face was there – his mouth was just a line, his nose a squiggle below the heavy eyebrows and luxuriant moustache that dominated the page.

Oliver squinted at it, his head on one side. 'Hey, it's a dead ringer for you, Pommy. It's good. No, I mean it. Is this all he does – people?'

'Nah.' Pommy John smoothed his moustache, looking sideways at the sketch. 'I reckon he's taking the mickey. Says 'e's painting the country's soul, whatever the 'ell that means. Told you, bastard's mad.'

Jim didn't think so. He had watched the artist, whose name was Gunther, wandering about the place, stopping at the stable yard to examine a morticed post and rail, fingering the grader tyres, running his hands over a ripple of corrugated iron. He even squatted to feel the grass, pulling it through his fingers and staring at the seed heads as if they were something new, made only that day. It was the way Nipper looked at things, Jim thought, and something he himself had copied. Gunther was like a kid, even though he was quite old, examining everything as if seeing it for the first time. To him, everything was new and interesting. And the proof of it was the day Jim found him on his hands and knees peering at little funnel-shaped holes in the sand.

'What is this, pliss?' He raised alert, pale eyes to Jim, who folded down to sit cross-legged beside him.

'It's an ant-lion trap.' He looked about and reached to pick up a passing ant, which bit him as he flicked it into the hole.

Gunther watched as the ant struggled to climb the walls of its prison, but the sand kept shifting. The ant slipped, there was a flurry at the bottom and it was jerked from sight. The tiny moving granules settled and the trap became static, awaiting its next victim.

'So, it is deadly, no? If you are the ant.' Gunther got to his feet, two patches of sand on his bony knees, and waved his hand, saying gravely, 'I paint it all, you understand. Everything. What is empty, what is lonely, even the little ant. You like pictures, hmm? What is your name?'

'Jim. I dunno. They're all right, I suppose.'

'Hah, Jim.' Gunther took a sketchpad from one pocket and a pencil from another and put a dozen flowing lines on a page. He tore it off and presented it to Jim.

'What is it?' He looked at it with curiosity.

'It is you, Jim. Like the tree, see?'

'How come?' He wasn't even standing in the sketch. Gunther had drawn him as he sat, in a twist of arms and legs, his hat half over his face. 'Doesn't look much like a tree to me.'

'Nevertheless,' the artist made a meal of the word, 'it is you. I look before I draw. I touch, I feel, and I am thinking, How this thing is made? And why this thing is so? And I see you alone, like the tree, and sitting like the black pipples, waiting, yes? So this is Jim, who is different to the one with the eyeglasses, and different to the big cook who thinks I am mad.' His eyes twinkled and suddenly Jim found himself smiling back.

'Matter of fact he does. But my dad says you have to worry about what *you* want to do, not what everyone else thinks you ought to.'

'He is wise then, the big boss. We have only one life for drawing, or anything else.'

'Not *him*,' Jim said sharply. 'My dad's away, he's coming back later.'

'Ah, so that is why you wait. Like the tree waits for rain. Well, it is good, *nein*? For something special to be coming far off?'

'Yeah.' Jim loaded the word with irony. Scooping up a pebble, he flung it across the paddock. 'If you like waiting, that is.' Pommy John was right after all, he decided, the bloke was mad.

The following day, a non-school day, Jim and his cousins made their visit to the old mine. They timed their trip for when Rob was out at a new bore site with the drilling contractors, setting out straight after an early lunch to ensure they were back before he was. On the way they detoured to Bell Creek, south-west of the homestead. There were all sorts of yarns about the place, according to Oliver.

'Some reckon it's haunted. The blacks won't go near it and the stock don't like it either. Barney says that's because it's all rock and scalded country. A man's supposed to have perished there. They reckon he must've kept following the bell sounds, thinking it was his horses, and got bushed in the scrub and couldn't find his way out again.'

Bell Creek certainly wasn't like other creeks Jim had seen. It was a deep gully spilling out of the range in a tumble of stone. A mass of timber rose above the low scrub on the flats, casting the gully into perpetual shadow. The creek bed was filled with sand and had got its name, Oliver said, from the sound that could be heard when the wind blew through a pattern of holes in the rocks. But you had to go further in to find them, he added, and they didn't have time for that. 'Besides, there isn't any wind right now, so it's no use.'

Jim thought of the eternal curiosity of the strange little artist. 'I bet old Gunther would draw this.' He would have liked time to explore, but his cousins were anxious to reach the mine.

They headed on, and by mid-afternoon came to the sheds and gantries of the old treatment plant, with a midden of bottles and rusted tin where the rubbish heap had been. Dismounting to explore, they left their horses – Jake; Oliver's black, blaze-faced gelding Koel; and Mandy, the fat pony mare Rosemary rode – in the shade of the biggest shed, where Rosemary's slippery dip was. Bars of sunlight striped the ground through gaps of missing iron and a butcherbird carolled from a roof strut, the sound echoing through the vast building. Jake snorted; his velvet nostrils rounded as he stared at a pile of roly-poly gathered in a corner.

'Don't be stupid,' Jim admonished. 'It's only a plant. It won't hurt you.'

'He's cute, isn't he?' Rosemary said, and he glared at her.

'He is not *cute*. And,' he added as she reached to pat him, 'he doesn't like girls.'

Right on cue Jake nipped her. Rosemary yelped, then swung the flat of her hand hard against the astonished horse's jaw, sending him jerking back with a snort of surprise. She shook her fingers, giving Jake the eye. The blow, landing on bone, had stung. 'You do that again, you'll get it again.' Then, to Jim's chagrin, she put her grubby paw on Jake's nose and rubbed it, and he thrust his head up against the pressure, making no effort to bite.

Jim was breathless with loathing. 'You hit him again and I'll knock your block off.'

'You teach him some manners, then.' Rosemary stuck out her tongue and it was left to Oliver to make the peace and urge them back out into the autumnal sun. The green had gone from the grass now that the days were shortening towards winter, and the eastern arm of the range, seen up close like this, reared redly from the soil with no trace of the purple that dust haze and distance gave to it. Jim imagined miners working here on freezing winter mornings, being lowered into cold dark shafts far from the warming sunlight. Or maybe they had climbed down. Ladders, rotten with age, were still spiked to the walls of two of the shafts, but even without Oliver's warning he felt no desire to investigate. The hidden darkness of the old diggings put a shudder through his spine; it would be too much like being buried alive.

He said so and Rosemary, whose temper never lasted, nodded. 'There's a grave too. Come and see.'

There was no headstone on the oblong of earth inside rusted iron railings. They speculated on the cause of its occupant's demise before drifting off to inspect the dump. This was far more interesting. Jim found a lead soldier with a miniature metal drum lying beside it.

The paint had flaked off both pieces and the top of the soldier's rifle was a little bent, but they were otherwise perfect.

'You can even see the buttons on his coat,' Rosemary marvelled.

'There must have been a set.' Oliver turned the drum about. 'You can tell this isn't his because he's got his rifle at the ready. There might have been a whole band even. Let's see if we can find them.'

He and Rosemary searched without success, turning up a variety of useless items, including a bottle with a marble jammed in its neck and the twisted frame of a lady's sewing hoop. But Jim had lost interest, having suddenly remembered the clockwork train from the Christmas party. It had vanished in the accident, and was probably still lying in the wreck of the land rover. Maybe years hence somebody would find it and wonder about the boy who had owned it.

Oliver tossed the sewing hoop away, but on the way home he hid the bottle in a clump of rocks, which held a small collection of other stuff. Jim saw a nutcracker with jaws like a crocodile's head and the remains of a kerosene lamp.

'Why leave it out here?' he wanted to know.

'So Dad won't see it, of course. You reckon he wouldn't guess where it came from?'

Home again, they let the horses go and went up to the kitchen, which was empty save for Pommy John and Gunther, drawing at one end of the long table. The three of them slid onto the benches closest to the door. It might be well past smoko but Pommy John, unlike other adults, understood that biscuits neither ruined your teeth nor your appetite for the next meal. Rosemary, to Jim's initial alarm, was telling the cook about his find but he needn't have worried. By some strange osmosis, Pommy learned everything that happened on the station anyway, and his loyalties lay within the kitchen. Bosses, he'd already told Jim, were there to be shot at, an expression Jim knew to be figurative because it was Sandy's philosophy also. His father had always been on the side of the working man, the more so, he once told his son, because he'd done the work of three of them for most of his life.

Now the cook's big fist engulfed the little soldier and lifted it level with his face. 'Blimey! What we got 'ere?' Gently he pressed the crooked rifle barrel straight and set the little figure down on the scrubbed table-top. 'Part of a drummer's set too, eh? Can't really tell without the colours but I reckon he'd be a fusilier. Wonder how the 'ell he got out in this country? Makes you think, don't it?' He put the soldier next to the drum just as the screen door opened and Rob walked in.

Jim gaped at him, made a grab to snatch the pieces from view and found they were already gone. Pommy's hand emerged from his pocket holding a tobacco tin and Jim felt a surge of relief. He heard Oliver's quick intake of breath and it was only then that he saw the two strangers standing behind Rob. Pommy, grinding tobacco shreds against his palm with a spatulate thumb, nodded affably at the three men.

'G'day. Thought you wouldn't be back till after dark, boss?'

'Change of plan,' Rob said briefly. 'These blokes are the drillers, Pommy. They'll be camping in the quarters tonight. They missed lunch. Can you knock up a feed for them?'

'Yeah, course. What about you?'

'I'm right, thanks, I'll go to the house.' He cast an eye over the children. 'What are you three doing?'

'Nothing, Dad,' Rosemary answered virtuously.

'Good. You can give Barney a hand to get the killers up to the yard.' To Pommy he added, 'The rest of the camp'll be in tonight.' At the door he turned to look at his son. 'Don't keep Barney waiting.'

'As if,' Oliver said when Rob had gone. They grinned at each other in delight. It was great fun getting the killers in; the animals were wary of the yards and played up, guaranteeing some galloping for them all.

Pommy said hospitably to the strangers, 'Well, siddown. I got a nice bit of silverside.' Remembering the artist, he waved a meaty hand. 'This here's Gunther – draw you quick as look at you, he will.'

As if fulfilling a prophecy, the artist stood up, a charcoal sketch ready in his hand. It wasn't the drillers he had drawn, however, but the children – three startled faces staring at a huge fist disappearing into the pocket of Pommy's shorts. Gunther laughed at their expressions, which were almost as surprised as those in the sketch.

'He is quick to hide your secret, the big cook, yes? Tomorrow I go. And all of everything,' his sweeping hand took in the angular lines of stove, table, benches and, Jim understood, the world beyond the kitchen walls, 'is safe up here.' He tapped his head, then cocked it at the sketch. 'But this I am keeping to remember you by.'

'Well, I just hope he doesn't go showing it around,' Oliver worried as they walked back to see if their mounts were still on the trough. 'Strewth! Blind Freddy could tell we'd been up to something.'

'He'll be gone tomorrow,' Jim said. And suddenly he wished that the strange artist had arrived months earlier, before his father left. Then he might have had a picture of him to keep against his return.

And then it was May and the races. Jim, who had started writing to his father care of the post office at Mataranka in February, wrote two pages on the horses Kharko would be running at Goola. Oliver was helping with their training, and what Jim wanted most in the world, after a reply from Sandy, was to be his gangly cousin as he sprang onto the backs of those beautiful creatures in the half-light of a new day. The Rook had been entered for the Goola Cup, and a chestnut mare called Raygirl – out of Mountain Lass by Sunray, Jim wrote knowledgeably – would run in the Bracelet. And there was a three-year-old named Sweet Prue for the Maiden.

His hand was cramping up. He bit his pen and stared out the window, where Rosemary, a green jumper pulled over her shirt, was bouncing a ball in the garden. He wondered what to write next. He could tell Sandy about seeing Barney ride Mandarin, the station's worst buckjumper, or about the drillers finally striking water, but would his father care? He probably didn't even remember Barney.

Suddenly it all seemed too much effort. Jim was sick of it, he realised, sick of passing on news that for all he knew was never read. How did he know his father even got the letters? Because surely he would have written back if he had. He'd promised he would. Then again, perhaps he wasn't at Mataranka yet, or had already travelled on and the post office hadn't forwarded his mail.

Abruptly Jim dipped his pen to scrawl, 'I'm not writing any more letters because you aren't getting them. Your son, Jim.' He folded the missive into the prepared envelope (he always did the address first, while his writing was neatest), capped the ink bottle and put it away. Done was done, as Pommy John said whenever he pulled the bread from the oven.

But even though he no longer wrote, he couldn't stop himself haunting the corridor outside his uncle's office on Thursdays when the mailbags came in on the plane. At first he had waited eagerly, jigging from foot to foot, ready to grab the precious letter and run somewhere private to read it. But after weeks of hearing 'Not today, Jim' or 'Perhaps next week, dear' from Aunt Mary, and aware that she pitied his disappointment, he affected a more casual attitude. He preferred it when his uncle sorted the mail – he didn't care if you got letters or not. He'd slap the last one onto its pile on his desk, saying brusquely, 'That's it. You can take the school stuff back with you, Jim.' Or occasionally, 'Here, run this lot over to the bookie, will you?'

Pommy John never got letters either. 'Nothin' but trouble,' he said, punching the bread dough around on the zinc-topped table made for that purpose. 'Let's see, I been 'ere a bit over six years an' I never had a single letter. Not one. 'Cept,' he added darkly, 'from them bastards in the Tax Office. You can't get away from them.'

'So do you write any?' Jim asked, and the cook looked at him in astonishment.

'Wot the 'ell would I wanna do that for? I come out 'ere for a new start, not to drag me old life along with me. You wanna grease them tins?'

'How come you don't have any of the camp lubras to help you, Pommy? With the washing up and sweeping and that?' Jim wiped fat across the bread tins. 'Other stations do, even Mum did.' His voice wavered for a moment as he conjured a picture of Jenny wringing sheets over the laundry tubs with Meena, Nipper's mother, the two of them talking and laughing while they worked. He cleared his throat and continued. 'She used to get Nipper's mum to come up to the house and give her a hand.'

'Boss don't allow it, is how. Bit of a wowser, your uncle. He don't want the blokes chasin' 'em. Mind you, they can still go down the camp an' get it anyhow, but it means the sack, an' they know it. There's no velvet to be had on Kharko.'

'No what?'

For the first time in their acquaintance Pommy looked discomfited. 'Never you mind. 'Ow's the 'orses coming on? I expect to clean up big at the races, it ain't every year I get word straight from the stable.'

'Barney reckons they're going pretty good. He and Oliver did time trials this morning. Prue's got a bit of a knock on her hind fetlock but Barney reckons it'll be okay cos she'll have a lay-off while they're in the paddock. He's taking them down tomorrow. I wish I could go too, but we have to do school.' The classroom bell rang on the word and he heaved a martyred sigh and wiped his greasy hands on his shorts. 'See you later.'

Race day came at last and the whole station set off for Goola, the men filling the stock-camp truck, and the McAllisters in Rob's private vehicle, a canvas-covered land rover. A transformed Rosemary in a starched frock and knee-high socks sat between her parents, while Oliver and Jim, horribly self-conscious in their ties and braces, rode in the back.

It was a clear blue day, the line of the range bulking like an ochre wall beyond the racecourse. A score or more of vehicles were parked, noses in like drinking bullocks, along the fence behind the shabby stands. Barney was already there waiting for them, a dapper figure in strapped moleskin pants, a new shirt and what Jim recognised as his town hat. His riding boots shone, bright as the Rook's coat, and he grinned tightly as he greeted the boys. 'You right, Oliver?'

'Yeah.' He swallowed nervously. He was riding Sweet Prue in the Maiden. It would be his first race and now that the moment had come he looked sick at the prospect. 'How's her leg?'

'Just grand. You keep your head and she'll go like a charm. I had me first ride at fifteen. Nothing to it.'

'Didja win?' Jim asked.

Barney laughed. 'Would of, if the others had gone slower. Nah, we was second last, but that won't happen today. I'm riding two of Mike Kelly's nags as well, but he's got nothing in the Maiden so that's okay. C'mon, you'd better get changed, Oliver, they'll be calling the first race soon.'

They headed off, and Jim left the others to wander through the throng. He recognised some of the people in the group standing around the bookmaker – Dino was there with a fistful of notes, as was Des Hanks, Kharko's head stockman. Both men were studying the chalk board behind the bookie, a barrel-chested man with a moneybag hanging from a strap about his neck. The biggest crowd was clustered around the makeshift bar. Pommy John was there, and Jeff Tillet, stiff in his police uniform, and Bill Maddison, his skinny figure tense and spidery, his long chin sitting on his tie. Jim found Roy and Wally Maddison scoffing cake and soft drink at the CWA stand, and fishing out the money Aunt Mary had given him, he went to join them.

There was so much going on it was hard to know where to look first – at the horses, the vehicles still arriving, or the two men singing on unsteady legs halfway between the Gents and the jockeys' changing room. He and the Maddison boys were messing around at the back of the stands, where a cattle bitch in a box snarled at them over the heads of her week-old puppies, when the first lot of horses went out, their riders' silks shimmering in the sunlit breeze. Jim almost missed Oliver's race. He ran dodging through the crowd and squeezed onto the rails just in time to see the crouched green and white figure of his cousin surging up the straight in a storm of dust and flying tails.

'Left it too late,' a familiar voice muttered, and Jim glanced up to see Barney beside him. He was right. There were three horses ahead of the filly, the leader streaking for the post as the crowd cheered her on. Oliver's whip moved and Sweet Prue flew past the rangy chestnut in front of her, but the race was over.

'She nearly got there,' Jim said.

Barney, who'd been clutching the rail, gave him a tight, ferocious grin. 'Nearly don't count in racing. Still, wasn't the horse's fault.'

Barney rode in the next four races, alternating Kharko's green and white stripes with Mike Kelly's checked blue and yellow. Kelly ran Firepeak Station, just outside Alice Springs, and was a regular at Goola. When the jockeys were mounting for the second of Barney's races a woman's hat blew into the saddling enclosure, flaring right under the nose of his mount. The horses snorted or shied according to temperament, and Barney's horse, a big-boned bay from Firepeak called Nelson, dropped his head. Barney rode the first buck then vaulted from his saddle to grab the bridle and turn the horse so that his lashing hind feet missed the other animals. A flustered Kathy Colson retrieved her dusty hat and Mike Kelly threw Barney back onto the sidling Nelson while the rest rode out onto the straight.

'Did you see him?' Jim said proudly to the Maddison boys. 'That's Barney O'Dowd. He can ride anything.'

'Yeah, well, so can Jockie Barron,' Roy asserted. 'I seen him ride three winners in a row. And a horse has to sling the saddle to get rid of him.'

'He wouldn't be any better than Barney,' Jim said loyally. 'He rode a real bad bucker —'

He was cut short by the starter's pistol. Nelson reared and a man behind the boys said, 'Bloody useless dog meat,' and turned away, crumpling a betting slip in his fist. Nelson ran wide around the turn, flogging his tail as he chased the field and came in last. Jim, who'd been quite certain that anything Barney bestrode must win, perceived that there was more to the racing game than he had thought. Barney himself, pulling the saddle off the sweating horse, shrugged aside his commiserations.

'They come in all sorts, kid, slow as well as stupid, and this one's both. I was Kelly, I'd shove a pack on him. He ain't worth feeding.'

But all was redeemed in the Goola Cup. The Rook won with ease and panache. Squeezed between Rosemary and Oliver at the rail, Jim watched breathlessly as the big brown ran the opposition down and surged to the lead to win by a comfortable length. He screamed as loudly as his cousins, who were almost witless with excitement, grabbing him in turn to yell, 'He won! We won! He won the Cup!'

Did they think he was blind or something? Jim wondered, shoving Rosemary off him. Her hat had slipped to the back of her head, leaving her copper curls glinting in the sun. She had screwed the skirt of her dress into a knot, and one of her socks had sunk to her ankle but she was radiantly happy. His uncle, he saw, was smiling as he strode out to lead the Rook in. A couple of men, one of whom he recognised as Sam Colson, shook his hand and everybody clapped. Somebody took a photo of the horse and rider and then Barney, grinning widely, sprang down and with the other placegetters carried his saddle to the scales.

The noise level around the bar rose as the day progressed, almost drowning the voice of the man calling the races. A chestnut took the Bracelet, beating Raygirl to the post by a nose, then Barney brought the second of Mike Kelly's horses home in the final race. Dino, grinning owlishly at Jim, waved the fistful of notes he had won and with some difficulty separated one from the rest, handing it to him. 'You kids have a drink on me.'

'Cripes!' The boy stared at the first ten shillings ever to come his way. 'Thanks, Dino.' He made for the refreshment stall with Rosemary and the Maddison boys in tow. The Goola storekeeper's wife was serving and he gave her the note. 'Four bottles of sars, please.' His eye fell on the last tray of cakes; it was too good an opportunity to miss. 'And eight of those chocolate ones.'

Jim took his change, gave Rosemary the bag of cakes to carry, and he and Wally took the bottles. The crowd was thinning out around them. Pommy John could be heard loudly and drunkenly defending some point at the bar, where a desultory fist fight had started between two men, whose punches bruised the air. Jim saw the Rook's head hanging over his uncle's shoulder, and Barney, still wearing Kelly's colours, crossing towards the stalls. There was no sign of Oliver.

'Round here.' Roy ducked under the back of the stand. They squatted in the red dust, swigging at the slightly warm gassy drink between mouthfuls of sticky cake. Jim was finding it a struggle to get his share down. Earlier there had been watermelon, as well as sandwiches, and he had already consumed a quantity of soft drink.

'Not bad lolly-water.' Roy burped loudly and lowered his bottle. 'Who was that bloke who gave you the money anyway?'

'He works at Kharko.' Jim spoke faintly. He felt distinctly unwell and regretted that last cake. His head swam and a cold sweat covered his body as he lurched suddenly to his feet.

'You gunna spew?' Wally drew his feet back as a precaution but Jim, mouth filling with saliva, was already running. He made for the tin building marked 'Gents', then swerved aside. There might be somebody in there and he couldn't wait. He got almost to the back of it before his stomach heaved and he staggered against the warm corrugated iron, retching desperately, eyes tight shut and the sour fizz of sarsaparilla in his nostrils. When it was over he stayed leaning there while his stomach settled, trying to spit the taste from his mouth. He raised his head and waited till the horizon stopped swimming, then jumped as a voice spoke behind him.

'You been getting into the booze, kid?' It was Barney, dressed once again in his moleskins. 'You're not the only one neither, by the look of things.'

'Huh?' Then Jim saw the dirty legs and bare feet protruding from behind the tin hut. He had nearly been sick on them. 'Who's that?'

'Sammy Deane.' Barney's lip curled. 'General no-hoper. I'd say he's shit himself by the smell. You right, now?'

'Yeah.' Jim gave a final spit. 'Too much fizzy drink, that's all.' He stared, repulsed at the dirty figure with flies buzzing over it. 'What shall we do about him?'

'Nuthin'. His gin'll see to him. She'll be round somewhere. Rob's looking for you, he's about ready to leave. I'll see you at home,' he said and walked off.

'Right.' Jim stared a moment longer at the unconscious body sprawled amid the roly-poly and bindi-eye, at his blotched features and bristled face, his thin, scrawny limbs and lank hair. The man smelled dreadful. There was an empty rum bottle under his hand and he lay so still that if it hadn't been for the noisy snores he might have been dead.

With a sudden scalding fury Jim wished he was. He was just a stinking drunk. Why should a man like that live when his mother, who was good and kind and helped everybody, had died? A just God would have saved her and let drunken Sammy Deane die instead. Jim hawked in his throat and watched the gobbet of spit land on the man's greasy shirt. He rubbed his mouth hard on his sleeve and turned away, all the pleasure of the day ruined.

SEVEN

The races eventually wore out as a subject for reminiscence and then there was only the long desert of weeks and months until Christmas. Oliver went out to the stock camp in the mid-year holidays to help with the mustering, but neither Jim nor Rosemary was allowed to accompany him. It was reasonable enough, Jim thought, that Rosemary couldn't – after all, she was a girl, and just turned ten – but it should have been different for him.

He brooded on the injustice of it, then went to look for his uncle, finding him in the blacksmith's shop collecting the gudgeon pins that Charlie Attwood had made for the gates in the new yards at Duck Hole.

'Uncle Rob.' Jim stood in the doorway, his back to the light, and glowered at Rob in his pressed khaki and polished boots. Even the belt about his trim middle shone, and the buttoned-down sleeves of his shirt might have come straight from the iron.

'Well, what is it, Jim?'

'I want to go out to the camp. Why shouldn't I? If Oliver's allowed

I should be too. Dad always let me. He never said I couldn't. There's nothing to do here and I can ride just as good as Oliver.'

'Just as well, you mean,' Rob said. He frowned down at his nephew, trying for a conciliatory tone. 'I'm afraid you're still too young, Jim. It was different in your father's camp – that was smaller and he was there too. I won't be. And it's not fair to the men to put the responsibility on them.'

Jim's eyes flashed. 'I can look out for myself.'

'I'm sure you think so,' Rob agreed politely. 'But for all that, you're not going. The men aren't paid to chase after kids. Maybe next year when you're older you could camp out with them for weekends.'

The very suggestion raised the boy's hackles. 'I won't be here next year!'

'Then the question won't arise, will it?' Rob said with maddening reasonableness.

Jim scowled, kicking at the dirt as he turned away. He had a good mind to clear out, just saddle up Jake and go. He fantasised about riding to Arcadia and living there with Nipper and his family until Sandy came home, but of course it wouldn't do. His uncle would know where he'd gone and would waste no time dragging him back, and that brought him to the crux of the matter – Rob's easy assumption that Jim would still be here this time next year. Of course he wouldn't! When his father returned it would be to stay. They would return to Arcadia, which, according to Aunt Mary, had not been sold after all, stock up and start again. Once he got home to his own place, he would never come near Kharko again, and he would visit the blacks' camp as often as he liked and never wear shoes.

Lost in his own thoughts, Jim suddenly became aware of Rob's voice behind him. 'What?' he asked his uncle.

'I said, you don't have to spend all your time at the homestead. It's not the stock camp, but you could come for a run out to the new yards with me if you like.'

'I don't want to.' It gave him satisfaction to refuse the offer, but if he had expected his uncle to show disappointment he was wrong.

'Suit yourself.' Rob threw the pins into the back of the rover, dusted off his hands and nodded towards the flying figure coming through the garden gate. 'Rosemary does.'

Jim wished his refusal unspoken then, but was too proud to say so. With his hands in his back pockets and a scowl on his face, he watched the column of dust chart the rover's progress down the paddock. Even a girl's company was better than nothing. Barney had taken rations out to the camp and would probably stay there; Dino had gone off to help pull the rods on a broken-down bore. That left the bookkeeper and old Charlie, neither of whom liked kids, and Pommy John. Sighing heavily, Jim wandered down to the kitchen, only to find Pommy napping in his ragged armchair with a month-old newspaper spread over his face. Everyone, it seemed, had something better to do than be with him.

He sat on the loading dock for a while, kicking his heels back against the supporting timbers. Then movement at the trough caught his attention – the horses had come in and suddenly he knew what he would do, where he would go. He wasn't supposed to ride alone, but nobody would even notice he'd gone. His uncle wouldn't return before dark, his aunt was busy, and he'd be back before she began to wonder where he was. He set out purposefully for the saddle shed where his bridle hung.

But his conscience was not altogether clear and he argued briefly with himself as he bridled Jake, who leaned stubbornly back on the reins and had to be coaxed into following him. He had often ridden alone at Arcadia. But only in the horse paddock, an internal voice reminded him. Well, this was still a paddock, wasn't it? Bottom lip stuck out in indecision, he glanced at the angle of the sun – there was all afternoon to get there and back. His mind was made up.

He slapped the saddle into place, had a drink at the stable tap and was ready to go. He could get to Bell Creek, explore and be back well before his uncle got home. When he didn't turn up for lunch Aunt Mary would think he was in the kitchen with Pommy, and Pommy, if he thought about it at all, would assume he was up at the house. Swinging into the saddle, Jim kicked Jake and cantered swiftly away, until the bulk of the stockyards hid him from sight. Then, reining his pony to a brisk walk, he turned him towards Bell Creek.

It was pleasant to be abroad alone, with the sun warm on his back and arms and only the regular tread of hooves for company. He wished Nipper was with him to see the little scurryings and sudden freezes of movement about him as he rode: the flick of a lizard's tail, the stealthy rustle of insect life. Kitehawks hung as if from threads in the blue above him, and euros' ears twitched as he passed. Jake snorted comfortably, reaching at the bit, while Jim daydreamed, imagining his father riding beside him, the creak and jingle of his saddle gear chiming with Jim's own, and the whiff of his tobacco on the light breeze. That was something else he missed. Most of the men at Kharko smoked, but his uncle didn't. He would have liked him better, Jim thought, if he did. At least he would smell right. He and Nipper had tried it once with flakes cut from a plug of nikky tobacco, but it made them so ill that Jim had never touched it again.

It was no distance to the overgrown track that led on to the mine. Jake turned automatically towards it but Jim kicked him on, then picked a switch to reinforce the message. Sandy had said he could have spurs when he was older. Perhaps he had already bought them at Mataranka, or some other town, and would send them in time for his birthday. Jim had hinted as much to Barney, and of course Rosemary had been there and blabbed it all around the kitchen and now everybody knew. Jim grimaced at the memory. Trust her! It wasn't certain, and if she hadn't said anything it wouldn't matter. Perhaps he would write one more letter to his father, just to remind him.

He smacked the pony's shoulder again with the switch. The range was suddenly closer. The sand had given way to pebbly ground that Jake's hooves clattered over. Jim could smell the waxy, baked-stone scent of the range and hear the shrill of cicadas in the trees. He listened for the stone bells but they were silent. The air hung still and there was the buzz of flies.

At the creek, spindly gums shouldered each other for room amid a tangle of conkaberry bushes and black-stemmed beefwood suckers. Jake, pushing through it into the dimness beyond, snorted unhappily as his hooves slid on the water-smoothed rocks. He kept propping, ears like sticks, to stare bug-eyed into the shadows, until in the end it was quicker to walk. Jim swung down and hitched the reins.

'You wait here,' he said sternly. 'And don't rub that saddle neither.'

On the right bank of the gully was a sandstone ledge with a narrow euro pad winding down its centre. Jim scrambled along it, thinking there had to be soakage water somewhere. It was too rocky here, but perhaps further along he would come to sand. The trees squeezed tightly together, and when their foliage sighed in a little gust of wind his skin goose-pimpled with cold just as his ear caught the faintest echo of a bell. He stopped, head up, but the noise was not repeated. All he could hear was a tiny clicking sound, perhaps a borer in the tree beside him, and the far-off cawing of crows.

He needed the wind to blow. As it was, with the trees crowding his view, he might walk right past the bell holes without seeing them. Time fretted at him. In the gloom of the timber and high gully walls it was impossible to see the sun, but he seemed to have been hours in this shadowy world. He had been confident of his ability to find the holes but realised now that he could walk straight past them unless they were actually sounding. Perhaps that was what happened to the man who was said to have perished somewhere in here. He wished he hadn't thought of that, but it was probably just a yarn anyway.

The pad still ran before his feet but the slope at his right had turned into a solid wall of rock, which just up ahead jutted out in an overhang that forced the trees aside. He looked up, following the line of their trunks, and that's when he saw them – the shadows of blackfella hands on the ancient stone. They fanned ochre and white across the grainy rock, their spread fingers and partial prints as shocking as a shout in the silence.

The hair prickled on Jim's neck and his mouth was suddenly dry. Oliver had been wrong about this place and the reason the blackfellas kept away. It was spirit ground, where nobody but the old men should be. He took a careful step backwards and then another. The trees that had been simply a nuisance seemed all at once menacing, and in the dim light the air pressed down on him like an accusation. He half expected to see the bodies of the men whose handprints they were, and when the euro that had sat unnoticed behind him suddenly moved he turned and bolted, crashing away down the path.

He broke panting into the thinner scrub where he'd left Jake, but the pony was gone. He couldn't believe it: Jake was an old hand at getting his own way and had a habit of rubbing against whatever held him, but Jim had hooked the reins high, so to escape Jake must have snapped them. He swore. Jake would get home long before he could, and it only needed someone to spot the riderless horse and the roast would be ruined, as Pommy liked to say. His heart sank and he had a hollow feeling in his stomach. It was one thing to pretend that Sandy would have countenanced the expedition but he knew very well his uncle had forbidden it. He'd have to walk, and as quickly as he could.

He was hot, footsore and halfway home when a vehicle overtook him. He could have pulled his boots off and made better time had not six months of enforced footwear softened the soles of his feet to useless-ness. He plugged doggedly on, grateful for the cooling wind that fluttered his hat, but it also masked sound, causing him to leap like a startled deer when a horn blasted behind him. He spun about, heart thumping, and was relieved beyond words to see Barney behind the wheel.

'What the hell are you doing out here?' Barney jerked his head in disapproval, his eyes searching beyond Jim. 'Get in. Where's young Ro?'

Jim slid thankfully onto the seat and cleared his throat. 'She's with Uncle Rob,' he said uncertainly. 'They went out to the new yards. My mongrel horse cleared out on me, I woulda been home else. Cripes, I've been walking for hours.'

Barney's eyes narrowed. 'Riding by yourself?'

'I only went to Bell Creek.' Jim was aggrieved. 'Crikey, Barney, what am I supposed to do with myself? I can't make friends with the black-fellas, I can't go out in the stock camp, I've gotta have a girl tagging along everywhere I ride. If *he* knew he wouldn't even let us . . .' He bit his betraying tongue.

'Frig around at the old mine, y'mean?'

'You know about that?'

'Have to be blind not to.'

'How come you didn't say anything?'

'Like you're gunna take any notice,' Barney snorted. 'Besides, Oliver's got his head screwed on. He's dependable. The boss knows that too, so I reckon he lets you get away with it.' He changed gear, saying bluntly, 'You don't give him much credit, do you?'

'Who?' But Jim knew who he meant and wriggled uncomfortably.

'The boss. It's not his fault that he ain't your dad, you know. I've never heard you say a civil word to him yet. And the funny thing is, if you gave him half a chance you might even get to like him.'

'Huh!' Jim hunched his shoulders. 'That'll be the day. I suppose you're gunna tell me you do? Like him, I mean.'

'Matter of fact I do. You know, kid, I worked a horse like you once. He couldn't learn nothing either. Silly bugger had to be taught the same thing over and over. I was still at it when the rest of his mates was finished and gone.'

Jim flushed angrily but bit his tongue. Then Barney slowed

and pulled over. 'There's the pony now. Catch him and slip home. Think yourself lucky it was me found you and not Des, but if you ever pull a stunt like this again I'll tell the boss meself.'

Back at the stables Jim unsaddled Jake and let him go. The sun was sitting on the shed roof, and half an hour later dust on the road heralded his uncle's return. Rosemary was full of chatter, about the brumby foal she had seen and the emus on the fence line at the new yards.

'So what did you do?' she asked and Jim shrugged sullenly.

'Nothing.' But he'd been thinking. Barney's words had dug into him like fishhooks. Did he really dislike his uncle so much for what he was, or for what he wasn't? Barney had been right about other things – he had, Jim silently admitted, been right about today too. It had been stupid to ride out alone like that without leaving word. He could have slipped on the rocks and twisted his ankle, or broken it; he could have got lost. And in all fairness, how was his uncle to know about the freedom he'd had on Arcadia? He had never told him about life there. In fact, save for the common courtesies demanded by the meal table and living together, he had scarcely spoken to him at all. Perhaps, Jim thought, he might try to, if only to prove to himself that Barney was wrong.

Despite the letter of reminder, Jim's birthday passed without word from his father. Aunt Mary baked him a cake with eleven candles that he blew out at a celebratory morning tea. There was a card from Leo Baker, a book about racehorses from Oliver, a yoyo from Rosemary, and a large parcel from his uncle and aunt that proved to be a handsome saddle pouch with buckles shaped like stirrup irons. Later in the day

Pommy John gave him a pack of playing cards, and Barney a tobacco tin with a lid he had decorated by scraping off the paint and punching the shape of a horse's head into it.

'An old digger showed me how,' he said. 'He learned it in an Eyetie prison camp.'

'Were you in the war, Barney?' Jim squatted beside him, the rail at his back, and ran admiring fingers over the tin. The horse looked just like the Rook. 'Dad was.'

'Nah. I was only about fifteen when it finished. Heard from him, have you – your dad?'

'No.' Jim fiddled with the tin, not meeting his friend's eye.

'Well, I expect you will,' Barney said cheerfully. 'When I was up north the mail useta take its time. Supposed to be a weekly service but it never was.' He rolled a smoke with quick, clever fingers, lit up and leaned back, his face lifted to the sun and smoke leaking out of his nostrils.

'You know that day I went out to Bell Creek?' Jim asked suddenly, drawing his feet up under him.

'Yep.' Barney squinted sideways. 'See you been getting on better with the boss since about then.'

'A bit. He's not so bad, sometimes,' Jim admitted. 'Anyway, I've been wondering what you were doing out there that day. The camp wasn't at Benny's bore. And you said it might've been Des that came in, not you. How come?'

Barney grunted. 'Mostly luck – for you, that is. Nah, we were mustering the Number Two country. We yarded early and were riding back to camp when Des sent that lazy bugger Jacko over to the dam to fetch in some fresh horses. The country's flogged bare and we had 'em on the bit of feed in the dam enclosure. Well, Jacko was too tired to get off for the gate, so he tries to do it from the saddle. Hooks his boot under the head stick and it pops out of the loop and smacks the horse in the side of the face. It was that goose-rumped yellow-bay, kick the eye out of a needle, you know?'

'Jelly,' Jim nodded.

'That's her. She bucks into the gate, dumps Jacko and gets the wire round her hind leg. That brings her down, and when she falls she shifts the saddle. Next thing she's up and bolting with the saddle under her guts.' Barney shook his head, cigarette smoke curling past one ear. 'Criminal is what it was. The rest of the day was lost getting her back. The saddle was wrecked of course, flaps gone, stirrups gone, tree busted. The mare's leg was cut to the bone and when we finally run her down she was that stirred up I had to get a rope on her to catch her. See, accidents happen in this game and sometimes it ain't nobody's fault. But then you get some useless bugger like that Jacko . . . There just ain't no safe shortcuts. Remember that, kid.

'Anyway, we was short a saddle and out of meat, so Des stopped to kill and it was me that come home for the gear instead. And seeing we'd caught up with the mare more than halfway to Benny's bore, I come that way thinking I might happen on a few of the lost bits. The bridle was gone too, and the saddle pouch.'

He flipped his cigarette butt into the dirt and stood up in one sudden movement. 'Well, a breather ain't a day off, so I better get back to it. Enjoy your birthday.'

'Thanks. And for the tin.' With a last admiring look, Jim stowed his present in his pocket.

EIGHT

Summer came early that year. All through October the mercury in the verandah thermometer climbed steadily, and the winds came furnace-tipped from the desert. The touch of it crisped the skin and fell like a tangible weight on the body, closing even shaded eyes into a squint to cut the glare. In the middle of the month, Supplejack bore broke down and every available man was put to work, either on the bore or helping shift the thirsty breeders, many of them weakened from the effects of calving and the long daily trek to water.

Jim, driving with his uncle, helped catch the baby calves too young to walk. They rode in a slippery mass on the back of the trayback rover, bumping and tumbling as they tried to stand on tied feet, while their mothers bawled frantically after them.

Rob was not simply the desk manager Jim had thought him to be. The discovery surprised him; he had thought that the hired men did the real work on Kharko, while his uncle's part consisted of sitting in his office and talking to cattle buyers. Rob's appearance supported this: his khakis were always starched and his fingernails clean. Jim had frequently been scornful of the way his uncle was forever paring them with a little silver knife he carried on his belt. But out on the run, Jim learned to his chagrin, Rob could strip a diesel or change a mill as quickly as Sandy had ever done.

Now that Jim was around to notice, day's end showed a man not dissimilar to his father – a figure in dusty clothes, hands grimed with toil. It was somehow easier to respect him like this. He saw, too, that while his uncle could do all the men's jobs – except, perhaps, stick on Mandarin the way Barney could – none of them could do his. To Jim, raised to admire competency and resourcefulness, this put a whole new slant on things.

Being together more helped break down the barriers between them. Jim decided that there was one aspect in which his uncle was nothing like Sandy, whose conversation rambled gregariously, who commented, joked, instructed, all in the same easy manner with a casual twinkle in his eye. Rob, on the other hand, gave information like a man handing out tools. And if he'd ever ridden a buckjumper, seen anything unusual in the bush or played a practical joke on anyone, he never spoke of it. Only in racing was he given to speculation, and Jim knew too little of this to pursue it as a topic. But these days he was glad rather than otherwise that the two brothers were so different, for however long Sandy's absence, Jim vowed that he would never return to find himself supplanted. Jim guarded that shrine with the fierce jealousy of his years.

Now, weary from the exertion of catching and carrying calves, Jim travelled in silence to Swallow bore, the alternative watering point for the thirsty stock. Rob parked in the shade and they swung the doors open and sat waiting in the cab for the mob to turn up.

'Why's it called Swallow?' Jim's eyes followed the screeching birds wheeling about the mill. 'It should've been Galah.'

Rob wiped a thumb across his brow and flicked sweat through the open door. 'The driller named it. He lost a string of tools down it while he was drilling. Said the hole swallowed them up.'

'Oh.' Jim didn't ask whether they'd been retrieved because he knew his uncle would tell him and he was too hot to care. The sky glittered brassily and the cattle camped under the trees bulked like rocks in the shade. One cow, standing apart from the rest, had a newborn calf that butted at her hind leg, unable to find the teat. Watching its hopeful, bumbling search, Jim smiled. It was the sort of thing his father would have commented on, but Rob said nothing.

'You don't talk much, do you?' Jim said, and couldn't believe he had. He glanced quickly at his uncle and imagined he saw a glint of amusement in his hard green eyes. Then Rob turned to look at him and the moment was gone.

'I've never found that words butter much bread.' Then in the same level voice he said, 'We must be more alike than you think – you don't talk much either.'

Startled, Jim thought about this, and couldn't deny it was true. Rosemary never shut up, and both Pommy and Barney were always talking too. They told yarns about their past experiences, as all the men did, or just gabbed on about the day's events. Jim frowned, trying to decide how he felt about being like Rob. Did that mean he was less like his father? Or could he somehow be like both of them? He was aware that physically he resembled his uncle more than he did Sandy, and until lately he had resented the fact.

But there was no time to dwell on it, for dust was suddenly visible through the timber as the cattle from Supplejack came bellowing into the bore. Hoofs clicking eagerly over the last few yards, empty udders swinging, they rushed at the trough, the weaker ones straggling behind, where the shapes of riders were growing out of the dust. Jim scooted up onto the tray to untie the calves' legs, and when Rob lifted them down they stood spraddle-legged and bawling, midway between trough and vehicle, for their mothers to claim.

'Will they go back to Supplejack now they've drunk here?'

'Some of them.' Rob brushed calf slobber off his shirt and banged his hat to remove the dust. Kicking his boots against a tyre to dislodge dung, he gazed across the backs of the bony cows to the bare ground and pitiless sky beyond. 'Cow shit,' he said unexpectedly. 'It's what this job's about. That and worry. Well, hop in, lad. We've waters to check yet, and I want to be home by dark.'

In due time Supplejack was repaired and most of the cows drifted back to that ground.

'They like their own country, cattle do,' Barney said. 'They'll go home if they can get there.' He was whittling wood on the verandah of the quarters, his body sunk into a canvas chair much faded by weather. A sluggish breeze, too hot for refreshment, rattled the pannikin against the waterbag that hung near the tank and set the screen door to intermittent banging.

'There's not much to eat out there,' Jim said. 'We dragged three dead ones off the trough yesterday. One of them had a calf, but Uncle Rob knocked it on the head. Do you think the drought'll get worse?'

'Oh, it ain't a drought, just a bit dry.' Barney gazed critically at his wood and began carefully paring strips from one end. Jim, watching, couldn't divine what it would turn into. 'It's early days yet to be giving up on the rain and declaring drought.'

'But the cattle are dying, Barney. Every day there's another couple that don't make it off the trough. Uncle Rob says they get a bellyful of water and lie down and then they can't get up again.'

'I know. But there ain't nuthin you or me or the boss can do about it except wait for the rain. And while we're waiting the weak stock die. It's tough, but don't let anybody tell you this ain't tough country. Thing is, you just gotta be a bit tougher to handle it. Ain't a stockman worth his boot leather wants to see stock die, but what you can't change you gotta live with.'

'It won't happen to the horses, will it?' Jim asked in dread. It was bad enough seeing calves being killed, and the snig chain hooked to the stiffened, emaciated carcases of their mothers. He didn't think he could stand it if it were horses they were dragging away. He waited anxiously but Barney, turning his piece of wood and going to work on the other end, shook his head.

'Nah. They look okay. I was out in the broodmare paddock yesterday. We might lose a coupla old mares, but that's always on the cards this time of year. The Rook'll be fine. Boss said I was to get him in and feed him before he gets poor. And seeing as the paddock's cutting out here, you kids are to fetch your ponies in and chuck 'em a bit of hay in the afternoons. We've got a shed full of the stuff so they might as well eat it.' Barney smoothed a hand over his whittling, then folded his knife shut and slipped it into his belt. 'There, what d'you think?'

Jim eyed the proffered work, a silky-smooth length of timber with shaped and blunted ends. 'What is it?'

'Camel nosepeg. Only you're supposed to make 'em out of olive wood, not mulga.'

Jim knitted his brows. 'What d'you want a camel nosepeg for?'

'I don't.' Barney stood and went to unhook the pannikin, squinting across the paddock where phantom lakes beckoned. He shook his head and drank, swallowing noisily. 'Gawd! She's hotter than the hinges of hell. Shouldn't like to be out there today.'

Jim turned the peg between his fingers. 'So why did you make it then?'

'Fills in the waiting,' Barney said.

And that Jim understood.

At last Christmas was close, and each day Jim woke with a tingling sense of expectancy. The rain still held off and the deaths around the bores continued, but after all the long weary months of waiting, his father was finally coming back. He could be as close as a week's ride away. Or a day's. Jim hugged the knowledge to himself and fretted every time he was gone from the house, in case Sandy should arrive in his absence.

Every morning he searched the pale horizon for the first hint of dust, straining to distinguish that raised by a traveller from that caused by a willy-wind. They were everywhere, spiralling through the scrub and flinging handfuls of grit and dried leaves, tearing across the flats and growing taller and taller as they sucked the red dirt into themselves.

These winds were the sound of summer, the backdrop to the parched land and its brassy sky and bony cattle plodding long miles to water.

In the kitchen the tin roof made little cracking noises as it expanded. Pommy John wore a rag slung over one shoulder to mop his streaming face with as he shovelled bread out of the oven, or stirred the boilers of curry and stew on the stovetop.

'I dunno why you want to be a cook,' Jim said. He was sitting on the bench near the door, fanning himself with his hat.

'Neither do I most days,' Pommy agreed. 'Still, beats a few other jobs round 'ere.'

'Like what?'

'Swinging a fencing bar. Climbing mills when the metal's red-hot. Even sittin' on a horse out there.' Coming to stand in the doorway, he jerked his head at the swimmy horizon. His singlet was patched with sweat, his face bright red from the stove, and his moustache stuck limply to his face.

Jim was unconvinced but too hot to argue. He got up and wandered back to the garden, where his cousins were on the grass under the big pepper tree. Rosemary was flicking a yoyo about – *his* yoyo, he saw with annoyance – and Oliver, as usual, had his nose in a book.

'Hey, that's mine.'

'So?' She flicked it towards him and caught it back. 'I'm only borrowing it. You left it at the gate.'

'I was going to pick it up.'

'Well, I beat you to it. Finders keepers. But you can have it back soon as I show you a new trick. Can you do this one?'

'No,' Jim admitted. 'Let's have a try.'

It was cooler under the tree than anywhere else. Remembering Pommy's words, Jim was glad he wasn't out with Barney and Des and the others shifting cattle off Strangefellow dam. The catchment water was going back fast, Rob had said, so there'd be more such work before the rain came. It was just as well, Jim thought, that the working horses were being fed.

Tiring of the yoyo, he and Rosemary let it fall between them and lay down on the grass, squinting through the moving leaves at the dazzle of light overhead.

'Mum could do that.' Jim spoke unexpectedly, less a statement than something remembered aloud.

'Do what?' Rosemary asked.

'You know, with the yoyo. She said an American soldier showed her, when she was nursing. He gave her a yoyo.' It was red with a white circle and he suddenly wondered what had become of it. He pictured her standing before an audience of himself and his father, doing over-hand rolls and loops and smiling at their surprise in this hidden ability of hers.

'I wish she was still here,' Rosemary said. She looked so sad and sounded so forlorn that Jim stared at her. He had never given much thought to the idea that anyone else might miss his mother.

'Well, she isn't.' He scowled.

When their stomachs told them it was mid-afternoon they headed back to the kitchen, passing from black shade to brilliant light, the sun striking fire on Rosemary's hatless head as she ran to the wooden steps.

'You want sunstroke, Ro?' Oliver asked, and in reply got a piercing scream. Following his sister's gaze, he caught sight of the snake coiled like a whip below the steps, its head raised to strike.

The day seemed to freeze around them. Jim saw Oliver's legs make great leaping strides to the kitchen wall, where the shovel that was used to clean out the firebox stood. Rosemary was unable to move; only her scream went on as the head of the big brown flashed towards her. Oliver pushed her aside and brought the shovel blade down on the snake, pinning it to the ground. But he had got it too far back, Jim saw. Its head and at least two feet of its body were still free and it lunged at the blade and then at Oliver's legs, which were out of reach.

Then, to Jim's horror, it threw its upper body around the handle of the shovel and surged upwards, its deadly fangs falling just short of Oliver's hands. His cousin's face was ashen now, his freckles stood out like bloodstains on a sheet, his knuckles were white from the effort of holding the snake in place.

Oliver knew he would be bitten the instant he let go of the shovel. A brown that size could move far quicker than he could. 'Get somebody!' he cried desperately, and the other two, as if released from a spring, shot different ways.

'Mum!' Rosemary screamed, running for the house. 'Mum!'

'Pommy!' Jim roared, racing past his cousin and up the steps. 'Snake!'

The big cook was already on his way. In the absence of a weapon, he had snatched a pot of boiling potatoes off the stove and now, taking the situation in at a glance, he emptied the lot over the thrashing snake.

The brown gave a great hiss and its mouth gaped so wide Jim could see the loaded venom sacs at the base of its fangs. It fell off the handle, biting its own body, and Pommy, without pausing, lifted the heavy pot and slammed it down on its head, then twice more, mashing it flat. He took Oliver's hands off the shovel and patted him awkwardly on his shaking shoulder. 'It's all right now, mate. Big bastard, eh? Must be six foot.'

'Ro almost stepped on him.' Oliver's eyes were glazed, his teeth chattering. 'I hate snakes,' he said, and crumpled into a faint at Pommy's feet just as Mary arrived, breathless from running, with a garden fork in her hand. She gave a cry and the blood went from her face as she dropped the fork and rushed to her son.

'Is he bitten? Where?' She looked frantically at Pommy. 'Jim, run for the kit in the office. Top drawer, I've shown you. Quick!'

'It's okay, Missus,' Pommy said. 'He ain't bitten. Just keeled over from the shock like. He saved young Ro's life, no question of that. If he'd been slower, or let go that shovel, the snake would of got her for sure. There,' he added with satisfaction, 'he's coming round now.'

Oliver sat up slowly and went with Mary to the house. Jim, now that it was all over, took a proper look at the snake. Grabbing its tail, he stretched it out and saw that Pommy was right. It was every inch of six feet long and as thick as his wrist.

'Big enough to kill a horse,' the cook confirmed. He was looking sadly at his spuds. Some had been squashed and one or two lay in the blood that had leaked from the crushed head of the snake. He inspected the bottom of his pot, then squatted to pick up the rest of the potatoes, all covered with dirt as they were.

'You aren't gunna *use* them?' Jim demanded.

'They'll wash,' Pommy said. 'Have to, anyway. I'm making shepherd's pie tonight. Them's the last spuds we've got.'

'Yerk! Don't let on to Oliver then.' Jim pointed at the snake. 'Where'll I put it?'

'Far away as you can.' Pommy mopped his face. 'Some blokes reckon if you kill a snake their mates'll come to the body. Well, I ain't about to welcome a visit from none of his kin.'

Jim dragged the body away, amusing himself by rolling it from side to side so that its track in the red sand looked almost real. Jake was camped with his cousins' horses outside the stable, waiting for the evening feed, and he towed the dusty snake across to see how they would react. All three snorted then backed warily away, and Jake, not content with that, let go a blast of air that brought the Rook's head round.

'It's dead, you great ninny,' Jim said fondly. He dropped his burden to rub behind his pony's ears. 'I reckon I've seen brighter things than you on plates, with forks stuck in 'em.'

Back at the house again, he went looking for Oliver and came upon Mary instead, sitting perfectly still on a dining-room chair, her hands folded in her lap. This was so unusual that he stopped and stared, unsure whether to speak or not. His aunt seemed entirely unaware of his presence, and that alarmed him.

'Is . . . Are you all right, Aunt Mary?' The squeak of his boots was the loudest thing in the room, until she moved, turning a sorrowful face towards him. She had, he was startled to see, been crying. 'What's wrong, Aunty?' he said, going up to her.

'It's nothing.' She smiled palely at him. 'You're all safe, thank God. But when I saw how close Oliver came to . . . Well,' she reminded herself as much as him, 'he *wasn't* bitten. And neither were you, or Rosemary. Thank God for Pommy.'

'It was Oliver who did it. I mean, Pommy helped but Oliver had already stopped it getting Ro. He was really brave. I didn't do anything.' He was chagrined but honest. 'It all happened so quick.'

'And it's over now.' She got up. 'Are you looking for the others? I think they're out in the garden. Run along and join them.'

The snake was a talking point in the kitchen for days. Rosemary bathed in the reflected glory of having had her life saved, but her brother had no desire to dwell on it. He hadn't been brave at all, he told Jim curtly, just petrified. He was terrified of snakes and ashamed of having fainted.

Jim was perplexed. He would never understand his bookish cousin, whose only other interest seemed to lie in the stables. He didn't even like stock work, Jim thought aggrievedly. Here he was cracking his neck to get into the camp while Oliver, who spent entire weeks there, would rather have stayed home and groomed horses.

The Rook had come back in from the stallion paddock, together with Corinne, an old bay mare shortly due to foal.

'She belongs to Dad,' Rosemary said proudly. 'She's in foal to the Rook. Barney says the colt ought to be a corker.'

'What about her other foals? Were they any good?' Jim reached out to rub the rough velvet of the mare's nose. She breathed gustily upon him, her great dark eyes reflecting the light. He could see thick veins, like dark worms, under the skin of her enormous belly. She kept hitching her body from hip to hip, as if the weight of it were uncomfortable.

'This is the first she's ever carried to term,' Oliver said. He was mooning over the rail at the mare, picking at a pimple on his face. 'Look at those legs! If she births this one and it lives —'

'Still might be a dud,' Jim put in. There was something in the way his cousins carried on about Kharko's thoroughbreds that nettled him. It was as if no other type of horse was worth considering. He was aware that both Oliver and Rosemary looked down on Jake, counting him a poor second to their better bred mounts, and he wasn't surprised when they rounded on him at such heresy.

'Well,' he said smugly, 'it might. Look at Pharlap. Barney said his full sister was useless on the track. What's wrong with a stockhorse, anyway? When Dad gets here I'm gunna ask him if I can have Pansy or maybe Havelock to ride next year. I betcha even the Rook couldn't catch a cow quicker than they can. They've been trained, and all he knows is straight galloping.'

'Huh!' Oliver made the sound an insult. 'I'm talking about horses, not nags. That mare's bloodlines are better than . . . better than . . .' His inability to think of a comparison incensed him. 'I dunno how you can call yourself a McAllister! Or Uncle Sandy either, with all those plugs he owns. He hasn't got a horse fit to stand in the same yard with Corinne.'

'He has so!' Jim yelled, and the mare threw up her head with a star-tled snort. 'He's got heaps, and they *can* have foals. Whenever they want,' he declared, with more passion than truth. 'Pansy had a colt last year, and Charity's had three, so there! And done her work too. She's a camp-horse, not some spoiled useless galloper like Corinne.'

A disproportionate fury had welled in him at Oliver's words. It was part loyalty to cobby little Jake, still the dearest horse in the world to him, and part envy, for Jim was not so blind that he couldn't see the folly of matching a small, underbred pony with a thoroughbred like the one his cousin rode. Furious, he stooped to seize a stick lying at his feet and hurled it at Oliver. '*And* they had them in the paddock, instead of being coddled in a stable and fed and looked at every five minutes!'

'Because they're plugs,' Oliver sneered. He had dodged the ill-aimed throw and was looking round for a missile of his own.

Jim rushed at him with a howl of rage and they collided and fell to the hot sand, yelping like burnt pups as their skin touched it. Corinne blasted out a snort as she shied away from the rail. Jim heard her hooves skid on the packed earth, and Ro yelling something, and then a voice that cracked like a whip.

'Wot the hell do you think you're playing at?'

Barney's face was a thundercloud and his blue eyes snapped fire. 'Are you mad? Scaring her across the yard like that! You wanna kill that foal?'

They disentangled themselves and stood abashedly before him, Jim rubbing an elbow that had banged into a post. 'If the boss was here you'd be getting a damn good flogging for it,' Barney went on remorselessly. 'Call yourselves horsemen?' He spat in disgust. 'Clear off out of it. And don't come back till you've learned a bit of sense.'

They went, Oliver chastened, Jim aggrieved at the injustice of it. 'It's not like we even touched her!'

'We frightened her.' Oliver's brow was clouded with guilt. 'I heard her shy – what if she'd slipped and fallen, or maybe banged into the rails? Or what if you'd got her with that stick you chucked? It's Dad's last chance to get a foal from that bloodline.'

'Well, she didn't,' Jim retorted. 'And it didn't go anywhere near her.'

'It didn't go anywhere near me, either,' Oliver reasoned, 'so it could've.'

'Oh, shut up, both of you,' Rosemary begged. 'Barney's never been mad at us before. What are we going to do?'

'He'll get over it,' Jim said with a bravado he did not feel.

Anxious days followed. Jim, infected by his cousin's worry and by the thought of his uncle's reaction should anything go wrong with the mare, greeted each dawn with unease. According to Oliver, pregnant mares were prone to all manner of ills, particularly thoroughbred ones. Jim didn't like to think what his uncle might do if the foal were to die. And Barney would blame him – he would blame Oliver too, but it was one of those cases where sharing the fault scarcely halved it. Having grown used to spending most of his spare time in the stables, Jim now avoided them, and every time the side gate clicked shut his heart leapt into his mouth for fear it was someone bringing bad news.

Oliver, on the other hand, haunted the stables, fussing with Corinne's feed and repeatedly scouring the already clean water trough. Or just standing, pulling nervously at his fingers until the joints cracked. He was there when the mare went into labour, and later that day he burst into the kitchen where Jim and Rosemary were helping Pommy John mix the Christmas pudding.

'It's come! She's had the foal – a little colt. Dad's as pleased as punch.' Oliver's pale eyes shone and the freckles on his face seemed to glow. 'Barney's calling him Chester till Dad finds a name for him. Come and see him.'

They needed no urging. Jim abandoned his knife, Rosemary the fruit she was stirring, and the two of them rushed for the door.

Barney was leaning on the rails beside Rob, a proprietary light in his blue eyes. 'Look at the little beggar.' He spoke as if he had completely forgotten their last meeting. 'Didja ever see a stronger foal? The old girl's done us proud.'

Corinne, as if understanding the praise, turned her head to touch the wobbly little creature standing beside her, whickering softly as she did so. Jim drew a deep breath of delight. It looked so right, the leggy, long-pasterned foal with his birth string dangling beside the beautiful, lean-headed mare. Somebody – Barney, he supposed – had dragged the afterbirth from the yard and the crows were quarrelling over it, their raucous calls a harsh reminder of the cycle of birth and death played out endlessly around them.

The foal was a bay, like his dam. 'Chester.' Jim tried the name out loud and Barney nodded.

'Suits him, don't you reckon? Course he'll wind up with a proper registered handle, but that'll do to be going on with.'

Rob assented. He looked pleased as he leaned to pat Corinne, whose neck was still dark with sweat. 'That's my brave girl. All right, time to leave her in peace for a bit to get used to the foal.'

'Oh, Dad.' Rosemary's face fell. 'Can't I stay? He's the dearest, cutest little thing.' The boys made retching noises, which she ignored, gazing hopefully at her father.

He shook his head. 'No, Rosemary. She's birthed him safely. We won't take any risks with him now.'

'No,' Jim echoed virtuously. A load had rolled from his shoulders. He looked to Barney rather than Rob for permission. 'Can I come down and show Dad when he gets here?'

'Course you can. Just remember Corinne's high-strung and treat her so.'

'I won't forget,' Jim said gratefully. Barney nodded and he knew then that he had been forgiven.

But not even the excitement of Chester's arrival could keep Jim's mind from the calendar for long. Two days before Christmas his nerves were at fever pitch, eyes and ears tuned to the first glimpse of dust on the road, or horses crossing the paddock. A dozen times a day he visited the gate to watch and listen for his father's arrival.

'You'll wear the path out, lad,' Rob said good-humouredly as his nephew returned from yet another fruitless foray. The garden hung still and green about them, patterned with inky shadows under the trees. There were clouds overhead, bluish-bottomed cumulus piled like soapsuds in the afternoon sky, and Rob eyed them hopefully.

Jim had trodden in the mint patch, short-cutting a corner, and the cool scent of it on the air seemed to diminish the heat where he stood. He could see the bright glitter of sun reflecting off the store roof, and down in the shed somebody was working the forge, the hammer blows ringing slow and dull, as if the heat were a blanket smothering sound. He smiled sunnily at his uncle, his face luminous with happiness.

'I reckon he'll camp at Butler's bore tonight if he's coming on the Alice road. That'd put him here tomorrow, just like he said. Have I got any taller, Uncle?'

Rob ran his eye over the boy. 'A bit. Why?'

'He said I would,' Jim said smugly. 'I'll bet he's riding Dolphin. She's the fastest walker in the plant. He could get here for lunch if he was – from Butler's, I mean – but I suppose the plant'd slow him up. How far is it?'

'Whoa.' Rob shook his head. 'Let's just wait, eh? You don't know he's even coming that way.'

'I bet he is, though.' Jim's confidence was unassailable. His father was so close now he could almost touch him. Just another night and day. He'd be reaching Butler's pretty soon, turning the horses off the track as the evening blued around him. He'd water the plant and go on a bit to find feed for them, and unpack by firelight and swing the billy. And early tomorrow, when the morning star blazed in the east, he'd find the horses again and eat and pack up, and there'd be nothing but the last bit of red track between them.

'He might get here in time for lunch, even.'

'Or he might not,' Rob warned. 'Where are you off to now?'

'I'm gunna climb the mill.' Even the heat could not curb his energy. 'He might've got to Butler's last night. If he did I'll see his dust coming.'

But high on his perch, Jim watched in vain. The road stretched emptily westward and only the red columns of willy-winds strayed across it. He remained up on the platform, under the curve of the turning wheel, until dusk came to cloak the valley and it was too dark to see anything but the yellow squares of windows in the quarters. The third time Rosemary came to call him he climbed down, bounding up to the verandah where insects mobbed the pool of light.

'You look like a beetroot,' she greeted him. 'Your face is all burnt.'

Jim touched it, only now aware of the smart. He wiped sweat from his forehead, for the air was still cloyingly thick, and blinked as it ran into his eyes, the bite of it curling his lids shut.

'Dad says it's gunna rain.' Rosemary lifted her hair away from her neck. 'If he's right I wish it'd hurry up.'

He shrugged single-mindedly. 'Won't matter. A bit of rain won't stop him. He'll be here tomorrow.'

'Yeah,' Rosemary said, bored. 'So you keep saying.'

But next day Sandy still wasn't there. Nor was he the day after that. Christmas morning flew by with its strange bustle. Mary was cooking the lunch, which they would all share in the dining room, and she arbitrarily co-opted whoever was closest to carry chairs or fold napkins or make certain every place had a glass and cracker beside it.

'Can Dad sit next to me, Aunty?'

'Yes, of course, Jim. But we're not certain he'll get here in time. Set his place anyway.'

'He will. I bet I could see his dust now if I climbed the mill.'

Mary shook her finger at him. 'See you don't, young man. You're burnt enough already. And looking won't bring him any faster.'

Lunch, despite being delayed an hour, passed without sight of Sandy. Jim ate with most of his attention on the front gate and little to spare for the table, where Dino, Barney, Pommy and old Charlie made uncomfortable additions to the family. All four would sooner have been in the kitchen. They ate awkwardly, saying little and leaving their napkins folded beside them. Leo Baker had gone on holiday, as had Des, whose wife was expecting a baby in Alice Springs. Des, Jim knew, would be spending most of January with her. The empty chair beside Jim echoed his disappointment.

The rain began before they had finished eating and everybody, including Rob, pushed back their chairs and dashed to the verandah to watch. It was a sudden storm, sharp and intense, growing outwards from a small core until a white knife of lightning split the belly of the clouds packing the width of the land. The silvery rods of rain turned grey and solid, blocking out the shapes of buildings with a wall of water. The oleanders along the fence bowed before the deluge, and ten minutes later the ground was a running lake. Still the thunder hammered and the rain poured down, until the run-off rushed ankle-deep across the flat. Jim and Rosemary shed their footwear and ran shouting through it, squealing at the water's icy touch, and for just a few moments he was able to forget that half the day was gone with no sign of his father.

No one could stay indoors after the rain. Jim, breathing in the scent of washed air and wet earth, followed a trickling gutter down to the yards and climbed onto the cap-rail above the main gate, staring towards the road. Wide sheets of water filled the claypans down the paddock but the sand had swallowed the rest. A gentle breeze shook silver light from the mulgas, where wet leaves turned in the sunlight, and beyond them the range loomed so clearly that he could trace the thin lines of waterfalls down its sides. They too would be gone within the hour, and surely Sandy would have come by then.

But he hadn't. Night fell and the desert frogs dug themselves out of the damp sand, croaking and chirruping after their kind. The plovers that shadowed the storms clinked and cried in the night and a dozen times Jim started out of sleep to the sound of imaginary horse bells. Dawn came grey and cool, and throughout the day the blue-bottomed clouds built to the east. That night they watched from the verandah as another storm formed and broke there.

'Duck bore way,' Rob said with satisfaction. 'That'll spread the stock a bit – get them off the waters.'

Jim barely heard the remark. He could not speak past the

bitterness in his throat and was afraid to try in case he cried. Sandy's promise had meant nothing. He had never intended to keep it. Perhaps – and the stark thought was new and terrible – he was never coming back, had known it even when he promised. A sound escaped Jim at this and he gritted his teeth angrily, glad that it was dark.

Rob's next words when they came were unexpected. 'It's pretty hard to tell how long things'll take, Jim. Like the rain. When your dad said he'd be back at Christmas he could've meant a week or two either side of it. I wouldn't give up on him yet. It's a slow business shifting a plant about.'

'Barney said that.' His voice was tight with anger. He was grateful for it, as it drove the treacherous tears away. 'But he didn't say why he couldn't send a telegram. How long would that take?'

'Well, if he was anywhere near a wireless —'

'Oh, he wouldn't be, would he?' Jim said rudely. 'Like he could ride all the way from wherever to here and never pass a station?' Pain at the betrayal of his trust choked him and the tears were coming in spite of himself. 'And I believed him. He doesn't care that I waited and waited. He never meant to come. I hate him.'

His chair screeched under him as he leapt to his feet and bolted through the door, slamming it so hard that the window frames trembled. He didn't care. If his uncle called him back he wouldn't go. The misery that overwhelmed him could not be made worse by anything Rob might say or do. A desert of endurance and heartache stretched behind him. He had crossed it alone, on foot, only to discover when he reached the far side that it had all been for nothing.

More than a month passed and school had started again before the parcel came. During those long trying weeks Jim's misery vented itself in sulky silences, rude outbursts and open defiance of his aunt. It shocked them both the day she slapped him, and he stood for a moment, aghast, hand pressed to his stinging cheek, as he stared from her tightened face to the bottle of ink they each knew he had deliberately spilled. He had never seen her soft mouth so thin before, or her placid face so pink.

With icy disdain, she took a rag from the school cupboard and dropped it before him. 'Clean it up. Rinse the cloth. And do the lesson again. In pencil.'

Jim's face flamed. Rosemary, who was a year behind him, used a lead pencil for her work. For a moment he teetered on the verge of rage, but something in her face made him swallow and pick up the cloth. He wondered why he'd knocked the bottle over – but he already knew the answer. It had been there. And he hated composition. And the pain inside him pushed relentlessly at him so that it had been enormously satisfying to hit the bottle with his ruler and watch the ink flood across the corrected page.

He was almost sorry now that he'd done it. The slap seemed to have cleared a fog from his head and he saw that Aunt Mary's lips, though so closely pressed together, were trembling and her eyes were very bright. His mother had boxed his ears the week before she died. He remembered it clearly, but not her reason for doing so. Aunt Mary, however, had never raised her voice to him, much less her hand, and now they stood either side of that blow and all at once he felt not triumph but regret that he had pushed her to it.

When he'd left the horse-paddock gate open and 'forgotten' to close the feed-shed door so that Mandy had gorged herself dangerously on oats, Barney looked at him in disgust. He'd earned some fierce dressing-downs from his uncle too, for rudeness and for cheeking Leo Baker, and he'd been as nasty to his cousins as he could so that the house had rung with their discord, but none if it had helped. Because through it all he knew they were making allowances for him, telling themselves he was upset that his father had not returned. Rosemary was the exception – she gave as good as she got. But Pommy and Oliver had tried, unpardonably, to console him. It only fuelled the outraged hurt and shame he felt. They were sorry for him. The knowledge was intolerable. They didn't under-stand it was not pity he wanted but something to batter his rage against.

And now he had hurt his aunt and added guilt to the welter of emotions he carried. He could not apologise, particularly as his uncle chose that moment to appear in the doorway.

'Parcel for you, Jim,' he said briefly. 'Mary, have you seen that pump catalogue I had last night?'

'It's in the dining room.' Her voice came high and tight. Rob glanced quickly at her, and Jim's spirits sank further. She was really upset. The only other time he'd seen her so was after the snake episode, and then she had been crying for him as well as his cousins. A great wash of shame went through him and he opened his mouth to make amends, but she was already speaking. 'Wait,' she said to Rob, 'I'll find it for you.' And they went out together.

Jim stared at the soiled brown-paper wrapping of the package Rob had placed on the nearest surface, and the regret uppermost in his thoughts was replaced with indignation. Even from where he stood he could recognise his father's curiously shaped capital M.

'Well, aren't you going to open it?' Rosemary was out of her seat, prodding experimentally at the wrapping. She turned it over. 'It's from Uncle Sandy! Betcha he's sent us Christmas presents.'

'He hasn't sent you anything.' A suffocating sense of ill feeling filled Jim. If his father thought he could ignore him for a year, break his word, and then make it all right by sending a parcel, then he could think again. Whatever was in it, he didn't want it. He snatched the package up and with a single sweep of his arm sent it sailing through the air to the top of the high cupboard where the school supplies were kept.

'Hey!' Oliver cried in alarm. 'You might break it.'

'So? It's my parcel. I'll break it if I want.'

'But you don't even know what's in it,' Rosemary wailed. 'I'll have it if you don't want it.'

'Just try touching it, Carrots.' He used her hated nickname with heat, spacing his words into a threat. 'Just – you – try.'

She glared at him, until the sound of Mary's returning footsteps sent them back to their desks. Jim stole a look at her as she entered but her face was blank and her voice normal as she glanced at the clock.

'Time for your radio lesson, Oliver. Have you got your book ready? And you'll need last week's paper too, remember.'

It was all right for Oliver, Jim thought. His cousin lapped up anything in print, but lessons were less pleasurable for himself and Rosemary. It was even harder to care about schoolwork when you were unhappy or, in Ro's case, when you were daydreaming about Chester and going riding that afternoon.

For three days the parcel lay out of sight on top of the cupboard. Neither his uncle nor his aunt referred to it, for which, Jim deduced, hardly knowing if he wanted them to question him about it or not, he had Rosemary to thank. Or blame. It was always Ro, he thought. But curiosity ate at him, making it harder to maintain the rage of his resolve. His anger hadn't gone; it was more that it had settled like a doughy weight inside him, at once lumpy and opaque, so that he no longer saw the world as he once had, but greyly, through a cloud of misery.

Early next morning, reasoning that nobody would know if he looked or not, Jim padded barefoot and pyjama-clad into the schoolroom and stood on a chair to retrieve the parcel. He carried it back to his bedroom, where the morning light streamed in through the window. The string was knotted in half a dozen places. He picked carefully at it until it fell free, then suddenly impatient he ripped the paper with both hands. The contents were wrapped again in newspaper. He tore that aside too and reached unbelievingly to lift out the plaited bridle that lay there.

There was a note. He read it, half his attention on the beautiful object he held, then read it again.

Dear Jim,

It'll be a bit late but I hope you like your Christmas present. I've been making it for a while now. The conchos are real silver so don't go losing them. I got caught by the early Wet and couldn't travel but I'll be back to see you as soon as the country's dry enough. Give my regards to your uncle and aunt.

All my love, Dad

Bridle temporarily forgotten, Jim stood in the pale light holding the note with both hands as he read and reread its magical words. He felt as if something weighty and black had been plucked out of his chest, as if a smeary pane through which he had been looking was suddenly thrust open to give an unimpeded view. He blinked hard and swallowed, and his heart sang as he read Sandy's note yet again, moving his lips as if tasting the words. Everything he had thought about his father was wrong. He did care. He was coming, and he'd made the beautiful bridle with his own hands, just for him. Reverently he laid the note down and shook out Sandy's handiwork. There were hours of patient toil in it, for the kangaroo leather had been cut very fine. The reins and straps he estimated at sixteen strands wide. The silver conchos were on the brow band, and buckles shaped like horseshoes secured the reins to the shiny bit.

Suddenly Jim wanted to yell his happiness aloud; he wanted to show Uncle Rob the bridle and tell Aunt Mary he was sorry about everything, but mostly he wanted to try his new possession on his horse.

He scrambled into his clothes, grabbed his precious gift, and taking the stairs three at a time ran whistling into the new-made day.

Some four months later, on the last Saturday in May, Sandy finally returned.

Jim heard the bells first. He had been out riding with Rosemary and they were coming back past the sheds when the wind blew the sound to him. It meant nothing for a moment, then his mind caught up with his ears – the stock camp was out mustering and none of the paddock horses were belled.

'It's Dad!' He lapped the reins under his startled pony's belly and Jake gave a great leap, springing into a canter and then a gallop, his sturdy legs pounding the earth. They burst out of the clutter of buildings, leaving the stable on their right, and galloped towards the yard where horses milled about and a stocky figure in a blue shirt trudged among them. 'Dad!' He yelled. 'Dad! You're here! I got the bridle – it's super.' He was out of breath, his voice torn by the wind of his passage, but he went on yelling. The main gates were shut and he skidded the pony to a halt and flew through the rails, still shouting his news and greetings as his boots carried him across the churned sand to where his father waited.

He was just the same. It was like running into a familiar, well-loved place that would always be home – the smell of tobacco and sweat, the strength of his arm and the rough feel of his cotton shirt. In the confused first moments, Jim saw that he'd turned his spurs onto his insteps as he always did in the yard, that his face was thinner and lined in a way it hadn't been, and there was a hole in the brim of his hat.

He said, 'Jim,' his voice lighter in timbre than Rob's, different to Barney's. His hands ruffled Jim's hair. 'No hat?' It had blown off in his wild gallop to get there. Then wonderingly, 'How you've grown!' And Jim swelled with pride, as if his height were something he had achieved in order to please his father. Sandy seemed to have no more words, but Jim made up for that as he tried to squeeze the events of sixteen months into five minutes.

'Whoa, son. Steady the lead.' Sandy cuffed him affectionately. 'We'll have plenty of time for news. For now let's get the nags unpacked.

They've come a fair stretch today.'

'I'll help.' Jim seized the halter of the closest horse and unknotted the shank. 'I always help Barney with the Rook. That's the station stallion,' he explained, forgetting that the horse predated his father's departure. 'He's won a couple of races at Goola already. Where'd you camp last night?' And before Sandy could answer, 'You look different with the beard. Shorter.'

'You reckon?' Sandy's lips quirked. 'Wouldn't be because you're taller, would it? And I camped back up the road a bit. Not far, but the horses cleared out and I got a late start.'

'But . . .' Jim checked again to be sure. 'They're not all here. Where's Pansy? And Dolphin? And what's the black over there? He isn't ours.' He craned to see over old Billy's neck. 'Why, you haven't got half of them!'

'Not here. A few of the mares have foals so I didn't bring them. And I've swapped some, and lost a couple. That black's a swap – I call him Gidyea. His mouth's damn near as hard as the wood. The rest are paddocked up north.'

Jim's hands stilled on a buckle. 'Then you're going back? You aren't staying?'

Sandy dodged, hearing what was behind the question. 'It's where the work is, son. I'm droving now. I've the promise of a mob from Glencam next month. Good long trip, worth a bob or two. Twelve weeks down into Queensland.'

'Where's Glencam?'

'Big place up north. They send their steers down into the Channel Country to fatten. That's where I'll be taking them.'

Jim's breath stopped. When he felt it moving again in his chest something of the day's brightness had fled. 'So we aren't going back home? To Arcadia?'

'It's not home any more, son.' Sandy's face tightened. He turned his back to pull the girths free and lift the packsaddle down. 'That's all finished. The best thing you can do is forget about it.' And with that Jim had to be content.

Sandy's visit lasted four days. Jim, excused from school, spent every waking moment in his company, from early breakfasts taken, as often as not, in the kitchen with Pommy and Dino, to trips out to the bores to check a mill or look at cattle with his uncle. He showed his father the Rook, and Chester, still running with his dam in the house paddock under Barney's eye. They rode out together to Bell Creek and though they both knew the distance didn't warrant it, they stopped on the way home to boil their quart pots, stowed in the neckbag Jake carried. The silver conchos on the pony's bridle glinted in the sun, and blue smoke coiled in little tendrils through the bright air. Jim swigged manfully at the black tea, squatting on his heels as stockmen did.

'Could I have another horse, Dad? Jake's too little. I wish he wasn't, but he is.'

Sandy, who said less now than before, wagged his head in a sideways hitch of agreement. 'Noticed your legs were close to the ground. We'll see what we can do, son.' The skin of his face was peeling redly about his beard and there were touches of grey in the hair above his ears that Jim didn't remember seeing before.

'Which one?' he pressed. 'I was hoping that Pansy . . . But she's not here.'

'Don't worry, there'll be something suitable. Not Gidyea, he'd be too strong for you. Anyway, he wants some solid work. Fidget's getting old. There's Muskrat, he'd suit – only I think he could've got a dose of poison. I notice he's dragging his hind feet.'

'Will he die?'

'Not necessarily, but he won't be much good for fast work. Leave it with me. If there's nothing here I'll fetch you back one next year. I daresay Rob can find you something till then.'

'I could ask Barney – he knows all the horses. Dad . . .' Jim hesitated, and then rushed his words as if speed might carry the day. 'Could I come with you next month? Just for the holidays. Uncle Rob could take me up to wherever you were and – oh, please,' for Sandy was already shaking his head. 'I want to go with you.'

'It's too far, son. And they're coming up to the bullock muster here. And even if Rob could get away to drive you there, I'd still have to get you back, and in the middle of the trip too. It just wouldn't work, Jim. You stop here like we agreed.' Jim did not remember agreeing to that. 'And I'll come back through on my way home.'

For another four days? But he did not voice the question. He sat very still, swallowing disappointment and staring fixedly at several ants carrying a moth's wing as they skirted an ant-lion trap. One fell in, and when its frantic scrambling had precipitated it to the bottom, where death waited, he tipped the dregs of his quart pot on top of it.

'Can we go look at the old mine then?' he asked bleakly.

'Don't see why not.' Sandy drank the rest of his tea and stood up to drag sand over the fire with the side of his boot. 'I know it's a bit hard, Jim. But your schooling's important. And I'm glad to see you're getting on better with your uncle too.'

'Yeah.' Grudgingly Jim added, 'He's all right.'

One more day then – that was all he had before his father vanished for another twelve months. The thought put a fishhook in his throat. He turned his head aside to hide it, then climbed doggedly to his feet and took up Jake's reins. There was still the mine to show him. He would be able to remember that when Sandy was gone – how they had ridden there together through the wintry golden day. He smacked Jake into a smart clip, Sandy's grey broke into a canter, and as the pony followed suit, pounding the red soil with determined feet, Jim had the fanciful thought that the thudding hooves were trying to outrun tomorrow.

NINE

It was two years before Jim saw his father again. Sandy did not return to Kharko after the Queensland trip, sending a brief note instead to say that he was heading north immediately for a chance at another mob. A week after Jim's twelfth birthday, a telegram came for him, and then there had been nothing until the carved boab nut arrived at Christmas. This time there wasn't even a note, just 'Happy Christmas, son' scrawled on the back of a label from a rum bottle.

'Not a bad brand, either,' Pommy said. 'Likes rum, does he, yer dad?'

'No. Probably the only paper he could find.' The question nettled Jim, who had unconsciously absorbed Rob's attitude to drink. Truth to tell, he thought miserably, he had no idea what Sandy liked, but he was older now and would not parade his disappointment before his friends. Taking the parcel to the kitchen to show off the oddity his father had sent was an act of defiance on his part. They would see that Sandy had not forgotten him, that there was no question of his return, that Jim did not expect it and had therefore no need of their pity.

To change the subject, he turned the boab nut in his hands, carefully scrutinising the tiny carved figures. 'Looks like they're fishing, but the fish is bigger than the boat.'

'Blackfella stuff,' Pommy sniffed. 'Wot d'you expect? Now, I seen some nice coconut carvings in Africa. Tropical pitchers they was – boats and palm trees, that sort of thing. They was selling 'em in the harbour at Capetown. All done by natives. They'd paddle out to the ships and flog 'em to the passengers. Big black bastards they were – looked like they'd 'ave your 'ead orf for tuppence, but they knew how to carve.'

'It's a dugong,' Matthew Henderson said quietly. A dried-up little man with a scar on one pitted cheek, he had replaced Dino as mechanic some six months before. Old Charlie had gone too, and Yellow Jack the half-caste now had his job. 'Sea cow,' Matthew added by way of explanation. 'Good tucker. The coastal blacks hunt them with spears. Where'd you get it? It's a nice bit of work.'

'My dad sent it. He's a drover up north. Soon as I finish school I'm gunna join him.'

'Are you?' Matthew asked with interest. He refilled his pannikin from the teapot. 'Sooner wrestle crocs meself.' But whether that meant he'd tried it and didn't like it, or couldn't ride and didn't want to, Jim couldn't tell, because Matthew wasn't a man to talk about himself.

Carrying the nut back to his room, he thought of the answer he had given Pommy and scowled. He knew nothing about his father as he was now, not where he went or what he did. All he had were memories grown thin from constant handling, the way a coin might. He still yearned for Sandy's return but sometimes a whole week would pass without his thinking of him at all. Feeling a sudden guilt over this, he placed the nut carefully on his bedside table, rather than on the wardrobe shelf as he'd originally intended.

Some weeks later, Des Hanks broke his leg at the end of the bullock muster and was taken to hospital in Alice Springs by the Flying Doctor. Jim, who was now spending his weekends in the stock camp, had expected Barney to take over as head stockman and was indignant when another man, who'd only been three months on Kharko, got the job instead.

Barney seemed unworried about it.

'Don't you care?' Jim demanded. 'You're the best rider on the place! Uncle Rob had no business giving that bloke Des's job.'

'Why not? He's the boss.'

'But you've been here longer. He can't even ride much – one of Des's horses chucked him easy as pie yesterday.'

'Don't mean he can't run a camp.'

Their job at the moment was tailing the bullocks the men had mustered the previous day for the drover to take delivery of later that week. A thousand head fed across the flat in the afternoon sunshine, lifting their muzzles now and then to stare about, or twisting their bodies to lick at their glossy hides with rough tongues. There were four of them tailing; Jim could see the other two riders moving slowly across the face of the bullocks, checking their advance. The idea was to let them feed without losing control of them as a mob.

'Look,' Barney struck a match, squinting against the smoke of his cigarette, 'the boss offered it to me. That good enough for you? I told him I didn't want it, so he give it to the other bloke.' He knocked the burning tip of his smoke against his kneepad and looked consideringly at Jim. 'He's a bit like you, you know, the boss. There's times neither of you can see for looking.' Then, in a bewildering change of subject, 'Wotcha reckon Oliver wants to do with himself when he's grown?'

'What?' Jim stared, puzzled by the question. 'He'll work for the company, I suppose. Become a manager like Uncle Rob.'

'Yeah.' Barney's tone was dry. 'I've heard the boss say so.'

'Well, what else would he do?' Jim's black gelding shifted his feet, reaching at the bit, and he patted his neck, perplexed by the turn the conversation had taken.

'What he wants to do, and that's get into the racing industry and work his way up to trainer. Have a yard of his own. See, what you'd choose for yourself ain't necessarily what another man wants. I'm a horseman, and if I can't own 'em I'll work 'em, so it suits me to be a ringer. It don't mean I want to run a camp.'

'Oh.' Jim's face wore his surprise. He cast his mind back. 'But Oliver's never said he didn't want to be a jackeroo.'

Barney's brow lifted. 'You ever try asking him?'

'Well . . . no.'

'Nor nobody else, neither.' Barney's glance was hard to read. 'I seen young blokes like Olly before. When they think something's expected of 'em they don't like to upset nobody.'

'D'you think he will? Go training?'

'Depends if he gets a chance, which means if Rob gives him one. He's not much of a scrapper so he'll most probably wind up doing what the boss wants. Works that way sometimes.'

'Well, he better not want me to do that,' Jim said decisively. 'Because I'm going droving. In a couple more years I'll be finished school, and if Dad hasn't come back by then I'm going off to find him.'

Barney grunted. 'Figured you would. Meantime do me a favour, will yer? Quit acting like he's a brown snake. It's embarrassing. Man's only doing his job.'

'Who?' But Jim knew quite well what Barney meant. Flushing a little, he patted his gelding's neck again to bridge the moment. How was he supposed to know that Barney had turned down the job?

His horse sidled from a bush and he tightened the reins. Sandy had not provided the promised new mount but his uncle had, and Jake was now pensioned off in the spell paddock. The black gelding belonged to the station but Rob said he would do until something better turned up. He meant when Sandy returned. Jim knew his father would have forgotten all about it by then. He still missed him but his expectations were no longer what they had been.

Some months later, Jim's rashness provoked the ire of his uncle to an unprecedented level. Looking back, he could not remember whose idea it had been to make the carbide bomb. Probably his. He'd been learning about gases in school and it seemed like a good idea to test how explosive they really were. Rosemary had been a willing accomplice, and as carbide was used to fuel the stock-camp lights there was plenty available in the heavy, press-sealed drum at the back of the feed shed. Barney had drawn their attention to it ages ago, telling them never to touch it before handling feed. Carbide lumps resembled rocks but leaked a fine, silty powder that spread its unpleasant odour through everything it touched.

'Could it poison a horse?' Jim had asked, impressed.

'I dunno. It'd sure as hell put 'em off their feed, so mind you leave it be.'

Choosing the rear of the stock tank to make the bomb had certainly been Rosemary's idea. There they were safe from observation, and far enough away for the noise not to carry to the house. They used a three-pound milk tin for the canister, pressing the lid down firmly on its contents before punching a hole through it. Borrowing an idea from an adventure story, Jim took several lengths of baling twine and dipped them in Stockholm tar, which was used to treat horses' stake wounds, before winding the makeshift fuse twice around the tin. There was tar everywhere by the time they had poked and prodded one end into the prepared hole. Then, realising he'd forgotten about getting the water in, he punched another hole beside it. Finally, when all was ready, he looked at Rosemary crouched beside him in the narrow band of shade.

'That should do it. Ought to blow clean in half, I reckon. Course it'd be better if the lid was soldered on. Make more pressure. You got the matches?'

She shook them gleefully. 'Are you gunna put the water in now?'

'In a minute. Sort out what we'll do first. It'll heat up when the gas starts – the lamps always do, anyway. So I'll wait till it's really hot, then we'll light the fuse and chuck it as far as we can.'

'Bags I do that,' Rosemary interjected.

'No. You can't throw far enough. I'll do it.' Jim mimed an underarm bowl. 'The lid might blow off, of course, but I reckon it should explode and rip the tin open. I'll chuck it at the trees over there, and the minute I do we drop flat. Got it?'

'Course.' She wriggled impatiently. 'Don't fuss so. It probably won't even work. If it doesn't we'll make another one and *I'll* throw it.'

'It'll work.' Jim was positive. 'Give me the water.'

He poured slowly because the hole was small and he didn't want the liquid sloshing about on the lid and wetting the fuse. The carbide hissed as the water went in, converting instantly to a foul-smelling gas. The canister immediately began to bubble as the gas sought release through an aperture too small for its volume, and in seconds the tin was too hot to hold.

'Cripes! Matches, quick.' The lid, it seemed to Jim, must burst off at any second. He jammed his hand over the rush of gas, only to snatch it back with a cry of pain. 'It's red hot! Quick, light it up.'

Rosemary did so, kneeling to blow coaxingly on their makeshift fuse. The flame sputtered and almost went out, then a weak spark caught and everything happened at once. One moment the flame seemed on the point of dying and the next it was racing along the tarred string faster than Jim could think.

'Look out!' It was too fast, the fuse too short. It would blow up in their faces and blind them both. 'Run!' he yelled. And dithered for a horrible moment before snatching the tin up and hurling it not at the trees as he had intended but around the curve of the tank, because if it burst in mid-air the tank's bulk would protect them from the blast. 'Get down!' He ignored his own order and they were both still standing, staring at the spot where the canister had vanished, when it went off.

It sounded like the end of the world. A tremendous bang, and immediately behind it the thunder of hooves as the horses they had not noticed standing at the trough galloped away. Rosemary's hands flew to her mouth as their eyes met. Then both breathed again as the half-dozen animals slowed, tails high, to circle and snort, jumpy with fright. It was then, when they thought they'd got away with it, that they heard the thumping and panicky whinnying of the one left behind.

It was Chester. Jim knew it with numbing certainty before he saw the colt on the ground. He had never envisaged that the gas-packed canister could be so unstable, or explode with such force, but once it had he knew something terrible would result. There was an inevitability about it that brought a gripe of pain to his lower stomach as he moved on leaden feet towards the trough and the animal struggling there. Chester's near-side front hoof was caught under the edge of rail forming part of the float cover. Had it been round it might have slipped free, Jim thought, even as he saw that the colt's foreleg had snapped, the bone sticking, obscenely white, through the bleeding hide.

The world seemed to stop while he stared at the wet, splintered thing in fascinated horror. He knew a vet could not fix such an injury. In his head, in idiot repetition, ran the words he had heard at some time in the kitchen or quarters – *arse over tit and done his leg on the rail*. Only it had been the steel edge of the trough, coupled with weight and gravity, that had caused this.

Jim squeezed his eyes shut, amending the thought. The trough had simply been there; it was he and Rosemary who'd done this, mostly him. He wished he could run away, somehow hide from the result of his actions. The colt would die and Uncle Rob . . . He didn't want to think about his uncle right then.

Beside him Rosemary wailed something and bent suddenly to retch. Then Corinne whinnied and the sound broke him from his frozen trance. He darted to the colt's side and crouched there to lift his head and wrap his arms around it. In that position, with his poll on the ground, he could not hurt himself further by attempting to rise.

Jim held the face against his chest, feeling Chester's pain in the air that wheezed through his nostrils in little whining grunts.

'All right, boy, all right. Steady now, steady – that's it.' His voice croaked with dread. He looked up at Rosemary standing tearfully behind him. 'Get Uncle Rob.'

'Oh, no Jim!' The words were a whisper. 'He's going to be so angry.'

'I don't care if he kills us. Go and get him!' The colt heaved and thrashed his legs, the broken one banging sickeningly against the metal. Jim gulped. 'Get him, Ro – hurry. Tell him to bring the rifle.'

'He'll shoot us.' She was paper-white. Their eyes shared their terror as she wrung her hands. 'Oh, I wish we hadn't done it. If only you'd thrown it the other way.'

'Well, I didn't,' he snarled. 'Now, get moving.'

Swallowing a sob, Rosemary turned and ran, bobbing hatless across the flat towards the distant house, her red hair bright in the sun.

Left alone with the colt's agony and the glistening spread of its blood, Jim dropped his face lower until the wheezing breath blew against his cheek. He could feel the little tremors of pain rippling through the sleek body and he ground his teeth in self-hatred and despair. He'd break both his own legs if that could make Chester's whole.

'I'm sorry,' he whispered to the dulled eyes and lax lips. 'I'm so sorry.'

When next he looked up it was to see Rob moving towards him in deliberate strides. Dully he watched him come and saw that he carried not the big .303 they used to shoot the killers but the little Remington .22 from the office. His face was terrible as he looked down on the colt's heaving flanks. He worked the rifle's breech to load it. 'Get out of the way.' His voice was hard enough to cut stone.

Dumbly Jim released Chester's head and pushed himself upright. Blood caked his knee and stained one sock but he didn't notice this. He dared not look at his uncle as Rob placed the end of the barrel behind the colt's ear and pulled the trigger. Jim heard the breech click open and followed the golden spin of the spent shell as it struck the hide and bounced under the trough. Chester gave the smallest jerk and his body seemed to flatten against the ground.

There was scarcely any blood from the bullet hole, nor had there been much noise, but in a single second everything was over – all the hopes and plans and, for the colt, life itself. He was nothing now, not Barney's miracle, nor a future world-beater, nor Rob's last chance at the bloodline – nothing but carrion for the crows.

Jim was aware only of the polished boots and khaki-clad legs in his field of vision, and the dead Chester between them. He found the courage to raise his eyes, and quailed before the look he encountered. 'I'm sorry,' he said miserably.

'And you think that fixes it?' Jim's soul shrivelled at the sight of Rob's face, and at the cold scorn in his voice. 'That's a dead animal lying there. Unnecessarily. A valuable animal that shouldn't have died – wouldn't have died, if you'd showed a quarter of the sense anyone your age should have. And you're sorry!'

Jim's gaze fell again. 'I truly am. I —'

'Actions have consequences, Jim. I would have thought you'd know that by now. Things done can't be undone. There is no magic formula to wipe out regret. You make a decision you know is wrong – commit a stupid, dangerous act that might have maimed or blinded the pair of you – and manage to kill a colt that's been years in the breeding.

Then you tell me you're *sorry*. Well, there are some things those words don't cover.'

There was nothing to say. He was scorched by guilt, frozen with self-loathing. Flies crawled and buzzed over the caked blood on his leg as he stood there staring blindly at the dead colt and wishing his uncle would belt him. He had thought he would but he wasn't going to. Instead he jerked his head and said grittily, as if he could not stand to breathe the same air another minute, 'Just go. Get out of my sight.'

It was a long time before Jim could put the misery of his deed behind him. One day, perhaps, it wouldn't matter, or at least not so much, but he was learning that regret was the heaviest pack to carry. Oliver, he was certain, would never forgive him for Chester's death.

He was lurking in the garden immediately after the accident, too upset to face anybody, when his cousin found him. Jim had watched him come, his lanky body jerking towards him like a marionette, and sought for something to say, only Oliver didn't wait to hear it.

'Pommy told me, you murdering little shit!' he cried, and launched himself furiously at Jim, striking out wildly with clumsily knotted fists. His anger made up for his lack of skill and he caught Jim flush on the nose. Through the blinding pain that momentarily dimmed his sight, Jim saw that Oliver's face was bone-white, and that behind the wire-rimmed spectacles he was crying. It only deepened his wretchedness; he didn't want to fight his gentle cousin. He pushed him back and dodged the next punch.

'It was an accident. I didn't mean to hurt him.'

'The only accident was that you ever got born!' Oliver yelled. 'But seeing you did, I don't see why *we* should have to put up with a son of a bitch like you.' Oliver seldom swore and the oath came out stiltedly. One part of Jim's brain recognised its ineptness while the rest responded to its literal meaning. A blaze of pure fury swept through him and with it a certain relief, for Oliver was now a legitimate target. *All right!* He was sorry, he had said so. But not so sorry that he would hear his mother maligned. Forgetting everything else, he flung himself at the older boy, hitting every part of him he could find.

Afterwards he never quite knew how long it lasted. When sanity returned he sat gasping, feeling the pain of his puffy eye and socked nose and knowing there was blood all over his shirt. He glowered at his cousin, who was in no better shape, with a great welt along one cheekbone and a split lip. It was a miracle his glasses were still intact.

'You ever call me that again,' the words came pear-shaped through his tender lips, 'and I'll kill you.'

Oliver's rage had also eased. And being the peacemaker he was, he apologised. 'I'm sorry. I didn't mean anything against Aunt Jenny. I was too angry to think straight. I shouldn't have said it.'

Jim maintained his glower and ignored the olive branch. 'You better believe it,' he said ungraciously, then got to his feet and walked away.

Part of him wished he hadn't, that he had stayed and made it up with his cousin, said again how sorry he was for the accident. Because now, to his previous unhappiness was added a mild shame. He knew perfectly well that despite the difference in their ages he was far more capable of defending himself than Oliver was. Why, even Ro, he thought cynically, would be harder to beat. Still, what was he supposed to do?

His cousin had brought it on himself. He could at least have waited to hear Jim's side of the story before charging at him like a mad bull.

Only Barney had given Jim a chance to explain. The horse breaker had not needed telling, for thanks to Pommy the tale was all over the station. The cook meant no harm by it; the avidity with which he collected and disseminated news was a symptom of the isolation they lived in, and was common to most station workers. Jim had found Barney at the horse yards, drafting out fresh working horses for the camp with the aid of a stock boy. He waited to be noticed, standing by the rails until the job was done, although he knew Barney had spotted him the moment he appeared. He hoped Barney would stop and not walk past without speaking, although it would be no more than he deserved if he did.

Barney unchained the gate and called to the stock boy to take the remaining horses to the spell paddock. He pushed the gate open to let them out and trudged back through the heavy sand, rolling a smoke as he came. Unsmilingly he nodded a greeting. 'Jim.'

To the boy, nerves keyed to withstand either fury or scorn, Barney looked and sounded more sorrowful than angry. The slow realisation came to him then that it was the blue blood of Chester's breeding that his uncle and cousin mourned, while Barney mourned the colt himself. It made things infinitely worse.

He said huskily, 'I'm sorry.' He seemed to spend his life repeating those words, which were as useless as his uncle had warned.

'I bet you are.' Barney's face seemed planed from wood. He stuck a cigarette between his lips and struck a wax match against his thumbnail. Blowing blue smoke out, he put a hand up on the rail and scratched idly at the timber. 'What happened?'

Jim told him simply, without attempting to shift the blame, and when he ended Barney blew out another cloud of smoke and sighed.

'Well, it's done. Horses die. Pity it had to be him.' He shook his head regretfully. 'Coulda been a champion, that colt.'

'I don't think they'll ever forgive me – Oliver and Uncle Rob.' Jim sounded as wretched as he felt.

'Can't blame 'em.' Barney was forthright. 'You gotta learn to think, kid. The horse is bad enough. What if it had been young Ro, eh? Or you? You been down that road? I bet the boss has. You do bloody stupid things that hurt people, don't expect 'em to like you for it.'

Jim hung his head but Barney had no more to say. The matter was never raised between them again.

TEN

When finally Sandy did reappear, a year or so after the death of Chester, it was unannounced. He drove up in a battered Holden utility, parking as he always had under the shade of the pepper tree by the gate. Rob had gone to Goola with Oliver and Rosemary, and Mary was painting the pantry cupboards when the ute pulled up.

'See who that is, will you, Jim. Oh, damn!' She dipped a rag in turps and rubbed at a paint splotch on the floor.

Jim went down the path to meet the visitor at the gate. His father was the last person on his mind, and he stood for a second goggling, his greeting an uncertain question. 'Dad?'

'That's right, it's me, son. How are you? Planning on getting much bigger?'

Jim saw with bemusement that he was as tall now as his father. Intense joy swept through him, to be followed instantly by a hesitation that Sandy sensed, then solved by putting out his hand. They shook hands for the first time, like men.

'But what are you doing here? Where's the plant?' Jim peered past

Sandy's shoulder at the vehicle behind him. 'Who's the car belong to?'

'We can talk about all that inside,' Sandy suggested. He threw an arm round Jim's shoulder. 'It's good to see you, son. Your uncle home?'

'No, but Aunt Mary is. Where'd you come from, Dad?'

'North a-ways. Came down the Sandhill route. The track's a bugger – lucky the ute didn't bog outa sight.'

'You should have a four-wheel drive.' Jim pushed the screen door wide and entered shouting. 'Hey, Aunty! Come and see who's here!'

Mary came, still in her paint-spattered pinny, and after a second or two the blank look on her face was replaced by one of startled welcome. 'Sandy! Of all things! I almost didn't know you. You must be parched – come and sit down. I'll make tea.'

'It's all right, Mary,' he protested. 'I can see you're in the middle of something. I'll go down to the kitchen. Old Pommy still there? I'm sure he'll have the kettle on the boil.'

'You'll do no such thing.' Mary fisted her hips. 'You sit there right this minute while I get things ready. Jim, pour your father a cold drink. Rob will be back shortly. Why ever didn't you let us know you were coming?'

Her last few words were called from the pantry. Jim, taking advantage of her absence, put several questions of his own. 'Where's the plant, Dad? Is it far? Did you find that horse for me?'

Sandy dropped his hat under the chair and combed his hair with his fingers. His face looked thinner and his hair needed cutting. He coughed. 'The plant's gone,' he said. 'I sold the horses and gear last summer.'

'*Sold* them? You sold Dolphin?' Jim started to his feet in horror.

'And Peddler, and . . .?' He slumped down, pale with shock, his mind racing. 'But you're a drover. You can't just . . .' The future he had dreamed of crumpled before his eyes. 'I was coming to join you,' he cried. 'I'll be finished school in a couple of years. It was all worked out.'

'Well, son, you're better off on wages than working for yourself, you know.' Sandy uttered the heresy calmly while his thick fingers fashioned a cigarette. A part of Jim's mind noticed the broken nails and ingrained dirt like a stain across his palms – a working man's hands. But his father, as long as he had known him, had always worked for himself. He could scarcely believe what he was hearing.

'But you always said . . . about being a wage slave . . .'

'A man gets older, and tireder, son.' Sandy licked the edge of the cigarette paper, rolled it, and stuck it in his mouth. His eyes, Jim saw, were bloodshot and there were bags under them as if he had not slept. 'And even a bit wiser. There's a lot to be said for a regular wage.'

Mary came back with the tea, and while she poured it and set out biscuits Jim stared at his father. He saw a stranger, someone he barely knew. Sandy's strong, indomitable body had grown soft-looking and paunchy round the middle, and his once broad shoulders were permanently slumped. Even his hair was different, more grey than ginger. His trouser cuffs were frayed, his shirt unironed – as they were bound to be, Jim reminded himself with a flicker of loyalty. Dismay spread through him. How had his father got so old and beaten-looking? He said abruptly, hating the accusation he could hear in his voice, 'What do you do, then? Run a camp?'

'Well, I could.' Sandy glanced at him. 'Matter of fact Sid Miller asked me to take on the camp at Basingstoke, but my back still gives me trouble from a fall I had last year, so I turned it down. I do a bit of everything. Did the camp cooking there for three months, then moved into the kitchen when the stock work finished.'

'Basingstoke – you've been at *Basingstoke*?' Incredulity and anger warred in Jim's tone. Basingstoke Station was little more than ninety miles from Kharko in a straight line – a hundred and thirty by road. 'And you never came to see me? I thought you were somewhere like the Kimberley, or the Channel Country. Weeks and weeks of travel to get here, but all the time . . .' Jim sat clenching the starched tablecloth, and his face quivered.

'Perhaps your father couldn't get away, dear,' Mary said tactfully, covering her own surprise. 'You know, a cooking job —'

'Pommy does. He gets to Alice Springs, and that's a lot further away.' Jim glared accusingly at Sandy, who shrugged and set down his cup to touch his son's arm.

'You're right. I should've made the effort, and I'm sorry I didn't. But I'm here now, so let's make the best of our time. Tell me what you've been up to.'

But somehow it was difficult to do that. Jim's tongue was stiff and his words came awkwardly. He could not get over the fact of his father having spent so much time on what amounted to a neighbour's property without trying to see him. That, and Sandy's casual disposal of the plant, had rocked his world to its foundations. It was left to Mary to carry the burden of conversation until Rob arrived. Jim, wrapped in self-conscious silence, was racking his brains for something to say when he heard the front gate click. He leapt gladly to his feet.

'There's Uncle Rob. I'll tell him you're here.'

He did not return to the house with the others but wandered blindly down to the deserted stables, a prey to conflicting emotions. Rosemary might find him there if she were sent after him, but nobody else would. It was the summer lay-off time. Barney had gone to Adelaide and Des Hanks and his family were in Alice Springs. Yellow Jack was out pumping, so Pommy had only Matthew and a couple of stock boys to cook for.

Head bent, Jim kicked at the sand to dislodge the heel of a bottle. He bent to pick it up, rubbed it aimlessly on the weathered rails, then flipped it away and sank to his haunches with his back against the post, gripping his knees with both hands. He should have been happy to have his father back, but instead there was such a mixture of anger and hurt and humiliation inside him he could scarcely breathe. Why hadn't Sandy just stayed away if it was such a nuisance to visit him? Jim would have walked the distance to Basingstoke barefoot had he known Sandy was there. But he hadn't known, and that was the crux of it. It did not matter to his father that they were so close yet did not see each other.

Jim leaned his head back and let his eyes cling to the hawk circling above him, glad that Barney was not there to learn of his shame.

Sandy was waiting on the verandah when Jim returned to the house. He swung his legs down and sat up at the sight of him.

'Jim. I wondered where you'd got to.'

'Seeing to the horses,' he said untruthfully. 'And I wanted to talk to Matthew about a job we've got on tomorrow. We're going out to Duck bore. That's in the bullock paddock. He's teaching me about diesels.'

Sandy raised his brows and looked steadily at his son. 'I thought we might spend tomorrow together.'

'Sorry.' Jim shrugged. 'Matthew's expecting me, and Uncle Rob says I should learn everything the men'll teach me.'

'Well, why don't I come too?'

'What for?' It was Jim's turn to raise his brows. His eyes bored into his father's. 'I'll be back tomorrow night. Anyway, you can see me anytime you want to visit, can't you?'

Sandy winced and looked away and Jim felt a surge of vindictive pleasure. 'Dinner'll be ready soon and I still have to shower. See you later.'

The meal was an uncomfortable affair. Mary set flowers on the table and used the good china in Sandy's honour. Rosemary was so subdued that Jim was certain she'd been told by her father not to monopolise Sandy's company. Oliver was his usual quiet self; Leo Baker, who seldom spoke at meals, made an effort. But Sandy had little to say himself, and if it hadn't been for Mary's inconsequential chatter and Rob's contributions, the conversation would have collapsed. Jim answered half a dozen questions about his schoolwork but volunteered nothing on his own. Several times he felt his uncle's gaze upon him, but another discovery distracted him from Rob's possible displeasure.

He was ashamed of his father. He despised himself for it, but he couldn't help comparing Sandy's rumpled, threadbare appearance with Rob's pressed neatness. His father had not showered or combed his hair with anything other than his fingers before coming to the table. Jim watched hot-faced as he knocked over his water glass, spilt gravy on the good cloth, and chewed absentmindedly as he talked. He wished his father's shirt was cleaner, and that he'd hold his fork a little higher, and thought how he would be more at home with the rough manners that prevailed in the kitchen.

Afterwards, despite the early hour, Jim would have slipped away to his room had not Rob taken him firmly by the shoulder. 'Let's sit in the lounge. It's a bit cool to be outside now. You haven't told your father about your holiday yet, Jim. Why don't you run up and get the photos? Mary took the kids to Adelaide for ten days last month, Sandy. They had a great time.'

'Good,' Sandy said heartily. 'If you're going upstairs, son, bring down the bottle in my room. It's on the chest of drawers. And fetch us the glasses there too.'

Jim did as he was asked. Sandy held the bottle up to his brother. 'Rum. Not your tipple, Rob, but you'll have a snort?'

'Think I'll pass, thanks.'

But Leo Baker, Jim saw, sipped his like a cat at the cream and accepted another as soon as it was offered. The generator engine thumped and Jim caught the odour of tobacco on his father's clothes. When Sandy belched Jim smelled the rum on his breath. Wishing only to be gone, he tapped the pile of prints to square them up, then dealt them briskly onto the coffee table. He had taken them himself with the box Brownie he got for his last birthday, a present from his aunt and uncle. From his father he'd received nothing.

There were shots of the ocean, an out-of-focus tram, Rosemary eating an icecream, a man selling balloons. He remembered how he'd felt taking the pictures, anticipating this moment and the things he would tell Sandy about his first ever visit to the city. He'd been stunned by the sheer size of it; bewildered by the crowds, the shops, the traffic, the neon nightscape, and had longed to tell his father about them. But that was when he believed it was distance rather than inclination that kept Sandy away. He placed the final snap on the table – Rosemary and Aunt Mary on the beach – then immediately tidied them back into their folder.

'Pretty good, son.' Sandy lifted his glass again, eyes creasing into a smile. 'I always meant to take you south one day. You had a good time, did you?'

'It was all right,' Jim said woodenly. He picked up the photos and looked at his uncle. 'Think I'll put these away before I forget. See you all in the morning.' He shut the door with finality behind him.

'That was *dreadful*.' Mary crossed the bedroom to fling the lacy curtains wide and close the louvres against the chilly night air. 'Poor Sandy. If only children weren't so unforgiving.'

'Well, and hasn't he plenty to forgive?' Rob shook his head. He and Jim had put the death of Chester well behind them. 'The man's a soak. I can't believe . . . If Jenny could see what he's sunk to —'

'Oh, for heaven's sake, Rob.' Mary's eyes snapped with a sudden, unaccustomed temper. 'If Jenny were here there'd be nothing *to* see. I don't expect Jim to understand that, but surely you can? He lost everything when he lost her, including the will to carry on. And if taking a drink helps, then I for one don't blame him.'

'There are other ways,' Rob began.

'Like what?' Hearing her voice rise, she lowered it again, conscious of the silence in the listening house. The diesel had been switched off and only the soft glow of the kerosene lamp lit the room. She tugged savagely at the skirt of her dress, the folds of which muffled her words as she peeled it over her head. 'Go and see the padre, you mean? The only time Sandy ever set foot in a church was to be married, you said so yourself. Perhaps if he had somebody to talk to – that's what a woman would do. But you men have to be so self-sufficient! In any case, I can't see him chatting it over with the neighbours, can you? If any of them were even capable of listening – and that includes you, let me add.'

For once Rob was on the defensive. 'I only meant —'

'I know exactly what you meant.' Mary's face was bleak in the lamp-light and she looked suddenly tired as she shook out her dress. 'And I know exactly how you'd behave in his shoes, but not everybody's like you, Rob. They can't just turn to and work grief out of their system like they were tuning up a cranky engine. His heart is broken, can't you see that? And in ten years' time it will still be broken. That's something we can't help, but *you* could help Jim understand the reason for his father's behaviour.'

'Hah! I think he's pretty clear on that already. Sandy's dropped his bundle. And I'm certainly not excusing him conduct I can't condone.' Rob pulled his belt free of its loops and dropped it onto the chair beside the bed, following it with his trousers. 'Anyway, it wasn't the grog that upset Jim tonight, it was finding out that his father's been living so near for so long and hasn't come to visit.'

'I know.' Mary sighed. 'If he wasn't going to come he should at least have let him know where he was. Poor Jim.' An afterthought occurred. 'Did you know?'

'I heard talk, but I thought it was someone else.' He reached for the lamp. 'Are you right?'

'Yes.' Her voice came softly through the sudden dark, repeating, 'Poor Jim.'

Sandy stayed five days. Rosemary spent the first one with him while Jim worked miserably with Matthew, wishing himself alternately back at the station and as far from it as he could get. He returned in the late afternoon to find his cousin ensconced at Sandy's side with Pommy, and he stamped off to wash, furious with them all.

But over the next few days his anger cooled, for there were still occasional flashes of the old Sandy – a look shared, a lift of the eyebrow that wordlessly included Jim in some trivial observation not worth speaking of, the hint of a smile when Rob got onto racing and preached some breeding doctrine at his brother.

Jim was acutely uncomfortable the first time this happened, fearing that Chester's fate would surface, but it never did. 'You can depend on the boss,' Barney had once told him, adding, 'that's why I work here.' Jim now knew what he meant. His uncle stood behind his word, he saw with pride, and was loyal to his family, the company and the men he employed.

Once he would have said that his father owned the same qualities. But they had got lost somehow with his mother's death, Jim thought, or Sandy would never have sold his horses and let his son slip away to the recesses of his mind. It still hurt that Sandy should grieve so greatly for his wife and yet think only intermittently of him. It was as if, with

Jenny's death, the wellspring of his father's being had snapped and nothing really mattered to him any more.

On Sandy's last morning they drove into Goola to restock his tuckerbox from the little all-purpose store there. Coming down the steps with the groceries, they met Bill Maddison, whose long face lit up at the sight of his old neighbour.

'The mulga-wire's not working too good,' he said by way of greeting. 'I had no idea. When did you get back?'

'Friday last week.' Sandy dumped the groceries in the ute and shook hands. 'Just a quick visit to catch up with Jim here. I'll be pushing off tomorrow. So how've things been going?'

"Bout the same. More work than quids, nothing's changed in that respect. We miss you at the dances. Still got the old accordion?'

'Nah. Hard thing to hump around in packs.' He squinted at the sun. 'Better keep moving. Gotta pack this afternoon. How's the family?'

'They're good, thanks, real good. Boys are growing like weeds, same as your lad. You gunna drop by for a visit? Maggie'd love to catch up with you before you leave.'

'Like to, Bill,' Sandy said. 'Have to see how it goes.' They shook hands again and parted. Jim waited until the ute was moving, throwing its column of dust behind it, before speaking.

'What packing? You've only got to sling your swag on, Dad. We could drive to Condamine this arvo and have time to drop in at Arcadia on the way back. The main road's much better than it used to be, you know.'

Sandy shook his head. 'I don't think so. Anyway, he won't be expecting us now.'

'Well, we could still see Mrs Maddison and the boys,' Jim argued.

'And if we took the back road past Strangefellow we could cut across to Arcadia and come home that way. Oh, go on, Dad. Let's.'

'Not today,' Sandy said firmly. 'I've told you before, son, that's all finished. And as for the Maddisons – well, maybe next time.'

'And when's that gunna be?' A touch of his earlier defiance coloured Jim's question. 'I don't see why you can't just get a job on Kharko, then you wouldn't have to go away.' It was an argument they had already had and Sandy sighed.

'It's no good, Jim. It wouldn't work. A bit of Rob goes a long way with me.'

'He's all right.' Jim spoke hotly in his uncle's defence.

'He's doing a great job with you, anyway, and I'm grateful.' Sandy swerved to dodge a hole in the road. 'I might've been a bit careless of you, son, but at least I got that right. You're a credit to him and I want you to know I'm proud of you, even if I'm not here to tell you so. And I'm glad you get along with old Rob the way you do. The two of you are a bit alike, come to think of it.' He reached to ruffle Jim's hair, and the old gesture dissolved the awkwardness between them.

It was only after Sandy had left the following day that Jim realised he'd never answered his question about when the next visit would be.

In July of 1961, Oliver packed the old leather suitcase that had served for years on the family's infrequent visits to Alice Springs and left for his first job. Eighteen now, he was going to Knolly Downs, a hundred and fifty miles to the north-east of Kharko, to be a jackeroo. Knolly Downs was owned by the same company that owned Kharko, and the job was the first rung on the ladder of management. Jim, holding his tongue whenever the subject came up, remembered Barney's words and wondered if it was what his cousin wanted.

On Oliver's last morning at home Jim found him packing in his room, from which the photographs of horses and most of his books had already been removed. Jim fingered a bare shelf and looked about him. He was almost as tall as Oliver now and suddenly he wished that they had become better friends over the three-and-a-half years he had been there. Somehow he had been too occupied with his own problems, and Oliver was somebody it was easy to overlook – unlike his fiery-natured sister. In the interim his dreamy, pliant cousin had become a young man, who was free to roll his swag (smoothing the nap flat with his usual finicky care) and take charge of his own life.

Except he wasn't really doing that, Jim knew. He was going off to Knolly Downs as Uncle Rob had planned, and in twenty or thirty years, if he didn't make too many blunders, he would become a company manager and perhaps forget that he'd ever wanted to train horses for a living.

Jim settled himself on the stripped bed and thumped the bulging suitcase beside him. 'Sure you got everything? You don't want to stick a racing pad in too?'

'Very funny.' Oliver reached for the straps to buckle around the canvas cylinder of his swag. He was bony still, and stick-thin, but there was a wiry strength to his frame for all that. Weaklings, Jim knew, couldn't hold in half a ton of galloping horse, and it was his boniness that allowed Oliver to make the weight as a jockey. He had lost and won many races since that first nervous ride those years before.

'Did you want something?' He looked enquiringly at Jim.

'No. Well, that is, I just wondered why you're going to Knolly. You don't *have* to be a jackeroo, unless you want to. If I were eighteen I wouldn't go jackerooing, I'd be heading off to work with Dad. I thought you wanted to be a trainer? They don't have racehorses at Knolly, you know. Matthew told me that – he worked there.'

Oliver snugged the buckles tight. 'I know. But why should you worry? You've always reckoned stockhorses are better, anyway.'

'Yes, but . . .' Jim floundered, then blurted it out. 'Why don't you just tell Uncle Rob you're not going? I mean, if you don't want to – well, you're grown up, aren't you? It's not like he could stop you.'

His cousin stood the swag on one end and put his elbow on it, his angular face set and his pale eyes glinting. 'That's what you'd do, is it?'

'Too right.'

'Well, just suppose for a minute it was Uncle Sandy and he wanted you to, to, oh, work in a shop or something, and you knew he wanted that and had planned it from the moment you were born, and he'd been training you for it for years. You'd just walk out on him to go climbing mountains or something else you fancied, would you?'

'Girls work in shops,' Jim objected. 'And anyway, he wouldn't want me to do anything like that.'

'Ah, forget it.' Oliver picked up the swag and tossed it onto his shoulder, his gaze once again dispassionate. 'You're the most single-minded, self-centred person I've ever met – you realise that? All that matters is what you want. But other people have claims on you too, as you'll maybe find out one day.' He lifted the suitcase with a grunt and stood for a moment surveying the room, then turned and left.

Jim, miffed by his criticism, picked up the coiled whip and bridle lying near the door and followed him downstairs for the family farewell.

For somebody who'd barely noticed Oliver's presence most of the time, Jim found the homestead strangely empty once his cousin had gone. He wandered aimlessly between the stables and the big house, then finally sought out Rosemary, who was washing dishes as slowly as possible.

'If you're going to stand there,' she snapped, 'then you might as well do something useful and wipe these.'

'What's biting you?' He picked up the cloth and began drying.

'It's Mum.' She flounced a dish into the drainer, sending a spray of soapsuds up the wall. 'She's come over all prudish. Now that Oliver's gone I'm not allowed to eat in the kitchen with the men any more. I have to keep away from the quarters. I'm a big girl now, and so on. Does she think Pommy's gunna grab me, or Barney? Maybe it's old Charlie she's worried about?'

Charlie Attwood, who came and went, was currently back at the station.

'Not likely,' Jim laughed. 'The cranky old bugger hasn't spoken to us since we broke his pipe that time. So what are you gunna do? I suppose you're still allowed to ride?'

'Yes, but only with you, or at least if you're there. And I have to learn to sew and make bread and crochet stupid doyleys, and I'll never be allowed to do any of the things I want.' Her voice wobbled, and to his great surprise Jim saw that she was on the verge of tears. Rosemary, who never cried, and whose tough little fists he had often felt in argument.

He said awkwardly, 'It's because you're growing up.' She had never been pudgy, but the planes of her face were now visible through its childish roundness and he was aware of the small hills of her breasts beneath her shirt. 'Aunt Mary probably wants to make you more . . . more, ladylike,' he finished lamely, one eye on the dishcloth, for Rosemary usually retaliated with the closest thing to hand. 'Girls have to learn these things, or how would they know them? My mum sewed everything at our place, and she baked cakes and made jam and put flowers in the house – all that sort of lady stuff. It won't be so bad once you get started.'

'You think?' she cried bitterly. 'They're sending me away to school. I suppose that's not going to be so bad, either? Months and months away from home. I'll have to wear a dress every day.' Tears spilled down her cheeks now. 'And I won't ride Mandy or see Barney, and Mum says I'll have to learn deportment and not to swear.' She put her soapy hands to her face and sobbed.

'Aw, come on.' Jim was at a loss. It was so unusual to see his self-sufficient cousin in tears that he gave her a clumsy hug. 'When are you going? It's the first I've heard of it.'

'Not till next year, but that doesn't make it any better.' She had soap in her eyes and wiped them with the hem of her shirt. 'It's not fair.'

'No,' he agreed. 'I'll miss you,' he added truthfully. 'What's deportment, anyway?'

'How should I know? You're lucky you're a boy, Jim. I wish I was. Oliver didn't have to go away to school.'

Jim was reminded of his original purpose by the mention of his cousin's name. 'Here, tell me something. Your brother said just before he left that I was self-centred. Do you think I am?'

Rosemary sniffed and blinked her soap-stung eyes. 'Of course you are. You always have been, so why worry about it now?'

'Well, thanks a bunch.' He flipped the tea towel over the rail. 'You can finish the rest yourself.'

Before the start of the following school year, Rob, Jim and Leo Baker were left to eat alone while Mary went with Rosemary down to Adelaide. She showed a mutinous face the day she left, flouncing and dawdling by turns throughout the morning, and slamming into the rover without once looking back at the group assembled at the gate.

Rob clasped his daughter only briefly and pecked a kiss on her forehead as she glowered at him. 'Behave yourself, Rosemary. I expect a good report at year's end.'

Guilty that he was staying when she had to go, Jim was indignant on his cousin's behalf. Rob was an undemonstrative man but surely he could have tried harder than that. Jim hugged her awkwardly to make up for it. 'I'll look out for Mandy,' he promised. 'And write you the news.'

Her glower softened slightly. Jim found it hard to tell with Rosemary when she was frightened and when she was just plain mad, but this time he thought she was frightened. There was a fixed look to her mouth, and against her brilliant hair her face, with its dark hazel eyes, seemed pale. She and her mother would travel to Perishing Downs that afternoon and stay overnight there with the Colsons, then drive on to Alice Springs the next day, catching the plane south that evening.

Things were comfortable enough in Mary's absence, if dull without Rosemary. Pommy, his temper restored by a visit to Alice Springs over the Christmas period, made a special effort with the cooking, and Des Hanks's wife kept an eye on the house, which turned echoingly empty overnight, as if mourning its womenfolk's departure. In the first few weeks, before he became accustomed to it, Jim was surprised at how much he missed his cousin. She might have been wilful and argumentative, always wanting to do things differently, but she had been company when nothing better offered.

Pommy missed her too and disagreed with her going. 'Crool, that's wot it is. Bit of a kid like that being sent orf on her own. Sobbing herself to sleep ev'ry night, I shouldn't wonder.'

This was altogether too much to swallow. 'Huh! The only ones doing any sobbing will be the teachers, if I know Ro.' Jim bit into his scone. 'Come off it, Pommy. Pull the other one.'

The cook lifted his singlet away from the taut curve of his paunch to reach up and scratch his chest. His bald head shone as if polished but there was a dolorous look to his face, and even his moustache seemed to droop. 'I miss having her round the place. I useta mend her dolls for her when she was a little tacker.'

'Yeah? I never saw her with a doll.' Jim was sceptical.

'An' she useta come in when I was baking and try me cakes. Iced 'em for me sometimes too. Won't be no more of that, anyroad. The buggers I'm feeding now do nuthin' but whinge. They'll be dead lucky if they get bread, never mind cake.'

'You show 'em, Pommy,' Jim said. He carried his mug to the sink, rinsed it and took another scone on his way out. Still, he frowned, there was a lot of truth in the cook's words. The easy friendliness of the kitchen had changed lately. He couldn't put his finger on why, but the men were cranky in a way he hadn't seen before. There had always been good-natured grumbling at the men's table; it was their prerogative to bitch about the boss, the food, the long hours, but nobody took it too seriously. Or hadn't until now, when suddenly everybody did. And it wasn't just grumbling, Jim thought, the men seemed to be nursing real grievances, and the easy camaraderie of the kitchen, which had attracted him from the start, had vanished.

The first fight occurred one day in March when Casey, the new ringer, swung on Des following a reprimand for jamming cattle through the gates in the stockyard. Des, who'd cut his teeth working camps up north, wasn't one for talk. One punch from him took Casey down, and the ringer quit before he could be sacked, going straight to the office for his cheque.

'An' good riddance too,' Pommy growled, but it was he who dropped Casey's replacement, a man known as Turps who had an unpleasant tongue and a drinker's blotchy veins across his cheeks. It happened in the kitchen, where Pommy snatched up a billet of stove wood for the purpose. 'An' there's more where that come from,' he bellowed. 'Scum like you ain't fit to sit at me table.'

Rising slowly, Turps resumed his seat in front of the puddled mess of his dinner. Jim watched open-mouthed from the sidelines, uncertain whether it was Turps's endless insults or the act of tipping his meal onto the freshly scrubbed tabletop that had roused Pommy's ire. Jim knew how much work went into keeping that table clean.

Turps stayed on at Kharko, but if he did nothing further to provoke the cook outright he still goaded with snide comments. It was a man called Roger Lawson, though, who was the real cause of the problems.

He was a flashy, trouble-making show-off with a high opinion of his own abilities. He could stick on a rough horse, Jim grudgingly admitted, but he wasn't as good as Barney, not as a rider or a horseman. You never saw Barney's horses bleeding from the spurs, or with their mouths torn from the bit, no matter how hard a day they'd had.

Jim wasn't the only one to dislike Lawson. 'A cocky little git,' was how Pommy described him. 'Wants to be top dog at ev'rything. You don't want to pay no mind to nuthin' he says,' he told Jim.

'I don't.' Jim was determined that Lawson would not drive him from the kitchen. He had as much right to be there as anyone, even if Lawson didn't see it that way.

'So what've we got here, fellas?' he had asked during his first few days at Kharko. 'A wood'n'water joey?'

Yellow Jack, catching Jim's affronted eye, answered on his behalf. 'That's Jim, the boss's nephew. He's learning the trade. Turning into a useful ringer already, and a smart lad with a rope. He often eats with us.'

'Be buggered!' Lawson affected amazement. 'McAllister's got his head screwed on, ain't he? His own little spy right in the middle of us. How about that, boys? Every fart reported soon as you break it. The boss dresses like a pansy, seems he thinks like one too.'

Jim flushed scarlet. 'That's a filthy lie! If I ever tried to tell my uncle anything I heard here he wouldn't listen anyway, he —'

'Lay off, Lawson.' Des's heavy voice cut him off. 'You got a beef with the boss, take it to him. The kid's welcome in the kitchen, and the camp. It remains to be seen whether you are.'

'I just might at that. See McAllister, I mean.' Lawson gave Des a hard look, then turned to the men. 'What you've gotta remember, boys, is that the station don't run without us. Hey, great dinner, Cookie. Tucker's gunna be good here at least.'

Jim fumed as he listened but there was nothing he could do. His own words ruled out the option of telling Rob, and what could he report, anyway? That Lawson had called him a pansy? Or that he needled Barney and made sly digs at the others in their absence?

After that it never seemed to stop, in the kitchen or in the camp. Lawson bragged of his riding ability and marvelled that a place the size of Kharko should still have someone like Barney O'Dowd handling their breaking.

'Wood at the top,' he said, pointing to his own head. 'It might have worked ten years ago but McAllister ain't thought about it since. Typical company man. They tell me old Barney's *been* good – well, a lot of blokes talk a good ride – but he's getting on a bit to be topping off buckjumpers. Slowing up and getting windy. Only natural.'

Jim, who'd been standing unseen at the fire, could hear no more. 'Barney O'Dowd could ride you to a standstill blindfolded, any day. He was riding rough horses when you were in your pram.'

'Well, that's what I'm saying, isn't it?' Lawson's voice oozed understanding. 'He's past it, is all.'

Barney himself seemed willing to let the matter go. 'Can't stop a man talking,' he said, lying back on his bed in the quarters. But his gaze was bleak as he ashed his cigarette and winced into a sitting position. 'Besides, maybe it is about time I packed it in. First it was my shoulder, now it's my back. Pulled a bloody muscle in it. The smart ones quit before they get hurt, not after. I've been thinking it's about time I hung up me spurs.'

'Give up riding?' Jim was flabbergasted. 'But you're only – what? Twenty-nine? Thirty?'

Barney grunted. 'Thirty-one. Nah, not stock work, just the breaking and the rough horses. As for Lawson, ignore him. You're playing into his hands else.'

It was easy to say. Harder to practise when, at smoko a few days later, Lawson broke off a conversation he was having with Turps and Yellow Jack to glance across at Jim as he took his seat at the table and greet him as if they were old friends.

'There you are, Jim. I was just telling Jack here, I seen your dad. Didn't pay attention to the name at the time or I'd have told you sooner, seeing the boys reckon he's not round much.'

Jim stiffened. 'He comes when he can.' He was aware of Pommy's head turning from the stove, and Barney's sudden stillness at the end of the table. 'Where'd you see him?'

'Getting chucked outa the Stuart Arms, just before I left town.' Lawson wagged his head admiringly. 'Gotta say, he can put away the rum, your old man. That right he had a property once? Makes you think, don't it?' He was no longer speaking to Jim but to the room at large. 'Station owner, on the streets in the Alice now with the arse outa his strides. And trouble getting a job, he's been sacked from that many.'

'Why, you lying —' Jim lunged at him across the plates of buttered buns but Des seized his arm and hauled him back.

Lawson sat straighter, brows rising. 'Hey, I'm only passing on a bit of news,' he said, all innocence.

'Why don't you shut your mouth, Lawson.' Barney was on his feet, his right hand clenching into a fist. 'Before I shut it for you.'

Lawson shrugged, palms raised. 'Okay, okay. Well, *sorree*. Damned if I ever seen such a place. You oughta have a list of rules in here, you know that? Man might have some idea then what he can't say.'

'Right, get back to it you lot,' Des ordered. 'Lawson, you bring those colts up from the paddock. Jack, you and Barney give a hand with the loading. Turps . . .' When the room had emptied save for themselves and the cook, he let Jim's arm go, giving it a friendly shake. 'Let it drop, kid. The bloke's a mongrel. He likes to stir, so why give him the satisfaction of seeing he's succeeded?'

'Because it isn't true!'

'Nothing to worry about then, is there?' he said reasonably. 'Just cool down.'

Seething, Jim watched him walk off, thinking about the odd way Pommy's head had turned, like a man listening to something he'd rather not hear. Barney too. What did they know that he didn't? And suddenly Jim was less angry than afraid.

ELEVEN

The stock camp was leaving that afternoon, but just as the bell rang for the midday meal Jim saw Barney heading back to the quarters. He followed him.

'What?' his friend asked. He was looking around the room, pocketing a spare tin of tobacco, the bag for his riding boots tucked under one arm. Barney was as fussy about his boots as he was about girths and stirrups. Jim had never met another ringer who oiled and waxed his boots and kept them in a bag the way Barney did.

'Did you know?'

'Know what, kid?' Barney sounded irritable. 'Look, whatever it is, can't it wait? The bell's gone.'

'No, it can't. Is it true – what Lawson said? I saw you back there at smoko. And Pommy too. Who else knows my old man's an alcoholic?'

Barney sighed and sat down on the bed. He looked up, rubbed his cheekbone and sighed again. 'All right, yeah, I knew. He drinks a bit. Fact, talk is he hits the bottle pretty hard.'

'And gets thrown out of pubs and can't hold a job?'

'Yeah.' This reluctantly. 'A lotta men drink, Jim. It ain't a hanging offence. Did you ever see old Pommy on the hops, for instance? He —'

'Pommy's not my father. I suppose it's all over the country? No wonder he didn't want to go to Condamine when he was here. Is it true that he left Basingstoke?'

'Far as I know. It's what I heard.'

'Was drink the reason?'

'I dunno. Maybe. But I'd reckon it's why the boss never took you over to visit. Look, Jim, I – what now?' Jim was staring at him in disbelief.

'He knew? All the time Dad was there, Uncle Rob knew?'

'How the hell do I know if he did or he didn't?' Barney, at the end of his patience, stood up. 'But yeah, probably he did. Talk spreads fast about something like this. There's a few that'd find it funny, the boss being the way he is about grog.'

Jim said nothing. He was remembering the rum bottle Sandy had kept in his room, and the other one wrapped in a towel behind the seat of the ute. He remembered the disapproval with which Rob had refused a drink. 'Think I'll pass,' he'd said that night, and Jim wondered how he could have forgotten what everybody knew – that to bring grog onto the station meant instant dismissal. No wonder Sandy hadn't wanted a job on Kharko.

'Nothing you can do about it, kid,' Barney said more kindly. 'I been there. Drunks have gotta want to help themselves before anyone else can. Now, I'm late. I gotta move, or the mood Des is in I'll be getting the boot meself.'

Jim watched him leave. Later, from the homestead garden, he

saw the truck with the men drive off. He was glad they were going. Yesterday, Lawson notwithstanding, he would have felt the loss of their company. Now he didn't care if they never returned.

A bell rang insistently and with a start he remembered school. He had missed lunch too, but food would have choked him just then. Slamming an impotent hand against the trunk of the pepper tree beside him, he returned, heartsick, to the house.

Late summer passed into autumn as the slow round of the camps continued. The nights grew cold and Barney had horses back in the stable in training for the races. Jim helped half-heartedly, listening to Barney reckon their chances and harp on the career of a horse called Tulloch, which he maintained would be remembered as long as Pharlap was.

'Thirty-five wins he's had, and that's outa fifty-two starts. They're retiring him this year after the Brisbane Cup. My money says he'll win that too.'

Jim couldn't have cared less. If it had been Oliver standing there in his place he and Barney would have canvassed the matter to death, but it was just words to him. He said peevishly, 'How d'you know all this stuff, anyway?'

'It's in the papers. Just cos a man's up the scrub don't mean he can't follow what's going on.'

'Bet you never see a paper under a month old.'

'So? Don't change a race result, do it?' He dropped his cigarette butt and toed it into the sand. 'You want a change, kid. A day out. Good thing the races ain't far off.'

Jim made no reply. He was dreading the annual meeting, and when the time came he went in an aggressive mood, ready to attack the first person who mentioned his father. But nobody did. If Sandy drank to drown his heartbreak, few men besides Rob would blame him for it. And Rob himself never spoke of the matter. Only Mary was able to criticise Rob's attitude, and only in the privacy of their bedroom.

'You're too hard on him, Rob. You've got to make allowances for grief.'

'Do you think so? How much allowance would you suggest? He's had five years' worth already. And during those years he's chucked away a property, lost a plant and had more jobs than I can count – and that's only those we know about. And how do you think Jim feels knowing his father's a drunk?'

'Perhaps,' Mary said quietly, 'you should talk to him and find out. You've done nothing but disapprove – and let him see that you dis-approve. A little tolerance might help right now.'

'Damn it,' Rob exploded, 'of course I disapprove. He's wrecking his life – how am I supposed to approve of that? It's not as if he's the only one. Jim's lost out too. And accidents happen, tragedies occur, every day of the week. If we all gave up and took to the bottle, what good would that do? The man's a weakling. He never could stick at anything; it was always easier to duck out, move on.'

'He loved her.' Mary's grey eyes watched him steadily. 'And there's the difference, I think. The greater the passion, the greater the loss. Not everybody has your ability to switch their feelings off, Rob.'

'It's a pity then,' he said curtly. 'Because the way Sandy's going he'll drink himself to death.'

Mary sighed. 'Talk to Jim, Rob. Try to explain.' But the door closed on her words.

Jim was too tightly wound to enjoy the races. In any event it seemed strange without Oliver's dithering presence. He knew how disappointed his cousin would be at missing the Goola meet, which had always been the highlight of his year, despite the anxiety it brought. Oliver fretted about last-minute sickness in the horses, or an injury in the paddock, and every start held the potential for his mount to be left at the post. He had even, Jim recalled, worried that his lanky frame would have outgrown the set of colours his mother sewed for him a week before-hand. Now he wrote home regularly from Knolly, and in the passages Mary read out from his letters there was always more about the horses he rode than the work he did.

Jim paid only cursory attention to this year's program, and took his place on the rails more out of loyalty to Barney than any real interest in the outcome. There was an upset in the second race when a chestnut fell and brought Sam Colson's leggy grey down with him. And Barney's current pet mare, a dark brown with a beautiful body and an elegant head, ran lame in the last. A drunken Turps, having backed her, lurched into the empty straight to abuse Barney, who'd jumped off at the first furlong post when he felt the mare's stride break and was now leading her home.

'What happened?' Jim had slipped under the rail to join him. Barney, squatting beside the horse, was examining her leg, turning a deaf ear to Turps's torrent of invective, which was mostly concerned with his inability to ride anything faster than a pig.

'Dunno. Something seemed to give. Just after the off. Her knee's swollen up. Hot too. Won't take her weight.'

The mare had eased her foot clear of the ground. 'Can we still load her?' Jim asked.

'Might – just.' Barney scrubbed a hand across his jaw and stood up. The latch of his helmet swung loose as he turned his head. 'See what the boss reckons.'

'And yer owe me five quid, yer useless bastard,' Turps suddenly roared, and to Jim's surprise Barney, who had seemed relaxed enough despite his concern for the horse, whirled on the other man and seized a fistful of his shirt.

'Piss orf,' he snarled, jerking Turps's slack-jawed face within inches of his own, 'or I'll break your bloody neck!' He opened his hand and gave Turps a shove and he fell, frightening the mare into throwing her head and stumbling onto her injured leg. 'Easy girl, easy.' Barney shook his head in disgust. 'Bloody drunks! Between him and Lawson I dunno if the job's worth it any more.'

Jim was shocked. 'You wouldn't leave?'

Barney's mouth pinched together and his eyes were like blue stones. 'Don't bet on that, kid.' He tugged gently at the mare's bridle. 'Better get her home and get some heat onto that swelling. Might help.'

Turps didn't return from the races, whether of his own initiative or because he was sacked, Jim neither knew nor cared. Barney's mare gradually recovered, although her racing days were over.

Shortly afterwards, a cattle buyer who came to look at Kharko's bullocks left influenza behind him. Pommy went down with it, and Mary, and Leo Baker, but Jim and Rob escaped. It ravaged the blacks' camp as well and three of them – two stock boys and an old woman – were picked up by the Flying Doctor and flown into Alice

Springs. Rosemary, arriving home for the school holidays, found her mother in bed, Pommy wheezing unhappily about the kitchen, and her father and cousin absent, Rob out working on a broken-down bore and Jim jubilantly filling in on the stock camp, a temporary part of the mustering team.

Unable to replace the manpower he'd lost, Rob went to Jeff Tillet, who acted as the local protector of Aboriginals, and borrowed a couple of stock boys from the permanent camp under his jurisdiction, a half-mile downriver from the Goola soak. Rob collected the boys, signed the paperwork at the single-roomed police station, and went straight on out to Helm's Yard where the camp was mustering. Jim, looking up from the branding fire, watched the newcomers jump down from the back of the rover, lifting their swags after them, and found himself staring into the face of his childhood companion.

Nipper, taller now, was as lean and long-legged as ever but looked unfamiliar in hat and boots. His dark eyes, widening at the sight of Jim, were still merry. 'G'day, mate,' he said, grinning with pleasure.

Jim felt a rush of joy that was immediately replaced by despair. He felt horribly self-conscious under the eyes of the men, one half of him sharing his old friend's delight in the encounter, the other painfully mindful of stock-camp etiquette that forbade fraternisation between the races. 'G'day,' he returned curtly. None of the men around him would, he knew, waste words on a blackfella. It just wasn't done, and should he transgress the unwritten rule Roger Lawson was right at his shoulder to make capital from it later. Jim turned deliberately aside to speak a word to Yellow Jack, who was shaking out his leg rope in preparation for the next big weaner coming in, and from the corner of his eye he saw

Nipper look down, his brow clouding as his face assumed the shuttered aspect most blackfellas wore. Jim was sorry then, but it was too late.

Des, coming in on the bronco horse with another calf on the rope, jerked his head at Nipper and his mate and they scurried to obey. Jim felt an aching regret, remembering the honey tree and the plans for a canoe, then he shrugged the memory aside. Those days were over. Things were different now.

At the ramp the struggling weaner thumped down onto its side, scooping a flurry of dirt into the air. The leg-ropers leaned back on the greenhide while a dusty figure grabbed the ear-marking pliers and bent to the animal's head. Somebody yelled, 'Brand!' and Jim grabbed the irons and ran. Afterwards, as the newly branded beast kicked to its feet, he laid the irons carefully back in the fire and spat dust and the stink of sizzling hair from his mouth, but the faint taste of betrayal lingered on.

He had no further contact with Nipper, but that night, back in his own bed at the homestead once more, sleep came slowly to Jim. There was no reason, he told himself, to feel guilt. Nipper should have known how it would be. It wasn't as if the two of them were still ten years old, free to eat and play together as they once had. Jim had learned from a wider world to distrust the idyll of Arcadia, and the days when he had openly counted a blackfella his equal were long gone.

Throughout the holidays, now coming to an end, Jim had scarcely seen his cousin, except at the meal table. Rosemary seemed to spend a lot of time in the house with her mother, or messing about with her hair and clothes. Once she went out with him on Mandy to bring the killers in, and another day she accompanied him on a bore run, bouncing in the passenger seat of the battered truck Jim was now permitted to drive. Neither occasion had lent itself to much conversation, but on their last day of freedom he came across her sitting at the foot of the pepper tree in the garden and he dropped companionably to her side.

'So what's it like being at school, Ro – better or worse than you thought?'

In typical fashion she ignored his question to make an observation of her own. 'You've grown taller.' She leaned closer, an imp of mischief in her eyes. 'That's not a bit of hair on your lip, is it?'

'Lay off.' The second word came out squeaky and he coughed and frowned to cover his confusion. 'Anyway, you have too.'

'What, started a mo?'

'Don't be daft. Changed. Grown. You used to look like a mop handle on fire at one end.' He eyed her judiciously. 'You look more like a girl now. So how is school – really?'

She stared past him, considering the matter with narrowed eyes. 'All right, I suppose. I mean, I like having girlfriends, and there's new things to do. I'm learning the piano and we have singing lessons, and I like the sport. I'm gunna make the netball team, Miss Johnson says. But . . .' She linked her arms about her knees. 'I dunno, the city's different. It's really horrible, Jim. You feel like you can't breathe. All those sharp edges and crowds – and the traffic! There's hardly any real ground left, you know. Dirt, I mean. It's all asphalt or concrete or people wherever you look. No space, no *real* space, like there is here.' She waved a hand to encompass the flat with its sun-blistered sheds and the ochre range beyond.

'Well, you don't have to stay there for ever.'

'No.' She fell silent for a long moment. 'It was strange coming back on the mail plane. I was watching out the window as we were landing. Everything looked so small at first, like a tiny little fort or something, with Indian country right up to the door. But then it turned back into paddocks, and the homestead grew again, and everyone here's the same. Pommy and Barney – I miss them most, I think. After Mum, of course. And the horses. School's all right, but it's not home.'

'How d'you mean, it grew? Buildings can't grow,' Jim objected.

'Well, I know that! You're the most aggravating . . .' Rosemary sighed and settled against the tree again. 'You've got as much imagination as a duck, Jim,' she said, but not as if she wanted to quarrel. 'When you've been gone for months and months, places *do* seem different. You think they're bigger than they are. I bet you'd find that if you went back to Arcadia now. They change – or you do.' Her voice sounded forlorn all at once. 'I'm scared that one day I'll get off the plane and it won't grow back how it used to be. It won't be home any more. I don't want it to shrink. I want it always to be the same, right down to old Baker sniffing and moaning about the weather at every meal, and Pommy pretending he doesn't love us.'

'He does not either!' said Jim, revolted.

'You're so dumb.' She spoke witheringly. 'Of course he does. We're his family. But how do I know he'll always be here when I get back?'

He stared at her. 'Why wouldn't he be? Anyway, if anyone pulls out it won't be him, it'll be Barney. Now, if you want to talk about change . . .' It was a relief to talk to somebody after the long weeks of worry. 'It's just not, I dunno, like it used to be,' he finished. 'Everybody's more ready to snap and take offence. It's like Lawson's poisoned the place. And,' he added bitterly, 'when he told me that Dad . . .' He stopped. Rosemary didn't know about that. And then she surprised him again.

'He must be a *pig*.' She studied her toes inside her sandals. 'Mum told me about Uncle Sandy, you know. She says he only drinks because he loved Aunt Jenny so much.'

'Huh!' Jim's voice sounded strangled.

'She says,' Ro continued to gaze at her feet, 'that he's grown old and tired and sad, and the drinking helps him forget. And we shouldn't blame him for it.'

'That's nice. And what does Uncle Rob say? You don't happen to know that too, I suppose?'

'Don't be such a dill, Jim.' This was the old Rosemary speaking. 'You always want to fight everybody. You know Dad, so you know what he thinks. No, it was just what Mum said when we were alone. She told me so I wouldn't talk about it and upset you.'

'So that's what you're doing, is it? Not talking about it.'

'Oh, grow up.' She sounded exasperated. 'Mum always wants to smother things – you must know that. It doesn't mean we have to. You know, I'd never have found out about my other brother if Oliver hadn't told me. He came across some photos one day and asked Dad who the baby was, and that's how we learned we'd had a brother who drowned. He'd be almost grown up now. It's funny to think of, isn't it?'

'It's not quite the same as your old man being a drunk. Try thinking about that.' Jim threw a piece of gravel at the post of the tennis court. 'He's gone through everything – the horses, the gear. There's nothing left. All he's got now is his swag and a beat-up old ute. He can't even hold a job any more.'

Rosemary hesitated, then spoke slowly. 'Maybe he can't help it, Jim.'

'Of course he can help it! Nobody has to get drunk. He's weak, that's all.' Disgust quivered in his voice. 'My mum's been dead four-and-a-half years, so whatever Aunt Mary says, that's not much of an excuse either.'

Rosemary's eyes flashed. 'You know, you sound just like Dad. And before you think that's a compliment, let me tell you something else. We have this stupid hymn we sing at assembly every morning – "I Will Walk in the Ways of Righteousness" – all about being stern and scorning sin and following the light. And you know what? That's what Dad is – righteous.' She jumped to her feet and glared at him. 'And you'll wind up just the same. In fact you already are. If he was a little more . . . more . . .' She searched vainly for the word and stamped her foot in frustration. 'If he didn't expect everyone to be perfect, if he let people make mistakes, or excused them occasionally when they did, maybe Mum wouldn't hide things away. And she might even be a little happier.'

'What are you talking about?' Jim said blankly. 'Who said she isn't happy?'

'I do,' she yelled at him. 'Boys! What do you use your brains for? Have you ever, for instance, heard her laugh? Of course not! She doesn't. She never has since I can remember. She's got that tired sort of smile she pins on and that's it. She's like lukewarm tea. She's never excited, she doesn't even get mad – except after that Christmas Uncle Sandy didn't turn up when you thought he would and she cracked you one in the schoolroom. Do you know what I used to wish when I was little?'

Jim, utterly bewildered, stared at her. 'I used to wish I belonged to Uncle Sandy and Aunt Jenny,' she went on, 'that I could be their little girl for always. I wanted a mother like you had, one that got mad and laughed and shouted and squeezed me in hugs. I would've,' she swallowed, 'given anything to be you. To have Uncle Sandy tell me stories and swing me up on his shoulders and tease me, the way he did you. And now all you can do is blame him. Just like Dad. Well, I reckon you deserve each other. So there!'

Her voice cracked and she spun on her heel and ran towards the house, leaving Jim gaping after her.

Next day she was gone again, this time with her father, who would put her on the plane to the city. Jim approached her warily when it came time to say goodbye, but she had overcome her exasperation with him enough to aim a friendly punch at his arm and caricature Pommy's vowels.

'Look out for Mandy, mate. I'll 'ave yer guts fer garters if yer don't.'

'Rosemary!' Mary protested, while Jim grinned and promised to do his best. Her eyes were overbright as she tossed her head and got into the rover, fluttering her fingers at the cook as he stood watching from the kitchen step. Maybe Pommy did love her, Jim reflected. You either had to do that or loathe her. She was too turbulent a personality to ignore.

That day there were only three of them at the table for lunch. Jim stole occasional glances past old Baker's silent form at Mary's placid face, wondering if there was any truth in Rosemary's claims. It would be just like a girl to imagine it all, but her words had startled Jim into remembering things. It was a long time since he'd thought to criticise his uncle, and the knowledge that Rosemary had done so from the first, and that she had envied him his own parents, staggered him. He no longer recalled his reasons for so disliking Rob. He had almost forgotten the life he enjoyed at Arcadia, until his cousin reminded him of it. His mother *had* laughed and hugged and cuffed him; she'd made the world come alive with her stories and songs. The very air around her had vibrated with life, in stark contrast to the quiet woman sitting opposite.

When Leo Baker had consulted his watch and said, as he did every day, 'Well, I must be getting back,' Jim helped his aunt gather up the dirty plates.

'Are you unhappy, Aunty?' he suddenly asked.

Mary blinked. 'Unhappy? Oh, you mean without Ro? I miss her – of course I do, but you're still here and that helps.' She picked up the napkins and lifted the tablecloth, eyeing him strangely. 'Whatever made you think I mightn't be? Can you bring those plates in? And then you'd best get on with that essay.'

He hesitated, then persisted. 'So you are happy?'

'Ecstatic.' Her tone was dry. 'Are you all right, Jim? What's come over you?'

'Nothing.' He felt suddenly foolish and carried the plates into the pantry, aware that she still stood, tablecloth in hand, staring after him.

Roger Lawson's sneers and belittlement of Barney had finally done their work and the two were now in reckless competition, each determined to prove himself the better rider. Lawson went so far as to help himself to Barney's saddle in order to put on a showy ride on a buckjumping mare. Jim heard of it from Pommy, who got it from the camp cook when he came into the station for rations.

'What happened?' Jim asked.

'After? Barney belted 'im one.'

'Serves him right.'

'Then he took the horse himself to work,' the cook added.

Jim frowned. 'Why? He said he was gunna give it up. He said he was getting on and it was time to quit.'

'Yeah, well, he can't hardly now,' Pommy observed.

And that was the problem. Jim, back and forth between the station and the stock camp but always on the fringe of things, was worried for Barney, who had grown curt-tongued and touchy these days and was riding in a manner that a month before he would have been the first to condemn. Helpless to intervene, Jim watched the men outdo each other, risking falls for the lead, opting for the roughest horses and the worst ground over which to ride them. He thought of tackling Barney about it and had just enough sense not to.

Briefly he pondered involving Rob, but dismissed that also. His uncle would not interfere; he couldn't. The camp was Des's business. In the end he went to Lawson, knowing it would do no good but bound to try. He caught him on the trough after they had yarded, sluicing the dust from his face as his horse drank beside him.

Jim got straight to the point. 'Why don't you stop it, Roger?' he said brusquely. 'It's stupid.'

Lawson affected surprise at his presence. 'Oh, it's the pup. Out for a run with the dogs, eh? Stop what? Did the old fella send you? Pace getting too hot for him, is it?' He gave a bark of laughter, water dripping off the dark stubble of his jaw. 'He oughta learn when to quit, then.'

'Barney's ridden every outlaw on the place. Everybody knows it.' Jim gritted the words out. 'Why don't you just give over before somebody gets hurt?'

Lawson smirked and gathered the reins. 'Man wants to be top dog, he's gotta work at it.' He fitted his boot into the iron and swung up, flowing into the saddle in one smooth continuous movement. 'Let him pull out if he don't like it.' He reined the gelding cruelly about. 'That's what they make scrapheaps for, you know – old has-beens.'

The next morning, sitting his horse with the rest of them to wait for Barney, who was changing the girth on his saddle, Jim wished his action undone. If Lawson were to tell anyone that Jim had tried to intervene, Barney would never forgive him. It would seem a deliberate humiliation, as though Jim thought he was past it too. He squeezed his eyes shut, wondering how he could have been so stupid. And opened them as the hated voice jibed at the man they were waiting for.

'C'mon, for gawd's sake! You don't get on him soon, he's gunna die of old age.'

Barney lowered the stirrup iron and pulled the horse a few paces. He didn't look round but the back of his neck flushed an angry red as he gathered up the reins. If they didn't kill each other in the paddock, Jim thought, they would do it with their fists – and sooner rather than later. Des must have thought so too, for he fixed Lawson with a cold look and jerked his head at the fence a hundred yards from the camp.

'You're in such a damn hurry, go open the gate.'

'Anything to get moving.' Lawson jammed the spurs into his grey and thundered off.

Knowing he wanted them all to watch, Jim looked the other way and so missed whatever miscalculation it was that cost Roger Lawson his livelihood. Jim heard a confused thudding, a blasting snort, and then a whinny of terror as the grey went into the fence. The horse was thrashing in the wire with his shoulder laid open when they got to him. Lawson lay on the ground, sweat-slicked and moaning in agony.

Jim expected that to be the end of it. The accident had lifted a great weight from his shoulders and overnight, it seemed, the miasma of bad feeling went from the camp. Now they could get back to normal. He felt no sympathy at all for the injured Lawson, who had broken his hip in the fall and was transported on the back of the camp truck to the homestead. From there the Flying Doctor had flown him to hospital in Alice Springs.

'Best place for him,' Des said briskly.

Nobody, in fact, was too upset by the incident, and the absence of the vague, unarticulated dread that had hung about Kharko for months made Jim almost light-headed. It wasn't until he heard Barney tell Des that he'd take on the rest of Lawson's string that he realised nothing, for Barney, had really changed.

TWELVE

For his sixteenth birthday Jim got the new horse his father had promised him years before, but it was Rob who gave her to him. She was a half-sister to Corinne, and like her a deep red bay. He called her Pearlshell, naming her even as he stammered out his thanks.

'She's beautiful.' Dumbly he ran his hand over her silken neck, his eye tracing a line from her pricked ears down to her velvety muzzle. She wore the plaited bridle Sandy had made, for Barney had stabled her the night before, bringing her up to the house just as a grey light was breaking behind the trees.

Rob had greeted him as punctiliously as always. 'Good morning, Jim. Happy birthday. Barney's outside, I believe he has something for you.'

Jim hadn't guessed even then, and now he looked at the lovely mare and turned a shining face to Rob.

'She looks good enough to race.' He said it because he knew it would please his uncle, but Barney took him at his word.

'She is, kid.' Folding his arms, he tipped his head to one side, the better to view the mare's lines. 'Pearl.' He tried it out, pursing his lips. 'Don't sound too bad.'

'It suits her.' Jim stroked his hand down the thin blaze and felt the warmth of her breath on his fingers. He looked at Rob standing by the gate. 'I'll never have a better horse.'

'Well, if it comes to bloodlines that's probably true.' He gave his wintry smile. 'But we're keeping your aunt waiting. You'd best come in now.'

It was on the tip of Jim's tongue to say he would eat in the kitchen, where he could tell Pommy and Matthew about the mare, but then he thought of Mary. He hadn't forgotten her casual avowal of a year ago that she wasn't unhappy about Rosemary's absence because he was there. He had felt guilty hearing it, having paid her scant attention over the years, and he felt guilty still, knowing he did not deserve the declaration. She had always cared for him as if she were his own mother, treating him just as she did her son and daughter. He'd never once put himself out to please her, and the first time he'd thought to enquire into her feelings she'd been so surprised she asked if he was ill. His neck prickled with shame. The kitchen could wait.

'I'll put her in the stable and fetch her back after breakfast. Maybe Aunt Mary would like to see her too.'

His other gifts were on the sideboard when he went in: a sweater from his aunt, a card from Rosemary, a telegram that had arrived the previous day and been kept till now – *Happy birthday, mate, parcel in mail* – from Oliver. There was nothing at all from his father, but he no longer expected there would be.

Sandy returned to Kharko for the last time a month or so later. Once more his arrival came as a surprise to Jim, who was fully occupied with work, school and Pearl.

He had become a bore on the subject of his mare, Jim knew, but nothing could dent his pleasure in the splendid lines of her, the intoxicating smoothness of her gait. 'When you're riding her it's like her feet never touch the ground,' he confided proudly to the kitchen at large.

Barney grunted. 'Old Corinne's the same. Built to stretch out.'

'But it's not only that,' Jim pursued eagerly. 'When we were drafting the other day I asked Des to give me a go. She worked like a charm. Didn't overrun the beast once. And turn – she's like a cat on her feet. What with school and all I've only ridden her with stock a dozen times, maybe less, but she's a natural. Born for it.'

'Try chucking a bit of the credit my way,' Barney said. 'It was me broke her in. And learned her the game.'

'Yeah, course. I forgot.' Jim was unabashed. 'I'll bet she handled well right from the start, didn't she?'

'Stone the bloody crows,' said Matthew. 'Have you checked to see she don't shit gold dust?'

Jim looked at him, hurt, then glanced questioningly at Barney, whose grin was sardonic. 'You do go on a bit, kid.'

Rosemary alone seemed to appreciate Pearl's finer points. At any rate she regularly answered the long letters he wrote her about the mare, and his first attempt at drafting, and the traveller who got lost on Condamine Station. In a strange way her absence seemed to have brought them closer, made them better friends. If she were home, he thought, they'd squabble as they always had, but this way they seemed to be able to say things without trying to score points off each other. She wrote about her friends, the interschool sports competition, and excursions into the city. He chuckled over her description of an unpopular new science teacher, and made a mental note to answer her urgent questions about Mandy's wellbeing, the fate of a colt with a jinked neck, and how Barney and Pommy were going. *Mum doesn't tell me anything,* she complained, by which Jim knew she was referring to the stables, the kitchen and the men.

It was Rosemary who suggested he register Pearlshell. *In case you ever want to race her,* she wrote. 'Fat chance,' Jim muttered, reading her neat script, but afterwards he thought more deeply about it. The mare was fast and her mother had been a champion sprinter. Perhaps it would be interesting to give her a run at Goola. He could help Barney train her and it would please Rob to see her on the track. It might even make Oliver regard him as less of a changeling. And if she won he'd have a photo of her, like the ones already in pride of place on the dining-room walls. She'd be up there with the Rook and other winners, only this time it would be his name as owner instead of the company's.

He put the question casually to Barney. 'What's it cost to register a horse?'

'I dunno. Coupla quid. You seen that spare collar anywhere? Bloody thing oughta be in the saddle shed and I can't find it. Camp's going out and half the bronco gear's gone walkabout.'

'Charlie's got it. I think some of the stitching was bust or something.' The old boundary rider was a skilled saddler. None of the Kharko gear ever left the station for repair; Charlie stitched and riveted on demand, counterlining saddles and plaiting the finest kangaroo-hide whips Jim had ever seen. 'You leaving today then?'

'This arvo.'

'I'm gunna register her. Pearl.'

'Makes sense,' Barney said, unexcited. He picked up a coil of rope and jerked his head at a bag of hobbles. 'Bring 'em, will you? We've got fresh horses in, we'll need 'em.'

The following day was a Sunday. Jim, out riding on Pearlshell, mulled over alternative names. He had to provide five on the registration form, according to Rob, and even so they might all be rejected if other horses had already been assigned them. Jim wished he could talk it over with Barney, and that he'd thought to ask Rob about racing colours – did you make up your own or did they have to be registered too? He rather thought he'd like sky-blue and gold. Or maybe he'd ask Mary what her favourite colours were. In any event he'd want Barney to ride her. That was a given. At a gangling six foot with big hands and bigger feet, Jim was far too heavy for the task himself.

Reaching the stable, he swung down and led the mare into the yard to drink, then hesitated, one hand on the girth strap. Perhaps he'd leave her saddled and find Rob – he could give her a gallop around the training track while his uncle watched her action and got an idea of her speed. Rob would never agree to the time and cost involved in training the mare unless he was satisfied she had a chance of winning. Racing was his hobby, but only fools, he said, let their passions rule their pockets. Barney, Jim knew, would gladly embrace the chance to run Pearl, but it was Rob who'd be paying for the feed and nomination fees.

Hitching Pearl's reins to the rails, he patted her shiny neck. 'Be back soon,' he told her. He'd never lost the habit of conversing with his horses. The mare turned her head and nickered and his heart squeezed with love. 'Ah, you're a queen,' he said. 'A real Irish queen.' It was Barney's highest praise. 'You'll run the socks off 'em all.'

Whistling his way down past the bookkeeper's office, Jim thought of the last time he'd seen Oliver, which was when he came home for Christmas. He'd seemed more interested in a girl called Yvonne, whom he'd met at Knolly, than in racing. Rosemary teased him mercilessly, until Aunt Mary told her to stop. Oliver was always so earnest that it was somehow hard not to poke fun at him.

Just then he saw a utility, or at least the hump of its load, sticking up behind the loading dock. It had a battered tarpaulin over it, and between the ropes that held this in place Jim glimpsed swags and buckets and billies and a couple of what Barney called bagman's suitcases – corn bags tied shut with wire. The tyres were worn and the duco dented; it was clearly a battler's turnout. Then something about the look of it prodded his memory. His gaze swivelled to the crumpled edge of the near-side mirror, and with an unwelcome shock he knew it for his father's.

Jim hesitated, then trod quietly around the utility to the cab, to satisfy himself that Sandy wasn't in it. He couldn't have said why but he didn't want to meet him like this, unprepared, with no time to work out what his response should be. If he were honest he didn't want to meet him at all, it would be so much simpler if his father continued to stay away. That way the question of where Jim's loyalties lay need never be faced. Suddenly his eyes widened and he stopped dead, staring at the woman in the passenger seat.

Long afterwards he would remember that the first thing he felt in that moment was neither horror nor dread but a surge of thankfulness that the stock camp was out. It meant there were fewer to witness his father's shame. Of course they would hear about it – the whole bloody world, Jim thought savagely, would hear – but at least it gave him a breathing space.

For an instant he saw his mother, black hair tumbling and face alight, being swung like a child in his father's arms, and himself, laughing delightedly, in the background. Other pictures came crowding: the three of them round the stove on winter nights while the tin roof cracked in the cold; sunlight blazing behind the cheap muslin curtains in the kitchen, and catching the ginger hairs on Sandy's forearms as he worked at something on the table. He saw a flowered pinny with his mother's vague shape inside it, and the powerful heft of his father's shoulders in the days when love for him had ruled Jim's world. He saw Sandy's laughing face imposed upon the store shelves, and, high up on the wall, the patch of red and gold where the accordion hung.

He blinked and the pictures faded, but the moment's clear recall only made the betrayal worse. He stared at the woman in the car with her coarse hair, her thick, flattened features, her black skin.

'Shit!' He was unaware he had spoken. The woman's dark eyes, clear whites glistening with health, fell shamed and frightened before his glare. She was blacker than any billy, he thought wildly, but far worse than that, she was pregnant. Her cheap cotton shift strained across her body, and through the gaping buttonholes he could see the shiny dark mound of her belly. She cringed from his stare, folding slender hands across the bulge, and Jim closed his eyes in anguish, knowing she would not be there, riding in the cab of his father's ute, unless she was his gin. Blackfellas ate outside, rode up the back, kept their place. It was as simple as that. He knew what black velvet was now, and he knew too that however many clandestine visits were made to station blacks' camps in quest of it, no white man openly took up with a gin. Not without paying the price in ostracism and public disgrace.

From behind him, in an incredulous bellow he scarcely recognised as Rob, Jim heard, 'Are you out of your frigging *mind*? You're living with a *black* woman?'

'An Aboriginal woman, yes.' Sandy's voice, lighter, but with something defensive in it. 'I don't expect you to understand.'

Jim turned his head to where his uncle and father stood in the blacksmith's shed, some yards to his left. Clumsily, as if his legs belonged to someone else, he trod that way, the row escalating as he went. He had never known his uncle to swear, but now Jim discovered he could curse as crudely as any of the ringers. Sandy was the one who was more in control, but the resignation in his voice clawed at Jim with a nameless hurt, and suddenly he didn't want to listen. He stood unseen, staring into the shed where the two men faced each other, the anger almost palpable between them. Rob's back could have been moulded from iron, but it was to his father that Jim's eyes were drawn, and that first look confirmed his worst fears.

Sandy was defeated – it was the only word for it. *Mum says he's grown old and sad.* Ro's words rang in his head. It was true. He seemed to have aged ten years since his last visit. His hair was uniformly grey, the bags under his eyes had sagged into folds of loose skin, and his face was mottled across the cheeks and nose with a drinker's broken blood vessels. He wore a patched cotton shirt, jeans that had been cobbled at the knees, and broken sandshoes laced with wire.

'. . . and how you *dare* parade her here before my wife and your own son beggars belief.' His uncle's voice was glacial with disgust.

'Well, what would you have me do, dump her? That's my kid she's carrying.' For an instant Sandy seemed to have regained his old self, face as tight and voice as hard as his brother's. 'You're so bloody puritanical and *right* about everything – is that what you want me to do? Or is it the association you're worried about? The high-and-mighty manager has an abo-loving brother? Won't look good, won't *sound* good round the bars and campfires, is that it? Well, you'd better get used to it because she's staying with me; she's a kind and generous woman. I came to see Jim, that's all. I don't want your hand, I never expected a welcome, and you can shove your bloody tea if you were thinking of offering it. Though I'd have to drink it on the woodheap now, wouldn't I? I'll see my son and then I'll go.'

In anguish Jim shut his ears to his uncle's rejoinder. When his voice registered again he was shouting. 'You're not dragging Jim into this. Why come now? You weren't so keen last year, or the one before that. If Jenny could see, if she could know, what you've sunk to —'

'You leave her out of this.' The malevolence in Sandy's voice was like a snake coiled to strike. 'You're not so lily-white yourself there, are you? Did you think I was blind all those years? Or that Mary was? Did you think we didn't notice the way you looked at her – at my Jenny? Funny, isn't it? You take the high moral tone every time, Rob, but it never stopped you lusting after your brother's wife.'

Jim heard a half-cry, then the smack of flesh. He saw his father stagger back into a furious clatter of falling metal as his outflung arm brought down the collection of pritchels and cold chisels on the shelf behind him. His back hit the wall but he kept his feet. A red patch bloomed on his cheek and his nose began to bleed as Rob cocked his fist for a second blow.

'Speak her name again and I'll kill you!' he roared. 'You've dishonoured her memory enough.'

'And you didn't? Sniffing after her like a randy dog, committing adultery in your heart.' Sandy swiped angrily at his nose, spreading rather than staunching the flow.

'*Stop!*' Jim screamed. '*Stop it!*' The blood had fled from his face, leaving his vision patchy and laboured.

Rob's fist froze mid-strike and the heads of the two men turned to gape at him. Jim registered the horror on both faces, followed quickly by guilt and shame. Blood continued to run from his father's nose, through his beard and onto his shirt. He said uncertainly, 'Jim? Listen, son —'

But Jim had whirled and was running, feet falling erratically, breath coming in ragged sobs. Rob's voice followed him, calling words made inaudible by the pounding of his heart, their only effect to drive him on. Past the homestead he ran, and the bookkeeper's office, where Leo Baker's head popped out to watch him, down to the stables and the waiting mare. She snorted and backed from his rush, eyes rolling whitely. The need to calm her steadied him a little, then he had the reins up and a foot in the stirrup and she was sidling uneasily, tossing her head, made nervous by his tension. He put her at the open gate just as Rob appeared, winded, hand outstretched to stay him.

'Jim.' His face was crimsoned from effort, his chest heaving so much he could only gasp out single words. 'Wait.'

'Out of my way!' Feeling his heels, the bay sprang forward, her raking stride carrying him past the feed shed and stockyards and far down the paddock. The wind blew cold on his tears. There was a tight, hard hurt inside him.

He had no destination in mind; his one aim was to get away. At the bottom gate the track forked: left to the main road and right to the old mine.

He took the right. The steady thudding of Pearl's feet was muffled slightly by the grass that overgrew the track. She was blowing, lather creaming on her neck and dripping in gobbets from her bit, and under the saddle flap he could feel the thunder of her heart. Sanity returned and he pulled her down to a walk. He patted her neck, slick with salty sweat, feeling the heat of her and the energy coiled like a spring within. He felt light and unreal, as if shock had somehow thinned him, and he shivered.

Slowly he became aware again of the world around him – the scent of dust and the feel of the air, still and warm in the curve of the range. Over the pounding of blood in his ears and the chink of bit rings as Pearl tossed her head, he heard the whistle of kitehawks and the drone of a faraway engine. He wondered if it was his father leaving.

When he reached the shed where the gantries and conveyor belts were he reined in and stared about him. It had been two years since his last visit. In that time more iron had lifted from the roof, but the crumbling concrete vats and rusting machinery he had played on as a child were the same. He was ten when he first came here, his faith in Sandy solid and unshakeable, one of the verities of life. With wondering pity he examined that younger self – had he really been naïve enough to believe in Sandy's return then?

He drew a steadying breath but it didn't help the ache in his throat, or the heat of his anger. If Sandy had ever truly cared for him he wouldn't have left in the first place. And if his uncle . . . He clutched at the possibility that his father had been wrong, but he knew he was fooling himself. He had read the truth of the accusation on his uncle's face. Both men had betrayed him. Humiliated and furious, he couldn't decide which of them he hated most.

It was dim inside the shed after the clear light of the valley. He got down from the saddle and stood leaning into the comfort of the mare's neck. Pommy would know of Sandy's visit by now, which was one step away from everyone knowing it. Sandy would be gone for good. He would never return – which didn't bother Jim at all – but the disgrace would remain.

He opened his fingers to rub the reddened grooves where he'd gripped the reins too tightly, and had an idea. He yanked the girth strap loose. He couldn't ride Pearl without a bridle but she knew the paddock – she would take herself home.

Denuded of gear, the mare bumped her head against his chest while he rubbed her ears. He wished he could spend his life with horses and never have to meet a human again, particularly those he knew. Even Aunt Mary. He shut his eyes on the thought and stamped his foot to start the horse. She was cantering within minutes, her whinny reaching back to him down the track.

He pulled out his stock knife, and moving to the mineshaft, hacked the plaited bridle into pieces, flinging each separately down the shaft. The bit with its shiny rings followed, along with the silver conchos from the brow-band. If he could have cut up the memory of the morning he'd first seen it he would have flung that down too.

Afterwards he never knew how long he sat there in the bright sunshine with his head on his knees and his arms wrapped around them. He seemed to have run down like a clockwork toy – like the train he got that Christmas and never played with. His mind was a chaotic whirl of memories, of pictures far off and small, and scraps of conversation. *My dad's a drover*, he'd boasted. *When I grow up I'm going droving with him*. He had a mental glimpse of the road to Arcadia, of the ramshackle house with the waddi tree beside it, and his father saying, *There she is, son. Home with the fire lit*.

He covered his ears to stop the voices but the words kept trickling through his head. Rosemary, younger only in years: *When did you last hear her laugh? She doesn't*. Was it something other than Todd's death that had stolen the spirit and the laughter from the young woman who'd once ridden racehorses and been pretty and lively? And over and over: *Did you think I was blind? Did you think I was blind?* No, but he, Jim, had been. *Like a randy dog,* his father shouted unforgivingly in his head, and the tears fell wet again on his cheeks. How could that have been going on? How could his mother have done it? Why had his father not stopped it?

Hours passed. When hunger made him conscious of time, he could not remember whether breakfast or lunch had been his last meal. It didn't seem to matter. For no reason he suddenly remembered the old German artist with his knee socks and intense, childlike stare. *I paint everything, even the emptiness*. Well, there was plenty of that to go round.

The grey space of misery in his head could have filled a continent. He closed his eyes but the light still danced beyond his lids, showing him his father, shirt open at the neck, eyes squinted half shut as he sleeved his forehead dry. *She's a bugger of a country, son.* And then, with ludicrous alarm, *Now, don't let your mother hear you say that* . . . He opened his eyes again to banish memory and sat on, trying to think of nothing, trying to keep his mind a blank.

Fooled by his stillness, a crested pigeon winged to within a few feet of him and began to feed. He watched the shift of the light on its feathers, the liquid shine of its eye, which every few moments turned aloft to scan for danger. But when it came it was so sudden that neither boy nor bird had warning. Feathers exploded under the hooking talons and for a single heartbeat Jim stared into the mad, wild eyes of death before the hawk lifted off, talons dragging under the weight of its kill.

The incident broke his torpor. The shadows were lengthening and time suddenly made sense again. He judged it to be past three o'clock. He almost wished he'd kept riding, but the practical streak in his nature knew it wasn't that easy – you couldn't run away if there was nowhere to run to. Tiny, blue-grey feathers eddied about him as he got to his feet, settled his hat and headed back.

Pearl was waiting at the gate for him when he reached it. He let her through into the horse paddock and trudged on, concentrating on the dusty track, wondering if Rob would continue the lie he'd lived all these years. He had passed the stable before he lifted his head, and his heart sank at the sight of the truck parked in front of the store. The stock camp had returned. He could see a little knot of men clustered before the bookkeeper's office and recognised old Baker and Matthew, and the burly form and high-crowned hat of Des Hanks. They would have heard all about it. He swallowed dryly and forced himself to keep moving through the gate and up the path to the house.

The side door looked no different than it had that morning. He was faintly surprised by this – by the idea that anything could be the same. Automatically he wiped his boots on the mat and reached up to remove his hat. Anger still simmered like a stoked fire inside him. One way or another he would have the truth of it, although he was certain he already knew. He'd been halfway home when his physical resemblance to Rob suddenly assumed a new significance. The signs of his real parentage had been there all along, only he'd never had cause to read them. *You're just like Dad*, Rosemary had said, and even his mother had told him he took after his uncle. Oliver, with his pale eyes and ginger hair, might be inches taller than Sandy but he still looked more like him than Jim ever had. And if Jim wasn't Sandy's son, then it would explain so much of his father's behaviour. Why should he care for another man's get? Jim ground his teeth in helpless rage. His uncle would lie about it – of course he would. But his aunt mightn't.

Mary was in the dining room. He heard her footsteps and took two quick paces through the door to confront her.

'I want to know if it's true.' His voice came hoarse and loud. 'Did he . . . was he . . . did he and my mother . . . ?' He couldn't bring himself to say it, not to someone who'd been as much a victim as himself or Sandy. 'Him – your husband.' He could not call him uncle. 'Is he my father?'

'Oh, Jim.' The sorrow in her voice was like a knife in his heart. 'All that was years ago.' Sit down, dear, I want to talk to you. Something's happened.'

'I know, I was there,' he gritted. 'Well, what's the answer? Do you know what he said?'

She sighed. 'Sandy was angry. He wanted to hurt. People do when they're angry. I'm sorry you were there to hear it. But Jim, the stock camp's come in —'

'I know,' he repeated impatiently. 'I saw the truck. So is he my uncle or my father? Which is it?'

'Jim, I'm trying to tell you there's been an accident.'

'What?' The shift was too sudden for him to take in.

'In the stock camp.' She swallowed, and for the first time he noticed the pallor of her face, the strained tightness of the skin around her eyes and mouth. Foreboding filled him and he opened his mouth to stop her, to stave off whatever she had to tell him, but she was already saying it. 'I'm so sorry, Jim. It's Barney – he's been killed, dear. They brought his body back an hour ago.'

THIRTEEN

It was Rob who eventually gave him the details of the accident. There weren't many. Nobody had been with Barney at the time and it wasn't until his mount, still towing its grisly burden, had burst into the mustered mob that the tragedy was discovered.

'Where is he? I want to see him.'

'No, you don't.' Rob spoke flatly. 'Anyway, the police have to investigate an accidental death. Jeff Tillet came. He's taken the body back to Goola for now and it will be flown to the Alice tomorrow. We'll arrange to bury him there.'

Jim was speechless in his grief. How could this have happened? To his best friend on the station? No one got killed like that, especially not Barney. Had he held out against that mongrel Lawson only for this?

Rob was studying him. 'Death doesn't wait for an invitation, Jim. The horse might have fallen. Or perhaps Barney just got careless for once – it happens. It was that chestnut gelding with the white stockings.'

Nippon. That was his name. Nip on him and be sorry – that's what they said in the camp. He had a habit of rearing. Only last year Barney had declared he wasn't worth the risk of saddling. The horse must have played up and gone over backwards on him before he could move. Jim had seen Barney ride the chestnut only once and that was in the station yard. Nippon reared, the whole sixteen hands of him going up, front hooves raking the sky. The circle of watching men stiffened, taking a collective gasp as the horse hung poised at the point of balance before crashing backwards onto the rails. Nimble as a cricket, Barney leapt clear. He had the girth yanked free and the saddle off and over his arm in one continuous movement, before the thud of Nippon's fall.

Half of it's knowing what not to get on. Barney's voice was a ghostly echo in Jim's head. If he shut his eyes he could see him, lean and wiry in moleskins and cotton shirt, blue eyes squinched in the shadow of his hat, rubbing his cheekbone in thought or killing a butt under his boot, springing onto the Rook's bare back at almost his own height. Grief choked him. Along with the pain of not knowing. He would never know. Barney was the only one who could explain why he'd chosen to saddle that horse.

Jim spent the rest of that day and most of the next wandering wretchedly about the station. The men had brought Barney's saddle in from the camp. It sat forlornly astride the rail in the saddle shed with a shattered tree and a broken kneepad. He was glad there were no bloodstains. Somebody had cleaned off the dirt but the stretched stirrup leather and crushed iron told their own story.

Pommy's grief was almost as great as Jim's. Even his moustache seemed to droop, and he couldn't stop shaking his head in disbelief. 'Don't seem real some'ow.' Propped against the table on one meaty fist, he ran his tongue around his lips and sighed. 'Poor bugger. Christ, I could use a drink. 'Ow's me little sweet'eart gunna take this, eh? She was a great mate of Barney's. You both was.'

'Aunt Mary sent a telegram to the school.' The thought of Rosemary's pain only increased his own.

He wandered back to the house and found Mary in Oliver's old room, going through clothes in the wardrobe. As he watched she laid a white shirt on the bed, then sensing his presence she looked up and nodded gravely.

'Come in, Jim. You might have a better idea of sizes.' She held up the shirt. It had been his cousin's best before he grew out of it. 'Something to bury him in,' she said simply.

Jim swallowed. 'It looks about right. Bit long maybe.' He wondered how she could worry about mere clothes, but supposed she'd had practice at funerals. As an only child she must have seen to her parents', both of whom were dead. And there had been his mother's and little Todd's as well. He had never mentioned his dead cousin to her but now grief swept his reticence aside. 'Aunt Mary?'

'Yes, Jim.' She sighed and sat on the bed, patting a spot beside her. 'If you're going to ask me why it happened, I don't know. Nobody does.'

'I wasn't.' He remembered the hawk killing the pigeon – was it only yesterday? It must have been like that for Barney, the instant snuffing of life and light. At least he hoped so. 'I just . . . well, Mum told me about your little boy, about Todd. And I've never said how sorry I am about him dying like that.'

'Thank you, dear.' Beyond the window the light was failing. Soon Matthew would start the diesel, but sitting beside her in the stillness of the darkening room it was possible to speak the things he could not say in broad daylight. 'She said – Mum did – that was why you changed. That you used to be different. Lively and . . . not so quiet,' he finished lamely. 'But yesterday, when Dad was arguing with Uncle Rob, he said . . . He was very angry, they were fighting, and he said —'

'I know what he said, Jim. Your uncle told me, and he's bitterly sorry you heard.' She put her hand on his arm. 'It didn't mean what you think. Your mother was never unfaithful to your father, or Rob to me – except in his heart. He loved her, yes. It was very easy to and I doubt if he'd ever met anyone like Jenny before. She was so alive. Such a gay and carefree spirit. But she loved Sandy, nobody else. There was no affair, Jim. I knew how Rob felt about her, and so did your father. It hurt me at the time – very much.' She pleated a fold of her dress, speaking with difficulty. 'It's not easy for a woman to be second best with her husband, but it was nobody's fault.'

'It was. It was his. He was married to you.'

Mary sighed gently. 'Yes, but he loved her. You musn't think he wanted to, but loving isn't something you do to order. You'll find that out when you're older. And perhaps it was partly my fault, once we lost little Todd like that. Sometimes couples turn away from each other after a child's death. Your uncle's an honourable man, Jim, you should know that. But adult relationships can be complicated.'

'Ro says he's righteous. She thinks he makes you unhappy.'

'No, he's not righteous.' She shook her head and patted his hand again before rising from the bed. 'Unbending, perhaps, with rigid principles. But principles aren't worth having unless they're kept. It's why he can't feel any sympathy for your father. But we won't talk about that now. The dear Lord knows there's enough sorrow to go on with.' She hesitated. 'You don't have to decide now, but would you like to go to the funeral? Sometimes it helps.'

He hadn't given any thought to it but suddenly Jim knew he needed to go. To make his last farewell. He went to the window, where the first stars were pricking out above the shadow of the mill wheel that creaked ponderously in the breeze. Yellow squares of light shone out from the kitchen windows and the rooms of the quarters. Only Barney's was dark. It didn't seem possible that he could have lost both his friend and his father in the one day.

Staring into the darkness, Jim wondered where Sandy was now and what would become of him. And he knew with the certainty of his years that they would never meet again. Rob would not permit it. And anyhow he didn't want to. A vast desolation filled him but he told himself it was for Barney and no other that his eyes smarted and misery clutched at his heart.

Oliver came back from Knolly Downs for the funeral but Rosemary stayed at school. It would upset her too much to attend, her parents claimed; she was better off staying away. Jim, who knew it would upset her a great deal more not to be there, held his tongue. He wrote her a full account of it: the flowers Mary arranged for the top of the coffin, the hushed air of the church, the scraping of feet as people stood for the hymns, the sad strains of Bill Maddison's fiddle on 'Shall We Gather at the River?' Jim hadn't known the words and doubted Barney would have either.

Old Charlie Attwood surprised them by turning up in a suit – shiny at the knees and lacking a tie, but still a suit. The Tillet twins wore ribbons on their plaits, and while Rob was reading the eulogy their little brother fell off his seat, bellowing like a bull as he hit the floor.

Rob waited silently while Brenda quietened her son, then continued speaking, his words falling clipped and precise into the artificial hush. It sounded too ordered and cold to Jim – a list of Barney's virtues but nothing of his essence. He wanted to stand and shout, 'He was more than that! He was the best!' The best at handling horses, the best at making you feel good about yourself, especially after something terrible happened. And the best at teaching you things. Pommy could have done a more fitting eulogy than his uncle, in the rough vernacular of the kitchen, only Pommy was on a crying drunk down at the Stuart Arms, too devastated to attend.

Back at Kharko, ordinary life slowly resumed. The routine of work was a welcome distraction. Jim took the damaged stirrup leather and iron off Barney's broken saddle and dumped them, but the saddle itself he stowed high on a cross beam in the feed shed. The heat of the roof in summer would soon dry and crack the leather but the saddle was past repair anyway. It was one of the few tangible reminders of Barney and he could not, as yet, bear to have it thrown out. Already another man had Barney's room in the quarters, sat in his place in the kitchen, and dumped his hat on the long line of hooks near the door.

Jim took Rosemary to see the saddle when she returned for the summer holidays. She stared at it silently for some minutes while he sat on the hay.

'I'm glad you saved it. Seeing it like that helps me realise he's gone.'

She sniffed and wiped a knuckle across her eyes. 'I keep expecting to meet him, you know, at the yards, in the kitchen. But seeing his gear like that – well, I know he's dead. Can you imagine Barney with cobwebs all over his saddle?'

'No,' Jim agreed. 'Do you remember him carrying on years ago when I left mine on the ground and the horses walked on it?'

'Yes! And the time I put my saddlecloth to soak in the trough and old Memories grabbed it in her teeth and scared herself silly dragging it out? He had a lot of patience with us.'

'Yeah, and he never let us get away with any bullshit.'

'James Alexander McAllister!'

He gave her a shove. 'Like you've never said worse.'

Rosemary sighed. 'It's a combination of Mum and that stupid school. Young ladies aren't supposed to know words like that.' She grew serious again. 'Thanks for writing me about the funeral. I don't think I could've borne it – not being there to say goodbye – without your letter. I've made Mum and Dad promise they'll take me to see his grave on my way back through Alice.'

'When you do I've got one of the Rook's old racing plates. Take it with you and leave it there with him, from me?'

'All right. And speaking of plates, what about Pearl? Are you going to race her?'

Jim shook his head. 'I don't think so now. If Barney . . . I fixed up the papers to register her the evening before he died, you know, so she's in the studbook. Uncle Rob said we'd run a time trial but . . . It was a good idea,' he added politely, remembering that it had been hers. 'It just doesn't seem to matter any more.'

'I know. And anyway, who would train or ride her? Even if Oliver was home he's probably too heavy for a maiden race. Besides, he probably thinks more about girls than racing these days. I expect it won't be long before he marries.'

'What, just because you made his life miserable over that girlfriend he had last Christmas?' Jim snorted. 'Honestly, Ro, where do you get these ideas?'

Her hazel eyes rested speculatively upon him as she swung her leg over the edge of a bale. 'Do you know, if you stopped moving I think you'd fossilise. I've got a friend at school like you. Julie. She never thinks outside the minute. She can't imagine anything ever being any different. School will go on for ever and we'll always be there, half-way between one class and the next, wearing our hideous uniforms and being told how to behave.'

She had bewildered him. 'What's that got to do with anything?'

'It's called growing up. That's what we're doing, Jim. Don't you have any plans for the future now that you've finished school and can please yourself? I have. I bet you've never even thought about what you'll be doing in three years' time, have you?'

'Course I have.'

'And?'

'Well, I'll be here, won't I? Working for the company.'

She gave him a knowing look and his ire rose. 'What else would I do? I like stock work, and I'll make a far better cattleman than your brother, that's for certain. So if he winds up managing a place I don't see why I shouldn't. And in three years I'll be . . .' Where would he be? His long-held plans had all been overturned by Sandy's actions and he'd made no more since, letting the days drift by, comfortable in the knowledge that his uncle expected him to follow his cousin into the company. 'I'll be on another company place, I expect,' he finished. 'Doing my time, like Oliver. What about you?'

'Office work,' Rosemary said decisively. 'It's quicker than nurse's training, although I thought about that too. Shorthand, typing and simple bookkeeping. Wherever there's a city there'll be a job, so I can find work anywhere.'

'You never liked sums,' Jim objected.

'But I can do them if I have to. It's a pity you're such a stick-in-the-mud, Jim. If I was a boy . . .' She sighed, then added, 'Maybe I take after Uncle Sandy. He's a wanderer at heart. Have you —?'

'Don't ever mention his name again, you hear me?' He turned his back and strode from the shed.

It was a bad summer that year, with what little rain there was falling late and patchily. Rob got the drillers back in and they punched down three dry holes before striking water in the fourth. The camp was busy for weeks on end, shifting cattle about to maximise the use of feed and water. A truckload of grain and chaff and lucerne hay came in and Jim helped stack it in the shed, sneezing in the sweet powdery dust the bales exuded. They were piled so high they hid from sight the saddle on the cross beams, but he was fiercely thankful for the size of the load. This was what it meant to be a company station. No working horse would starve on Kharko – the company would spend its way through the dry, conserving their breeding and working stock. He need not worry that Pearl or the Rook (soon to be replaced with another stallion) or dear old Jake would suffer. Condamine and Perishing Downs he knew would be less fortunate, unless real rains came.

Riding behind the weakened stock, or squatting in the shade while the mob rested and the men waited for their quart pots to boil, Jim wondered about his future. Once, it had all been set out for him but now the page had been wiped clean. Rosemary was right, he had to admit. It was up to him to choose. He could follow Oliver into the company, doing his four years as a jackeroo before moving up through the successive stages of head stockman, overseer and, perhaps one day, manager. Or, his mind ranged over the possibilities, he could go off-siding for the drillers and learn the trade, or take himself into town and start an apprenticeship of some sort. But he felt no desire for either of those. The land was his future.

For an instant he played with the notion of returning to Arcadia, supposing the lease were still available. But that was a child's wish that the years had soured. Before Sandy had sold the plant, it had been Jim's dream that they would go droving together. Then, after a few years, and with time on his side to wear down his father's opposition to the idea, Jim would coax him back to their old home, where they would rebuild their future. But that was pointless fantasy now. There was nothing to be found along that track but ghosts.

Around him the mob of bony cattle stood licking listlessly at fallen leaves in the mulga. Their coats were harsh and the ribs of the older cows stood out like fence pickets. One thing was certain: he might be finished with school and rising seventeen but he could not go any-where until it rained. The station blackfellas, sick of the dry and the unremitting labour, had already cleared out, gone off on their own business, and Des needed every man he could get to work the stock. In two months, or three or six, he would sort something out, but until then nothing else mattered but rain.

As the summer passed and hope faded, the wireless chatter reflected the prevailing mood. There came a point in February when people began to admit aloud the fear they had secretly nursed: that this year the rain would not come. Diehards like Bill Maddison insisted there was time yet, that he'd seen the storms build as late as March, but Rob, listening with one ear as he read the paper, muttered that it was desperation talking.

'But I remember March rain,' Jim objected. 'I'm sure I can. It was an extra-good year and the wildflowers came right to the garden fence. Mum dried some. We had big bunches hanging everywhere under the verandah. Dad said —' He cut himself off.

'That was '53. A bumper season, best in a decade.' Rob folded his paper. 'But the storms started in December. Bill's talking about a March start, and that's something I've never seen. Ah well,' he dropped the week-old daily, 'others have troubles too. I see some aircraft carrier's cut a ship in half. You wouldn't be worrying about rain if you'd sailed on the *Voyager*, seems to me.'

Mary tutted and reached for the newspaper. Jim, blotting sweat from his chin, stared out at what he could see of the brazen sky, thinking of the calves they'd shot that morning. It was the only way, he knew, to save the cows. The trouble was there was no guarantee it would, if the dry hung on. And it could. Old Charlie Attwood talked of a station in the Corner Country where drought had lasted five years, and when it finally broke the only thing left alive on the place was a camel team that had been brought in to delve the dry, silted dams. Drowning seemed an almost pleasant alternative compared to the suffering drought entailed.

In the end he stayed at Kharko for the rest of the year. Patchy storms blew inland from the coast the following January, filling one of the dams and bringing small relief, but apart from that the skies stayed obstinately clear. Rob, turning an iron face to the dusty paddocks, shook his head forebodingly and plotted to make the best use of his country. Wherever neighbours met, the men stood apart, wearing worried faces, the weather their chief topic of conversation. Race meetings were cancelled by common consent – everybody was too busy keeping their stock alive to spare time, or money, for racing. Bill Maddison, lean and desperate, camped out, cutting scrub for weakened breeders, and carrying orphaned calves home across his saddle pommel for his wife to rear on the goats. His eldest son, kicking discontented heels against the steps of the Goola store, told Jim that he was through with the place.

'The old man wants to kill himself, that's his business.' Wally scowled at the barren countryside. 'Me, I'm heading for town and a job on the council. I can drive anything – hell, I'll drive a garbage truck if it gets me outa swinging an axe all day. Christ, a man's gotta be mad to want to run cattle in a bloody desert anyway, and I dunno why the old fool can't see it for himself. '

His brother Roy was staying put. 'Hasn't got the gumption to get out,' Wally said contemptuously. 'Be the best thing for the family if he did. The other kids are too young, so the old man'd have to give up then. What about you?'

'Working in the camp,' Jim said briefly.

'Thought you was heading off after your old man?' There was an ambiguous tone in Wally's voice and Jim's colour rose.

'Well, I'm not. I'll see the season out here, then my uncle's getting me a place jackarooing for the company.'

'Nice for some,' Wally said. 'I don't reckon you'd do so well if it was your dad asking instead.'

Jim stood up. He had the advantage in height and weight. There was a rash of acne on Wally's brow and a sulky look to his features. Staring straight into them, Jim said fiercely, 'I don't give a monkey's what you think of my father but you'd better not couple him with me unless you want a good pasting. It's up to you.'

'Ah, siddown.' Wally looked shamefaced. 'I didn't mean nothing. It's just . . .' He shrugged. 'Well, I feel a proper turd leaving the old man, but what the hell am I supposed to do? I don't want to spend my life slaving my guts out the way he has. But if I stay for the drought, when *do* I leave? When prices go down? When the bore packs it in? There'll always be some reason, and the older he gets, the worse it'll be.'

'Yeah, I know.' Jim watched a willy-wind rush between the gums, lifting bark litter and leaves as it went. The verandah shade fell like a black bar, and beyond it the landscape lay achingly bright, the fierce light painting the turning gum leaves silver. Across the road, a bony cow foraged between sun-blistered houses while crows watched from a branch overhead, as if measuring her for a meal. 'Perhaps it'll rain,' he said.

'Yeah. Pigs might fly too.' Face tight, Wally screwed the heel of his shabby work boot into the dusty ground.

A dance was held in the Goola hall that December, to mark the Christmas season and to replace the party by the river, which had been dropped as the children in the district grew older. There was an old upright piano in the hall and this, played by Gina Colson's fresh-faced governess, together with Bill Maddison's fiddle, provided the music.

Oliver was home for the occasion. He had left Knolly Downs and moved on to Windamere Station, a property further north and out of reach of the drought. He liked it well enough, he said, though the boss was a bit of a bastard. The town of Katherine was their centre. He went to the race meetings there and talked wistfully of the old days at Kharko and the runners he'd helped train. He was as freckled and ginger as ever and spoke repeatedly of Fiona, a girl he was seeing on his infrequent trips to town.

The second time he heard her name, Pommy had eyed him mournfully. "'E's the marrying sort,' he said darkly afterwards.

Jim, thinking about it, decided it was true. His cousin had always seemed incomplete in a way his sister never had. Perhaps a wife would redress the balance.

Rosemary too was back for the dance, school finally behind her. Coming downstairs with his tie straight and his hair slicked down, Jim was taken aback at the sight of her.

'Hey!' He eyed with approval her bare shoulders and slim legs beneath her party dress. She had been fortunate with pimples and her skin was as clear as a ten-year-old's. Her red curls were burnished from brushing. 'You look pretty good.'

'I know.' She smiled complacently and appraised his own appearance. 'You've scrubbed up rather well yourself. You used to be all knobby, and your ears stuck out. They don't seem to any more – maybe your head's grown to fit them?'

'Thanks.'

'Don't mention it.' She grinned. 'Have you got a girl to dance with tonight? Because if you haven't,' she continued without waiting for an answer, 'you can partner me. And that's a pretty good offer. I was always very popular at the school dances.'

'They liked big-headed carrot-tops there, did they?'

Once at the hall they slid amiably onto the dancefloor, to Wally Maddison's envious stare. The last time he'd seen Ro, Jim thought, giving him an airy wave as they swung hands in the gypsy tap, chances were she'd been trying to black his eye or best him in some game.

The night was kind to the land, cloaking the burnt claypans and barren flats in silvery light, and even the air seemed to have lost some of its tortured dryness. Moonlight softened the sharp edges of suffering, so that for a brief time you could imagine there was feed out there, and that the bores were not ringed with desiccated carcases.

At midnight, when the music had stopped and the women were laying out a cold supper in the annexe, there was a general exodus to the cooler air. Jim drew it gratefully into his lungs, loosening his constricting tie. He could feel sweat trickling down his ribs but Ro, he was chagrined to see, looked unaffected by the heat. She leaned her forearms on the handrail of the steps.

'Has it been as bad as Mum reckons, Jim?'

'Yes,' he said matter-of-factly. 'From here to Alice it couldn't be much worse. Uncle Rob sent the steers off in June. They've gone for agistment on a place down the Channel Country. If it hasn't rained by next month he's looking at moving a wedge of breeders across to Arcadia. He's been onto the Lands Department about it – the company would make the payments owing on the lease and fix up the bores. There's plenty of dry feed there, apparently. I daresay poor old Bill would've done it first if he'd had the money.'

'What about Uncle Sandy?'

'What about him? He hasn't paid a thing since he left the place, so I don't reckon the department's gunna lose any sleep over him.'

'Do you ever think about him, Jim?' she asked, low-voiced. 'I mean, I know how you felt —'

'You think you do. Look, I don't want to talk about it. If you want to feel sorry for someone, try Bill Maddison. Wally's cleared out, he's had it with battling the drought.'

'Poor Wally. But everyone has to decide for themselves what they'll do with their life.'

'So have you found a job yet, now you've finished school?'

'Oh, I'll have a year home with Mum first. Dad's already decided that. Then I'll get a job and start saving. I'm going to see the world – all of it. Africa, Spain, the UK. I'll work my way round once I get started.'

'On your own? Your father will have a fit.'

'Let him.'

'Sometimes,' Jim said, 'you sound like you hate him.'

'No, just the way he thinks he's God.'

February brought tantalising fragments of storms but for a third consecutive summer there was no substantial rain. At Kharko they had two inches in the bullock paddock, twenty-one points at the house, and a scattering of showers across half the station, enough to make short green pick for a brief while. One dam was filled and water lay on claypans and hollows for a few precious days, and then the stock were back on the bores. The hope of further rain passed with the summer. Bill Maddison had opened his fences and let the rest of his cattle go to fend for themselves.

'That's it,' he told Rob when they met on the side of the road where he was patching a worn-out tyre. 'They gotta take their chances now. I can't do no more.'

'What about your horses?'

Bill's eyes were hard with hurt. 'Poor buggers are starving. I've weaned the colts off the mares, shot a coupla young foals that should never have happened, but still most of 'em won't make it.' Squatting in the thin shade, wrists dangling over his bony knees, he stared at the harsh landscape and sighed deeply. Then he shrugged. 'A man can only do so much.'

'There's a bit of grass left in the Ten Mile,' Rob said gruffly. 'You fetch 'em over and run them there till the rains come. They won't eat any more than the damn roos are right now.' The sudden hope in his neighbour's face was painful to see, and he turned aside to pull the tailboard down and heave the spare tyre off the back. 'You better borrow this to get home on. That tube won't stand another patching. I'll pick it up sometime when I'm over your way.'

March passed and the stock camp, moving slowly in crippling heat, began shifting breeders onto Arcadia, where the mills had been replaced or repaired. The camp travelled mainly of an evening, nursing the cattle over the stages, but Jim was gone by then, packing his bags as

Oliver had done before him to start at Knolly Downs as a first-year jackeroo. Rob offered to drive him across to his new job but he refused.

'I'll ride the mail, Uncle. Turning up there with you, the boss might think . . . Well, I mean, I don't want any favours because I'm a McAllister.'

On his last morning Jim said goodbye to Pommy, kissed his aunt, pulled Rosemary into a rough hug, and shook hands with his uncle before shouldering his swag. The carrier was waiting by the loading dock where he had delivered the road mail, along with another ton of chaff and oats that Leo Baker was signing for. Jim waved to him as he sprang aboard the truck and took a last look around. Des and the camp were out, old Charlie had retired, Yellow Jack and Matthew were gone. Station hands were a transient lot, and if a man moved around enough he would inevitably find in other kitchens men he'd known elsewhere.

Jim's gaze returned to the gate where his family waited, while the mailman tested his ropes. Ro, bright hair uncovered in the early light, waved to him and he stuck up a thumb. Aunt Mary called, 'Goodbye, Jim. Take care, dear. Goodbye.' And then they were moving and Rob, standing like a pillar of hewn stone, lifted a hand in salute. Even after they'd mended their fences they'd never had much to say to each other, but strangely it was the picture of his face, with its hard eyes and firm lines, that Jim carried away with him.

'New job, eh?' The mailman slowed for the horse-paddock gate.

'Yeah.' Jim waited until the dust settled, then pushed open the door.

'Ah well, you won't find it no better than here,' the man warned. 'She's a bugger of a country and no mistake.'

FOURTEEN

The earth at Knolly Downs was as barren and parched as it was at Kharko, and the same dispiriting round of labour continued. They fed truckloads of molasses to the breeders – all that were left on the place, the rest of the herd having gone off for sale or agistment in Queensland. Jim grew to hate wrestling the dead weight of 44-gallon drums in the loose sand, and the stink of the molasses glugging into the feed troughs. They ran Herefords on Knolly, and nothing, Jim decided as another winter advanced, looked as bad as those particular cattle when they were in poor condition.

Knolly's manager was Chris Landers, a heavy big-bellied man; a one-time fighter run to seed. He did most of his managing from the seat of a land rover. He had a voice that could make itself heard across a cattle camp, and a short way with lazy men and slipshod workmanship. In the kitchen he was known as Grease, for the manner in which he sacked the incompetent. 'You better grease your swag straps' was an invitation for a man to call round at the office for his cheque. Jim liked him well enough, but as Mason Andrews, the other jackeroo, pointed out, he knew what he was doing so there was no reason not to.

Mason was from the city and had only six months' experience in bush living when Jim met him. He had a mop of curly brown hair above guileless eyes and a snubbed and peeling nose, and his face retained some of the chubbiness of childhood. He was perennially cheerful and proved to be a quick learner – and just as well, Jim thought, as he had a great deal to learn. They shared a room, for at Knolly the jackeroos lived separately, taking their meals with the manager's family. Mason would have been content with the men's quarters and the kitchen, and was agog to learn he needed an invitation to both.

'For God's sake, why?'

'It's customary.' Jim frowned. 'Where've you been all your life, anyway?'

'Adelaide. I learned to ride on a farm my mate's dad owned. Then I got my dad to pull a few strings and he came up with this job. Mind, he reckons I'll be back in twelve months. Fact he's counting on it, but I've got news for him.' Mason gazed contentedly around the spartan room, which contained only their beds, a chest of drawers, and two towel rails screwed to the wall. 'This'll do me.'

'What's his job then, your father?'

'He's a lawyer. Thinks I'm gunna be one too. What about yours?'

'Dunno. Haven't seen him in years.' Jim shrugged. 'Mason – what sort of name's that?'

'Hah! That was my grandfather's occupation. That's why I'm supposed to be a lawyer. We pull ourselves up by our bootstraps, we Andrews, with our eye constantly on the goal – no diversions or side trips permitted. We signpost our successes as we go. I expect I could call a son of mine Jack Aroo Andrews. Anyway, I generally answer to Mace.'

'Right.' Jim thought he would like his new companion. A brassy clanging broke upon their ears and he stood up. 'There's the lunch bell. We'd better get up to the house and meet the missus and the book-keeper. And I see the padre's here as well. I recognised his vehicle coming in.'

'You're kidding?' Mason's face was a study. 'God, I thought the one thing I'd be safe from out here was soul-savers.'

'Oh, Padre Don's not like that. In fact I've never met a bush preacher that was. Forget your churchy blokes. That side of him's there if you want it. He'll baptise you or marry you – even bury you,' he added with sudden soberness, remembering Barney. 'But if he didn't wear the crosses you probably wouldn't twig he was a padre. He's just like the rest of us, except he's ready to help when he's needed.'

'Well, that's a relief. For a moment there I could just see him handing out tracts and reporting back to my dad.'

After lunch they met Pete Patterson, the head stockman. Thin and lugubrious, he suffered from piles and carried a swagful of medi-cines about with him, but he ran an efficient camp. The station cook, whose right arm was missing below the elbow, was called Lefty. What remained of the limb had shrunk to the size of the bone, but he man-aged his work and wasn't a bad cook.

'Mad bugger,' Pete warned the two young men, 'but at least he ain't gabby. Gawd, I can't abide a gabby cook.'

The rest of the men changed as regularly as the months. Only Pete and Lefty and the two jackeroos stayed on through the grind of that first winter and into the start of another summer of flies and heat and dust-stained skies. Jim, standing on a mill platform to grease the head, thought the country looked as if it had never been rained upon, nor ever would be. As far as the eye could see, the land stretched barren as the moon. Only the willy-winds moved upon it, in red spirals of heated air, and all he could hear above the buzz of flies was the maddeningly repetitive cawing of crows.

They all hated the crows, and the dingoes grown sleek and bold on the stock's misfortune. The first time Jim had to shoot an old mare that had had the living eyes pecked from her head by crows after going down in the paddock, he'd been sickened to his soul. But he discovered as the months went by that you got used to even that. Death was their daily companion. You shot the dying and towed them away to make room at the troughs and in the shade for the tottering living, and you gritted your teeth and knocked on the head those few foals and calves that were born. The paddocks reeked of death, part of the grim economics of survival. In the war against drought only the strategists survived, and not always then.

Mason, muscles harder and face leaner, endured grimly beside him. He had never killed so much as a fish, he confided the day Pete shot a brumby mare and her newborn foal and left the jackeroos to burn the carcasses.

'What are we doing this for, anyway?' He dumped an armful of wood over the emaciated hide. 'There's gotta be thirty or more dead cattle unburnt back there.' He jerked his head at the country north of the bore. 'Come to that, why shoot her? She's only a brumby.'

'And good for about another week, by the look of her.' Jim sleeved his forehead dry and splashed diesel over the pyre. 'Then she goes down and dies over a coupla days and the foal starves. You ever see a horse die like that, eyes pecked out, digging at the ground trying to get up? That's why he shot her. Brumby or not, she's a horse, and Pete's a horseman.' Gazing at the skinny neck and staring ribs, he said softly, 'I knew another bloke like him once. He would've shot her too.' He struck a wax match against his boot, dropped it onto a little scraping of mulga leaves and watched the oily black smoke billow into the dust-hazed sky. 'God, I wish it'd end.'

His voice was suddenly wistful and Mason eyed him in surprise. He had thought Jim too pragmatic for sentiment.

'You should see this country after rain, Mace, you've got no idea. It's the most beautiful . . . The feed, and the flowers . . .' He waved a hand to express what he could not find words for, finishing lamely, 'Well, I was born here. I suppose I'm biased.'

'I'll have to take that on trust, won't I?' Mason swung himself into the saddle. 'Right now I'd swap the lot for half a mile of beach. If I thought he could control the weather I'd reckon my old man had planned it this way to turn me off the whole thing. Lawyers don't have to worry about droughts.'

Jim squinted ahead at a wavy line shimmering above the mirage on the claypan: cattle coming in to drink. 'On the other hand, you're seeing the worst it can be nice and early in the piece. I had a mate who worked on that theory. Tackle the touchiest horse first, he used to say. It saves on your nerves in the long run.'

Mason, who had been thrown off every horse he'd saddled,

looked sceptical. 'Oh, great – and if they're all touchy? Where's your friend? Maybe he'd like to try my string?'

'Dead,' Jim said curtly, and Mason, surprised by the sudden change of tone, let the conversation drop.

The drought lasted four years, and that fourth year was the longest Jim had ever lived through. It was late November 1967 before it finally broke. Three weeks beforehand the four of them, Pete, Lefty, Mason and Jim, had been sitting around the kitchen table listening to a static-filled broadcast of the Melbourne Cup, won that year by a five-year-old chestnut called Red Handed.

'Christ,' said Pete at the end of the broadcast, an irritating roar of fragmented speech, 'I only heard every fourth word of that.'

'It's called static,' Mason offered. 'Caused by weather or sunspots or the hand of God.'

'Funny bugger, ain't you? Weather? When's the last time we seen any of that?' Pete rose stiffly from the bench and walked with his peculiar spraddled gait to the door.

Jim crowded his shoulder. 'That's not cloud, is it?'

'Yep.' Pete scratched at his ear. 'But it don't mean nothing yet.'

He was right. The few wisps of white were high and far off to the east, and could have little effect on the radio reception, Jim thought. The day felt no different around him, the air was still furnace-dry, but the cloud's very existence planted a seed of hope in his heart.

'Won't come to anything,' he scoffed, not yet daring to admit that it might.

'Give it a month,' Pete grunted. 'You young blokes, think yer seen it all. But the end of every drought's gotta have a beginning, and I reckon this might be it.'

He was right, although his timing was out by a week. For three glorious days rain pounded down upon the stricken country, filling dams and creeks, turning claypans into lakes, and washing the dust and smell of death from the land all the way from Alice to the border. For the first time in four years a cerulean sky, washed clean of haze and dust, arched above the mulga, and almost as they watched, the nine-day grass came pushing through the steaming earth. Within days there were fresh shoots on the trees and ducks planing down onto waterholes. The country burst and chirruped and sang with life, from the little brown frogs that dug themselves out of their desert cocoons to the strident row of the cicadas in the big gum outside the jackeroos' quarters.

Lefty baked a cake to celebrate, although only Jim, Mason, Pete and the mechanic were there to eat it. The pumpers, cut off at their lonely posts by the mud, could not leave until the roads opened. The windmill expert was bogged halfway between Trident bore and the homestead, and the station blacks had gone walkabout the moment the rain stopped.

They drank a toast to the cake and the cook and the ending of the drought with black tea, Pete shifting uncomfortably on his piles on the wooden bench.

'Well, I reckon this means we can get the steers home again next year,' he said.

'And a man might get a bit of decent beef in the meat house for a change,' Lefty said. 'You couldn't feed a bloody dog on what's been coming in.'

'We know,' Mason said. 'We've been eating it.'

The cook pointed his stump threateningly at him. 'Cheeky young bugger. Watch yer lip.' But he spoke without heat; everyone got along with Mason.

Afterwards, luxuriating in enforced idleness on his bed, boots off and hands crossed behind his head, Jim said, 'There won't be anything much doing here for a while, Mace. Where are you going for Christmas – back to the city?'

'For a couple of days, anyway. To see the family. Then I don't know.' He raised his knee to cock it over his other bent leg, and watched a fly circle lazily above his head. 'Cripes, this is the life. Nothing to do and all afternoon to do it in. Makes a change for a hard-working ringer, don't it?'

'When you are one,' Jim suggested derisively. 'Anyway, if there's no hurry, stop off with me for a day or two at Kharko. Have a look at the place and meet my uncle. There's a good chance you'll do at least a year of your time with him. Besides, there's bound to be a dance, and I've got a very good-looking cousin. She'll be home.'

'A dance? Music, you mean? And girls?' Mason rolled his eyes. 'I'll be in that, mate. Tell you the truth, I was starting to wonder if there were any girls out in this country. I've seen nothing female – in a dress, that is – since I got here. Apart from the missus of course.'

Jim grinned. Mrs Landers, gossipy and friendly and matching her husband in girth, was no oil painting.

Riding back home in the mail truck, Jim marvelled afresh at the changes the rain had wrought. Green feed carpeted the red earth, a scattering of white clouds softened the glare, and the cattle, stringing along the pads to water, were visibly improved from a fortnight before, their coats cleaning up, their apathy lifting. When a bony young heifer standing in the road put up her tail and bucked over the verge, he felt like cheering. He wondered how Bill Maddison was doing, and Sam Colson and the rest of them around Goola.

Dropping down out of the truck at Kharko's loading dock, Jim was vaguely surprised to observe that nothing had changed. It was two years since he'd left, the drought having prevented him returning the previous Christmas, but there was old Baker's head popping out like a tortoise from its shell at the sound of the motor, just as it always had, and the pepper trees still guarded the gate, and the smoko bell was a clanging racket.

He tossed his swag onto the platform and threw Mason's beside it. 'They'll be right there,' he said, slapping dust from his clothes. 'C'mon, let's go find my aunt.'

Mary, writing at the dining-room table, looked up with a glad smile at her nephew. 'Jim. Welcome back, dear. And this must be Mason?' She rose to shake his hand. 'I'm pleased you could come.'

Jim hugged her. 'Aunty, you look great.'

She folded her reading glasses and said, 'Shopping list. We're going into the Alice next week. Your uncle will be back soon. He's gone out to the Ten Mile. How long can you stay?'

Just then Rosemary came in and her discontented expression changed at the sight of them. 'So it's you – how are you, Jim? Nice to meet you, Mason. Wasn't the rain marvellous?' Then, before he could answer, 'I've got another job. The new Riverside Hotel in the Alice. They don't open their doors until mid-January, so I'm here till then.'

She had worked that year as a governess for the Tillets, after spending her obligatory twelve months at home on Kharko. Experience as a governess, she had reasoned, would widen her chances of finding work abroad.

'Good for you,' Jim said. 'What's the job?'

'Oh, general dogsbody – running messages, taking bookings. Not,' she mimed horror, 'working in the bar. That's the first thing Dad thought, of course. Anyway, it's a start. I'll find something better later on.'

'I'll make tea,' Mary said. 'Take Mason through to wash, Jim.'

But Mason, head tilted, was looking curiously at Rosemary. 'Won't you miss the life out here?'

'Probably. But I don't have a choice. You should try being a girl sometime, it's pretty restricting.' She shook her head. 'Bathroom's through there. Jim'll show you. I'd better help Mum.'

As at Knolly, everyone at Kharko was renewed by the change in the weather. In the kitchen Pommy was tracing the station brand into potato mash on an enormous cottage pie. The wood range behind him gave out a steady blast of heat, making the perspiration gleam on his bald head. Loaves lay cooling on a wire rack and there was a mug of half-cold tea on the table beside him.

'There y'are, Jim,' he said, unsurprised. 'Heard you was back. Get a bit of rain too, did you?'

'Six inches.' They shook hands and Jim nodded at the branding on the pie. 'What's this?'

'Tryin' to take their minds orf the meat. Gawd, you oughta seen some of the killers we've 'ad. Mince is all they're good for. I've forgot what fat meat looks like – reckon most of the country has, come to that.' His eyes went past Jim. 'Who's this bloke?'

'Mate of mine.' He introduced Mason and they sat down to drink tea and catch up with the news. Pommy, as always, knew everything about everyone's affairs. The rain had been general. Dams throughout the district had filled, Sam Colson was already talking about buying young store cattle to replace stock lost in the drought, and Kharko's own steers would be coming home at the start of the new season.

Jim turned his pannikin on the scrubbed wooden tabletop. 'And old Bill? Things were pretty bad on his place – how'd he get on?'

'Well, 'e's still there. And he's bound to get some of his stock back.' Pommy pursed his lips, adding wisely, 'You leave 'em be, it's marvellous how cattle'll hang on. Course the boss took care of his nags. They been paddocked in the Ten Mile most of the year – thin pickings, but more than Bill had left. He's done some fencing for the boss as well, so I seen him off and on. I think he mighta been with the camp for a few days even, when they shifted the cows over onto your dad's old joint.'

Mason stayed five days, long enough to attend the dance. Finding Rosemary alone in the garden, he asked her to partner him, adding hopefully, 'I've got party manners and a clean shirt. And we Andrews never step on ladies' feet. It's quite an article of faith with us, that.'

She looked at him, lifted one shoulder. 'Well, why not?'

'Good. That's settled. Tell you the truth, I thought I'd have to fight the big fella for the privilege.'

'Clown. Jim's my cousin but he might as well be my brother. We grew up together. I shoved him out of this tree when I was nine. He knocked a tooth loose and got so wild he came after me with a cricket bat. I shot up the mill tower, because I knew he couldn't climb while he was hanging onto the bat. He was always very easy to stir up.'

'I'll bear that in mind,' Mason promised. 'The cook said something about his father's property – whereabouts is it?'

'Oh, that was years ago, when he was a kid. He came to live with us after his mother died. Uncle Sandy walked off the place. Jim never talks about it – or him.'

'I noticed. I thought you might.'

'No.' Her tone was decisive. 'It's his business.'

'Fair enough.' Mason gave an exaggerated sigh. 'I suppose you have to take this job in town? I mean, Jim reckons the company'll shift us around. Next year, the one after, I could be here – who knows?'

'Well, I won't be. I'll be halfway to Europe by then.' Sudden irritation edged her tone. 'We're going to a dance, Mason, not starting a life-long relationship.'

'True. But the one sometimes leads to the other, and I'm an optimist. Is there a boyfriend?'

'Not with me it doesn't,' she said, ignoring his question, 'so don't be tiresome. If you are I can always dance with Jim.'

The atmosphere at the dance was markedly different to the last one Jim had attended. There were streamers and balloons in the hall, and the conversation ran from satisfaction to outright joy at the miracle of rain. Going around the floor with Mary, Jim heard snatches from the older men gathered obstinately in the corners, ignoring both their wives and the dancefloor.

'. . . over the spillway of the dam . . .'

'. . . four inches at the very least, swept the crossing to hell, had to run every cable again . . .'

'. . . wettest it's been in thirty years . . .'

'She'll be a bewdy season . . .'

Streaks of grey hair showed in the brown as Mary tilted her head to look up at her nephew. 'It will be too. I'm just so thankful it's come. It's been a big strain on your uncle, Jim, getting through this drought.'

'I'll bet it has.' He glanced across the room to where Rob stood in conversation, his back to the dancefloor. 'Who's that he's with?'

'Where? Oh,' Mary stopped craning, 'you wouldn't know him. Willy Bell. He manages Basingstoke.' The name reminded her and she eyed him carefully. 'Did you . . .? Have you heard from your father at all, dear?'

'No.' It came out more curtly than he had intended. 'I don't expect to, either. He's gone for good.'

Her attention was taken by latecomers at the door. 'Oh, there's Jeff Tillet, and Brenda and the girls. He's being transferred, you know. Well, of course you do, I remember writing you about it. I must speak to her.'

Jim swung her out of the dance and found himself shaking hands with the blocky policeman and congratulating him on his promotion to sergeant. He tipped his head at Mrs Tillet and grinned at the twins. 'Hello there – which of you is which?'

He danced with them both, and then a little later he noticed Gina Colson. It had to be her, he thought, staring at the slight, ethereal figure seated beside Kathy Colson, although who could have guessed that that timid, pudgy little girl would turn into such a swan? She would be seventeen, he supposed, and was reed-slim and lovely, her hair the colour of ripe wheat and caught into a twist at the back of her head. She used to have untidy, whitish-looking hair that either clung damply to her face or stuck out in pigtails. He started across the room to ask her to dance, finding it hard to believe he'd ever called her fatso and wondering what strange metamorphosis had brought her to this.

Mrs Colson, a big, forthright woman, greeted him unsmilingly. 'Hello, Jim.'

'How are you doing, Mrs Colson? I heard you got good rain. We had six inches over at Knolly – the frogs had to learn to swim again. Hello, Gina,' he smiled. The music swung into a waltz and he tapped his foot. 'Have this next one with me?'

Kathy Colson's hand closed over her daughter's wrist. Gina showed no sign of rising. Her face had crimsoned and she was shaking her head in rapid little movements, her eyes not meeting his.

He stared uncomprehendingly, 'Why not? Come on, Gina, you can waltz as well as any of them.'

'But not with you,' Sam Colson said at his elbow.

Jim swung to face him, feeling a rush of heat to his face, and then a sudden coldness as realisation sank in. And somehow it worsened the insult that Sam's expression should show regret rather than scorn or anger. That he should in the same breath call into question Jim's fitness to dance with his daughter while speaking in so kindly a tone.

'It's nothing personal, Jim. I'd wish it otherwise myself. Good God, I count your uncle a friend, but I have to protect my daughter's name. You can see that, can't you? It's not your fault that your father's . . .'

He didn't finish his sentence, but he didn't have to. Jim knew what he meant. And it wasn't just Sandy's alcoholism.

By an effort of will he unclenched his fist and turned away. Another second, he thought, and he might have driven the man's teeth through the back of his skull. Or tried to, anyway. He felt as though he stood naked in the crowded room – only it was worse than that, for the scalding shame was inside him as well. Sam's appearance had been no accident; he had been waiting to warn Jim off. The knowledge made his humiliation complete. It showed that the Colsons had discussed the matter. How many others present tonight had done the same? Which of the girls in the room would refuse, or were forbidden, to dance with him?

He had almost reached the door when Rosemary seized his arm. 'Jim! Dance with me.' She stepped in front of him, put one hand on his shoulder, and gave him a little shove to halt his advance. 'Come *on*,' she hissed, 'move your feet. You want them all staring?'

'I don't give a shit!' he gritted. But still, he was obeying her, blind instinct turning him and lifting his feet as the music directed, the couples around him appearing through a blur of rage. The colours of the balloons ran together and he felt giddy from the pressure of blood in his head.

'You never think, Jim,' Rosemary told him, keeping her voice low. 'You couldn't pick anyone else to dance with but Gina Colson, could you? Knowing the way her parents are about her, what did you expect? A crown prince would have to show his pedigree to get past Sam. And you looked like you were going to sock him.'

'I was,' he said furiously. 'If he'd said one more word.'

'Oh, that would have been wonderful! Hit first and holler after, that's our Jim. It never occurred to you that Mum and Kathy Colson have been friends for years? Or that Dad's got a position to keep up?'

'I'm not stopping him from keeping up anything he wants.' Jim sounded defensive even to himself.

'You will be if you drag this out into the open and make a scandal of it. The company doesn't approve of your father's actions either, you know. But as long as it's kept quiet they'll overlook it. Next time you feel yourself insulted, Jim, just count to ten and think of my father's job first. You owe him that much, surely.'

Flushing, he nodded dumbly. She was right, of course. He had never once thought of his father's shame except as it affected himself. The music stopped and she took his hand and squeezed it. 'It was a rotten thing to do – I'd thought better of Sam Colson. But it's done now. Let's get out of here and go for a walk.'

Through his affronted pride he felt a surge of affection for her. That was Ro: kick your head in and then stick a bandaid on the damage. 'What about Mace?' he asked.

'He's found the twins. He won't even notice I've gone.'

FIFTEEN

Jim spent a further year at Knolly Downs, taking time off with Mason in May for a trip to the Goola races. Oliver came home, his gangling presence as unobtrusive as ever, slipping quietly back into his old place at the table as if he'd never left. Jim looked curiously at him. It was twelve months since they'd last met. His cousin was broader across the shoulders these days, and his features had firmed, but his manner was as diffident as it had always been. He shook hands with Mason and looked Jim up and down. He had to move his head to do so for they were now of a height.

'You gunna give up growing soon? God, you're the spit of the old man. How're you finding Chris Landers, then?'

'Oh, I don't have a problem with him. It's only slackers and Mace here who cop it. Course he wanted to be a cowboy, so he's only got himself to blame. This is the bloke who gave up a law career to shove cows around. Can't ride either, poor sod. Still, takes all sorts.'

'It does indeed.' Oliver met Mason's engaging grin. 'That right? You actually want to work stock?'

Mason looked surprised. 'Well, of course. Wouldn't be here if I didn't. You bushies can't keep it all to yourself. Sure, the horses are a bit tricky but I'll get the hang of them eventually. I'll take cattle over the law courts any day.'

'Good luck to you.' Oliver hitched himself out of his chair. 'I'm taking a run out to the mare paddock. You want to come for the ride? Room for three.'

'Count me out,' Mason said, turning to follow Rosemary's progress across the lawn. She too had come home for the races and was returning the next day. 'You two go – I'll make do here.'

'He's a good bloke,' Jim said as he and Oliver drove off. 'Nothing gets him down. Just about every horse on Knolly's slung him but he bounces up and gets back on every time. So how's Windamere?'

'No worse than anywhere else.' Jim saw his cousin's big, sun-splotched hand tighten on the wheel as he changed down, thrusting the gearstick with unnecessary force. He had always been a rough driver. 'Truth to tell, it's pretty deadly. Your mate must be touched in the head; at least we had the racing to look forward to here. Look,' he poked his chin at the corner window, 'the bay mare with the foal – that's Pearl, isn't it?'

'So it is. Uncle Rob said he'd put her to the stallion. Strong foal, too. No more than a day old by the look of it.'

'We won't disturb her then.' Oliver steered wide of the mare and Jim watched the interest kindle on his cousin's face as more horses came into view.

'Why don't you just chuck it in, Oliver? Uncle Rob'd get used to the idea. Mace's father's had to – he must've guessed by now he's not getting another lawyer in the family. Just quit and do what you want.'

Oliver grunted. 'It's a bit late for that. They're making me overseer. The bloke who's got the job's dying of cancer. Only forty, poor bugger. But it means we'll have a house.' Sensing Jim's incomprehension, he said, 'To live in. Fiona and I are getting married.'

'Are you? You know, Ro once said . . . But never mind, congratulations. Have you told your parents?'

'Not yet.' He looked sheepish. 'I dunno why I told you, actually. We're keeping it quiet until her family gets used to the idea. They aren't too keen on her doing the Never-Never bit.'

'But why let a promotion stop you doing what you want?'

'And then what? Keep my wife in a tent? If I pull out I've got no job, no prospects, and no place to live either. Better to stick to what I've got. I'm used to it, God knows.'

Jim shrugged and gave up. 'Your funeral then.'

That evening after dinner, Oliver passed around his latest photos. The Windamere homestead was an old house with wide verandahs and palms flanking the steps. There were shots of mares and foals on a trough and a nice-looking horse silhouetted prick-eared against a sunset. There was another of the same horse in the round yard.

Oliver tapped the snap. 'That's Bruno the stallion. His sire's grandfather won the Oaks years ago.'

There were many of Fiona, a small, thin girl with a sharp-looking face, and others of strangers at a dance, or crowded onto the bonnet of Oliver's car, and one of Oliver grinning self-consciously, one arm around Fiona and the other raising a glass.

'I'll get that one copied,' Mary said. 'Who's the girl? She's very pretty.'

'Fiona Hocking. She works in town. I see her now and then.' Oliver blushed as he took the photo back.

She was as plain as a post, Jim thought uncharitably, but Mary had picked up on something. She smiled and repeated, '*Very* pretty. If she's a good friend you must try and bring her down for a visit next time you come.'

Oliver beamed. 'I'll work on it. Maybe I can take a week after the bullock muster. There must be some perks in the job.'

Rob rattled the newspaper he'd picked up. 'Precious few, I'd say. Between the markets and the weather a man's lucky to get a day off a month, and overseers don't have it much better.'

'I haven't noticed jackeroos do, either,' Jim complained.

Those few days at home were to be his last break until the June long weekend, during which he and Mason drove furiously into the Alice to catch as much of the rodeo as they could. Rosemary put them up in the old house she was renting not far from the hotel where she worked. It was a ramshackle affair with very little furniture and she shared it with another girl. Jim and Mason rolled their swags out on the verandah and queued for the bathroom, where it was easier to shower in freezing water than wait for the arthritic heater to work.

'It's a bit of a dump,' Ro said without apology, buttering her toast. 'Mum carries on about it, but I daresay Africa will be worse.'

Mason, lifting his cup, cocked his head. 'You're still going? I didn't think you meant it.'

'Certainly I do. Why shouldn't I?' She spread honey lavishly on her toast and bit into it. 'As a matter of fact it won't take as long as

I thought. Getting there, I mean. I've got a new job, starting Tuesday. The pay's half as much again as what I'm getting at the hotel.'

'Doing what?' Jim asked, and to his surprise she gave a sudden spurt of laughter and nearly choked on her toast. He was bewildered. 'What's so funny, then?'

'Oh, Jim – you are. Here's a riddle, everybody. What's the difference between my cousin and my father? About thirty years. *Doing what, Rosemary?*' she mimicked. 'Well, it's a very proper job in a real-estate office and not whatever you were thinking.' She wiped her eyes and leaned across to tap his hand. 'Dad'd be proud of you. He might even make you my official chaperone.'

'I wasn't,' Jim began, but he could hear the echo of his own voice and it *had* sounded like Rob's at his most censorious. But the trouble with Ro was you never knew what she might do – it could be anything from being a barmaid, which Rob would certainly forbid, to joining a trapeze troupe. He shook his head and stood up. 'We can't win here, mate,' he said to Mason. 'Let's get moving.'

'Not so fast.' Rosemary raised a finger. 'There are dishes, remember? And it's you boys' turn to see to them.' She licked honey daintily from a thumb tip and smiled at him the way she had when they were kids and she'd just succeeded in dropping him in it. Resignedly Jim began collecting plates.

Back at Knolly again, the year dragged. After the drought there were few calves to brand and no bullock muster, as those cattle were sold off from their place of agistment. The steers came home, round and rollicking fat, white faces gleaming in the pale sunshine. The stock camp met the drovers at the boundary and Pete looked with pride upon the young cattle spread across the red sand country, where the feed grew winter-gold amid the flowering mulga. The steers fed slowly past where they sat their horses, one plumping itself down in the grass occasionally to chew its cud, another turning its head to lick its thick coat back into rippling waves that shone damply on its red hide.

'Never think it was the same mob of starving clatterbones, would you?' Pete leaned a forearm across his black gelding's neck and beamed upon the day.

The station men shared the drovers' fire that evening, and their stories of the road and other places, but after weeks of nightwatches and dawn-to-dark days, the men mainly wanted to sleep. Long after the fire had sunk to coals, Jim lay wakeful, listening to the night sounds and the heavy breathing about him. The black stockboys' fire had long since turned to ash, and at their own Pete snored and one of the men muttered and ground his teeth in his sleep. Out beyond the camp the horse bells rang busily as the plant fed and a little wind walked the darkness, filling the night with its voice. Later, when the temperature dropped, the bells would still as the horses drew into the shelter of the timber, and cold would grip the earth.

Jim, rearranging his pillow, thought of the steers and their long tramp homewards from the channels of the Georgina. He envied the drovers their life, picturing the mob's steady swinging progress and the freedom of a new camp each night. Such a life might have been his, and on the heels of that thought he wondered where Sandy was now. He had been half afraid as the talk ranged around the fire that somebody would bring up his name. Stockmen travelled widely, and despite it being a big country the population was small, the chances of meeting old acquaintances high.

Overhead an owl whooshed by on velvet wings and a sudden memory came to him of summer nights at Arcadia, lying listening to the eerie wail of curlews along the creek and knowing, because of his father's steady breathing alongside, that there was nothing to fear. He felt a pang of loss, followed immediately by a quick anger at his need. Turning his pillow again, he sought to banish his memories in sleep.

The new herd bulls arrived in August, and Chris Landers began making plans to hire a sinker for another dam. They were either in short supply in the area or extremely busy, for word came back from Harry Freeman, the contractor, that he couldn't get there before the end of September.

'Time enough,' Landers said expansively. 'We'll have it finished before the rain. Might even get it full come summer.'

The cold nights vanished as the weather warmed towards the end of August. Mason, riding a fresh horse in the station yard one morning, was thrown into the rails, breaking his arm as it made contact with a post. The horse, a black with three white feet and a crooked blaze, bucked away as Mason stood up, hatless and green about the gills. He was very pale and cradled his arm protectively against his body. Pete swore and jumped down from the rails, looked at Mason's arm and swore again.

'For Chrissake, boy! Can't you do anything right? Looks broken to me. Take yourself up to the house and see the missus.' He turned to Jim, jerking his head at the snorting horse that stood, reins trailing, in the corner of the yard. 'Jim, get on that bloody animal and give him a pasting. Then we'll see if a day's work don't mend his manners.'

Jim, a competent if not a great horseman, trapped the trailing reins under his boot, caught them up and swapped the saddles over. Pulling the horse to the centre of the yard, he reined him tightly and swung smoothly into the leather. The black humped about, squealing and raising dust, sweat breaking along his neck and flanks; he bucked straight ahead and was easy to stay on. Jim lapped the reins under his belly then drove him at a hard, fast canter around the yard. When the horse felt loose beneath him he reined him in and stepped down, the sharp scents of dust and wet horsehide in his nostrils. The black jerked his head, eyes rolling whitely. Jim patted the slick neck. 'Serves you right,' he said, then hooked up the reins and went to see how Mason was getting on.

He was in the kitchen being poured a cup of tea. Jim went in, nodding a greeting to the cook. 'Morning, Lefty. What's the verdict, Mace?'

'Broken, my lord. The doctor's on his way. I'll be in the Alice before you're halfway out to Winter Creek.' He shifted carefully. His arm was splinted with rolled newspaper and secured in a sling about his neck. 'Ride the tail off that horse for me, will you? I don't suppose he chucked you, too?' he added hopefully.

'I'd need shooting if he could.'

'Yeah, well, I miss all the fun.' Mason brightened suddenly. 'Might run into Ro, though. She's still in town, isn't she?'

'Far as I know. Right, I'd better be off. See you when you get back. If you do see Ro tell her I said hello.' He swung on his heel, then paused indecisively. 'Don't get too hung up on her, Mace. I mean, she's fair dinkum about leaving. Long as I've known her she's done what she's said she will. Just so you know,' he finished awkwardly, seeing Pete approaching the open door.

To Jim's surprise the head stockman came in and sat down with a groan on the bench. 'Got a pot of tea going?' he asked Lefty. Then added without rancour, 'Seeing young Mason here has buggered the start, we might as well have smoko before we leave.'

Contrary to Jim's expectations, Mason did not return on the mail truck the following week. A note came instead to say that he was being transferred to Kharko, and could Jim get his gear together and send it on? Rosemary, he wrote, was well and waiting on her passport. She was planning to leave in summer. Briefly Jim wondered if Mason had heeded his warning. He was certainly going to miss having him around. Not counting Ro, he was the only real friend his own age he had.

A week after Mason's letter, the dam-sinking contractor moved onto the station with his wife and three children: a ten-year-old boy, a moony girl of fifteen with acne-rashed cheeks, and her elder sister Kate. Suddenly Jim felt the absence of Mason a lot less. Kate was brown and lissom, with dark hair that she wore pulled back in a ponytail and a direct, challenging gaze. It was a combination that took Jim frequently to their camp to deliver rations, to ask if they had mail to go or needed anything from the store.

'You must think Mum's the worst manager in the Territory,' Kate said on one such visit. Jessie Freeman had bustled off into the mess tent behind the truck to bring the smoko things, while Jim and Kate sat on folding chairs under the shade fly. The fire burned behind a break, and downwind of them the roar of big machinery provided a constant background rumble to life in the camp.

'Of course I don't.' Jim coloured. Kate was very like Rosemary, blunt to a fault. Sometimes he wondered whether the similarity, which he had immediately recognised, was part of the attraction.

'It's just that this is the third time this week you've come to check if we're running short of something.'

'Yeah, well, seeing I was going past . . .'

'Like you were Wednesday? Let me see, you'd been out to the pumper at Number Three, wasn't it? That's west of the station, right? And we're east, and a touch north. I thought I had my directions wrong.' She smiled, showing a dimple in her left cheek, and her eyes glinted mischievously. 'And here you are again, so maybe it's me you're coming for?'

She was laughing at him. Jim reddened again, then shrugged at the truth of it. 'Well, it's not for your brother, is it? I like you, Kate. I like your family too. Your parents remind me of mine.'

'Well, that's all right then.' She stretched and jumped up. 'Let's walk down and tell Dad it's smoko time. You'd yell yourself hoarse before he heard you, and he never thinks of stopping for a break, bless him. What's your dad do?'

Jim was unprepared for the question. It was the Freeman family's ease with each other that prompted his incautious remark, and now an answer was called for. His silence seemed to stretch endlessly; any moment she would be asking if he was deaf. He could see her right eyebrow lifting and knew he had to say something to prevent closer enquiry. His mouth opened. 'Oh, nothing exciting. He's a manager, been running Kharko for years. I did my schooling at the station, had my first pony there, and the job just sort of grew out of my background, I guess.'

'Well, lucky you. Manager's son, eh? And I suppose you're going to be a manager yourself some day?'

'That's the general idea. What about you, Kate?' She was waving her arms to catch her father's eye. They were still some distance from the dam site, where the scraper shook the chewed-over earth from which dust plumed in a red cloud. The machine was halfway up the forming bank before its driver noticed them. He lifted a hand and Kate turned back while the behemoth roared on behind them.

'He'll dump the load first.' She looked sideways at him. 'What about me? We're nothing flash, you know. My dad's a contractor. The few times on a job that we get to visit the station, we eat in the kitchen. Not like you nobs up in the big house. Camp born and bred, that's me.' She winked at him. 'Though we do get under a roof in summer. Dad's got a shed for the machinery in the Alice and we rent a house. It gives Mum a break and the kids get a bit of time in a proper school.'

'But don't you get tired of the camp, and the travelling? Your dad told me his next job's a couple of hundred miles north of here. What do you do with yourself all day?'

'Oh my,' Kate said. 'Like that, is it? Mum's the cook so I must be idle, eh?' Her eyes sparked combatively. 'You drive a grader, Jim? No, well I do.' She thrust her hands at him, palms up. They were strong hands, small and brown, with calluses at the base of each finger. 'I work, that's what I do. Bulldozer, scraper, the lot. I might be – I probably am – the only female operator around, but that doesn't worry me, or my dad.'

'You're amazing,' Jim said, and meant it. He glanced guiltily at the sun. 'Look, I'd better not stop for tea. Can't you run out of something pretty soon so I have an excuse to come back?'

Her dimple showed itself again. 'Maybe I'll work on it.'

Kate's dam, as Jim privately called it, was a long job. They were still at it a month later, but however many meetings Jim contrived they were inevitably brief, and he and Kate had little time alone to talk. Twice the scraper had broken down, necessitating a dash into the Alice for spare parts and depriving Jim of her company for a week. She and her father returned on a Wednesday with a replacement for the hydraulic hose that had split and new bearings and a seal, and by Friday noon the work was continuing. Kate, Jim saw when he met her in the shadow of the idling scraper, was wearing a new hat and a green shirt that matched the feathers in her hatband.

'I like it,' he said. Under the brim her eyes sparkled and her honey-brown skin was soft. She was a head shorter than him and close up like this had to lift her face to meet his eye. His heart beat fast. He had never kissed a girl before but suddenly his arms went round her and first their noses and then their lips bumped. Hers tasted of dust. Jim adjusted his position and Kate's new hat fell off and she pulled back laughing.

'Whew!' Her face was flushed and she looked extraordinary with her white teeth and shining eyes. 'Let's not get carried away, because I truly can't stop, not even for you. Dad's done his back in and we're behind to blazes. Right now the job's costing us more than we're making. Besides, one kiss is enough to be going on with.'

'Two.' He held her again and she let herself be kissed before springing away. She placed a boot on the step set forward of the scraper's wheel and reached for the grab handle near the door, swinging herself effortlessly into the cabin.

'Hat,' she mouthed, and he tossed it to her. The engine bellowed and the great tyres rolled down the steepening slope.

The following Monday, when Jim returned from a bore run, the Freemans' shabby red truck was parked at the end of the store. It was Kate who had driven in and he met her coming out the door, a half-sack of onions under one arm.

'Kate!' His face lit up. 'I didn't know you were coming in today.'

'I bet you didn't.' Her look raked him from head to toe and there was loathing in her tone. He stared flabbergasted as she clutched the onions and kept walking, forcing him to step out of her way.

'Kate, wait!' His bewilderment was complete. 'What's up? Talk to me! What's the matter?'

'I daresay you wouldn't consider it much.' She rubbed unconsciously at her lips. 'A manager's son, are you? You dirty, lying . . . What's he managing then? A blacks' camp? You make me sick. I never want to see you again.'

Jim watched her stalk past, her spine rigid with disdain. He would have gone after her but no explanation was going to help. Not after what he had seen in her face, and the frantic way she had rubbed at her lips. As if she had learned too late that his own were contaminated with some loathsome disease. He heard the cab door slam, the motor whirr to life, and the crash of gears as she roared off. She'd take out a gate-post the way she was going. Serve the silly little fool right, he thought furiously. He cursed his father, and then himself for lying about him. Not that in the long run it would have made much difference – she'd made that perfectly plain.

He wondered who had told her. Everyone at Knolly, from Landers down, probably knew, but he doubted it had been intentional. Given that stupid lie, it would only have taken one passing comment for somebody to correct it and cause the next question to be asked. Sooner or later it had been bound to happen.

Jim turned blindly on his heel and strode away. Even if he wanted her to, he knew she would never speak to him again.

He left Knolly Downs at the start of summer and spent Christmas at Kharko, where he met Fiona for the first time. Her parents had been won over, and the engagement was now common knowledge. They made an incongruous pair, his beanpole cousin and the girl whose head came to the top of his breast pocket. Jim, still smarting from the manner of Kate's rejection, found Fiona a little sharp for his taste. She liked having the last word and was very protective of Oliver. Mary, he saw, thought it an endearing trait but Jim inclined to the belief that Fiona disapproved of her fiancé's gentle nature and did not intend to have it imposed upon. And it was plain, from the beginning, that she didn't like Rob.

Jim, curious to know how his uncle felt about the match, waited his opportunity to ask, which came as they sprawled at ease on the veran-dah chairs. 'What do you think of your daughter-in-law to be? Oliver seems pretty happy about it all.'

Rob grunted agreement. 'She'll wear the pants,' he said. And would not be drawn further on the subject.

Rosemary came home for two days only, getting a ride out with Wally Maddison and going back in with the current mechanic. She had made the arrangement herself and was impatient with Jim's offer to take her into town. 'For heaven's sake, he's a station man, not Jack the Ripper. Do you think I'll be getting a police reference from everyone I meet overseas? Don't be tiresome, Jim. What do you think of Fiona?'

'I guess she suits Oliver.' He pulled a face; he could always be honest with Ro. 'Still, he won't need a boss with her around.'

'No.' She stretched her arms luxuriously, gazing up into the branches of the pepper tree. 'Poor old Olly, he always makes the wrong choices. But I suppose he loves her. God, it's good to stop for a bit. I've spent every night of the last fortnight waitressing at the pub for extra money. With that and my other job, and trying to get packed up, I'm dead on my feet. When I'm freezing in London what'll you be doing?'

'Heading up to Darwin.' He tilted his hat to cut the glare. 'I'll be working round Katherine next year. They're sending me to a place called Ralston Hills. It'll be different.'

She snorted. 'Why? You reckon they'll run giraffes or something? Anyone'd think you were forty, Jim.' She eyed him judiciously. 'You know, you ought to fall in love. Look what it's done for Oliver.'

Jim rolled his eyes. 'Oh, sure. Why don't you take your own advice?'

She looked smug. 'I don't need to. I've got more interesting things to do.'

Darwin was a whole other world, with a different feel and pace to the homely Alice. Jim spent several weeks there, enjoying the strangeness of the colourful frontier town with its torrential downpours and exotic Asian influences until, tiring of idleness, he took a job picking fruit at a government experimental station called Pelli-Pelli. It was an eye-opener, the Top End, a place of violent tropical storms that ripped the night sky apart in hour-long displays of lightning, of intolerably muggy afternoons, of palms and pandanus along waterways where scaly crocodiles waited in the turbid waters about their roots. He shot buffalo with one of the Pelli superintendents, fished for barramundi, and feasted on tropical fruits. It was hotter than the desert but in a different way – a cloying, enervating heat in which his sweat sprang at the slightest movement and the air itself was as soggy as wet linen.

Oliver and Fiona's wedding was a small affair, held in her hometown of Waikerie in the first week of the new year. Rob and Mary attended; Rosemary and Jim sent gifts. Ro was flying out in mid-January and couldn't afford the trip to South Australia anyway, she told Jim. He'd rung her from a phone box in the main street of Darwin, with the door propped open for air and sweat dripping off the bakelite handpiece. The line was noisy. 'It's worse than the wireless,' he yelled, digging more coins from his pocket. 'What date do you go?' Her voice came tinny and distant in bursts between static.

'Flying . . . Be in . . .' Then something about Singapore and sixteen hours and the rest was lost.

'Well, take care,' Jim roared. 'Send me a telegram if you get into strife, run out of money – anything at all, Ro. I mean it.'

'I'll remember. Keep an eye on the parents.' She sounded as if an ocean already separated them. 'See you, Jim – and thanks.'

'See you, Carrots. Are you scared?' He heard a laugh, followed by silence.

'A bit,' she said at length. 'Nothing I won't get over.'

The static buzzed, and when he could hear again she'd hung up. He stood for a moment listening to the surflike roar on the line before placing the handpiece back on its hook and stepping out into the street, his shirt like a wet rag and sweat running down his face. He felt – illogically, he knew – as though he'd been left flat-footed at the starting post. Oliver was married, Ro off to foreign countries – only he remained. And suddenly the glamour of Darwin palled and he saw it as just a shabby town at the end of the bitumen, not the exotic location he had imagined it to be. Another couple of days and he'd be heading off to his new posting at Ralston Hills. That at least would be different, he thought, then winced as he remembered Rosemary's tart dismissal of his new job.

Strolling back along the shady side of the street, he wondered if the newly-weds were back from their honeymoon and settled into the overseer's cottage at Windamere, which was only ninety-odd miles from Ralston Hills. Feeling lonely, Jim promised himself he'd run over and visit them during the year. Kharko was too distant for weekend jaunts.

It struck him as ironic that, having spent his boyhood pining for Arcadia, it was the shade trees and wide verandah of Kharko that sprang to mind now when he thought of home. He had not seen the old place since he was ten, but there was little point. Arcadia was in the past and he was a company man now, with an easier life and better working conditions than he'd ever have as a solo battler. He knew it, but occasionally, on the verge of sleep, old memories called to him and he half regretted not the life he had chosen but the chance at the life he had lost.

Ralston Hills was the smallest of the company properties, red-gravel country interspersed with wattle and box scrub and spinifex ridges. The homestead, a low, compact structure with verandahs on all four sides, was backed by a distant escarpment whose purple and ochre colouring reminded Jim of Kharko. The kitchen was an old bush-built building connected as usual by a covered walkway to the house, with the men's quarters a little distance behind it. The sheds, all crooked beams and dipping rooflines, were set somewhat incongruously to the fore of them all. Visitors to Ralston Hills encountered first the stockyard, then the sheds and petrol dump, the kitchen, and finally the homestead. It was more functional than either of the other properties Jim had been on.

'There's no frills here, son, so don't go expecting 'em,' the manager growled. 'You bunk on the back verandah and eat in the kitchen with the men. There's a shower under the tank and the doings are down the back.' Kevin Gaunt was a tough-looking middle-aged man with leathery skin and a grizzled crown. His wife Paula was younger, a tired, pallid-faced woman with lank hair who strove ineffectually to keep her two sons in order. The only other woman on the place, apart from those in the blacks' camp, was the cook, a half-caste called Linda who wore shapeless garments in vivid reds and blues and walked spraddle-legged to accommodate the size of her thighs. The head stockman was Buck Moody, a blockily built man with an unfriendly manner who offered his name like a challenge to newcomers.

'Not Rogers?' Jim suggested pleasantly, and realised from the fish-eyed stare he got in reply that he'd made his first mistake. To cover it he added, 'I'm Jim McAllister.' Buck Moody was making no effort to meet his outstretched hand so he let it drop. 'I was at Knolly Downs last, Kharko before that.'

'Which your uncle runs.' Buck nodded. 'I worked with his son last year and a dozy bastard he was. Nose buried in a book half the time.' He scratched the growth of hair in the V of his shirt neck. 'Well, whatever you did there it don't mean we need the benefit of your wisdom round 'ere. A first-year jackeroo don't know spit from —'

'Fourth, actually,' Jim said.

'Smart-alec too.' Moody looked him up and down as if he were a horse he'd decided not to buy. 'Keep your trap shut and do your work. That's all I want from you.'

In the kitchen the first face Jim saw was a familiar one. Matthew Henderson stood to shake hands across the table, looking up at him to do so. 'G'day, Jim. Knew you'd grow into a big 'un. How's life been treating you?'

'Pretty good. Been here long?'

'A while.' Matthew spoke with his usual economy. He had changed little since his time as the mechanic on Kharko, and if Jim had to run into anyone from the old days he'd rather it was Matthew than some. The man could give a stone lessons in staying silent.

In the months that followed, Jim had reason to be glad of the thorough grounding his years with his uncle had given him. Stock work had come naturally to him and he'd learned from old Charlie Attwood how to work hide and splice ropes. Matthew had taught him to strip a diesel engine, Barney to butcher a carcase, and he could mortise posts and rails for the repair of yards. It was just as well, for Buck Moody, finding nothing to fault in his stock work, seemed determined to catch him out elsewhere. He got the dullest and dirtiest jobs: if they were making camp his allotted task was to fetch the firewood, if they killed for meat it was Jim who pegged the hide and cut it into strips for hobbles or rope making. They used pack saddles to reach the camps furthest out, where the roads did not run, and Ralston Hills, Jim thought with grim humour, must have had the best-greased packs in the Territory. Working the warmed fat into the dirty leather was another of his jobs.

He could have complained or pulled out but was determined to do neither. Buck had no power to sack him, so it was just a matter of waiting him out. Eventually the head stockman would realise the futility of needling him this way, or get over whatever was bugging him.

It was hard to believe that Jim's connection with Kharko was responsible, but even Lester the camp cook, a rheumy-eyed alcoholic, seemed to feel himself slighted by mention of the larger place. He had never noticed it at Knolly, but it was as if Kharko, by its mere existence, had the power to diminish Ralston Hills to a poor relation. It was ridiculous. Ralston might have been smaller, with fewer paddocks and roads and no big machinery of its own, but that was no reason for it to suffer by comparison. On Kharko, when Des Hanks had the camp, every man in it rode for the brand, loyal to the boss and the station that paid them.

Buck had a different way of doing things, but after a while Jim came to see that what he had taken for envy was a sort of inverted pride in the station. The stockmen were not so much resentful of their parent property as determined not to be looked down upon by a newcomer used to, as Harry the windmill man put it, 'A joint where they've got every spanner a man can use.'

It was easy after that. Jim was pleasant and did his share and the men thawed towards him, save for Buck, who continued to treat him as an unwanted interloper.

Kevin Gaunt was an excellent manager. There was far more to the job, Jim knew, than signing the monthly pay cheques. Like a ship's captain, a property manager was responsible for everything from the daily running of the station to the morale of the crew. Kevin had the men's respect, which in itself was an indication of his capability.

Jim worked as hard as the rest of them. The post of jackeroo was no sinecure, more an apprenticeship to every task that arose, from pulling bores to drafting stock. His Sundays off, when they occurred, were spent in domestic chores. Well-greased packsaddles meant, by the time the dust had settled into the grease, a lot of very dirty washing, then there were shirt buttons to sew on, ripped jeans to mend, and his riding boots to care for. And there were the young Gaunt boys, who gave nobody any peace.

'Young buggers need a good flogging,' Buck said frequently, and Jim was inclined to agree. As kids, he and Rosemary had picked up the odd swear word from the kitchen and quarters, but he had heard few men as profane as the Gaunt youngsters. Their mother was unable to control them and her husband did little beyond threaten his sons. Paula seemed permanently tired, and judging by the swell of her apron was pregnant again. Jim felt sorry for her but was glad of the kitchen that kept him free of their bickering and domestic upsets. It was no wonder the boss spent so much of his time out on the run. On the other hand, if he stayed home occasionally or did something about the boys, perhaps his wife might nag less.

Observing the Gaunts, it occurred to Jim what a singular marriage his parents' had been. He had not met another couple as close or as happy as he remembered them being, or a couple so much in tune with each other's needs and moods. Rob and Mary were . . . companionable. That was the word that came to mind. But there was nothing of the incandescent force that had been so visible between Sandy and Jenny. When she died it was as if a fire had gone out in Sandy. Jim could still recall the light in his father's eyes as they rested on Jenny, and suddenly he understood what a burden life must have become for him once she was gone.

He shifted uncomfortably. He preferred not to find a justification for Sandy's behaviour, for at the back of his mind was the fear that to understand might mean to condone – and that was something he would never do.

SIXTEEN

In the winter of that year, the last of the decade, Paula Gaunt's sister arrived at Ralston Hills. She was driven out to the station by her brother-in-law, who left her standing with her suitcase while he put the ute in the shed. Riding up from the horse yards on a skittish colt, Jim saw Paula come out onto the verandah, one hand up to shade her gaze, the other pressed into the curve of her lower back from which the swell of her body depended. He heard her faint, glad cry and watched curiously as she hurried clumsily to the steps while her sister ran to embrace her. Then his horse snorted and propped, limbs trembling nervously at the appearance of a tractor, reclaiming his attention for the job at hand.

Later he bumped into her – quite literally – in what passed for the garden, a couple of straggly oleander bushes and a poorly kept lawn. He was walking back from the kitchen after the evening meal when she knocked into him from one side. Startled, he took a step back.

'Sorry, wasn't watching where I was going,' she said. 'I was too busy looking at the stars. I've never seen anything like them before.' She had a pleasant voice but it was too dark to see her face.

'Haven't you?' Automatically his gaze lifted to sweep the familiar sky. 'I saw you earlier. I'm Jim McAllister, by the way. I work here.'

'Yes, I know. Paula told me. I'm her sister, Ruth Petlow. And you're the jackeroo?' There was a faint upward inflection to her last words.

'That's right, Miss Petlow.' He hesitated as a thought struck him. 'Or is it Mrs?'

Her laughter was warm and bubbly in the night. 'Miss is correct, but please, call me Ruth. Paula says everything is very informal out here.' She had turned her head and was studying the sky again. 'I didn't know there were so many – that it was so big. You never see anything like this in Melbourne. Which is the Southern Cross?'

He showed her, pointing his arm above the dim shape of her shoulder. She was about medium height, a little taller than Ro, and her hair gave off a faint, pleasant scent. Or perhaps it was her talcum powder. He shifted his feet, edging discreetly back from her, conscious that he'd gone from the day's work to the kitchen and had yet to shower. Between the cow shit on his boots and the dried blood staining his jeans he must stink like something a dog had dragged home.

'How long are you staying?' His words came out awkwardly. What in daylight would be a courteous question seemed somehow imbued with significance in the dark. He could almost see the words hanging there in front of him in letters of fire. She must be wondering what business it was of his. 'I mean . . .'

'Just a few days to give Paula a break. A sort of holiday for me too. Although,' she added lightly, 'I'm not so sure of that with my nephews around. I've just got a teaching post in Katherine,' she explained. 'Been there a term. It's show holiday and Queen's Birthday all on the one weekend. It seemed too good an opportunity to miss. At least it did. I've already had a sleepy lizard in my bed.'

'That'll be young Jack, no doubt. Well, if you need a stockwhip at any time,' he offered, and she laughed.

'It might come to that. I'll let you know.'

'Well,' he said again. He lifted his hat, then realised the gesture was wasted in the dark. 'I'm overdue for a shower so I'll leave you to it. I expect I'll see you around.'

'Yes. Goodnight, Jim.'

'Goodnight,' he said. 'Ruth.'

Next morning Lester, the camp cook, was drunk. 'Passed out cold,' Harry informed the kitchen. 'Jeez, I thought he was dead. Seen his boots sticking out the door and went in to check. Cranky old bugger's had a heart attack, I tells meself. Bet on it. But he ain't – been at the metho by the smell of him.'

'Useless bloody bookie left the store unlocked again, I'd say,' Buck growled. 'Unless . . .' He looked accusingly at Linda.

'He got nothin' from me,' the big woman declared. 'I don't keep more than a cupful to light the primus. And that's in my room.'

'He's finished,' Buck said. 'Tell him I said so when he comes round. He can catch the first ride out of here.' Jim opened his mouth and he narrowed his eyes. 'Something worrying you about that?'

'No. It's just I was thinking of slipping into town myself on Sunday. I could give him a lift.'

'Not Sunday you won't. We'll be bringing the Six Mile cattle back then.' Buck's voice was rich with satisfaction. 'Only place you'll be going, sonny, is out to the camp.'

Benjy, the young ringer sitting beside Jim, whacked his shoulder as he got up. 'Nice try, mate. Wouldn't mind a day in town meself.'

Jim stood. 'It'd beat shoeing horses, anyway.' He carried his mug and plate to the sink then headed down to the horse yard, where a fresh working plant waited to be drafted and shod for the second round of mustering.

It was hard work shoeing, especially with fresh horses that pulled away and kicked, or danced at the end of their reins. Jim collar-roped the worst of his to get at their hind feet while Benjy, scarlet-faced with exertion, clung grimly to the bent front leg of a chestnut mare, getting in quick whacks at the nails between her staggering hops as she dragged him around the yard.

'Bitch!' he swore when his hat was knocked off and an unclinched nail ripped clean through the leg of his jeans. He let her foot go and straightened up with a groan of relief, saying hopefully, 'You wanna finish this one, Jim?'

'Like I haven't got enough of my own?' Jim plucked the last nail from his pursed lips and positioned it in the hole. 'Use a rope. At least it stops 'em leaning on you.'

'A bit less belly-aching and a bit more effort, that's what you need.' Buck was leading his own fully-shod roan across when his eye was caught by something across the yard. He didn't see the mare startle or the kick that caught him full on the side of the thigh. The roan snorted and plunged sideways, ripping the reins out of Buck's hands. Benjy said, 'Jeez!' in a tone of wonder and started towards the fallen man.

Jim was already there, extending a hand to help him up. 'You right, Buck? Where'd she get you?'

'Course I'm bloody right!' But Buck's face had gone a dirty grey and he was slow in getting up. He limped across to the rails, where he clung, head down between hunched shoulders, breathing heavily.

'I'll bring a vehicle,' Jim said. 'We'll get you back to the quarters.'

Buck glared out of the cheesy pallor of his face, which was shiny with sweat. 'If I wanna go to the quarters I'll get there meself.'

'I'll bring it anyway.'

Buck had got through the rails when Jim returned but had sunk to the ground, his leg out straight before him. He let himself be helped without further protestation into the cab of the land rover. Benjy sprang up behind and Jim drove slowly, trying to minimise the bumps. When they had Buck on his bed back in the quarters, breathing like a broken-winded horse and still the same alarming colour, Jim said, 'You need some codeine or something. Shall I get the missus to come down and have a look?'

'Her? Fat lot of good she'd be,' Buck grunted. 'You can tell the boss if you want.'

'Right.' It had to be pretty bad, then. Jim turned to leave, only to be stopped by Buck's grating voice. 'See you get the bridle off that roan. And the shoeing finished. And don't go letting anyone knock the horses about neither.'

'I'll see to it, Buck.' Jim kept the surprise from his voice. Being left in charge was the last thing he'd expected, and hearing the sudden gasp of pain behind him as Buck shifted on the bed he wondered if the kick had affected his brain.

Kevin Gaunt was in the bookkeeper's office. Jim passed on the news, adding, 'I dunno if the leg's broken. He was walking on it but it looks pretty painful. I reckon it needs checking.'

'Righto.' Kevin stood up. 'I'll have a word with him and call the doctor – he'll probably want him in town. Just carry on with whatever you're doing, Jim.' He glanced at the wall clock. 'They'll be on air with the next list in ten minutes. I'd better go down there and get some details off the old bugger.'

Back in the office, Kevin radioed the Katherine base station and reported the medical, all other radio traffic halted while the flying doctor weighed the description of Buck's injury. Some thirty minutes later, Jim glanced up from the shoe he was shaping to see the station vehicle pull up at the quarters. He dropped the hammer, sprang over the yard rails and walked across.

Kevin helped Buck struggle down the steps. Grey-faced and gasping, the head stockman hung over the bonnet while the door was opened for him, then inched carefully into the seat. Jim caught up Buck's swag and dumped it in the back.

'What did the doc say, boss?'

'He wants an X-ray. Could be a crack in the bone but he doesn't think it's broken. Probably major tissue damage. He can't pick him up because the plane's already been called out for a kid with suspected appendicitis, so I'm running him into town.'

'Right. Well, best of luck, mate.'

Buck eyed him coldly. 'Just see you get that shoeing finished.'

Jim returned early from work that evening to shower and shave in the primitive bathroom beneath the tank stand. He dumped his dirty clothes under his bed and went round to the cane chairs on the side verandah. Here he could look out over the garden, which, he noticed, was dusty no longer – the sprinklers had been running all day on the lawn and the result was already visible in a freshening of the grass. A step sounded on the boards behind him and he stood watching Ruth approach, thinking that she looked very much like her voice – pleasant and warm and rounded. She had brown hair cut in a fringe across her forehead, wide cheekbones and arresting dark eyes. When she stood smiling beside him, he saw a dusting of freckles across her nose.

'Ruth.' He patted the back of a cane chair. 'Are you busy? Can you spare a minute?'

'Hello, Jim.' Her gaze was frank and friendly. 'Of course. The boys are in the bathroom. That'll occupy them for a while.' She sat down and gazed out beyond the garden at the vista of purpling range and shadowed scrub, smiling at the wild cries of the black cockies winging to roost. She drew a long breath. 'It's such fascinating country.'

'So you're from Melbourne?'

'Yes. I applied for a posting in Katherine because I wanted to see this part of the world, and because Paula was here. What about you?'

'Oh, I'm a Territorian, born and bred.' But he didn't want to talk about himself. 'I was wondering if there'd been anything on the wireless about Buck? That was a nasty smack he took.'

Ruth shook her head. 'Not yet. Paula said there'll probably be a message in the morning. Kevin won't be home before tomorrow evening at the earliest, Paula thinks, because he has to hire someone?' She finished on a questioning note.

'Another poisoner. Sorry, camp cook. The last one was sacked.'

'That extraordinary man who swears so much? He went with Kevin too.'

'That's him. As for his language, I figure he learned it off the kids.' Jim grinned. 'How's the monster-taming coming on?'

She laughed. 'It will take a while. You know, I envy you working out here – it's such a vibrant, different life. But I haven't seen anything yet. Paula hates it,' she finished.

'Not everyone's suited. Particularly not every woman,' Jim said. 'My cousin Ro, for instance —' The clangour of the bell cut in and he stood up with regret. 'Excuse me, I have to go. There's only one rule that really counts on a station. You ignore it at your peril.'

'Oh, I see.' Her eyes danced. 'And what's that?'

'Never keep the cook waiting.' He picked up his hat. 'See you later, maybe?'

'Yes.'

It sounded like a promise. Thinking it so, he went whistling off to tea.

Next morning, Sunday, the wireless brought a message from Kevin, which Marty Grange, the bookkeeper, delivered to Jim as he sat on the verandah polishing his boots. Kevin had found another camp cook and would be returning with him that evening. In the meantime Jim needn't worry about the cattle at Six Mile but should check the level of the tank at Mary-Ann bore and if necessary start the diesel there. Jim's heart rose as he read the message. It couldn't have suited him better. 'Consider it done,' he told the bookkeeper cheerfully. 'I'll just have to see the missus first.'

Paula was not so pleased to see him. Holding the screen door against her she said snappily, 'Yes? What did you want?' She viewed the men with suspicion and was not popular in the kitchen. Marty alone escaped what Jim mentally dubbed her lady-of-the-manor act.

'Morning.' He touched his hat. 'I was wondering if Ruth was around.'

'Well . . .' Her tone was reluctant. 'I don't think so. Why?'

'I'd like to speak to her. If she's not busy.'

She stared at him, a hint of animosity in her gaze, and Jim saw that she wanted to deny his request. 'If you could just check,' he suggested, then stood waiting as she shut the door in his face and vanished inside. He heard a quick, low exchange and then Ruth, her colour a little heightened, came smiling out to greet him.

'Good morning, Jim. Another lovely day.'

'It's that all right.' He turned his hat in his hands, unsure all of a sudden if he was taking too much for granted and about to make a fool of himself. 'I have to run out to one of the bores.' The words came out more abruptly than he intended. 'You mentioned you haven't seen much of the place, so . . . Well, I wondered if you'd like to come with me.'

Her face lit up. 'That would be wonderful.'

Her answer came so spontaneously that he found himself smiling back, unaware that Paula stood in the doorway behind them, lips pressed together in disapproval.

'Get your hat then and I'll bring the rover round. Okay?'

'Okay.'

He crossed the verandah, boot heels loud on the boards, sprang down the steps and strode off whistling.

Mary-Ann bore was in ridgy country west of the homestead. Jim drove slowly, pulling up to let Ruth examine whatever took her eye – anthills scattered like frozen life forms through the scrub; the pattern of spinifex rings across a ridge; a white calf, ears spread and tail high, fleeing before them down the track. She laughed, clapping her hands like a child, then cried in quick concern, 'Oh, don't chase it too far. What if it loses its mother?'

'It won't.' Nevertheless he stopped, then pointed through the windscreen. 'Look there. Eagle – a big wedge-tail.'

'Oh, yes.' Ruth stared upwards, her lifted face exposing the lovely line of her throat. Jim stared and felt his ears redden when she swung suddenly to look at him. 'How do you manage to notice everything? I mean, you're doing the driving and I didn't see the eagle, or the roos back there, until you showed me.'

'Just habit. You get used to looking. There's the bore now.'

'Where?'

'Watch above the trees.' He pointed. 'There's a glint of silver – that's the mill sails turning. It's a couple of miles yet. And see, here on the road, see how the pads are getting deeper and more of them are coming in from the side? The stock make them walking in and out to drink.'

She smiled. 'So simple when you put it like that.'

The tank was down a sheet. He started the diesel and stood for a moment, listening critically to the *doem, doem* beat of it as the arms of the pump-jack rose and fell, lifting the mill rods. When the water was splashing into the tank he wiped his hands on the oily rag carried for the purpose, stuffed it away behind the seat, and went to stand beside Ruth in the shade of the tank.

'How would a cup of tea go down?'

'Very well, thank you. Don't tell me you brought a thermos?'

'No, but I've got a billy. I thought we might go on to a rock hole I know, about twelve miles from here. It's a nice spot for a picnic – if your sister isn't going to worry about how long you're gone.'

'Oh, she's doing that already,' Ruth said dryly. Catching his look, she shrugged. 'Well, she's not very happy, as I'm sure you've noticed. Paula's meant for city life. All this,' she waved a hand to encompass the arch of sky, range and grey-green scrub, 'frightens her. She needs people and bustle and traffic around her.'

'But you're different?'

'Oh, yes. I love this,' she cried with passion, then laughed self-deprecatingly. 'Listen to me. Two days and I know everything. The other night you said you had a cousin. Is she on a station too?'

'Maybe a railway station.' He held the door for her, then got back behind the wheel. 'Last I heard she was making for Greece – by way of Italy, I believe. With Ro you expect the unexpected. When we were little . . .' He talked as he drove, telling her about life at Kharko, and Mary's struggle to tame her daughter, and even about Jake, his pony, now long dead. Pulling up under the scrappy shade of a gum at the rock hole, he realised he'd talked the whole way.

'Sorry.' The ease he had felt a moment before while recalling Mason's exploits at Knolly suddenly deserted him. 'I don't usually run on like that. Talk about a tongue hinged in the middle. Sit in the shade while I get the fire going.'

Ruth linked her hands about one knee and leaned back on the flat rock she had chosen. Her face was dappled with shadow as she stared about her, eyes moving slowly from the narrow, sandy-bottomed pool in the creek bed to the red curve of ridge against the sky. The smoke curled blue between them as Jim set the billy on the fire and she sniffed appreciatively.

'Gum sticks.'

'Yes. We always burnt gum on our picnics. My mother —' He changed tack. 'But it's your turn now.'

She talked while he poured the tea and snapped a green stick to stir it with. Her parents were still living in Melbourne, where they ran a newsagency three blocks from the primary school she and her sister had attended. Paula had done an apprenticeship as a hairdresser while Ruth opted to train as a teacher. Biting into a piece of fruitcake Linda had provided, she broke off to say, 'Mmm, this is good. How did you come by it? Surely it's not standard equipment on bore runs?'

'Nope. Just the reward of staying on the right side of the cook.'

Her brown eyes twinkled at him. 'It's worth it.' She brushed crumbs from her skirt and sighed happily. 'It's all so different. I think I've said that a few times already, but it is. Paula and I have the wrong lives. She just wants to go home to Melbourne, but Kevin will never do that.'

'Bit hard for a cattleman to find work there,' Jim agreed. He squinted at the sun and got reluctantly to his feet. 'Time's getting on. We'd better go.'

The return trip ended all too soon. Jim dropped Ruth off at the garden gate and drove the vehicle into the shed. Having switched off the engine, he sat for a moment gathering his thoughts. This time, he resolved, he must do things properly. He would tell Ruth about Sandy at the first opportunity.

Kevin Gaunt returned in the splash of gold that was the setting sun, red dust writhing like a giant serpent behind him. Jim, coming back from the shower, dumped his dirty clothes and headed to the kitchen, where the rover had stopped. A stranger – the new camp cook, he supposed – limped behind Kevin, but there was no sign of Buck. He didn't know whether to be pleased or not. He assumed that Alf McKenzie, an able enough hand in his forties, would get the camp, although he was a bit too careless in his stock handling for Jim's taste. Say what you liked about Buck, he'd been bred in the same school as Des Hanks – they were cattlemen both from their boot soles up.

Kevin met him at the kitchen door. 'There you are, Jim.' He jerked his thumb at the newcomer. 'Holiday's over, I found you boys a cook. How was the bore?'

Jim scarcely heard him. The years had taken their toll on the man who was to be the new camp cook but there was no mistaking that hateful smirk. His hair was thinning and his body, well padded now with flab, was pitched permanently sideways from the damaged hip, but Roger Lawson, stepping forward with his hand out, was as unctuous as ever.

'Well, if it isn't young Jim.' He shook his head, marvelling. 'All grown up and dangerous to know, eh, Jimmy? Bet you give the girls a run for their money. Good to see you again, old mate.'

'I'm no mate of yours, Lawson.' Jim ignored the proffered hand and turned his back, earning a raised eyebrow from Kevin. He dredged through the fury in his head for the last thing Kevin had said to him. 'Oh, yeah, boss – Mary-Ann. It was down a sheet and a half. I started the diesel. There's a bit of a crack coming in the float. Saw it when I was checking the trough. It's right where it joins the stem – looks like something's given it a decent bump.'

'I'll look into it.' Kevin's gaze followed the newcomer, who having shrugged at Jim's rebuff was crabbing awkwardly up the steps to the kitchen. Then he looked at Jim. 'You've met before.' It was a statement, not a question. 'Something I should know about? Or is it personal?'

'He's a troublemaker,' Jim said bluntly. 'As bolshie as they come. I've seen him at work. He makes the bullets then gets somebody else to fire them. He was ringing on Kharko years back. That's where he got smashed up.' He drew a long breath through his nose, adding reluctantly, 'Of course that doesn't mean he can't cook.'

'Let's hope so. There's nobody else in town. So do you think you can work with him? If I give you the camp?' Kevin removed his hat to rub the itchy patch on his brow where the sweatband rested. 'Well?' he said as Jim just stood there. 'Can you handle it?'

'Me?' Jim asked as if his hearing were at fault. 'But I thought Alf McKenzie . . . ?'

'It calls for a bit more nous than Alf's got.'

'Yeah, but . . .' Jim got a grip on himself. 'I can handle it – and thanks. I appreciate the chance.'

'That's settled then.' Kevin rolled his shoulders to ease the stiffness there, his face hard and unreadable in the fading light. As he turned away, curiosity overcame Jim.

'Did you tell Buck you were gunna give it to me?'

'It was him suggested it,' Kevin said over his shoulder. 'I'll see you up at the house when I've had a feed and we'll plan your musters. If you stick to the way Buck did it you won't go far wrong.'

He was gone before Jim remembered that he hadn't asked how badly his predecessor was injured. But satisfaction at his promotion, however temporary it proved, ousted all other considerations. He stood for a moment, head raised and hands on hips, smiling at the faint prickle of stars becoming visible in the eastern sky. His thoughts darted like fish, gone as soon as glimpsed. Who would have thought the cross-grained Buck would recommend him for anything? He'd have laid odds the old bugger hated the very sight of him. It might only be for a few months, but head stockman! He would tell Ruth – in a fairly casual way, he decided. And Rob would be pleased. He'd find time before mail day to write home, maybe even drop a line to Mason.

A shout of laughter through the open kitchen door broke into his reverie and he felt the muscles of his face tighten. He'd almost forgotten Lawson, who by the sound of it was already worming his way into the fabric of station life. The man's presence was enough to spoil the sweetness of the night. He'd bet a quid he was at it right now, ingratiating himself before sowing dissension with his innocuous-seeming 'misunderstandings' and sly hints. And once he learned of Jim's promotion, Lawson would do his best to undermine him in the camp.

He tried to shake the thought, to recapture the triumph he'd tasted a moment before, but worry teased at him as he made his way back to the house. If a man as experienced as Des Hanks had been powerless before Lawson's malice, Jim could not imagine that he would fare any better.

The camp truck was loaded next morning, the black boys sent on their way with the horses, and the camp itself went out. Ruth, Jim was gratified to notice, watched from the verandah as they pulled away, her own bags packed beside her. They had spent the previous evening together, after Paula retired early with a headache, and a further hour before breakfast talking softly in the half-light on the verandah. He told her about his promotion, which she already knew of, having heard Kevin discussing it with Marty Grange, but she congratulated him warmly, looking pleased on his account.

'Chief stockman. Is it a big step, Jim?'

'Head,' he corrected. 'It's one of the stages of becoming a manager. Head stockman, overseer – it's all experience. Not all jackeroos run camps and not all head stockmen are jackeroos, quite the reverse. It's down to the company, really. Back at Knolly the manager was never a jackeroo. He went to the place as a head stockman and they eventually promoted him to manager. That was, I dunno, fifteen, maybe twenty years ago. It's not so common nowadays, working your way up from wood-and-water joey to boss, but he was a good manager for all that. Knew his cattle and his country inside out.'

'I see.' She caught his glance at the clock. 'I mustn't keep you. A scream of rage came from one of the boys, piercing their eardrums. 'That'll be Jack. Well, good luck with it. Maybe I'll see you next time I visit?'

Jim's heart leapt. 'You'll be coming back then?'

'Oh, I hope so. I haven't been asked, but it's school holidays soon and the baby's due a few weeks later. She hasn't said so yet but I expect Paula will need a hand with things here. If she does I'll come.'

'I'm glad.' He touched his hat and left, smiling at her answer. A flush of gratification warmed his cheeks. They had only met three days ago but she might have been the first girl he'd ever seen – her existence as great a marvel as the clear-edged morning, or the parabolic flight of the rainbow bird snatching insects from the air above the meat house.

Whistling, he swung into the truck – and found Lawson already there, his body screwed sideways in the passenger seat to favour his bad leg. He winked at Jim.

'Making up to the big house sheila, eh? Smart young fella like you could do worse.'

It was like seeing a dirty rag smeared over something precious. Jim felt the anger leap in him and his words came sharp and cold. 'Do your work and keep your trap shut, Lawson. Because if you don't, cripple or not, I'll shut it for you. I'm not a kid now. You got that straight?'

'Hey, there's no call for that.' Lawson's face sagged into exaggerated lines of hurt. 'Honest to God, Jim. I'm making allowances but still. I mean, new at the job and all, you got no call coming the boss over me. Not when a man's only trying be pleasant.' Injured innocence coated his words but did nothing to hide the flash of malice Jim glimpsed in his fleshy eyes.

'Shut,' he reiterated, and trod on the starter as if it were Lawson's face.

It was the pattern of days to come. If Jim had hoped the man would not know his job or be unable to sustain the pace – particularly when it came to packhorsing it once they abandoned the truck and rode to the campsites – he was disappointed. Lawson was an unexpectedly good cook and he made excellent bread; even Jim looked forward to his sweet yeast buns. Within two days of going out, Benjy was good-naturedly helping Lawson with the heavier tasks, packing up and carting firewood, and when Jim, goaded by the look of complacency

276

on the cook's face as he watched the youngster toss swags onto the load, told Benjy to get on with his own work it was Benjy and not Lawson who protested.

'Hey, can't a bloke lend a hand?' He threw the last swag up and glanced across at the horse camp. 'They aren't ready yet, so nobody's waiting on me.'

'Getting wood and packing up is Lawson's job, not yours.' Jim sounded petty, he knew, but that was the effect the cook had on him. Somehow Lawson always managed to wrong-foot him. And it didn't help that he knew his reaction was the very thing Lawson desired. The bastard didn't need help loading up, he thought in a fury. He just wanted to make Jim try to stop it, to set the others wondering why the boss had it in for a man with a gimpy leg doing his best for the lot of them. But by not asserting his authority, Jim knew he would lose control of the camp. Lawson's poisonous tongue would succeed in turning them against each other, until they were fighting or quitting on him or both.

As it was, Benjy gave him a troubled look as they rode out. 'What you got against Roger anyhow, Jim?' he burst out. 'I reckon that's a bit unfair, chipping a bloke for lending a hand. And him with a bad leg and all. Can't be his fault he's crippled, can it?'

'You don't think so?' Jim's eyes pinched down in a manner that those who knew Rob McAllister would have recognised. 'If he hadn't been trying to do a good man down he wouldn't be crippled, so don't expect any sympathy from me for the bastard. You'd be better off steering well clear of him.'

Benjy glared, affronted by Jim's manner. 'You reckon? Well, I'll make up me own mind about that.' His eyes sparked and his colour was high as he yanked his mare sideways and turned her to join the gaggle of black boys riding at the rear.

Jim ground his teeth. It was as if Lawson, far back with the packhorses on a quiet mare, rode smirking beside him. He wished passionately that old Bluebell would shove both feet in a hole and fall, breaking Lawson's other leg. Jim's mount stumbled, forcing his attention back to the job and the faint smudge in the distance that he knew would be cattle feeding into the scrub.

But Bluebell kept her feet and Lawson proved as adept with the billies and Bedourie ovens of the pack camp as he had with the more commodious equipment carried on the truck. There was no doubt his injury pained him, but though he resorted frequently to the papers of Bex powders he kept tucked into his hat band, he made no complaint. Not, Jim thought sourly, that he needed to with Benjy falling over himself to help. But he let things be, knowing that his initial interference had succeeded only in driving the two together.

Lawson, for the most part, kept his nose clean, although Jim knew without having any way of proving it that at least two vexatious incidents – a set of sliprails knocked out of their slots, resulting in the loss of a yarding of cattle, and the smashing of his personal saddle – were down to the cook. It was possible, but unlikely, that Jim's grey gelding had bolted from the tree he was tied to; the greater likelihood was that he'd had a whip laid over him. But about the yard there could be no mistake. Jim had slotted those rails home himself, and only hands had lifted them out again.

Lawson was apologetic about the escape of Jim's horse, which was recaptured later that day. 'I seen him go,' he admitted, shaking his head at his inability to catch the animal. 'Done me best cos I knew it was your saddle, see? I mean, the station can afford it, but it's a bit different for us working men. Any rate, I'm knocking me bread down and I hear this racket and seen him go.' He slapped his lame leg. 'A man's a bit handicapped when it comes to sprinting. I tell you, I've backed faster horses and still done me dough, eh boys?' The men laughed.

Jim seethed quietly. He was lucky, he supposed, to have got the big grey back. It was unfenced country and a certain number of working horses inevitably wound up with the brumbies, but it was mostly carelessness that got them there. The gelding had either fallen on the saddle or hit a tree with it in flight, for the nearside knee-pad hung by a flap. The saddle pouch, and the dee rings it depended from, were missing, and Jim could feel that the cantle was cracked. The saddle would have to be stripped and rebuilt.

The following week, Benjy had a fall when the mare he was riding turned turtle in a dry swamp bed. Jim saw the heifer Benjy had been chasing burst out of a tangle of brush and rust-coloured grass and he swung his own mount to intercept it. It was only when he'd turned the beast that he saw Benjy and his horse limping into the open, Benjy favouring his right leg and the mare her near shoulder.

'You right?' he called, cantering over.

'Yeah.' There was dirt on Benjy's hat. He lifted and settled it, wincing at the movement. 'Bitch of a thing went arse over tit. Shied at something in the grass and next thing I'm flying.'

'Well, she won't carry you far now, by the look of that leg,' Jim said. 'Better get her back to camp. Catch something else and wait for us there.'

He cantered back to the receding mob, thankful Benjy hadn't been hurt. Falls were common, and commonly disregarded, but there was always the chance of real injury. This time the mare had taken the brunt of it.

She was still lame when they arrived back at the station some ten days later. Jim had the black boys drop her off in the paddock on their way in while the rest of them rode back in the truck. They pulled up with a certain flourish before the quarters. Instantly, it seemed, the two Gaunt boys were there yelling vociferously above the engine. One of the ringers swore wholeheartedly at the welcome.

'Not them little buggers again.'

Jim grinned, but not at the remark. He'd caught a glimpse of sky-blue skirt on the verandah and a shape that did not belong to Paula. It was only a little after ten in the morning, so if the boys were out of school then the holidays had begun and the woman must be Ruth. The nagging worry of Lawson and the crippled mare vanished as he jumped from the cab. He marvelled at how, in such a short space of time and without knowing her feelings, or for that matter anything much about her, she had become necessary to him, as the sun was necessary, and sleep, and the harsh beauty of the land about him. He wondered if his father had felt the same blinding moment of recognition when he first saw ex-nursing sister Jennifer Grantly coming through the peas towards him with the smoko billy in her hand.

'Right, you bludgers,' he called cheerfully. 'Grab your gear or you'll be carting it back from the shed. Benjy, you'd better see to the knives and I'll let Linda know we're killing tonight.'

Kevin's land rover was in the shed, which meant he'd be round the place somewhere – probably in the office, Jim thought. He garaged the truck, hoisted his swag onto his shoulder and tramped up to the house, eyes searching the side and front verandahs for sight of Ruth. She wasn't there, but before his disappointment could register he glimpsed her in the garden, crouched beside a row of pots. She saw him at the same moment and stood up, dusting soil from her hands, a smile breaking on her face.

'Jim. How nice to see you again. How's the new job?'

'Hello, Ruth.' She was as lovely as he remembered, hatless, and slender in blue, the sun glinting on the fine hairs of her forearms. 'Pretty good. And you? What's this – planting a new garden?'

She laughed ruefully. 'I doubt it will survive the boys, but the place is so bare. I thought a few shrubs along the wall here, perhaps a flower-bed. I brought some cuttings out with me. Easy-care stuff Paula could see to. We always had flowers at home.'

'Well, if you want any digging done while I'm here.'

'Would you?' Her face lit up. 'That would be marvellous, Jim. The ground's hard. I was going to ask Kevin, but I don't think . . .'

'Me either.' Station gardens were the cowboy's province, together with butchering and the woodheap, but the best that Ralston Hills could boast in that department was an old blackfella who chopped the wood for the kitchen stove. With a jolt Jim remembered he hadn't told Linda there'd be fresh meat that evening. 'Look, I'd better go. It's Sunday tomorrow, I'll give you a hand with the garden then – if the boss hasn't figured things otherwise. I'll see you later.'

He carried the memory of her smile as he ran up the steps and dumped his swag in the latticed corner of the verandah. He made straight for the kitchen, aware that the smoko bell had rung a little while before. The men were all there about the table, listening, he realised as he entered the room, to Roger Lawson holding forth to an audience of Matthew, Harry and Linda on the recent muster.

'Course you gotta put in the time before you can run a camp. Stands to reason. But these company johnnies, they'd promote anybody. Well, he's cluey enough, Jim – for his age. But you and me,' he looked across at Alf McKenzie, the senior stockman there, 'both know it's experience what counts. What've we had this time out? A yarding of cattle lost, horse loose with a saddle, another one crippled. What I'm saying is he's a fair enough ringer, young Jim, but the job needs an older head.'

'Yours, for instance?' Jim said witheringly, and the men's faces jerked guiltily around to his. 'I don't recall you were much good at stopping horses coming down yourself. But try your luck if you like.' He helped himself to tea and stood sipping it, ignoring the others. 'Linda, I came to tell you we're killing tonight – unless the new manager here decides otherwise.'

'No cause for that.' Lawson sounded reproachful as he looked around the table. 'Dead ringer for his uncle, our Jim,' he confided sagely and clicked his tongue. 'Old Rob never had much humour neither. A man had to tread a pretty fine line on Kharko, I'm telling you.'

'Only what you'd expect on them big places.' Alf nodded agreement and the men's interest picked up again, leaving Jim to shake his head and wonder how Lawson did it.

They brought the freshly killed meat in at dusk, stacking the corn cuts on the salt tray and hanging the rest to cool in the screened meat house. Jim washed for tea with the others, lathering the grease and blood from his hands, then sat down to a huge mixed grill of rib bones, liver, milk gut and sweetbreads, the traditional fare on killing nights. Afterwards he shaved and showered carefully, and in clean jeans and shirt trod with a slight quickening of his senses along the verandah to where Ruth sat, her hair shining in the light of the bare bulb above her.

Kevin Gaunt and his wife were also there, together with Marty Grange, who was holding a newspaper to the light as he read. Older than Kevin, Marty was tall with thinning hair and a closely trimmed moustache. His past was a mystery he never spoke of. Jim had a vague idea he'd been an accountant in another life, but not from anything Marty himself had said. A city man of his obvious education in a backwater like Ralston Hills usually meant an escape from something – debt, drink or a maintenance order, perhaps. It was something you learned not to ask. There were many reasons a man took to the bush, and a lot of the men had a past to bury.

Jim took the only spare chair, which was beside Paula, who was sitting back with her feet propped up, looking sallow and unwell in the artificial light. Her body had ballooned in the past few weeks and fleetingly he wondered if she was carrying twins. He looked across at Ruth and felt torn between pleasure at the sight of her and the nagging need to tell her about Sandy before she heard it from someone else. The longer he left it, the more it would look like he was attempting to conceal the truth. Not that telling her would necessarily help – it could well have the opposite effect.

Then again, perhaps it would be different with Ruth. She *was* different to other girls he'd known. He had already imbued her with all the virtues, tolerance among them.

Kevin and Marty were discussing the weather and Jim spoke under the cover of their voices. 'I'm glad you're back. How long have you got?'

'Another week. Kevin's been showing me a bit of the station. He was going to take me out to see the branding on Wednesday but something came up.' Her tone was slightly reproachful.

Paula, who had overheard, said sharply, 'You haven't missed anything, believe me. I went once. It's filthy work – the dust, and the smell of burning hair. It was horrible.'

'I'd have found it interesting,' Ruth said mildly. 'I'm sure some women must.'

'That reminds me.' Marty broke off to reach into his pocket, from which he extracted a folded paper. 'Speaking of women, there's a wire for you, Jim. I picked it up this arvo.'

'For me?' Jim straightened in his seat and took the message. It could only be from Kharko. His stomach felt suddenly hollow. He heard his cousin's voice, faint and tinny on the phone – *Look out for the parents for me* – but as his eyes skimmed the telegram it was his jaw that dropped, not his heart.

'Good grief!' He read Marty's neat capitals again, noting that the message had originated in some unpronounceable place in Greece. 'HAVE SAID I DO STOP HIS NAME IS KEN STOP WISH ME HAPPY COMMA PHOTO FOLLOWING STOP.' Beneath it was the signature: 'RO (GILBERT).'

Ruth was watching him. She said, 'Not trouble at home?'

'It's my cousin Rosemary. She got married.' He stared blankly at her, his astonishment complete. 'In Greece. To somebody I've never heard of. Her father will have a fit.'

'She's married a Greek?' Paula looked dumbfounded.

Ruth cut in sharply. 'Why shouldn't she? As long as they're happy – and I'm sure they will be. From what Jim's told me of her, she sounds like she knows what she wants.'

'And generally gets it.' He smiled, suddenly delighted at the thought of Ro dodging the fuss of orange blossoms and veils, which she would hate, by marrying beyond the reach of her family. Perhaps she did it in sandals and a cotton dress, he thought, given that it would be summer over there now, with a few flowers in her copper hair. He'd read about weddings like that. 'I don't think he can be a Greek, Mrs Gaunt. Not with a name like Gilbert. Well!' He smiled again. 'Good on her. She always beat me to everything when we were kids. I'll write a reply – if you could get it off for me Monday, Marty?'

'Righto.' The bookkeeper heaved himself to his feet, patting a yawn. 'Well, I'm off. Goodnight, all.'

Jim rose too, not to leave but to take the vacated chair next to Ruth. She welcomed him with a smile, but despite his fervent wish that Paula would also retire it didn't happen. The talk turned to places they'd seen, books they'd read, and what turned out to be a shared preference for Scrabble over other board games.

'Ro's brother, Oliver, taught me to play,' Jim said. 'He was a great reader even as a kid, and he'd make these words I'd never heard of. I don't think I ever won a game against him but I got to like it.' He was speaking only to her now. 'You'd like Olly – everybody does. He's over at Windamere now and I've been meaning to get across to visit.' A happy thought struck him. 'If you want to see a bit more of the country you could come too. He's married,' he added. 'They've got the overseer's cottage, so there'd be somewhere for you to stay and it's less than a day's drive. Do it in a weekend, easy.'

'It sounds fun. I'd enjoy that, especially meeting his wife. How long have they been married?'

He thought for a moment. 'Must be about six months now.'

'Still a bride, then. What's she like? I mean, what sort of person is she?'

'Hard to say.' Jim lifted his shoulders. 'I only met her the once.'

'Well, isn't that enough? You must have formed some opinion. Is she like Ro, for instance?'

He gave a snort of laughter. 'Believe me, Ruth, nobody's like Ro. And a good thing too. You'll see what I mean when you meet her.'

And it wasn't until later, when he was lying in bed watching the moonshadows of the latticework striping the floorboards and playing the evening over in his head, that he realised Ruth had not contradicted that *when*. He thought of Rosemary herself then and hoped she had chosen wisely and would be happy. And he wished suddenly that he could tell her about Ruth.

When he eventually fell asleep it was with a head full of memories of his cousin glowering at him across the school desk, shoving him out of the pepper tree, racing him up the mill. But it was of Ruth that he dreamed.

After breakfast next morning, with the sun on the tree line and the air like cold needles against his face, Jim walked to an open stretch of ground behind the house and shook out the wet hide of the beast they had killed. He pegged it flat, and beginning in the centre cut it into a thin, continuous strip for rope-making. He worked contentedly, despite his numbed fingers, for Ruth, cheery in a red woollen jumper, kept him company. Perched on a convenient log, she listened to him explain what he was doing and why.

It was the perfect opportunity to tell her about Sandy. He knew it, but his mind shied away from the task and he decided to put it off until the rope was finished. He would choose a better, a more private, place. Anybody – the boss or one of the men – might wander over to watch his knifework or pass a comment on the hide. They were in full view of the station if the station cared to look and it would be wiser, Jim decided, to leave it until he wasn't squatting on a greasy hide or in danger of interruption.

Ruth's voice broke into his thoughts. 'You work very hard out here.' She rubbed her fingers briskly and tucked them into her armpits for warmth. 'Didn't Kevin say you were all having the day off? Listen, there's somebody else working too.' She turned her head as a whip cracked sharply beyond the house.

'The hide won't keep. Station work's like that. The job's finished when it's finished, not when it's five o'clock or Saturday night.' A faint shout overrode his last words and the whip cracked twice again in quick succession, bringing him to his feet. 'That sounds more like a rifle than a stockwhip.'

Ruth's bright colour paled suddenly. 'Oh, my God!' She leapt to her feet. 'That devil Jack was playing with a gun this morning. I took it off him . . .'

She was running before Jim could snap his knife shut. He dropped it on the hide, yelling, 'Ruth! Wait!' When she paid no heed he legged it after her. He overtook her at the garden fence, hurdling it without pause to dash past the dusty oleanders and find the narrow pedestrian gate. The sheds now lay before him, and the fuel dump, but the shots were coming from across the track to the right, where the empty fuel drums, as well as the two currently in use – one of household kerosene, the other of petrol – stood in the old hen house.

He could see the rifleman now, and it was not young Jack but a man with an unbalanced body taking aim at the drums.

'Lawson, you idiot!' he roared. Then the rifle crack sounded again and the hen house seemed to open sideways to make room for a blossom of scarlet and yellow. The blast shook his ears and he was knocked off his feet, his face slamming hard into the ground. There was dust and flying debris all around and he wondered frantically where Ruth was. He pulled himself to his feet and then saw her standing, frozen, halfway through the gate.

His hat lay a few yards away; he snatched it up, yelping as a shard of burning timber touched his hand. Blood trickled from a cut on his face and everywhere he looked there was fire – up the trees, across the paddock. He glanced around for Lawson and saw him climbing to his feet a short distance away. Now Ruth was running again, towards him. Her legs seemed to move in slow motion and her eyes had widened in horror, as if she couldn't comprehend what had happened.

'Get the men! Tell the boss!' he yelled at her, too shocked to realise that only a deaf man could be unaware of the disaster. There was a heavy smell of burning fuel and at the centre of where the hen house had stood was a blackened hole, in which bits of red-hot metal cooled to grey as he watched. The drums – even the empties – had been either torn apart or flattened in the explosion and now littered the paddock, setting fire to all they touched. Thank God it wasn't the full fuel dump, he thought, swinging to look, and the breath stopped in his body. The fire was there too, racing through the ring of short grass inside the cleared break where thirty or forty assorted drums of petrol, kerosene and diesel stood.

There was no time and not even a shovel to hand to stop it. Jim skipped across the flames, feeling the heat of them through his boots, and began shifting drums like a madman, wrestling them onto their sides and rolling them over the burning grass to the relative safety of the road beyond. Before he had the second one clear, Benjy was working beside him, then Alf and Matthew arrived, and Kevin, with a brow like thunder and curses to match.

'What the bloody hell happened here?'

'Lawson. Shooting into the fuel.' Movement distracted him and Jim saw Linda coming towards them as fast as her size allowed, a corn bag in one hand and a long-handled shovel over her shoulder. And he saw something else – flames licking the uprights supporting the shed roof. 'Christ!' he bawled into the fury around him. 'Boss, it's in the shed.'

'Get the vehicles out. Where the hell are the bloody blacks? Linda, take yourself over by the homestead and start shovelling a break. Ruth, get those sprinklers going – turn on every hose we've got. Where are the kids?'

'Here, Dad.' The two boys bobbed importantly behind him, trailing green branches almost as big as themselves.

'Well, clear out,' his father said furiously. 'Get home to your mother. And if I find you had a hand in this I'll have the skin off your arses.'

The vehicles were out. Alf was rolling tyres after them and Benjy, slopping water as he ran, was flying back from the trough with a four-gallon bucket in each hand. Water was the only certain way of extinguishing timber burning vertically, especially wood that was cracked and fissured by forty years of weather. Jim seized the second bucket and at last had time to pause and take stock. The paddock was still burning. Smoke hung like a blue fog below the canopies of the trees and the smell of it, pungent and alarming, coated his throat. Already the hawks had gathered above, planing down through the heat eddies after lizards and grasshoppers fleeing the flames.

'Well.' Sleeving sweat from his heavy features, Kevin surveyed the scene, face hardening as he gauged the spread of the fire. 'That'll take some stopping, but it's no use rushing off like blue-arsed flies and having it start again behind us. Harry, you stay here. Get the blade on the tractor and cut a decent break around the homestead and quarters.'

Linda was still shovelling, her shoulders rolling easily to the swing of the blade, and Kevin jerked his head in her direction. 'Tell her to knock off, Jim. She'd be better employed packing us lunch. Where's the stupid bastard responsible for this?'

Roger Lawson, who until now they had all forgotten, was a sorry sight. The blast had taken his eyebrows and half his hair, singeing one side of his face a bright scarlet that contrasted with the sooty streaks on the rest of it. His shirtsleeves hung in tatters and the skin of his arms and hands was blistered with superficial burns.

'It was a snake,' he whined. 'A brown. I was just trying to stop one of the kiddies being bitten. How did I know the fuel was gunna explode?'

'*Any* idiot would know better than to shoot up a bloody fuel dump,'

Kevin roared. 'What are you, a halfwit? Stone the bloody crows!' His face had reddened to the point where it seemed to radiate heat of its own. 'Go on,' he jerked his head in disgust, 'get over to the house and have the women fix you up. And pick up that rifle and clean it while you're at it.'

Lawson grimaced as he shuffled across and bent to retrieve the firearm, fumbling clumsily with his left hand. Looking for the sympathy vote, Jim thought cynically, but he would find little of that now. A fire at this time of year, with the feed tinder-dry and no rain to be expected before Christmas, was a serious matter, the more so because it would have to be fought by hand. There was no grader on Ralston Hills, and by the time they got a borrowed one there half the station would be burnt.

The rest of the men were already loading the land rover, tossing long-handled shovels, rakes, old feedbags and the water drum onto the back. There would be time while the drum was filling to pick up food from the kitchen, strap the waterbags onto their hangers, and retrieve his knife from where he'd dropped it on the hide. The rope was a washout now – and so too was his day with Ruth.

SEVENTEEN

It took the rest of the day and half the night to stop the fire. The flames powered across the grass country, trailing blackened ground behind them like a cloak, but it was when it reached the ridges where the spinifex grew that the fire really exploded. The wax of the plants forced the flames higher, driving the men back, and they stood helpless, gasping and scarlet-faced from the heat, as their enemy raced away through the silver-leaf box, igniting the low trees and bushes and doubling the ground it held.

Backburning was no good while the wind blew, but the moment it dropped Kevin drove ahead of the fire with Matthew, searching for a break in the fuel supply and finding it where a horse pad crossed a few hundred yards in front of the flames.

They lit it up, but as if through malice the wind immediately returned and the fire leapt effortlessly across their pitiful barrier and surged away again, driving the men before it.

'Lot of bloody use that was.' Alf got a lungful of smoke and bent double in a painful bout of coughing. The air was full of particles of burnt matter that marked their skins in streaks of soot. Ash danced in the heat eddies above them. Alf's eyes were streaming as Benjy tugged at him.

'Move, you silly bastard! You wanna fry?'

'No worse than choking to death.' But he shambled clear of the fire's path, still hacking as if he meant to cough his lungs up, while the rest of them resumed their attack with shovels and branches and the long wearying day drew on.

Dusk came prematurely, the sun vanishing into the smoke then slipping from sight altogether. The wind had stilled. The dense, fire-born cloud, in shades of dirty yellow to black, hung stationary in the darkening air with the wide red glow of the fire beneath. The air stank of smoke and ash and was filled with the crackle of flames – a sort of crunching sound, Jim thought, now that the wind had quietened and the pace of the fire moderated. They worked doggedly on in the cooler air, mopping up little islands of flame outside the main fire, shovelling dirt over the smouldering trunks of fallen trees.

At full dark they were ten miles out, working on a spreading front. Kevin Gaunt returned to the station in the rover to pick up the camp truck, the tuckerbox, and their swags, but it was Harry who returned some two hours later, headlights boring holes though the darkness and lighting up blue curls of smoke rising from the blackened ground. The fire was burning back on itself by then, the far-flung perimeter having been turned towards its centre, giving them time to stop for a meal. Harry slapped the billy up against a burning stump, then laid out bread and cold meat and a large brownie richly speckled with fruit.

'Get into it, fellas,' he said. 'I ain't in the market for fancy meals.'

'It'll do me.' Benjy wiped an arm across his sweaty, soot-stained face. 'There was a big old goanna shot out of a hollow back there. If he'd been a bit slower I'da had him for dinner. My belly's been complainin' for the last hour.'

Jim took a swig of black tea and sighed with satisfaction. 'The boss coming back? What's he doing?'

'Oh, yeah.' Harry scratched his head vigorously before replacing his hat. 'I was just getting to that. He's took the missus into Katherine. She had pains. He seemed to think she was gunna drop the kid and he didn't wanna risk waiting till daylight for the doctor's plane. The young lady went with her to look after the boys. And your cook went too. Says his burns need a doctor's attention.' Harry sniffed. 'Bloody maniac. You ask me it's his head wants the attention. Anyway, the boss said to tell you he'd be back tomorrer.'

'Right.' Jim was disappointed to learn that Ruth had left, but it was understandable that Paula would want her sister with her. And that meant taking the boys too. With Harry joining them on the front, that left only Linda and Marty at the homestead, and he couldn't see either of them volunteering as babysitter. He hoped the Gaunts made it to Katherine before the baby came; it was a long drive.

'Okay,' Jim said, one eye on the glow of the fire, 'let's make sure we've got it out by the time he's back.'

At midnight the country lay dark under the moon, save for intermittent pillars of fire where standing trees still burned. The weary men traipsed back to the truck and fell into their swags, rising again with a little daylight wind and turning anxious eyes to a sky that showed only blue.

'Well, thank Chris' for that.' Alf held his back and stretched gingerly. 'Me feet'll never move again. I musta done fifty miles yesterday and last night.'

'Yeah, well, credit where it's due,' Jim said. 'While you're feeling sorry for yourself, don't forget Linda.' According to Harry's account, the station cook had rousted half a dozen blacks out of their camp and, shovelling beside them, had held the station end of the blaze until Harry got the tractor blade around it. 'Wasn't for her, we might be starting again this morning.'

'Wonder how the missus is doing – if she's had the kid yet.' Benjy stretched, his shoulders cracking.

'I'd sooner know who's gunna be doing the cooking from now on,' Alf grumbled. 'Man's been up half the night chasing fires, 'e wants a bit more than straight corn meat for breakfast.'

'Get it into you,' Jim said, 'and we'll go home and find out.'

The homestead drowsed quietly amid its oleanders and patch of lawn that now stood out vividly in the surrounding black. There was nothing left of the horse-paddock feed, Jim saw, and half the fence was burnt away. The horses themselves were hungry but unhurt. Stock seldom suffered in grass fires unless they got themselves pinned by the flames against a fence, or up a gully. Still, he'd have to move the animals out of the paddock today.

A glance at the vehicle shed showed the land rover still missing, which meant Kevin hadn't returned yet, something Marty verified when Jim reached the top step of the verandah and spun his hat onto the bullock horns mounted on the wall.

'You look like you've had a night of it.' The bookkeeper was sitting at a table outside the office, working at figures with the wireless running inside.

'Yeah.' Jim dropped into a chair and yawned. 'It's out, anyway. Any news?'

Marty jerked his head at the gabble of sound. 'Just waiting on the telegrams now. Thought there'd be something before this.'

'Well.' Jim stopped for another jaw-cracking yawn. 'Better tell him things are under control here. He mightn't quite see it that way, though, with the Six Mile burnt out and half the bronco yard gone as well. Not to mention the horse paddock – there isn't a strainer post left on the eastern side. Still,' he sighed, 'could've been worse. There was a moment there when I thought the sheds and the rest of the fuel was gone. I cannot *believe* what Lawson did.'

'Ah well, people make mistakes. It's nothing a couple of men and a good downpour won't fix,' the bookkeeper said tolerantly.

Jim stared at him, but let it pass. The rain was months away. Still, you couldn't expect a city bloke to have the outlook of a stockman. And he had a more immediate interest than Lawson's transgression. 'Nobody left any messages for me?'

'Not that I'm aware of.' A fleeting look of surprise, then Marty's brow cleared. 'Oh, what to do – well, I know which pub he stays at. I can send Kevin a wire if you want instructions.'

'I don't.' Jim got to his feet. 'We're taking the horses out to Pincher's Yard. The fence is down in their paddock and there's bugger all left to eat. We'll camp there and muster across to Mary Ann. Tell the boss, will you?'

He fitted his hat and clumped across the verandah. He'd hoped

Ruth might have left a note, but given the circumstances of her departure he wasn't too troubled that she hadn't. He'd see her next holidays, perhaps.

Weariness vanished at the thought of it, and he whistled as he strode over the flat to where three of the black boys were waiting with the horses in the corner of the ruined paddock.

It was a week before Jim saw Kevin Gaunt again and they were still at Pincher's. Kevin drove up to the yard, nudging the rover through the low scrub along the track, just as Jim was towing the last calf into the branding ramp. He flicked the head rope free and booted his mount towards the fence, coiling the greenhide as he went. Behind him the men swung their leg ropes, Alf wielded the ear-markers, and Benjy stooped to the fire. Then came the stink of burning hide as he applied the brand.

Jim nodded at Kevin across the rails. 'G'day, boss. How did it go – boy or girl?'

'Another boy.' Kevin lifted his hat to scratch his scalp, the rays of the westering sun full upon his florid features. 'We've called him Mark.'

'Congratulations. Missus okay?'

'She's fine, thanks.' He spoke shortly, his gaze on the cattle. 'Looks like a good yarding. I've seen that brindle cow at Mary-Ann, and that snaily-horn one there – a few of them must've shifted over since the fire.'

'Yeah. Noticed it myself. Have you seen the extent of the burn? The stock'll be doubling up on a few of the bores, I imagine. Still, might get early storms, eh?' Jim squinted at the sky.

'You never know. The fire certainly did a job on the horse paddock. I've got a bloke coming out to replace the fencing. Feed will be the main worry if we cop a late Wet. That the last of the yarding?' He nodded at the newly branded weaner rising groggily from the dirt at the foot of the ramp. It shook its wounded ear and bounded away, the Ralston Hills brand now plain on its hip.

'Yep. We've about finished here.' Jim swung down and began pulling the bronco gear off his mount, wondering how to phrase his next question. Nothing subtle occurred, so he asked outright. 'How's Ruth?'

'Who? Oh, fine. Back at school, I should think. Paula's having a couple of days with her before Patterson brings her home.'

Jim nodded. Ben Patterson was their eastern neighbour, whose way ran past the Ralston Hills homestead. 'Sending the girls back, is he?' Ben had three, all of whom, as Rosemary had done, attended a boarding school in Adelaide.

'Yeah. Must cost him a packet. Anyway, your cook's back. I dropped him off in the camp.'

'I see,' Jim said curtly. That was the end of that hope.

'Look, if there'd been anyone remotely capable of replacing him I'd have sacked the bastard,' Kevin growled. 'But we're stuck with him, at least for the time being. You know how it is.'

Jim had to concede his boss was right. It was the middle of the stock season and every station needed a cook, often two. It wasn't a job anyone did for the love of it. You became one by default, because you couldn't do any other work. There were never surplus cooks in the bush, and now that he thought about it, perhaps Buck had been a bit hasty sacking Lefty the way he did. You couldn't work men hard without feeding them well, and cooks usually got away with things that others didn't. Station men were used to handling whatever came up, as long as they got a good meal at the end of it. They'd grumbled a few times about Lawson's stupidity but he was a good cook after all, and that counted for a great deal.

The men were mounting, getting ready to let the cattle out. Jim stuck his toe in the iron and swung up. Kevin turned back to the rover, calling over his shoulder, 'I'll wait at the camp till you're through.'

One of the black boys had the gate open and the cattle surged out, pushing dust like fog before them. Then one of the black boys' chestnut gelding dropped his head, putting in a couple of curly bucks that had the leaders scattering about him. Jim swore and spurred his mount, only to relax as Benjy slipped neatly around the lead, steadying them back. Spitting dust from his throat, Jim felt the big horse's gait jolting his spine. He watched the other riders blacken into silhouettes against the dying sun and yawned widely. He was dog-tired. The only good thing about having Lawson back was that he need no longer spend more of his nights cooking than sleeping.

Next day they packed up and moved on to Bulrush camp, where the earthen turkey nest that served in lieu of a tank was choked with rushes. Seed-carrying fluff glittered silver in the tops of the grass on the sloped sides of the mound, and floated gauzily with every puff of wind. Jim, sitting his saddle while his horse drank at the trough, put up a hand to catch a piece. Its softness made him think of Ruth. Not that he needed much inducement – he couldn't get her out of his head, and was constantly composing letters he didn't have time to write, hugging to himself the hope that she would have written herself, and that any day now a letter would be waiting for him at the station.

When his horse finished drinking it blew a great gust of air through damp nostrils, then shook itself hard enough to rattle the saddle pouch against its ribs. Jim gathered the reins and headed for the camp, which lay beyond the prickly bushes behind the yard. It was an orderly affair, set out the way he liked, which, if he stopped to analyse the matter, was exactly as Des Hanks's camps had been, with the fly rig standing square on to the side of the truck and the fire downwind of both.

Jim hooked his reins to the branch of a whitewood at the edge of the horse camp and poured himself a drink from the waterbag, noting that the billies were already on the fire. Lawson, his forearm still ostentatiously bandaged, called a greeting that Jim acknowledged with a grunt. It irked him that the man knew his job, but then he had as a rider too – only he'd been a horse-killing show-off then.

'The boys will be about five minutes.' He spoke curtly but Lawson, annoyingly, never seemed to notice.

'That's fine,' he said agreeably, as if Jim were asking rather than telling him. 'Lunch's ready for 'em. Hey, the boss came by again this morning. Brung out those rations I wanted and a bit of mail. One for Benjy. He gets so many letters, that kid. Must be his mum writing him. Nothing from your girl, I see, but you've got a coupla papers.'

'What are you talking about?' Jim demanded roughly and Lawson cocked his head like a watchful bird.

'Ah, come on, mate. Who're you fooling? She fixed me arm up, Ruth did. Real gentle hands she's got, and pleased as Punch when I said I knew you from before. Questions! I tell you there wasn't nothing she didn't want to know about you and your family. Course I was glad to oblige, you having been a bit shy with the personal details, she said.' He shook his head wisely. 'Big mistake, that. Stands to reason they're gunna ferret out everything in the long run. Born inquisitive, sheilas are.'

Jim felt his fist clench of its own accord and had to turn away to avoid driving it into that hateful leer. He cursed the opportunity he let slip the day of the fire. Why had he not told her then? At least she'd have heard it from him and not second-hand. From Lawson, as it turned out, who hated him. Jim's soul writhed within him. He could well imagine with what unctuous sympathy Lawson would have unfolded Sandy's shabby story to Ruth.

He breathed out slowly. It was all his own fault, but knowing it only made matters worse. And there was no use pretending he'd lacked the time to mention his father. He could have told her on any number of occasions. He could have written her the sorry details many times over, but he hadn't. And now, he knew, as he stood there listening to the blood thump in his head, it was too late. Lawson had stolen any chance he might have had to prove to her that he was different, that he was not like his father.

Rage boiled in him. If only he'd been open with Ruth. He imagined her mortification on hearing the tale, and how fortuitous the timing of Paula's labour must have seemed to her – a heaven-sent excuse for a dignified exit. He winced, thinking how glad she would have been to go, how thankful to avoid the embarrassment of meeting him again.

The rest of the men had arrived, the black boys peeling off to their own shade tree, Benjy and Alf stooping as their heads came under the canvas. Benjy, striding long-legged to the waterbag, said, 'I seen the tracks. Who's been out? They bring any mail?'

'Yeah.' Jim nodded at the table. And seeing the eager way Benjy pounced on the envelope and bore it off, a mixture of jealousy and anger harshened his voice. 'This isn't a bloody reading room. Get your dinners into you. We've got a long afternoon coming up.'

'Aw, c'mon, man. There's plenty of time,' Alf protested. 'There couldn't be fifty calves in that yarding. We'll knock 'em over inside two hours.'

'Which is why we're mustering the eastern country this arvo. A night in the yard won't hurt them. We'll brand tomorrow, when we've enough to make it worth lighting the fire.' They gaped in surprise as he ripped the knife through a loaf and slapped meat onto his slice of bread, and though he knew Lawson was loving the helpless fury that drove him, he snarled, 'Get moving, damn you.'

'Jeez,' Benjy reflected, wide-eyed. 'I dunno what bit him, but whatever it was I don't wanna meet it.' His words were meant for Alf and Lawson alone, and a look of comical dismay crossed the easygoing youngster's features at the sight of Jim's lifted head and bleak expression. For a long moment their gazes locked, then Jim turned away. It was Lawson he wanted to kill, not Benjy. Scrapping with him would achieve nothing but the loss of a good hand.

They were late getting in with the cattle that night, and wound up yarding in the dark with a good deal of galloping and cursing. Buck Moody would not have approved, Jim thought morosely, any more than he did himself. It had been a stupid decision to take and both he and the men knew it. Disgusted with himself, he kicked his swag open and sat down on the nap to pull his boots off.

Long after the camp slept, he lay wakeful in his swag. His mind pulled this way and that, intent one moment upon immediately writing to Ruth and the next on letting matters ride. A letter would achieve nothing but prove he cared, which, if she already despised him, was the last thing he wanted. And what, anyway, could he say? However Lawson had told it, the truth was bad enough. There was no way he could justify or excuse it. It would be better to see her, but that wasn't likely to happen until the Katherine rodeo in – he counted it up – three weeks' time. So he could write or he could wait.

The decision was still unmade when bodily weariness claimed him and he slept, pursuing strange dreams of loss and dislocation in which Ro, her head crowned with flowers, sat on a ledge above him eating exotic fruits and reading from a book whose title he could not see.

Somewhat prophetically, by the time the camp returned to the station a couple of weeks later the promised letter from his cousin had arrived. It was the only one, and Paula, to Jim's heightened awareness, seemed to deliberately avoid any mention of Ruth. His heart leapt at the sight of mail, but turning it in his hands he instantly recognised Ro's distinctive loopless writing. She'd sent it to Kharko and Mary had forwarded it on, her even script filling the corner of the coarse brown envelope. There wasn't much in it, just a flimsy sheet wrapped about stiffer photographic paper. Well, postage was probably dear.

Aware of Paula's inquisitive gaze, Jim moved away to slit the envelope open and pull the picture out. He had expected a wedding snap but it was Rosemary smiling under a wide-brimmed white hat that cast a bar of shade across her eyes. She was standing beside a dark-haired young man dressed casually in trousers and a short-sleeved shirt. They were backgrounded by pine trees growing on a slope beside a white wall with a spill of geraniums down it (he recognised the flower, if not its name, from his aunt's garden) and a patch of blue sky in the corner. Rosemary looked happy, Jim thought. He studied Ken, who might have been in his late twenties and was tall with a long Australian face, his dark hair brushed to one side. There was no clue in his appearance as to what he did – he could be anything from a carpenter to an accountant – while the brief note that accompanied the snap was Ro at her most aggravating. *Here we are, the happy couple. He's a great bloke, Jim, and I love him to bits. Heading for Rhodes tomorrow. Might be home sooner than I planned. Why don't you write? Ro.*

He slid the contents back into their envelope, all his tortuous thoughts of the past fortnight suddenly clarified. *Why don't you write?* Of course she meant why didn't he write to her, but the words were just the push he needed to make a decision about Ruth. He would write tonight. The letter could go out on the mail tomorrow. And on the weekend he would be in Katherine for the rodeo. So she would have time enough, if she were prepared to, to mull the matter over before he got there.

Heartened, Jim hurried away to find pen and paper while the impulse was strong upon him. He had reached this stage a dozen times already before changing his mind, but this was different – almost an omen – and he would treat it as such. Thank God for Ro! She was a lot of things – he totted them up in his head. Stubborn, aggravating, ruthless, but she was loyal too, and clear-sighted, and she had always understood a great deal more about people than he ever would. In any case, he reasoned, he had nothing but pride to lose. Ruth was worth that, and much more.

He had known it for some weeks. Kate's rejection, painful though it was, had only wounded his self-esteem. With Ruth it was different altogether. If she were to reject him too . . . But that was something he wasn't prepared to contemplate.

EIGHTEEN

Katherine, perched astride the narrow strip of bitumen linking Alice Springs to Darwin, had exchanged its everyday somnolence for the feverish activity of rodeo weekend. Dust hung like a red stain in the air above the yards, and bush hats predominated in the crowd. A show had come to town with its merry-go-round and rides and shooting booths. Or perhaps, Jim thought, wandering down sideshow alley, it was part of the rodeo and travelled along with the buckjumpers and riding gear between the widely scattered centres of the north.

His search was taking longer than he'd expected, for the Katherine he'd experienced on his earlier visits was not the crowded centre it had suddenly become. Entertainment was too rare in any bush town to miss and he knew that nobody would be sitting at home today. Still, it ought to have been easy to spot her in the crowd. A dozen times his heart leapt at the glimpse of a slim waist or the back of a head, but none of them were Ruth and now, aware of passing time, he must try another way.

He found a likely-looking boy at the shooting booth, standing with two companions and wistfully watching an older lad try for one of the prizes stacked on the open shelves. Jim judged him to be about ten; he was bare-footed and freckle-faced with a cloth hat over tow-coloured hair. As he stood there considering him, the older boy shot, shrugged, and with a rueful look laid the rifle back on the counter.

'I coulda done better'n that,' the boy asserted and Jim pulled a handful of change from his pocket and moved up beside him.

'You want to try?'

'You bet,' he agreed. Then added suspiciously, 'Why? Whatcha want?'

'Maybe you can tell me something. D'you go to school here?'

'Course I do.' He looked at his mates as if seeking confirmation. 'We all do. So what?'

'So who's your teacher? Is it Miss Petlow, for instance?'

'Nah.' It was one of his mates who answered but the boy qualified it. 'Not any more. She's gone.'

Jim stared in blank astonishment. It was the one answer he had not expected. 'How do you mean, gone?'

'Left. Went away. And now we've got this mad army bloke. Always making us do PT and hauling us out to be caned. I wish *he'd* leave, bloody oath I do.'

'Right. Thanks.' Jim dumped some coins into the boy's hand. 'Have yourself a shot.' Shock turned him clumsy; as he turned away his boot caught on the guy rope supporting the booth and he stumbled. That was it then. If she'd quit her job and left town to avoid him, no amount of letter writing was going to bring her back. Through the sudden emptiness inside him he felt a burn of anger at the sheer injustice of her action. He might as well wear a bell and sign proclaiming: *Unclean*.

At the grog tent, with its scarlet and gold XXXX banners flapping above the entrance, he had a beer, and then another, carrying the second one clear of the jostling bodies about him. He found no pleasure in the taste, nor did he have any desire to drink himself insensible. That, and his lip curled at the thought, was something he could safely leave to Sandy.

A little later he spotted Paula pushing a pram through the dirt towards the car park and he went after her, less to help than to find some answers.

'Let me, Mrs Gaunt.' Effortlessly he lifted the pram and carried it to her car. 'There you are.'

'Thank you, Jim.' She lifted the baby out, cradling his head into the hollow of her shoulder. 'I just want to change him.' Then, as he continued to stand there, she asked brightly, 'Are you enjoying yourself?'

'I've been looking for Ruth,' he said bluntly. 'But it seems she's left.'

'Oh, well, yes. Didn't you know?' She nudged the door open and fished one-handed in a carry bag to bring out a folded nappy. 'She's gone back to the city.' Deftly she laid the baby down and unpinned him, whisking his plump bare limbs and rounded bottom this way and that as she cleaned him. 'I think she found the bush life wasn't for her after all.'

'So have you got a phone number for her, or an address?'

'No.' The baby woke and started to cry. Paula rocked him in her arms, her eyes steady on Jim's, and smiled with a hint of triumph. 'Not until she gets a new school and finds somewhere to live, and that could take ages. She was going to stay with a friend until she found somewhere, but I'm afraid I don't know who that would be. Still, if she gets in touch . . .' Her hair fell forward, shielding her cheek from view as she bent to cup the crying baby's head in one hand. She lowered her face to kiss his angry brow. 'There, sweetie. Hush, Mummy's made it better.' She looked sideways at Jim, as if surprised to find him still there. 'Sorry I can't help.'

'Right.' Jim touched his hat and moved on. If she was sorry so was the ground he walked on. Baffled, acknowledging defeat, he made his way back to the rodeo ground. It had been a waste of his time coming; there wasn't even a chance of running into Oliver, since his cousin had thrown in his job and taken his wife to live in Alice Springs, where he had work in a stock and station agency. That, Jim thought moodily, must have caused a bit of an upset back home.

But he had more on his mind than his cousin's career. It would take a miracle to find Ruth now, unless she got in touch with him herself.

Which, a month later, was exactly what happened. His own letter had been returned unopened with 'Left address' written across the envelope. He thrust it angrily into the fire, wondering how a girl he had known so briefly could matter so much, and went morosely off to bed. Then, some weeks on, Marty flagged him down as he was passing the store. The bookkeeper had been flattening cardboard cartons into manageable piles to send to the dump, but he dusted off his hands and came forward, calling a greeting.

'G'day, Jim. Just the man I want to see. Lucky I looked out when I did.'

'Yeah?' Jim said, uninterested. 'Why?'

'Well.' Marty scratched his head. 'It's a bit delicate. You remember Paula's sister, Ruth?' Jim nodded dumbly. 'She's written to me – well, to you actually, but she sent it to me, if you see what I mean. There was an envelope addressed to you inside one addressed to me, with a request that it be forwarded on.'

Jim's hand shot out. 'Forwarded? Why? Where is it?'

'There seems,' Marty said, maddeningly slow, 'to be a bit of skulduggery in the wind.'

'What the hell are you talking about? Just give me the letter.'

The bookkeeper ignored him. 'I reckon it's Paula. She doesn't seem to like you. She told Ruth you'd left the place. There must have been a letter I didn't see that was returned,' he said meditatively. 'Anyway, she – Ruth, that is – contacted the company's head office and they gave her Ralston Hills as your place of residence. And she says she's written to you here since and had the letters returned.'

Jim was almost dancing with impatience. 'Returned? I never saw them.'

'No,' Marty agreed. 'Well, I can't see the boss interfering so that leaves me and Paula, doesn't it? And I haven't touched them. Just thought you'd better know.'

'Okay, so now I do. Where's my letter?' Indignation warred with joy as he added, 'She's gotta be barmy. I mean, I asked her specifically and she said she didn't know where Ruth was, that she'd packed her job in and she didn't have an address.'

'I see. Well, she doesn't know this has come.' Marty finally produced an envelope from his pocket. 'I suggest you give any reply to me, and have the young lady continue to send hers to me also.'

He hesitated, then said, 'Paula Gaunt's a very unhappy woman, Jim. I doubt her husband realises just how unhappy. I wouldn't be too hard on her, I fear she can't help herself in all this.'

Jim beamed at him, his world right side up again. 'You think so? The cow can grow another head and it wouldn't bother me. Not now.' Happiness tugged at him. Ruth cared for him. Enough to write several times and even check with head office as to his whereabouts. Holding the precious letter, he would not have been surprised as he headed for the kitchen to find that his boots were floating six inches above the ground.

Linda was there, overflowing a cane chair in the corner, her swollen ankles propped on a blanket-covered stool and a crochet needle flashing in her hand. Whatever she was making she'd been at it since Jim's arrival at Ralston Hills, but the basket of wool at her side never seemed to diminish. She groaned to her feet to make him a pot of tea, then returned to her work, the silence of the room broken only by her heavy breathing and the comfortable bubble of the kettle on the big, wood-burning range. Jim poured himself some tea, then careful not to damage the return address, which he saw was Melbourne, he used the blade of his stock-knife to slit the envelope. His hands trembled a little as he lifted the single sheet and began to read.

Dear Jim,

I do hope this letter reaches you. Paula told me you had left Ralston Hills but couldn't tell me where you'd gone. When I contacted the head office of the company they told me you were still there. So I'm sending this care of Marty, because he keeps the books and will certainly notice if he's lost a man (especially one as knowledgeable as you). At least I hope so!

I wanted to see you again before I left the station but everything happened so quickly – the fire, and then Paula going into early labour like that. I had planned to send a letter back with her but once I got the message from home there was no time to do more than hand in my notice, pack up the flat and jump on the bus. I flew back from Alice and Dad met me at the airport – so changed it frightened me. I've written twice since then, but when Paula rang for news she told me you'd left. Perhaps you have and this won't find you after all. I'll be sorry if it doesn't. Our friendship was new but it felt special to me.

Mum is much improved. It wasn't a very severe stroke, as strokes go, but her left arm is still affected. We have her back at home now and a nurse comes each day to give her physio – I am learning to do the exercises so I can take over. I've written to the Department explaining my situation and they've given me six months' leave of absence. That will take me up to first term next year, when hopefully Dad will be able to manage and I can reapply for a school out in your beautiful country.

I think of you often and the pleasant times we spent together. I hope you remember me and will write back.

Sincerely,

Ruth

'Yes,' Jim breathed. 'Oh, yes.' Warmth suffused him, spreading like strong drink through his veins. He read the letter again, then folded it reverently. Odd phrases ran in his mind and he immediately opened it to read them once more. *As knowledgeable as you,* she had written, and, *it felt special to me.* But most of all, and more than he'd dared hope for, that wonderful declaration, *I think of you often.* He wanted to run and shout like a boy, then found himself wishing he had somebody to talk to about his amazing good fortune. Six months – that was no time at all. In six months she would be back and he would see her again. See the bounce of her shiny hair, and the way her head tipped to one side in thought, and hear her musical laugh. Lawson's poison hadn't worked. She knew the worst and plainly it made no difference.

Then, before he could speculate on Paula's odd behaviour, another, even happier thought occurred to him. It needn't be six months at all before they met again. Why shouldn't he go to her as soon as the stock work was over? There would be nothing doing over the Wet, so he could take a month off. He realised he was grinning foolishly into empty space before him.

'Well?' Linda was watching him over her crocheting. 'You look like you got the cream, boy. A girl, is it?'

Jim winked at her and patted his pocket where the letter lay. 'As a matter of fact I was planning my holidays. Thanks for the tea, Linda.' He had forgotten to eat his cake and reached for it now, snapping it up in two bites. 'Your cooking knocks spots off Lawson's. You ever want a reference, come and see me.'

He swung jauntily on his way, forgetting the plate and pannikin he would normally have carried to the sink, and the big woman's bulk shook in her chair as she chuckled, nodding sagely. 'Seen he had the look. It's a girl all right.'

Station life was a patterned existence and necessarily so, for the work was geared to the rhythm of the seasons, from branding to bullock muster and, as the year drew on, the shifting about of stock as waterholes dried. Now, for Jim, there was a smaller, more intimate pattern inside the greater one as he wrote and posted letters and waited impatiently for Ruth's replies. They came regularly and were eagerly devoured. Being a teacher, Ruth was good with words, and Jim, writing after the evening meal at a corner of the kitchen table, or scribbling with the pad on his knee during dinner-camp breaks, surprised himself.

He had never lost his childhood ability, learned from his Aboriginal playmates, to really look at things, and this aptitude stood him in good stead now. In long, rambling letters he drew the country for her, the arid landscape sprawled under the dusty sky, the flavour of the stock camp, the complaints and rough humour, the mishaps and funny incidents that occurred. He wrote about the stock boys cornering the big perenti on the flat with a view to roasting it, and how Benjy, riding past, had been thrown when the creature, instinctively seeking height, ran straight up his horse's shoulder. He told her about the wild duck with the clutch of ducklings amid the reeds at Bulrush camp, and of seeing a brumby drinking there with its mane turned silver from the fluff of the rushes.

In her letters she wrote of the city and the day-to-day constraints of life in the sickroom where her mother struggled to regain her speech and the use of her arm. Her father had heartened into something like his old self and both parents were desperate to see Paula and the new baby, though Ruth doubted if her sister would visit while she was there. *She knows too well what I'd have to say to her.*

Ruth had been less forgiving than Jim of the lies contrived to keep them apart. They had discussed that, and Roger Lawson's disclosures, which had earned the latter not the encouragement he'd hinted at but a cool disdain. *Well, I already knew about your father,* she wrote. *Why do you think Paula was so desperate to keep us apart? I believe I'd heard the whole history of it from her before I'd even drunk my first cup of tea at Ralston. That doesn't make Lawson any less of a crawling maggot* (Jim blinked and reread the words, unable to picture Ruth's soft voice actually pronouncing them) *for trying to do you a bad turn, but it certainly made no difference to me. That evening in the garden when we first met, I already knew. I didn't have to wait there to bump into you . . .*

He blinked again. So it had been a contrived, not a chance, meeting. For a moment he didn't know whether to feel flattered or affronted, then he grinned. What did it matter? It was a question Ro might have asked; he almost could hear her exasperated tone in the words. The important thing, as his cousin would be the first to point out, was that he and Ruth had found each other, not once but twice. But he was aware that he had a good deal to learn about girls.

Thinking of Ro made him realise how much he was looking forward to introducing her to Ruth. She and Ken, a scrappy note on a postcard had informed him, would be back in Australia in November. *The rest of the world will keep for a bit*, she'd written, and then, almost as if she suspected his secret, *You never write. What are you doing with your life?*

'Are we working today?' Benjy suddenly demanded. 'Or are you just

gunna sit there grinning to yourself till sundown?' He winked elabo-
rately at Alf. 'My sister's a nurse. She reckons it's the start of softening
of the brain. First they grin, then they gibber, she reckons.'

'Get stuffed,' Jim said cheerfully. 'Anyone as ugly as you couldn't
have a sister.' But he settled his hat and got to his feet, squinting
through the heat haze at their waiting mounts.

'Musta meant me cousin.' Benjy was unabashed.

Jim shoved him good-humouredly towards the fly entrance.
'I reckon she'd scare the cows too. Climb onto your horse, sonny.
You want to work, we will.'

In November, when the air shimmered with heatwaves and the red
earth burnt through the thin soles of his riding boots, Jim accompanied
Kevin to Katherine to pick up a load of fencing material for the station.
When they were readying the truck he lifted his swag, but the manager
shook his head.

'Won't need that. We'll stop in the pub.'

'Righto.' It would make a change, Jim thought, to get away, even if it
was only overnight. He hadn't been off the place since the rodeo weekend months before, and his steps moved faster in anticipation not only
of the break from the daily routine but of the opportunity to ring Ruth
and hear her voice again. The last time they'd spoken was the day of the
fire, and since then there'd been only the remembered cadence of her
voice as he read her letters. He was hungry for something more.

He got the connection that evening, standing in the hall behind the
noisy bar. The phone rang interminably, and listening to it burr across

the distance separating them, his heart sank. She would be out, or gone to stay overnight with friends, and tomorrow would be too late, for they were leaving first thing in the morning. A stack of coins rested beside the phone and he fingered them nervously, wishing for greater privacy than was provided by the bar's open door and the occasional passage of people through the hallway. Restlessly he turned his back on them, then heard the ringing stop as the phone was lifted. Without waiting he said, 'Hello – Ruth?'

'Who is it?' The voice was masculine and he corrected himself.

'Mr Petlow, is Ruth there? Could I speak to her, please?'

There was a pause, then he heard the man speaking into the room behind him, his words echoing past the mouthpiece. 'Ruthie, it's for you. Didn't give a name. Should I tell him to ring back?'

'Wait, I'm coming.' Her voice somewhere in the background, a shuffle of movement and murmured instruction. 'She's waiting, you go . . .' Then, soft but clear-edged, just as he remembered it, her voice on the line: 'Hello. Ruth Petlow speaking.'

His heart turned over. 'Ruth. I'm in Katherine. How are you?' Then hastily, 'It's Jim here, Jim McAllister.'

'Well, of course it is!' she laughed. Then more seriously, 'You're all right, Jim? There's nothing wrong?'

'I'm fine.' Belatedly he added, 'And you're mother, she's —?'

'Yes, yes. She's fine. And Dad's getting better at coping.' She laughed again softly, 'It's so *good* to hear you, Jim. I've loved your letters but it's not the same as hearing your voice. Now tell me everything. When does Rosemary get back to Australia? Has the Four Mile been repaired? Did the mare recover from the stake? Just everything!'

It was his turn to laugh. 'I'd rather hear about you, but to keep it short, Ro flies into Darwin in a fortnight; yes, the bore's going again; and no, the mare's permanently crippled. It's a shame, though I expect the boss'll put her to the stallion. But I didn't know your family called you Ruthie. And I've just realised I don't even know your middle name.'

'It's Angela.' For a moment her voice faded into static, out of which he picked '. . . yours?'

Jim blushed. 'James Alexander. Ruth, I've got holidays coming in December. It's what I wanted to talk to you about. I was hoping – I mean, would it be all right for me to come to Melbourne to visit you? Apart from wanting to see you again, which I do very much, I'd like to meet your parents.'

'That would be perfect, Jim.' Her voice vanished again into static. He thrust more coins in and banged the side of the phone.

'I can't hear you.'

'I said yes. Yes. Come.' Then she was gone again, the line roared and he heard, '. . . write me details.' And '. . . can't wait. Mum and Dad'll want . . .' Then nothing more.

Desperation seized him. For the duration of those magic moments she had sounded so close. His voice deep and intense, he said, 'I love you, Ruth,' but the words vanished in the crackling and she had gone.

Her next letter mentioned the phone call but not whether she had heard his declaration. It spoke instead of his forthcoming visit and of the places they might go and the things they might do. Her enthusiasm spilled over the page and made his heart leap. Her father had a car they could borrow to see something of the country beyond Melbourne, and there would be plays and concerts and the cinema and marvellous book shops. *It's strange to feel I know you so well and still know nothing of your tastes,* she wrote. *You must tell me what you like, for you can't know my preferences either,* which made it easy for him to reply, *No, but we have the rest of our lives to find out.* It sat better with him than another bald declaration, and meant exactly the same thing.

NINETEEN

Rosemary Gilbert arrived back in Alice Springs the day before Jim left Ralston Hills to head south. The timing was good; it meant they would meet at Kharko. She had been gone a little under a year but it seemed much longer, Jim thought, reading the telegram Marty handed him as they sat on the verandah in the early evening.

The Gaunts were there too, seeking the cooler air, and young Jack was watching Jim with a cat's inquisitiveness. 'Is it about your holiday? Linda said you're going away.'

'Well, so I am.'

'Where are you going, Jim? And what you gunna do when you get there? *I'd* go for a ride on a train. And I'd find the sea. And when I did I'd get the biggest fishing net . . .'

'That's enough, Jack,' Paula said crossly. She was nursing the baby and now hitched herself higher in the chair, pushing irritably at her neck where her hair clung in sweaty tendrils. 'Mind your own business.'

Which was pretty good coming from her, Jim thought. Nothing had been said but he had not completely forgiven her for her interference.

Jack's face flushed in a sudden temper and he stamped a bare foot on the boards. 'I want to know,' he yelled. 'It's only an old holiday. Why can't he say?'

'Hold your horses,' Jim admonished good-humouredly. 'I'm pushing off to Melbourne if you must know. To see a friend.' Paula stiffened and he smiled pleasantly. 'I found her, you see.' He looked steadily at her until she flushed and turned her gaze aside. Satisfied, he said idly, 'What about you, boss? Planning on getting away this summer?'

Kevin grunted. 'Depends on the weather, and whether Marty stays. We might take a week in the Alice but that's about it. And only if it rains.'

Jim, with no such constraints, left the next morning. He packed the old rover he had bought six months before, waved goodbye to Linda and the Gaunts, and gunned the motor through the blackened paddock, heading for Katherine and the bitumen. It was not too early for storms, though none had come yet, and away to the north the sky was lined with banks of cumulous cloud. He was glad he hadn't waited an extra fortnight, as Kevin had initially suggested.

He camped by the side of the road that night, reaching the Alice late next afternoon. The agency where Oliver worked was closed for the day and his cousin's name, Jim discovered, was not in the phone book. He booked himself into a hotel and had a meal in the dining room and a drink in the bar before turning in, to dream of driving along an endless road that vanished into storm behind him.

Next day he made an early start, skipping breakfast at the hotel in favour of a meal from his tuckerbox along the way. The road had recently been graded, at least as far as the Yambah turn-off, and he was able to maintain a steady pace, so that a little before noon he found himself pulling into Goola for the first time in a year and a half.

The racetrack had been smartened up, he saw. There was fresh white paint on the furlong posts and along the rails of the straight. That would be Rob's doing, he knew. And they had finally got round to a decent refreshment room, with a corrugated-iron roof that glared in the sunlight.

In the town itself nothing much had changed. He stared around like a stranger as he killed the motor and let the quiet flow back over the vehicle and its smell of vaporising fuel. It was very hot. He mopped his face, observing the same old rickety hall and handful of tin shacks. Sun had blistered the paint off the hall doors but someone had slapped a new coat on the police house and there was now a fuel bowser in front of the store. The mill looked unchanged, and down by the trough on the riverbank what could have been the same cattle from two or even ten years before were chewing their cud amid the litter of gum bark and old cowpats. A pair of crows called discordantly above the tic of the cooling engine.

He remembered his father standing on the store steps, brushing off Bill Maddison's invitation to visit, and himself and Wally sitting there during the drought and the latter telling him he was leaving home. He wondered where he'd got to now. They had not met since the dance when Jim had almost socked Sam Colson. A baby willy-wind skirred down the road towards him, then tore sideways under the trees, scooping up leaves as it went. The crows, feathers blown like lifted skirts, launched raucously into the sky before it.

In the yard of the closest house he recognised old Charlie Attwood and walked across for a word with him. He could, for all evidence to the contrary, have been the only man in town.

'What do you want here?' The old man squinted dourly from the canvas chair in which he sat, hose in hand, watering his little plot of beans and melons. Bent and arthritic, he had aged gnomishly and was shrunken, white-haired, with a suspicious gaze and a thin rat-trap of a mouth.

'Just passing through, Charlie. You remember me, don't you?'

'Course I bloody do. Worked for your uncle long enough, didn't I? You think a man's senile or what?'

'Could be.' Soft words had never worked with old Charlie. 'It's been a while, after all. What's new round here? Apart from the facelift on the cop shop and the racecourse – and the new bowser across there?'

'That's enough, aint it?' Charlie growled. 'Country's going to buggery.' Grudgingly he added, 'Sam Colson sold out. Some big company's got Perishing Downs now. Gunna put down more bores, I heard, and play bloody hell. They'd of done better to keep Big Sam on to manage the joint and leave the waters as they was. That country won't carry a head more'n what's on it, but I daresay they'll bugger it up finding that out.'

'Has he?' Jim whistled. 'I thought Sam Colson was married to that place. Where've they gone, he and his wife?'

Charlie shrugged. 'Inter town. Wherever that girl of theirs is. What you doing back here, anyway? Thought you was running the camp on Stockton.'

'Ralston Hills, up Katherine way,' Jim corrected. 'So I was. But I'm on leave now and heading south. This is just a bit of a detour to see the old fella. Did you hear Rosemary got married?'

'I heard. Right little bugger she useta be. And you weren't no better.' He glared, cheeks fallen in over missing teeth. 'So Rob's the *old fella* now, is he? Bloody kids! Wait'll he's my age and then you can talk.'

'Figure of speech, Charlie.' Jim grinned at him. 'How old *are* you, anyway?'

'None of your damn business.'

'Right.' He rose from his heels and looked over the vegetable plot. 'Nice garden. You're looking pretty good too. I'll tell Rob I saw you, shall I?'

Charlie struggled with himself, then gave a grudging nod. 'You do that. I don't mind if he drops in for a yarn sometime.'

'I'll tell him.'

Driving on, Jim did sums in his head, trying to work it out. It was twelve years since he'd come to Kharko, and Charlie had appeared brittle and white-haired then, his hobbling form already bent and lame from a combination of arthritis and old injuries. The one thing he and Ro had agreed on back then, Jim remembered, was his age, which they had put down as a hundred. Well, he certainly couldn't be a day under eighty now, and he had enough spit and vinegar in him to see another decade out.

Jim clattered over the grid that had replaced the horse-paddock gate and then the green and white station buildings were before him – the same combination, he suddenly realised, amazed that he'd never noticed before, as Kharko's racing colours.

He pulled into the shade next to the gate, switched off the motor, and sat there for a moment absorbing the scene, before whistling his way to the side door and the welcome he knew would await him.

'Jim! Lovely to have you back! It only needs Oliver now and we'll have seen you all.' Mary hugged him and he stooped to kiss her cheek. Her hair was prematurely white and she had put on a little weight.

'You look so well, Jim,' she continued fondly. 'And very like your uncle when I first met him. Come in and sit down, I want to hear all your news. And guess what? Ro's here with Ken.'

'I thought she must be. So what's he like? Ideal son-in-law material?'

'Well, not exactly what I expected, but then people never are. He's nice, though, with lots of charm. I don't know when I've felt so easy so quickly with anyone. He's seven years older than Rosemary, and she . . .' Mary shook her head, a tiny frown between her brows as she looked across at him. 'Well, you know her, Jim. She's not one to wear her heart on her sleeve, and it sounds silly, but she *adores* him. I know it shouldn't but it worries me to see her so, so . . .' She smoothed the cloth of her dress in that familiar way, adding, 'Well, she always stood alone, my daughter. She never seemed to need anyone. I'm her mother, but loving her often felt like hugging a prickly bush.'

'She'll be fine, Aunty. You'll see. So what does he do? How does he earn a crust?'

'He's a photographer.'

Whatever Jim had expected it was not this. He blinked. 'He's got a studio and goes round doing weddings and stuff?'

'Good heavens, no.' It was Mary's turn to look surprised. 'He's a photojournalist, I believe the term is. He travels round the world taking shots for magazines. That's what he was doing in Greece when they met. They're going to India next year.' She shook her head again and stood up. 'Anyway, you can ask him yourself. Here they come now. Look at the time. I must set the table for lunch.'

And suddenly they were both there and Ro grabbed him and kissed his cheek. She wore a yellow shirt over khaki slacks, and open-toed sandals. She had her hair cropped short, her coppery curls like a halo about her neat head. Slim and vital, she glowed with wellbeing, but marriage had not dulled the ironic glint in her eyes.

'You look wonderful,' Jim said.

She grinned impishly. 'And this is Ken.' The man waiting behind her stepped forward to shake hands.

He was almost as tall as Jim but lighter-built, though not with Oliver's gangliness. His face was unremarkable, long-nosed and thin-lipped with dark, watchful eyes. There was a quality of stillness and ease about him that Jim instinctively liked, and without thinking he nodded approvingly as they shook hands, at which Rosemary gave a peal of laughter.

'Strike three for the family, my love. You've been judged and approved – again. There's only Olly to go now.'

Jim reddened and opened his mouth, but was suddenly caught with nothing to say. He shot a malevolent look at his cousin, who stood with the laughter bubbling from her. 'Oh, Jim,' she gasped. 'You're so —'

'Cut it out, Ro,' Ken said mildly, and wiping her eyes she came obediently to take his arm and hug it against her. 'I'm sorry, love. He's just so dependable, is Jim. Never done a devious thing in his life. He can't, actually, because you can see straight through him. But he's my favourite cousin for all that.'

'Which isn't saying much,' Jim grumbled to cloak his embarrassment, 'seeing you don't have any others.' He grinned ruefully at Ken. 'I don't know what possessed you, but I wish you luck anyway.'

'Oh, I doubt I'll need it.' Ken's long face lit up with a lopsided smile. He had a crooked front tooth, Jim saw, and a triangular scar beside his nose. 'We understand each other pretty well.'

'Well, that's more than I ever did. Congratulations, anyway.' And with a glance at Ro, 'You didn't get to see that much of the world after all. Where will you settle, Alice or the city?'

'Ken's got a place in the Adelaide Hills,' she said. 'But we don't intend to be there much. Most of his work's overseas, so you see my French won't be wasted. I'll still be travelling, only now I won't be alone.' Her eyes were on her husband's face as she spoke and Jim remembered Mary's words. But watching them over lunch, seeing the ease between them, the unconscious way Ro's hand found and was covered by Ken's, Jim thought that everything would work out for them.

Rob, who'd been out at lunchtime, came in as Jim was washing for dinner in the downstairs bathroom. He was unchanged save for a slight thickening about his middle and a touch of grey above the ears. They shook hands warmly, their eyes now on a level.

'Saw your old boneshaker out front,' Rob said. 'It's good to have you back, lad.'

'It's only for a week. I'm heading down to Melbourne then. My flight leaves Monday morning, so I'll have to be in the Alice the day before. How're things here?'

'Getting dry. The dams are going back faster than I like to see. What's the Ralston country like?'

'Short on horse feed.' Jim pulled a face. 'Remember a ringer called Roger Lawson, got himself smashed up here the year Barney died? He's camp-cooking now. Gaunt put him on the books and the idiot managed to set fire to the paddock country, so the nags are suffering a bit. We've had to run the working plant with the brood mares for the last couple of months. Started out feeding the stallion, then Kevin had the idea of loaning him out to Ben Patterson, who runs the place next door.'

They strolled into the dining room, still talking. It had been painted since Jim's last visit but the polished sideboard, the silver-plated cruet, the crisp, starched napkins, were as they had always been. Only the cooking seemed to have suffered. Looking at the underdone meat and the burnt crust on the bread, Jim felt a pang of nostalgia for other days. There was a stranger in the kitchen now; Pommy John had gone, as had Leo Baker, whose chair was filled by a new bookkeeper.

'How's old Olly doing?' Jim asked, and saw Rob's face tighten. It was Mary who answered.

'We haven't seen him since the move. But from his letters he seems happy enough. Fiona's expecting, you know.'

'Is she?' Jim had been as stunned as anyone when Oliver resigned from Windamere. He had gone to a rented house in the Alice, within walking distance from his agency job, and Jim suspected that his uncle blamed Fiona for the move. He said, 'I was going to look them up but the agency was closed and I couldn't get an address. I'd just made plans to visit him at Windamere when I heard he'd quit.'

Rob cleared his throat and began talking generalities, as if not wishing to dwell on his son. Jim helped himself to more meat from the platter before passing it to Ken. He said, 'I saw old Charlie Attwood in Goola. Cranky as ever. He told me Sam Colson's sold up.'

'We had a send-off for them at the hall.' Mary passed his refilled cup back. 'And a dance afterwards. Mason played for us. He's full of surprises, that young man. It was a nice evening.'

'How is Mace?'

'On holidays, but he's just the same. He'll be back some time in January. I think he mainly went for his grandmother's birthday. She's ninety-eight and seems to mean a lot to him.'

'Well, tell him hello from me,' said Rosemary. 'It feels strange not to know anyone here any more. I can't believe old Pommy's gone.'

'He stayed longer than most,' Rob commented. 'By the way, Jim, there's a letter for you in the office. It only just came.'

'I'll get it later.' Any mail addressed to him at Kharko would not be major. Replete, Jim leaned back in his chair. 'Did you hear what Colson's place brought?'

In fact it was not until after dinner the following evening, when the bookkeeper had returned to his quarters, that Jim was reminded of the letter. Rosemary and Ken had left for Adelaide that morning to meet his parents, so it was a smaller party that gathered for tea.

'What do you think of him?' Jim asked, stacking plates after the meal.

Rob nodded, knowing at once who he meant. 'I like the lad. He's probably just what Rosemary needs. I doubt she'll have all her own way with him.'

'Your turn next, Jim,' Mary said, whisking the cloth off the table and folding it, and it was on the tip of his tongue to bring Ruth's name into the conversation when Rob paused on his way out of the room to pat his shirt pocket and fish an envelope out.

'Here, almost forgot this.'

Jim turned it idly, and finding no clue to its sender used his thumbnail to slit it open.

'I could just wish he had a more settled job,' Mary said. 'I mean, India, and Ro was talking about a trip up the Nile after that. From the way she spoke they'll be spending more time abroad than at home. And I believe some of those African countries are – why, whatever's the matter, Jim?'

The colour had gone from his face as he stood staring at the paper.

'Jim?' She went to him, wiping wet hands on her pinny. When his eyes lifted to meet hers they were wide with shock.

'Dad's dead. Pneumonia. He was crook with the flu and it turned into pneumonia. Jesus!' he said blankly, unmindful of his aunt's presence. 'I can't believe it.' He consulted the letter. 'On the tenth, it says. That's three weeks ago and I didn't even know.'

'Who . . .?' Mary asked, and he looked down mechanically again at the sheet.

'It's from the Salvos at a place called Lynton Creek, in Queensland. That's getting down the Channel Country, somewhere on the Georgina River, I think. It's from a Captain Brogan.' His hands were trembling. He felt a wrenching sense of loss and tried angrily to deny it. 'This is stupid! Why should it matter to me if . . . ? I've only seen him a handful of times since I was ten.'

'Of course it matters. Family always matters. Come and sit down, dear.' Mary tugged at the strings of her pinny and took his arm to lead him to a seat in the lounge, where Rob sat reading a paper. He glanced up, saw their faces and stiffened. Mary spoke before he could ask.

'It's Sandy. He's passed away. That's what the letter was. I suppose,' she added, 'that he still had the address in his gear and the padre found it. He must've known about Jim.'

Rob put the paper aside. 'What . . . ? I mean, was it an accident, or . . . ? When did it happen?'

'He was in hospital.' Jim fumbled the letter open and passed it to him. 'It reads like he was ill already and the pneumonia was just too much. I can't believe it,' he repeated. 'He's dead and buried and I didn't even know. Of course I'll have to go over there.'

'Why?' Rob lifted his brows. 'There's nothing you can do. Like you say, he's dead and buried. Let it go, Jim. You owe him nothing, and any debts he's left will find their way to your door soon enough. That,' he finished dryly, 'always happens. Just bear in mind you are not responsible, not in the eyes of the law.'

Jim stared blankly at him as if his words made no sense. He smoothed and folded the letter, then put it down on the occasional table and sat staring at it.

'He wasn't old.'

'Alcoholics don't have to be.'

'I wonder what he was doing there – in Lynton Creek?'

Rob made no answer and Jim looked at Mary perched on the chair beside him.

She touched his arm. 'Perhaps there wasn't a reason. It might just have been a place to finally stop at. Although he must have had work of some sort to keep himself and . . . and the others,' she finished.

'I suppose.' He sat listening to the whirr of the overhead fan and wondered if that woman had ever become his father's wife and whether the kid had survived, and if so what they would do without a bread-winner. If his father had ever been that, of course, and then he thought of Sandy dead in his coffin and misery was a sudden hard knot in his chest. He got up, knocking the table with his knee, and the letter coasted lightly to the floor.

'I'm going out for some air. I'll be a while. No need to wait up.'

Jim got little rest that night. Memories pursued him into tangled dreams of his father, who rode through the darkness somewhere ahead of him. He heard him quite clearly, but before he could catch him up Roger Lawson was there, grinning spitefully at him across a campfire. 'I seen a gin jockey go by a while back,' he said and tossed the contents of the billy onto the flames. Steam and ash rose into the air and exploding coals banged like rifle fire. The cattle rushed, carrying the post and rails before them in a demented panic, and Jim felt the sting of the wind on his face as he flattened himself along the horse's neck and rode through the violent night, knowing he was too late; there would be no turning them now.

Silent branches slapped him out of the darkness, his heart pounded along with the hooves, and the wind tore tears from his eyes. Urgency beat at him, but even as he pushed her on the mare was slowing and through the dusty starlight he could see, he could *feel*, the way the mob was sliding away from Dolphin's flagging stride. Somewhere ahead Sandy was riding full in their path, and anguish hollowed his chest because he knew he could not save him. Then Dolphin fell and he with her, his stomach suddenly weightless as he tucked his head into his shoulder and crashed pantingly awake against the wall.

His heart was thumping like a trip hammer and his cheeks were wet. Breathing deeply, he let the terror of the nightmare fade. When his heart rate had slowed he bunched the damp pillow behind him and lay watching the dark beyond the window yield to grey amid the first tentative stirring of the birds. As a kid he'd often stared out the same window at the stars scattered like glass powder across the sky, holding to himself the knowledge that those same stars shone somewhere on his father's camp. It had seemed to bring him closer, and in doing so eased his loneliness. For despite Mary's best efforts, the friendship of the men and the company of his cousins, he had often felt alone. His father had done that to him, by taking away the sun of his existence, and not content with that he'd compounded his first betrayal with another by dying.

A great anger burned in Jim, mostly directed at himself. Somewhere in the back of his mind there had existed an unacknowledged plan to find Sandy and make a tidier leavetaking than they'd had the last time. He had known he would do it. It wouldn't change anything between them but he would at least give his father a hearing, let him explain whatever it was he had come to say and hadn't at their final meeting. *Couldn't*, an inner voice corrected now, *because you wouldn't listen.* But he had never thought there might be reason to hurry his search, and so had buried the guilt that occasionally visited him and let the months and then years that measured the span of his father's life slip from him until all were gone.

Now, when it was too late, Jim wanted him back. Regret seared like a brand. Unable to go on lying there, he flung the sheet aside and rolled into a sitting position to stare down at the patterned linoleum between his bare feet. Memories of Sandy that for years he'd forced himself to forget swept over him, and he covered his face with his hands as if that would blot them out. But still they slid past his inner eye, faded snapshots of his childhood. Sandy as a stocky shape on Dolphin, hat pulled down and eyes squinting against the glare. Behind the wheel of the old rover, his cotton shirt crumpled and sweat-stained. Seated on the verandah on summer evenings, squeezing tunes out of his accordion for Jim and Jenny . . . He had bestridden Jim's world, been all that a father should be in those early years. And yet in the end Jim had turned from him and run without giving him a chance to speak.

He sighed out his remorse from the hollow in his chest, wishing he could undo it, could take back the silent years that marked his own betrayal. Rob had been right, even though he hadn't been referring to that. *Someday,* he'd once told him, *you'll find being sorry isn't always enough.*

Skipping breakfast, he wandered down to the stable to sit on the top rail in a thin wedge of shade cast by the feed shed. He gazed around at the familiar scene. The stalls were empty, but alive with memories of the horses they'd held – the Rook, Corinne, his own Pearlshell. And memories of Barney too. Jim pictured him rubbing the lump on his cheekbone, ready with a kind word. *It's tough, kid, but it's life.* Pigeons cooed where the grass had seeded beside the water trough, and when he eased his position feeding galahs rose in a shrieking pink and silver cloud that whirled noisily over the stables before settling back into the yellowed grass. There were horses on the trough but they were all strange to him, like the men in the kitchen. A part of his life had gone. Old Pommy had been chased off the place, according to Rob, by a stout, henna-haired virago who arrived on the mail plane claiming to be his wife. Despite his grief, Jim smiled remembering his uncle's account of it.

'He got about three hours' start,' Rob said. 'A stock inspector had come through, and was heading back to the Alice. He was in the kitchen having a drink of tea when the plane got in and Pommy grabbed a lift out with him. Didn't wait for his cheque or to pick up his belongings. He saw her coming, legged it to the car and went.'

'Did she catch him?' Jim asked.

'I doubt it.' An unaccustomed glint showed in Rob's green eyes. 'Sheer bad luck if she did. The Catholic priest was visiting us and she got a lift out with him after lunch. I'm afraid I let her think – and so did Father Stillwell – that he and the stockie were heading in the same direction.' He sighed, pushing away his tasteless pudding. 'We've had about six replacements so far and none of them half the cook Pommy was.'

Jim shifted on the rail. He hoped his old friend had retained his freedom. Pommy had been a demon at the grog and had obviously run out on his wife, but he'd been kind to an unhappy boy and made him welcome in his world. Nor, Jim recalled, had he ever passed judgement on Sandy. He shifted again uncomfortably. Perhaps if he'd talked to Pommy about it instead of simply accepting Rob's reading of the unredeemable nature of his father's actions he might not be sitting here today vainly regretting the past.

He told them at lunchtime, waiting until the bookkeeper had gone before speaking abruptly into the clatter of clearing plates.

'I've made up my mind. I have to get over to Lynton Creek.'

'Why?' Rob's voice was hard with displeasure.

'I don't know. To see his grave, talk to his . . . family. I can't just walk away from it, Uncle.'

'Oh, Jim.' Mary put down a handful of used cutlery on the clean tablecloth. 'Of course you must if you think you should, but, well, will it make things any better? Shouldn't you just try to remember him as he was?'

'No. All I remember is the last time he came here. And I can't get past that until . . . I should have forgiven him,' he blurted angrily. 'That's why I have to go.'

'Some things,' Rob laid stress on the first word, 'don't deserve forgiveness.'

'No?' Jim looked levelly at him, his chest and shoulders tight from the effort of reining in the muddle of emotions that filled him. 'If it had been you, you know, he would have. He was,' the word came to him in a rush of enlightenment, 'a tolerant man. He didn't judge. He was like Oliver in that.' Anger squeezed his heart and he added viciously, for in that moment he hated his uncle's inflexibility, 'And you'd better hope that one day he feels the same – Oliver, I mean.'

Rob stared with a creased brow. 'What?'

'You don't even know! But you haven't forgiven him either – at least, you blame Fiona for it, which is much the same thing. But ask yourself who's done the greater wrong? Him for quitting the company or you for pushing him into it against his will? It's his life, you know. Not yours.'

336

Mary was staring at him aghast. 'What's come over you, Jim?'

'Nothing. Only now I've stopped hating Dad it's like everything's suddenly different. He wasn't perfect, he didn't pretend to be. But he wasn't . . .' Rosemary's word floated back to him. 'Righteous or unforgiving. He let people be what they were, without trying to make them into something he considered better.'

Rob pushed his chair back and stood. 'I don't know what you're getting at, Jim, but if this is some hare-brained complaint because I stopped you going after him when you were sixteen —'

'Of course it isn't! And you didn't stop me. Once he took up with that woman I never wanted to. I became a jackeroo to be like *you* – to be what he wasn't. All I'm saying is that you should've stopped me hating him sooner. You should've made me see that it was because he had no hate, because he loved too much, that he gave up. And now it's too late, for him and for me. That's what I'm complaining about,' he shouted furiously at the older man, 'that you made it too late for me. I was young and stupid and full of myself – why didn't you help me then?'

Silence held the room. Jim couldn't tell if it was anger or consternation struggling for expression on Rob's face. It was unfair to lay all the blame on him, he knew, but he couldn't help himself. His whole being keened with a loss so sharp that he half expected it to sound in the heavy air. It wasn't Rob's fault, he thought dully – he was who he was, a just and blinkered man with a code that made no allowance for human frailty. But even knowing that, Jim would not unsay the only words he had ever spoken in his father's defence.

Mary looked stricken, not, he knew, by the truth of his accusation but that it had been made at all. 'Oh, Jim.' She fumbled for a chair and sat.

'I'm sorry, Aunty. I know you felt differently about Dad. Ro did too, she tried to tell me once.' He looked at his uncle, who stood watching him under his brows. 'She said I was too much like you. And do you know, I was proud to hear it. Proud. I *wanted* to be like you. I didn't want to be the son of a failure, a dirty gin man that everyone despised. I was taught to despise him. And he died knowing that I did!'

Rob shook his head like a man recovering from a flurry of blows. 'Look, I know you're upset, Jim, but if you'd just listen to me for a moment —'

'No.' He picked his hat off the wall hook and slammed it onto his head, his eyes like marble. Halfway through the door, he turned. 'I listened before. This time I'm choosing him.'

TWENTY

Jim reached Lynton Creek via a rattly timber bridge spanning a deep dry watercourse after two days of hard driving. His anger was gone, lost somewhere far behind him, along the rutted dusty roads and scrubby gravel ridges, in an hour spent wrestling with a punctured tyre and another perched on his heels in the shade of a stock tank, gazing out over unfamiliar country while the engine cooled. He regretted his outburst to Rob, and guilt and sadness rode his waking moments, putting the taste of ashes in his mouth.

Ruth was also on his mind. He longed to talk to her face to face right now, and tell her how his world had changed. He felt intuitively certain she would understand his aching sense of loss. He wondered whether Roger Lawson's gossip had included mention of Sandy's child, and whether it would make any difference to her. Somehow he doubted it. But he wished she could have met the old Sandy; they would have hit it off, he thought, and for a moment his mind yearned after the impossible. Misery rose again within him, swamping his muddled thoughts. He would phone her tonight, he decided, just to hear her voice. His heart told him it would be filled with concern.

Lynton Creek, though substantially larger than Goola, was still a hamlet – a collection of iron roofs on the far side of the creek along which scraggy gums hung tiredly in the heat. Pads crossed the road and he saw cattle in the distance stringing doggedly across the bare flat, their rumps wavering out of focus in the swimmy air. There was a grid, a leaning sign – WELCOME TO LYNTON CREEK POP. 158 – and a corrugated stretch of road that continued straight through on its way south, leaving the scatter of buildings behind it like something unloaded there. There was a pub, a store, and an unpainted barn of a structure set on low blocks – that would be the hall. Also a tiny school, faded flag flying above the dusty playground; a handful of houses; and, right at the far end, screened by thickets of oleander, the police station set in a field of yellowing couch grass. Jim passed through without stopping, then made a U-turn and drove back to the pub.

The Goldrush Hotel had seen better days. Its wood had twisted in the heat of past summers so that its dim interior was barred with light where the planks had pulled and opened in the wall. A channel of air moving through propped-open doors cooled the room, and the muted light rested softly against Jim's eyes as he entered. He nodded to the barman, wound his long legs around a stool and ordered a beer.

'Coming up.' The man was absurdly thin, with a hooked nose that dominated a leathery face and cropped grey hair. 'Gunna be a hot one,' he said, sliding a glass onto the bar and uncapping the bottle with a practised flick. 'Come far?'

'From the Territory. Have one with me.' Jim waited while the barman procured another glass and poured. He lifted his own glass

340

in salute, then drank and sighed his appreciation. 'That hits the spot. Quiet little place you've got here.' He glanced around at the dartboard and faded posters, the bullock horns above the door, and the glitter of bottles and cellophane-wrapped tobacco on the shelves. Catching a glimpse through the inner door of a table and silver-frosted stove front, he remembered lunch. 'You do meals?'

'Bed and board,' the publican agreed. 'Thinking of staying?'

'For tonight, yeah. Do you have a room? Doesn't really matter, I've got my swag, but I wouldn't mind a decent meal.' Breakfast had been baked beans eaten from the can and he'd used up the last of his corned meat.

'Yeah, not much call for 'em but there's rooms. And the tucker's good. Got a yella woman does the cooking – Yella Stella.' He grinned, showing tobacco-stained teeth. 'Knows her stuff too. Going through then? Where you heading?'

'I just reached it.' Jim set the glass down, thumbed his hat back. It wouldn't hurt to test the local waters a little, see how his father's name was greeted here, and whether anyone had thought enough of him to make seeking out his new family worthwhile. The memory of Sammy Deane returned but he pushed it aside. He'd come this far, he might as well learn the worst. 'I'm looking for a bloke someone told me was out this way. Sandy McAllister – you ever run across him? Used to do station work, but he'd be getting on a bit now.'

'Well, bugger me,' the barman said, and his look was curious. He hooked an elbow on the bar and stared at Jim. 'You're the first ever did. Come looking, I mean.'

'You know him then?'

'Did,' he admitted, adding cautiously, 'if it's the same bloke. Cos if it is you're too late. He's dead.'

'Is that so?' Jim studied the bottom of his glass. 'What happened to him?'

'Pneumonia.' The man sucked his teeth as if debating whether to add more and Jim waited patiently. But he'd only been working out dates, for eventually he nodded. 'That's right. Be three weeks now. Bit more, maybe. You could see he was crook but the old fool wouldn't go up the hospital – didn't want to leave the kid, I reckon. He had this little kid, and a right taking he got into when he heard Sandy was gone. Screaming and kicking, almost had the roof down. The Sallies have got the little bugger now, and I'm looking for a new yardman. Y'aren't after a job, I suppose?'

'No.' Jim heard the sharp click of his glass as he put it down on the bar but it was as if someone else had performed the action. 'Just him and the kid? I heard he had a gin. And did you say he worked here, in the pub? The bloke I'm thinking of was a drunk.'

'It'd be him.' The barman was confident. 'Old alco. Bit shaky and his liver was shot, but he could do the yard work all right. I used to dole the grog out to him, just enough to keep him going and stop the shakes. He and the kid dossed down in a bit of a shed out the back and come up for their meals, and the kid went off to school every day. Seemed bright enough and terrible fond of his old man. I dunno what became of the mother. When he first turned up it was just him and the kid.' He sighed and scratched his neck. 'So you're not looking for work? I'm Bob, by the way. Bob Tyrell.'

'Jim McAllister.' He put out his hand, watching the barman's eyes as they shook. 'That's right, same name. Sandy was my father.'

'Yeah? You don't . . . That is . . .'

'Different mothers.'

'Ah.' Tyrell looked aside. 'Well, don't take it wrong if I spoke outa turn. If you'd said . . .'

'Yeah.' Jim got off the stool, the heels of his riding boots loud on the floor. 'What about that feed then? Sandwiches would do, or a bit of cold meat – and another beer to go with it.'

'We can do better than that, I reckon. Stella!' the barman bellowed, moving towards the door. He stuck his head through it and yelled again, then turned to look back at Jim. 'Be half an hour. While you're waiting you want to have a look over Sandy's stuff? The police came of course but all they took was the kid's gear. They said I should dump the rest.' He shrugged. 'Say truth, I never got round to it. It's only a few clothes, anyroad. The padre woulda took any papers, and there wasn't any money. Sandy wanted it that way, said he'd only drink it if he had it. He'd tell me when the kid needed clothes or he was running short of tobacco and I'd buy it for him. It's all on the books. I kept a running total and in fact there's a bit owing. I told the padre he can collect it any time.'

'It sounds like you were a good friend to him,' Jim said gruffly. 'Thanks.'

'Well, he suited me better sober than drunk.' Tyrell shrugged. 'At the same time he was a decent enough bloke for . . . Well, what he was. And he kept the kid clean, and himself. I can't bear a dirty drunk.'

Jim wondered why Sandy's son had not gone back to his mother's people. He said, 'If you'll show me this shed?' And followed the publican out through the door at the back of the bar.

There was a verandah behind the kitchen, overlooking a yard bounded by an ugly galvanised-iron fence. 'Past the tank.' Tyrell jerked his head and stood watching as Jim trod down the steps, his shadow short in the noon sun. The heat hit him like a blow. He squinted and focused on a patch of mint at the base of the tank, where a broken overflow pipe leaked down the side. A scraggly paw-paw tree leaned into the shade thrown by the shed, and a couple of yellowed tomato plants were staked along its wall.

Jim hesitated, fighting off his reluctance to enter the shed and plumb the depths of Sandy's degradation. The building was squat and flat-roofed, with double doors and a louvred window on the eastern side. It was meant, he surmised, for a garage and would be roasting hot inside. He lifted out the bent wire securing the doors and they fell wide of their own accord, showing a dirt floor and gloomy interior. His father's final home.

Its neatness caught at his throat. Sandy had always been neat; he kept his tools and his camps in apple-pie order, Jim remembered, and the same could be said of the scant belongings here. Two stretcher beds, one with a rolled swag on it, a couple of up-ended tea chests holding daily items, clothes hanging from nails driven into the wall supports. An emu egg, green as the grass that would normally camouflage it, rose from a small stand laboriously carved from mulga and was the only non-utilitarian object in the room. It sat on a rough shelf near the window. Jim remembered the day his father had found another such egg and his heart twisted.

He sat on the nearest bed and checked off the items on the tea chest: a stock knife with a cracked handle; a pipe, its bowl much charred;

a couple of plates and pannikins; and a lamp with smoke-streaked glass. A pair of sandshoes the worse for wear were placed neatly under the stretcher opposite.

The sadness of it tore at him but he found a fierce pride in his father too, for however poor he had been, however far gone in drink, the place was clean. He had not lost all self-respect. Yardman at some end-of-the-line pub mightn't have been the greatest job, but he had held it and cared for his son as best he could.

'Dad.' Jim said the word that for years he'd forbidden himself even to think. It came out sounding as small and lost as he felt himself to be. A sob rose in his throat and he choked it down. His father had battled a living for him and Jenny when there'd been more hope than money, and he'd done it again here without either. Not even the grog had killed his instinct for caring. He had made a home here – for that was what this was, however wretched by others' standards.

Jim picked up the stock knife and slipped it into his pocket, wondering if it was the same one Sandy had carried all those years before. That knife had cut whip-falls and shaved tobacco plugs, had castrated calves and scalped dingoes and quartered lemons from their garden tree. Jim gripped it fiercely within his pocket, but no feeling of union, no essence of the dead man's being, reached to touch him. It was a just a knife, the blades loosened from age, the bone grips cracked across.

He shut the door behind him, leaving the place as he'd found it for Tyrell to dispose of as he wished.

Lunch was ready in the kitchen when he got there, a generous helping of goat chops, tinned peas, spuds in their jackets and gravy. Stella introduced herself and joined him at the table, propping large elbows either side of a cup of tea. She was a big woman, with double chins above an enormous bosom and dark eyes buried in creases of fat.

'So you're little Eddy's brother.' Her voice was light, in contrast to her bulk.

'Oh, that his name is it, Edward?'

'Yeah. And you'd be Jim who's gunna manage a big station one day.' She sipped at her tea, eyeing him over the rim of her cup. 'No need to look surprised. Young Eddy'd talk about you by the hour. You were the only bit of comfort he had when they told him his dad was dead. Jim'll come, he said, after he stopped sobbing his little heart out. It took you a while but you got here.'

Taken aback Jim straightened, finding himself absurdly defensive. 'It was three weeks before I got the letter. That's hardly my fault.'

'No.' Her gaze was straight and he fidgeted under it.

'Tell me about him,' he said. 'My father. Had you known him long?' He found himself holding his breath as he waited on her answer.

'Fair while. He turned up about five years back with the kid. The arse out of his strides and a bad case of the DTs. The Salvo bloke, Captain Grogan, found him choked down by the creek. They took the kid off him and got him straightened out again. The captain told him the police would take his son away unless he took a hold of himself. I reckon he didn't want that, cos he tried to stay off the grog after. 'Course he never done it.' Her lips thinned mirthlessly. 'Once a drunk, always a drunk – and I've seen a few, believe me. But Bob give him the job here and shifted him into the shed, and pretty soon young Eddy was toddling round the place. It didn't seem no time then before Sandy was taking him for walks and carving him bits of toys. He kept to himself mostly.

Never said much, 'cept to the boy, and Eddy'd come babbling his stories to me. All about his big brother Jim. I reckon you were pretty important to 'em both.' She shot him a look and Jim moved uncomfortably.

'So what caused his illness?'

Stella snorted. 'Grog, what else? Sandy wasn't no different to others when the craving hit him. Usually some stupid bugger'd buy him a drink, or take a bottle round the back and get him started. Then the kid'd be banging on the door crying for me or Bob to come, and we'd find him choked down wherever he'd dropped. Last time was the worst – he was right out to it, but breathing sorta funny and his face was an awful colour. He'd been crook with the flu already, so Bob reckoned we oughta get him up the hospital.' Her shoulders lifted like hams rolling as she stared back at the events she spoke of. 'He died next morning.'

There was a little silence until Jim found himself asking, almost pleading, 'But did you like him?'

Stella shrugged again, her face hardening. 'He was a drunk. Me, I'm married to one. I've got five kids, and the grog ain't the only thing he hits. It's his way of getting square with the world.' For the first time Jim noticed the mottling of old bruises on her face and upper arms. 'Sandy was good to his kid, I liked him for that, but it's as far as it went. You can't depend on no-hopers, I learned *that* long ago.' Her voice softened suddenly. 'He'll be glad to see you, Eddy will. You taking him back with you?'

'With me?' Jim stared at her. 'Of course not.' He almost laughed at the idea, then realised from her face that she'd assumed it all along. He felt a momentary panic. Perhaps Tyrell also expected him to take responsibility for his half-brother? Good God! A worse thought intruded. Was it possible that this Captain Brogan had written with such an end in view?

He calmed himself. How could it be anything to do with him? He hadn't even met the boy. He'd visit his father's grave and look in on the Salvo bloke to check whether Sandy had left any debts Bob Tyrell didn't know about, then he'd get the hell out of here. He had no hope of making Monday's plane from the Alice but he could always reschedule. He'd tell Ruth tonight when he phoned.

He got to his feet. 'No,' he said firmly. 'I can't do that. But I expect the Salvos will find a place for him. Thanks for the lunch.' He picked up his hat and went out, conscious of the weight of her eyes following him.

Captain George Brogan was a stocky, red-cheeked man with a ready smile and the noncommittal gaze of someone accustomed to hearing people out before speaking himself. For all that, his eyes were shrewd behind their blandness and Jim, shaking hands with him at his front door, could not fault that. He'd have heard a few hard-luck stories in his time, and dealt with plenty of men like his father. In the bush, grog and loneliness went hand in hand. And that the bush had been the captain's stamping ground for some time was obvious. It took only moments for Jim to recognise in him that quality shared by Father Stillwell and the other travelling padres who had visited Kharko. Like them he would be non-judgemental and work beyond the strict boundaries of his Church.

'You got my letter,' the captain commented, ushering his guest into a shabby front room, its blinds drawn against the sun. 'I don't know how close you were to your father, Jim, but I'm sorry for your loss. And he must be a loss to you or you wouldn't be here. Would you like some tea?'

'Yes – that is, I mean, no. No tea, thanks, don't bother,' Jim said quickly. 'It was good of you to write. Of course I work away from the place now and the mails are slow so it wasn't until I got home . . .' He was babbling, he realised. He let the sentence die and looked for somewhere to put his hat, but there being no uncluttered surface he left it riding his left knee. 'I wanted to thank you for writing.'

'That was no bother, and neither's the tea. Ah, here's my wife, Anna. Eddy's brother Jim, my dear.'

Anna Brogan, who looked overworked, was the perfect foil to her husband's robust form: thin and pale with the blotchy skin of ill health. She had the tea tray ready in her hands.

'There, you see? Automatic, comes with the territory.' Brogan took the tray from her, placed it perilously on a chair and patted his wife's shoulder. 'I'll see to it. You go and rest.'

She smiled at Jim, who had risen to his feet, then murmured a few words and obediently left the room. Her husband served them handily enough while maintaining a flow of small talk about Jim's journey and the prospects for rain. It was only when they were both settled, the serviceable mugs in their hands, that Brogan's manner changed from host to padre.

'I couldn't discover what your father's religious beliefs were, so he just had one of our regular services when we buried him. I hope you don't mind?'

'Of course not. As far as that goes I don't think he had any. Any, er, formalised religion,' Jim amended, trying to remember if they had ever gone to church. There must, he supposed, have been a visiting padre during the years at Arcadia, for one had come regularly to Kharko, but his mind stayed obstinately blank. 'He used to say a man should help others and give where it was needed.' Embarrassed to be speaking of such things, he looked away, taking in the contents of the shabby room with its mismatched furniture and worn chair covers. He cleared his throat to change the subject. 'The publican said you might have some papers of his? There's probably nothing that matters but if I might look them over? He said you took on the boy too. What happened about that – is he still here?'

'So far.' Brogan crossed the room and ferreted through a battered filing cabinet from which he extracted a buff envelope. 'Here we are. I was going to send it if you didn't come, but I wanted to be sure first that my letter had reached you. Sandy seemed to set store by it. He was in a bit of strife when we met first.'

'I heard.' Jim couldn't keep some bitterness from his voice.

'Yes, well, we're all weak vessels, you know. With your father it was drink – and he knew his own weakness. He gave me the papers soon after that first episode. Said he didn't trust himself with them. And the address to send word when the time came. This was the end of the road for him. He walked here, by stages, carrying the little chap, and I think he knew he wouldn't leave.' Brogan tapped the envelope on his palm. 'It's his will, I believe, or maybe a last letter. At any rate it seemed too important just to send off to an old address.'

'Thank you.' Jim took the envelope with his father's name on it, written in what he guessed to be the captain's hand. It weighed very little to be the sum of a man's life, but then what had Sandy to leave? He said, 'About the boy – when I said here I meant in the house.'

'Eddy? Well, not right now.' Brogan consulted the clock on the wall. 'He's at school. But yes, he's staying with us for a little, until we find a place for him. It's the sergeant's job really, he's the local protector. But my wife and I said we'd look after him until the papers come through. You know how it is, anything official involves a mile of red tape.' A sudden thought seemed to strike him. 'Do you mean you want to see him?'

'No.' Jim spoke quickly. 'I was just curious. I'd thought his mother would still be around to care for him. What happened to her?'

'Your father never said. I imagined measles, TB, something like that. It's possible she just pined for her own people. Pined and died because she couldn't go back. I've seen it before.'

Jim nodded, relieved that this man at least did not expect him to take the boy. 'Bob Tyrell told me there's some money accumulated. I want you to collect it to . . . to defray expenses.' The next words came out before he could stop them. 'What'll happen to him – where will he go?'

Brogan sighed. 'Where all the abandoned ones go. The police will place him somewhere under protection – a reserve, perhaps, or a mission station. He'll be schooled and fed and clothed, but that's all. It will be shelter he'll get, not a home. A place, when he's older, to get away from. I'm afraid it happens all the time; there are plenty of unwanted half-caste children around.' He deliberated before adding, 'I shan't tell him you came. It will only upset him. He's got this notion in his head, which I'm afraid Sandy must have encouraged, that if anything happened to his father he'd go to live with you. I think Sandy may have told him that once when he was ill, to make his possible death less frightening to the child. So that even if the boy found himself alone, there would still be someone he belonged to. And then Sandy didn't correct it and the child never forgot, which makes it difficult. For you too, of course. You're not married?'

'What?' The question surprised him. 'No.'

'I thought not.' Brogan gave his jolly laugh. 'Your father meant it more for comfort than a done deal, I'm sure, but I'm afraid it will break Eddy's heart when he realises . . . Still, Man proposes, God disposes, eh?'

Shame surged in Jim, but not enough to drown the thankfulness he also felt. It was going to be easy, after all. Brogan would think of some explanation and he could walk away. He took up his hat and rose and the captain went with him to the door.

'Well, I musn't keep you. Should you want to visit the grave you'll find the cemetery behind the racecourse. See Bob Tyrell, he's the official groundsman. It wasn't a very big send-off, I'm afraid. Just my wife and young Eddy and Bob, and Mrs Hodges who cooks for the pub.'

'Stella? I met her.'

'A good woman – and very kind to young Eddy.'

'Well, thanks for the tea.'

'You're welcome.' A professional smile to accompany his words as he shook Jim's hand at the door.

Clutching the envelope, Jim walked across to the rover, aware only of his relief. He had done as much as any reasonable person could expect, and given ordinary luck on the road he would have time to call at Kharko and put things right with his uncle, and still make it to Alice in time for his flight. With each passing day, he regretted more deeply not the things he'd said but the manner in which he'd said them. It had been unfair to blame Rob when he had been as much at fault himself. Squinting in the light that hit like an axe blow at his eyes, he swung into the car and tossed the envelope on the seat. He was reluctant to open it; all he could imagine it containing was a plea on his brother's behalf.

At three o'clock he got up from where he'd been sitting in the dark shade on the verandah and strolled up the street to the school. The sun, halfway down the afternoon sky, glittered on bottle tops embedded in the dirt pavement. The flag lanyards tapped against the metal pole in an errant wind that stirred the faded cloth. Noise swelled as the door at the top of the steps opened and some twenty youngsters, ranging in age from around five to thirteen by the look of them, poured down the stairs.

Jim, who had never attended a regular school, watched them come towards him in a tide of hats and bags and running feet. Three of the boys and one little girl had skins darker than amber, with strong features and deep-set eyes. One of the boys was too old – ten or twelve, Jim judged. His eyes skipped impatiently to the other two, searching for a likeness, some hint that he was looking at his father's son. But there was none.

He expected to feel relief but was filled instead with an obscure disappointment. The boys passed him unheeding, shirts untucked, voices soft and quick, heads bent together over the arcane secrets of childhood. Jim almost called after them to ask their names, but the wind stirred and as he lifted his face to it the moment passed. Brogan was right. Better to let him think he'd never come.

He retraced his steps to the pub and let himself into his hot little room at the end of the verandah, switching on the sluggish ceiling fan. He left the door open, set the window wide, then picked up the envelope from the bed and worked his thumb under the flap. He did not understand his own actions. He had intended to visit the cemetery but had gone to the school instead, and now he wondered what possible point there could be in knowing which boy was a McAllister.

Coming here had been a mistake, but since he had he would see Tyrell about organising a headstone. That much he could do. Sandy should not lie in an unmarked grave. Tyrell would know who to contact, and the best way of getting heavy freight to Lynton Creek.

Sweat trickled from his brow, stinging his eyes, and he lifted his arm to dry them before tipping the contents of the envelope onto the bedspread. Three items fell out: a photograph, a sheet of flimsy paper on which he recognised Sandy's writing, and a heavier sheet folded across the middle.

He picked up the photo first. It was a small black-and-white snap of himself and his mother standing side by side in the garden at Arcadia. She had her arm around his shoulders and her head tilted to one side, smiling. He looked to be about six; the lemon tree, in brilliant sunlight, came barely to his shoulder.

The sudden jolt of recognition caught his breath. He touched the images, familiar yet distantly strange, like his younger self. There had been no photos of Jenny at Kharko, and the only photo he remembered from his childhood at Arcadia was the framed wedding shot that used to stand on the home-made dressing-table in his parents' bedroom. He had not thought of it in years. It must, he supposed, still be packed away in the tea chests Dino had loaded onto the truck the day his aunt had come to take him to Kharko.

Gently he laid down the photo and picked up the thin sheet of paper covered in Sandy's spiky script. His father's will. *This is to certify that I, Alexander William McAllister, do leave and bequeath . . .* It took only a moment to read. It was dated and signed five years before and witnessed by George Brogan (Captain) of the Salvation Army Citadel in Lynton Creek, and his wife Anna. And it left everything Sandy possessed to his eldest son, James Alexander McAllister.

Jim sat staring at the words, fingering the flimsy paper while a slow joy welled like spring water within him. It didn't matter that a broken stock knife was the most Sandy had to leave him, it was the words and intention that counted. They were the proof that his father had forgiven him, had thought of him and wished him well in his heart. Despite Jim's angry years, when he'd done his best to wipe Sandy out of his life, his father's love for him had stayed firm, if not apparent in his actions. It made Jim's loss the keener but went far towards assuaging his guilt. He read the will through twice, then laid that too on the bed and picked up the third and final paper.

It was a legal document, he saw, and he opened it curiously. Then straightened and sat very still, staring. In his hands was the Instrument of Lease for the pastoral holding known as Arcadia, with a description of its portions and boundaries, and his father's signature and that of a witness, together with the date of transfer – April 1947. The year that Jim was born.

He sat stunned, unable at first to take it in. He had assumed the lease had long been sold, or exchanged for drinking money, but here were the deeds. When everything else had gone Sandy clung doggedly to the land, knowing he'd never return to it himself. What reason could he have had to keep it, if not to leave it to his son?

Over the years, Jim had toyed with the idea of going back to Arcadia and reviving the station; of spending his life not as a cog in another man's empire but as the hub of his own, however small. But he'd never seriously expected it to happen, for once the selection of land by ballot ceased, its acquisition was beyond the means of ordinary working men. Now the opportunity was there, passed as a gift from his father's hand to his.

His heart beat faster as his thoughts flew to Ruth and a future with her. If she would have him they could marry now, and Arcadia could provide the home he must otherwise wait years to acquire. Even the company's comparatively generous standards didn't run to married quarters for jackeroos.

He tried to slow his thoughts, maintain a grip on reality. He was taking too much for granted even to think of marriage. Whatever her feelings for him, Ruth might not wish for that so soon, and she certainly might not wish for life in a tin shack in a place as lonely as Arcadia. He thought of Paula, discontented in a comfortable homestead only half the distance from town that Arcadia was. But Ruth was different, not just from her sister but from other women as well. His heart knew it. Different the way his mother had been. In the time they'd spent together he had sensed the strength in her. No, all he had to worry about was whether or not she would have him.

Outside, the glare had gone from the sky. The roof iron cracked in the cooling air. Jim placed the papers under the spare pillow in the wardrobe, pulled the door shut and went to see Bob Tyrell about a headstone for the grave.

'I can do that,' the publican agreed. 'Just gimme the words you want. What about the stuff in the shed?'

'Chuck it away, unless there's a tool or something else you can use. And here,' he handed some folded notes across the bar, 'I'll be pulling out early. Take my bill from this and put the rest in with what's owing to the kid – I don't want the Salvo bloke out of pocket. Do you have a phone here?'

'You're joking, mate. But there's a transceiver at the store. They'll send a telegram for you. You want dinner?'

'Yes, please. I'm going to drop by the cemetery, see the old man's grave. Then I'll get a wire off.' Ruth would have it tomorrow, he thought. He'd give her the details to explain his delay but the rest would keep until he saw her.

A set of steel gates that sagged a little on their posts enclosed Lynton Creek's graveyard. There was a padlocked shed just within the gates and a row of she-oaks spaced at intervals along the fence, through which the headstones were visible. Some were old, their corners rounded by time and weather. Other plots, like Sandy's, were marked only by a numbered stake. The raw earth had sunk a little but the grave still looked new. Somebody had spaded the edges clean and a faded plastic wreath had blown to one side, its momentum halted by a jam jar of dead leaves.

Jim squatted on his heels. It occurred to him that he had never visited his mother's grave, or Barney's, and now here was the final resting place of yet another person he had loved. He propped his forearms on his knees and sat listening to the wind through the she-oaks, and the distant cawing of a sky-blown crow, remembering Sandy. And with him all the ghosts of Arcadia – Nimrod and Diamond, Nipper and Meena, Dolphin and Jake, and the goats scampering up the trunks of the leaning ironwoods beyond the trough. His mother in the kitchen, his father at work in the shed – the whole idyllic world of his childhood. A golden island bounded by the sea of their love.

'It was good, Dad,' he said softly. 'Maybe it could be again?'

The stock knife in his pocket was digging into his leg. He stood and pulled it out, its worn handle slick and smooth to his palm, then he stooped and placed it on the grave, in the centre of the ring of plastic flowers.

The sun was almost gone, the air cool. Thin, raftered cloud had ridden in on the wind to bar the sunset with red and gold, presaging a dusty, unpleasant day to follow. The she-oaks thrashed and sighed as Jim shut the cemetery gate behind him and made his way back to town.

TWENTY-ONE

The return journey was no faster than the outward trip had been. Jim plugged along slowly, camping in gidyea country west of Mt Isa the first night, his swag rolled out beside the rover and his sleep disturbed by muddled dreams. He woke unrefreshed, with a crick in his neck, and sat on his swag massaging it.

He couldn't stop mulling over the past. In retrospect scarcely any of it since adolescence pleased him. Too many of his actions, he realised, had been dictated by selfishness, and he winced whenever he recalled the row with Rob. He had blamed everyone but himself: Sandy for leaving him, Rob for not somehow preventing his hatred, even Ro. She had seen the impossibility of either man behaving differently while he had not. But given their natures, how else could they have acted? He was amazed by how clearly he now saw this.

What about himself, then? Had he been equally bound to behave as he did? He had been little more than a child, after all. He frowned as he considered this. Perhaps he was less to blame than he thought?

He drove steadily through the heat, pausing at noon in the shade of a supplejack to let the motor cool and to eat a sandwich that dried as he made it. When he'd drunk his tea he kicked his swag open and rested, the heat like a wall around his patch of black shadow. It was too hot to sleep but he lay squinting out at the watery mirages shimmering across the parched earth, the sweat beading briefly on his skin before it dried.

Only dead men hurry in the desert. Out of nowhere Barney's voice came floating down the years. Jim had been about twelve when he'd heard that, on a November weekend just before the start of the summer holidays, with the air like an oven under a brassy sky. He'd been giving Barney and one of the black boys a hand to shift cattle somewhere and was eager to quit the dinner-camp and get back into the saddle.

How can they hurry if they're dead? he remembered asking.

They can't. They're dead because they hurried. Now, settle down, kid, and wait.

The words were like ghosts in his head. He owed Barney a lot and always would, for his companionship and guidance, for just being there when he felt he had no one else. Uncomfortably he wondered whether Eddy would have the luck to find somebody like Barney wherever he was sent. But he felt such guilt at the thought that he banished it and thought of Ruth instead.

It was mid-afternoon when he reached the turn-off to Arcadia. Scrub had narrowed the track and he had to buck the rover over the storm drain that had been cut across it, but once he was through the initial thicket of wattle the road's condition was reasonable. He drove carefully, having no desire to stake another tyre, watching the land and trying to recognise features he had thought forever branded into his brain. But his memory was wrong, or the scrub had grown and changed, for he came over the crest of the rise before he realised it and suddenly he was there.

The place had shrunk. That was his first reaction as he negotiated the bend and the open gateway in the sagging fence. All that was left of the gate itself was a tangle of rusty wire and half a set of hames that had been used to hold it shut. Nothing but the uprights and part of the back wall remained of the shed, which, Jim saw with a sense of shock, was no bigger than a suburban garage. It had seemed so spacious to him when he was small.

The mill wheel turned in the background, and to his surprise he saw sunlight glinting on a thin stream of water falling from the outlet pipe into the tank. The pump buckets would have been replaced in the drought, when Kharko had used the country, but it was a wonder the mill head hadn't packed it in for lack of grease. The house tank was still there, its corrugated iron streaked with rust stains, and a few paces to the side of it the house itself huddled in the shade of the old waddi tree. He got out of the rover and walked across.

The verandah had collapsed, and what had been the netting fence around the garden seemed inextricably mixed with thatch, dead roly-poly bushes and ant-eaten rails. Iron flapped on the walls where the nails had gone, and bats, lizards and euros had left their droppings in the kitchen, whose concrete floor was buried by sand. The shelves had warped clear of their screws and there was rust on the stove.

In his bedroom, a faded picture of Davy Crockett and his Mohican friend still survived on the wall. He found a mound of translucent scales where a snake had shed its skin; they crushed under his boots, releasing a faint, offensive odour. He pushed experimentally at the window shutter. It, like the balance of the structural work, seemed still sound, the timber undamaged by white ants. His father had built well, Jim thought, craning to inspect the roof supports. It wouldn't take much work to get everything back to how it had been.

Outside he strolled around, inspecting the trough and then the tank. It was one-third full, the surface of the water patched with virulent-looking green scum, but the walls looked solid enough. The trough seeped moisture at one end, where the rubber sealing had perished, and the pump, judging by the slow trickle produced by the rise and fall of the rods, needed new buckets. He dipped black oil in the crankcase of the diesel and turned the engine over by hand. The fuel tank was rusty and the canvas belting that drove the pump-jack had dried to a brittle, elongated hoop that could have been iron for all the give in it.

Jim spotted a grease drum and nudged it with his foot, expecting it to roll away, but there was weight in it and after a moment's struggle he prised the lid off. The contents were yellowed and a little runny but he grunted with satisfaction at the sight – it would do, for the moment, to grease the head.

Afterwards, scrubbing his hands clean on a rag from behind the seat of the rover, he strolled across to the shed. Somebody had camped there at some time, for charcoal was trodden into the red dirt and a pile of mulga sticks lay carelessly against the wall. He pushed at the bloodwood uprights, finding them as firm as the day they were sunk. Sandy must have poisoned their butts, as he had with the yard posts, to guard against termites. Bits and pieces of rusted steel were scattered about: a cogged wheel, the other half of the gate hames, a slew of old nuts and bolts, parts of a pump-jack. And, fallen down against the wall behind them, his father's pipe.

Jim picked it up and time stood still. He saw himself dancing with impatience to be gone while Sandy searched and patted his pockets for the missing item. *Nip down to the bore, son, see if it's there.* Jim had worried about it raining, about being late, about the missing pipe ruining the day – and had not known it would be their last.

He shut his eyes and felt again the steamy heat, saw the black women at the tank, the watermelon wrapped in wet bags, and Nipper's grinning face calling goodbye. But when he looked of course the flat was bare, save for a bush turkey stalking unconcernedly towards the seepage at the end of the trough. Jim watched it fold its legs to drink, then closed his fist around his father's pipe and strode purposefully towards his vehicle. If the roads had stood the passage of time he wanted to check both Two Bob and Marvell Creek bores while daylight lasted, and get a look at the fences too.

That night he camped under the gums on the bank of Marvell Creek, scratching a fire together from leaves and fallen sticks. He was carrying his own water but he took the shovel from the rover and trod down a euro pad into the creek bed, where he dug a shallow soak, spading aside the litter of leaves and gum nuts until he felt the blade slide crisply into wet sand. The water, when he squatted to scoop a handful, was sweet and cold. He filled his billy, then looked up to find himself staring into the eyes of a dingo watching him from the top of the bank. It had no fear of him. The pricked ears and dark eyes were steady, as if it watched game rather than man, and he could see the tiny movements of the dog's nose as it took his scent.

'You hang around, you're dead,' Jim told him. He picked up the shovel and the dingo, curiosity satisfied, trotted off into the dusk.

The moon rose early, sailing into view full and splendid in the east. Jim heated a tin and ate sitting on his unrolled swag beside the fire, listening to the night. Crickets chirruped from the sand, and from somewhere beyond the bore a boobook called repetitively. Occasionally he heard the thump of travelling roos, and once, far off to the south, the ululating cry of a dingo, answered a moment later from nearer at hand – probably the same dog he had seen, Jim thought. He tossed the dregs of his tea onto the leaf-strewn ground, stretched his long body and sighed, tired by the day.

He had been unable to check the paddock fence, or at least unwill-ing to once he saw the extent to which the scrub had overgrown the old wheel ruts, all that now remained of the track. But he'd greased the mill at Two Bob and turned it off, for the water it pumped was draining away through the rusted trough. Marvell Creek's mill was frozen, the tank a catchment for leaves, sand and the skeletons of small birds. The tank itself looked sound enough, though, and two out of three wasn't bad going, Jim told himself. He lifted his face to the black and white beauty of the night, feeling the slow excitement he'd been holding in for most of the day begin to build inside him.

He could do it, he knew. He could pick up where Sandy had left off, and given only average luck with the seasons, and enough time, he could turn the place around. There would be money owing to the Lands Department for rent and rates, but not that much, for Kharko had paid the arrears when the company agisted the property during the drought. To fulfil the lease conditions, he'd have to get stock back onto the country as soon as he could, and repairing the bores would cost too, and he'd need a working plant. It would mean going to the banks and it would mean hard work. Sustained hard work, but he had never shirked that. And it would mean having Ruth alongside him. He could do nothing without her.

When the fire died to coals he kicked his swag open, pulled off his boots and lay back. He watched the stars pale before the moon's passage, his mind too full for sleep. Moonlight silvered the branches above him and he thought of the harsh red country, clothed now in feed, stretching away to scrub-filled distances. He moved his hands to press them fiercely down upon the soil beneath his swag. It was an act of possession. He had forgotten until he saw it again how much he loved this land that had been his father's and was now his. And someday, he thought, his son's. His and Ruth's son; they would raise a family here.

Suddenly guilt overrode the pleasure of his dreaming, for the picture that came unbidden to mind was not his own faceless children but an orphaned child – his father's other son.

Jim sighed deeply, knowing he could deny it no longer. It had been there all day in the back of his thoughts, lying like a shadow over his calculations and hopeful plans. It was a pity he had ever spoken to Stella. The memory of his brother's words – *Jim'll come* – were engraved in his consciousness. There were so many reasons for taking the easy option. Public opinion, for one, would demand that he do so. He could just imagine his uncle's reaction if he took the boy in. But what of his father, who had saved the land for him?

With a shock of enlightenment Jim saw what he had missed before. Sandy had never been one for setting things out in writing; he had always been a man who let his actions speak for him and he had expected Jim to understand that the boy and Arcadia went together. Captain Brogan's words echoed in his head. *He thinks, and Sandy seems to have encouraged it, that he's going to live with you.* His father could have made that a condition for leaving Jim the property, but his faith in him had deemed it unnecessary.

He felt humbled by such trust and a little sick that he had almost proved it misplaced. He had driven away from Lynton Creek telling himself that whatever arrangements the State was making for Eddy's welfare were for the best. That he had done his part. He was appalled now at his callousness, but strangely, as he acknowledged what he must do, there came upon him a feeling not of resignation but of peace. Sandy, he saw, had known him better than he knew himself; had known that in the end, however bitter their last parting, Jim would forgive him. And having done so would take his brother in.

Jim breathed deeply of the night air. He felt that all the lonely years of estrangement had been leading to this, and now everything was falling into place. The way ahead might not be easy but it would be all right. He knew with an indefinable certainty that Ruth would agree.

The moon's face blurred as sleep stole like a shadow to embrace him. He lifted his head to bunch his pillow and a cat's-paw of breeze fluttered his swag nap and touched his hair, light as rumpling fingers, before his eyes closed upon the shiny night and he slept with the oblivion he had known as a child.

He broke camp at dawn, after a night undisturbed by dreams, and was back at the house in time to startle half a dozen brumbies off the trough. They wheeled, the sun striking their dusty hides and glittering on the droplets from wet muzzles. At the edge of the timber they turned and the stallion trotted out to stand, statue-stiff, and snort at him, the sound like ripping cloth among the morning shadows. Jim thought how Ruth would love them, for all the wrong reasons, when they were in fact pests that had to be controlled.

Slipping the clutch, he changed gear and headed up past the house to the old horse-paddock gate and the bumpy narrow track through the wattle that would have to be widened again by chopping the edges clear, and then graded.

But all that could wait. First he must mend the quarrel with the man who had raised him and then woo and win Ruth. After that he would keep faith with his father and lay the ghost of old betrayals and bring his brother home.

Pieces of Blue

When Kerry McGinnis lost her mother at the age of six, her father gathered up his four young children and left the city. For the next fifteen years the McGinnis family travelled the outback, droving, horse-breaking and living off the land.

Schoolrooms, comfort and civilisation are a long way off in this rugged country, but life for Kerry and her siblings is rich beyond measure, their experiences unique. But nothing stays the same, and with the memory of her mother ever present, Kerry begins her difficult journey to young womanhood.

> *Kerry McGinnis's personal – and personable – story offers insights into an Australia unknown by urbanites. And into the human values and verities that underwrite life there.*
>
> THE AUSTRALIAN

> *It is the author's word pictures of the sights, smells and sounds of the bush, and her perceptive rendering of the characters along the way, that make* Pieces of Blue *a book to be treasured.*
>
> SUNSHINE COAST SUNDAY

Heart Country

This second volume of Kerry McGinnis's memoir opens with her tired of the wandering life after years on the road, and yearning for a proper home. When her father, the irascible but loveable Mac, buys a property in Queensland's Gulf Country, it seems like she might have found one.

But not everything runs smoothly. The family is at loggerheads with each other, and Mac soon develops itchy feet. Kerry discovers that life as a young woman in a man's country is far from easy. At a time when she's expected to settle down and have a family, she must make some difficult decisions about love, marriage, and her passionate desire to write.

What makes this book stand out – apart from its compelling narrative of a vanishing way of life – is its lyrical description of the country and the elements that shape each season.

AUSTRALIAN BOOKSELLER AND PUBLISHER

A rare insight into the difficulties of life in the Australian outback during the 1940s and '50s.

THE WEEKLY TIMES

ALSO FROM PENGUIN

Burke's Soldier

Alan Attwood

Melbourne, 1871: John King is dying far from the deserts he traversed with the legendary Burke and Wills. Ten years on from that fateful expedition, King is finally ready to tell his story. The young Irishman had already endured the horrors of the Indian Mutiny when he signed on with the erratic Burke to explore a land he knew little about. As one of the advance group who were later abandoned by the rest of their party, King was with Wills as he penned his final letter; at Burke's side when he died. Then he was alone, the sole survivor, though barely alive when rescued by Alfred Howitt. But Howitt is a man who cannot let things be, and now he seems more inquisitor than saviour. He wants to know what King knows before it's too late …

Effortlessly blending fact and fiction, this gripping novel brings to life the forgotten man of the most mythologised journey in Australia's history.

A splendidly written and poignant side-view of history.

THEA ASTLEY

Unputdownable . . . a fascinating and long-neglected tale of an unsung hero.

GOOD WEEKEND

A must for lovers of Australian history and imaginative writing. In a word: exceptional.

KIM LOCKWOOD, HERALD SUN

The Stockman

Rachael Treasure

Rosie Highgrove-Jones grows up hating her double-barrelled name. She dreams of riding out over the wide plains of the family property, working on the land. Instead she's stuck writing the social pages for the local paper.

Then tragedy sparks a series of family revelations, and as Rosie tries to put her life back together she throws herself into researching the haunting true story of a nineteenth-century Irish stockman who came to Australia and risked his all for a tiny pup and a wild dream. Is it just coincidence when Rosie meets a sexy Irish stockman of her own? And will he help her realise her deepest ambitions, or will he break her heart?

> *This honest and heartfelt tale of life on the land captures the very essence of being Australian.*
>
> TANIA KERNAGHAN

Jillaroo

Rachael Treasure

After a terrible argument with her father over their family property, Rebecca Saunders throws her swag in the ute and heads north with her three dogs. A job as a jillaroo takes her into the rowdy world of B&S balls, Bundy rum and boys. When at last she settles down to study at agricultural college, her life is turned upside down by the very handsome but drunken party animal, Charlie Lewis.

Will she choose a life of wheat farming on vast open plains with Charlie? Or will she return to the mountains to fight for the land and the river that runs through her soul? It takes a tragedy for Rebecca to find a strength and courage she never knew she had, in this action-packed novel of adventure, dreams and determination.

One of the most refreshing Australian heroines ever . . .
By the end of this book you yearn for a ute, a pair of boots
and the wide open spaces.
AUSTRALIAN WOMEN'S WEEKLY